THE SEVEN DIALS AFFAIR

TRACY GRANT

The Seven Dials Affair

Ebook ISBN: 9781641972543
KDP POD ISBN: 9798394802522
IS POD ISBN: 9781641972673

NYLA Publishing
121 W 27th St., Suite 1201, New York, NY 10001
http://www.nyliterary.com

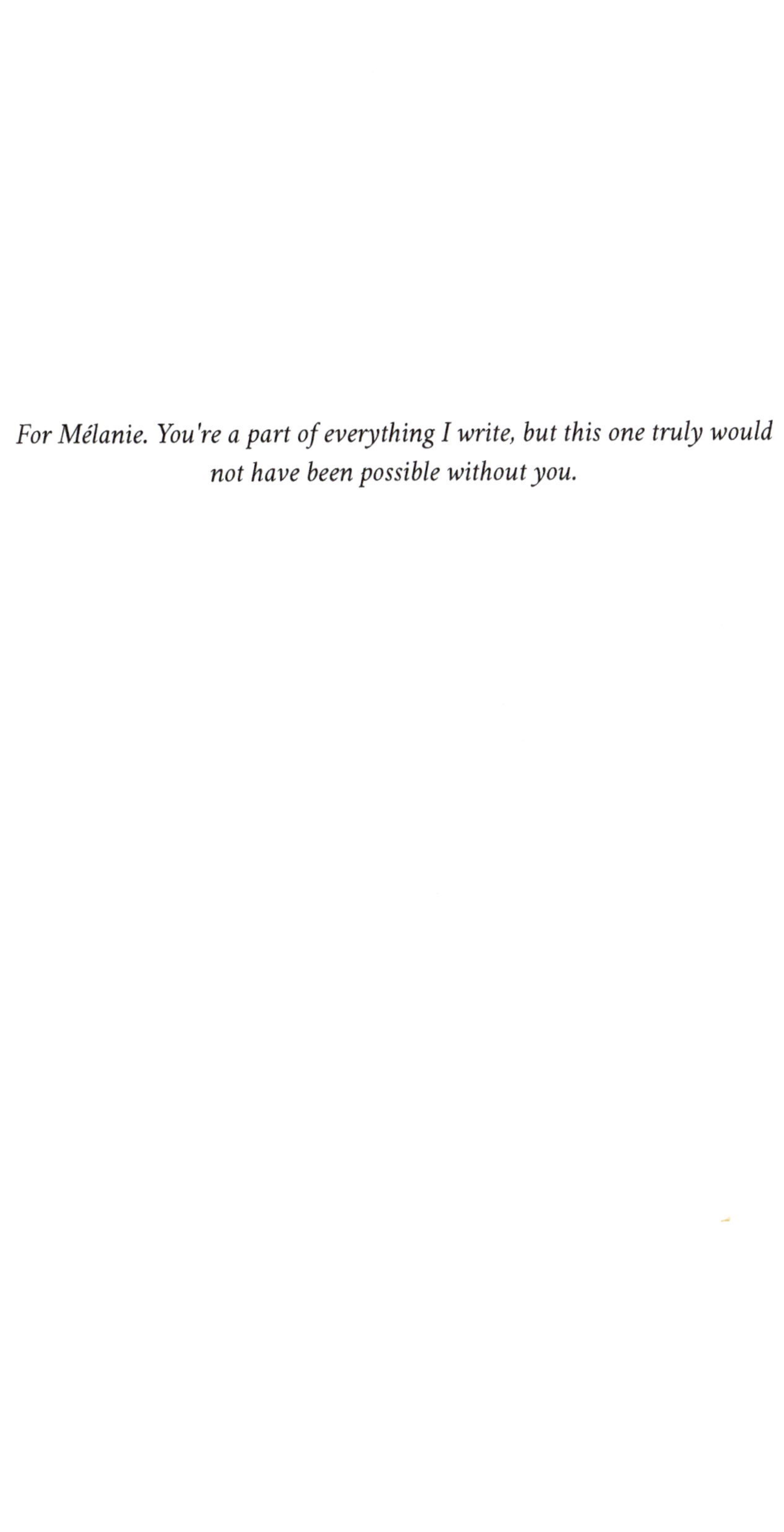

For Mélanie. You're a part of everything I write, but this one truly would not have been possible without you.

ered with the Rannochs with you and so appre-

ACKNOWLEDGMENTS

It takes the help and support of an amazing number of people to bring a book into the world. My amazing agent, Nancy Yost, has been a wonderful support to this series from the start. As always, huge thanks for her insights and brilliant eye for editing cover copy. Thanks to Natanya Wheeler, a brilliant Director of Digital Rights, for shepherding the book expertly through each stage of the publication process and once again working her magic to create a fabulous cover. It was particularly fun working on this one, finding the perfect image for Mélanie Rannoch, layering details that capture Seven Dials and the mood of the novel. To Sarah Younger for helping the book along through production and publication, and to Sarah and Christina Miller for superlative social media support. To Zoe Bryant for a great set of character and quote cards. And to the entire team at Nancy Yost Literary Agency for their fabulous work. Their creativity and dedication make all of them a dream to work with. Malcolm, Mélanie, and I are all very fortunate to have their support.

Thank you to Eve Lynch for the meticulous and thoughtful copyediting. I love sharing the Rannochs with you and so appreciate your care for getting their story right when it comes to everything from historical usage to series continuity.

Thank you to Kristen Loken for a magical author photo. This one is particularly special because we were back at the Merola Grand Finale after three years. Your brilliance never fails to amaze me, Kristen!

I am very fortunate to have a wonderful group of writer

friends near and far who make being a writer less solitary. Thanks in particular to Lauren Willig for sharing the joys of historical research and the challenges of juggling life as a writer and a mom. To Penelope Williamson, for sharing adventures (including wonderful writer escapes to the Oregon Shakespeare Festival), analyzing plots from Shakespeare to *Scandal*, and being a wonderful honorary aunt to my daughter. Thank you to the #momswritersclub for bimonthly chats that are energizing and inspiring, and especially to Jessica Payne for starting it and to Jessica and Sara Read for their wonderful #MomsWritersClub YouTube channel on which Mélanie and I had the fun of doing a guest interview. So excited I've had the joy of reading Jessica's and Sara's debut novels in the last year.

Thank you to the readers who support Malcolm and Mélanie and their friends and provide wonderful insights on my Web site and social media, and especially on the Goodreads Discussion Group for the series.

Thanks to Gregory Paris and jim saliba for creating and updating a fabulous Web site that chronicles Malcolm and Mélanie's adventures.

And thank you to my daughter Mélanie, for brainstorming *The Seven Dials Affair*, proofreading (including catching "Raoul says 1811 but everyone else says '06 or '07), and supporting me all the way through the process. I am so proud that my website now includes "Mélanie's Corner" for her stories, starting with her wonderful series *Talea's Mysteries*. From the time she could touch the keys, Mélanie has contributed something to each of my books. This is Mélanie's contribution to this story – "my mummy's stories are amazing, I am so so happy I got to help her with this one! Mummy is amazing at being my mom, writing, her job at Merola, and being the best person EVER! I am so lucky to be her daughter!!!!!!!"

DRAMATIS PERSONAE

*INDICATES REAL HISTORICAL FIGURES

<u>The Rannoch Family & Household</u>

Malcolm Rannoch, MP and former British intelligence agent
Mélanie Suzanne Rannoch, his wife, playwright and former
French intelligence agent
Colin Rannoch, their son
Jessica Rannoch, their daughter
Berowne, their cat

Laura O'Roarke, Colin and Jessica's former governess
Raoul O'Roarke, her husband, Mélanie's former spymaster, and
Malcolm's father
Lady Emily Fitzwalter, Laura's daughter from her first marriage
Clara O'Roarke, Laura and Raoul's daughter

Miles Addison, agent, Malcolm's valet
Blanca Mendoza Addison, agent, his wife, Mélanie's companion
Pedro Addison, their son

Valentin, footman

Mrs. Erskine, cook

Alexander (Sandy) Trenor, Malcolm's secretary
Elizabeth (Bet) Simcox Trenor, his wife
Robby Simcox, Bet's brother, groom at Carfax House

<u>The Mallinson Family</u>

Julien (Arthur) Mallinson, Earl Carfax, former agent for hire
Katelina (Kitty) Velasquez Mallinson, Countess Carfax, his wife,
former British and Spanish intelligence agent
Leo Ashford, her son
Timothy Ashford, her son
Guenevere (Genny) Ashford, Kitty and Julien's daughter

Hubert Mallinson, spymaster, Julien's uncle
Amelia Mallinson, his wife

David Mallinson, MP, their son
Simon Tanner, playwright, his lover (see also At the Tavistock)

<u>The Davenport Family & Household</u>

Lady Cordelia Davenport, classicist
Colonel Harry Davenport, her husband, classicist, and former
British intelligence agent
Livia Davenport, their daughter
Drusilla Davenport, their daughter
Cleo, their dog

Justine Lambton, classicist, their guest
Gerald (Gerry) Schofield, classicist, her friend

Archibald (Archie) Davenport, Harry's uncle, MP, and former
French intelligence agent
Lady Frances Davenport, his wife, Malcolm's aunt
Chloe Dacre-Hammond, Frances's daughter from her first marriage
Francesca Davenport, Frances and Archie's daughter
Philip Davenport, Frances and Archie's son

Judith Derwent, Viscountess Pelham, Frances's daughter from her
first marriage
Bobby Derwent, Viscount Pelham, Judith's late husband (see also
Others)
Serena Derwent, their daughter

Aline (Allie) Blackwell, Frances's daughter from her first marriage
Geoffrey (Geoff) Blackwell, doctor, Aline's husband

The Roth Family

Jeremy Roth, Bow Street Runner
Allegra Wainwright Roth, his estranged wife
Samuel Roth, their son
Dorian Roth, their son
Harriet Roth, Jeremy's sister
Cressida Caldwell, courtesan, Allegra's stepsister
Vincent Caldwell, Cressida's son

<u>**At the Tavistock**</u>

Simon Tanner, playwright and part owner of the theatre (see also
Mallinson Family)
Manon Caret, actress
Brandon Ford, actor
Letty Blanchard, actress

Will Carmarthen, actor, her husband
Eliza Bentley, actress
Tim Scott, assistant stage manager

At the Three Queens

Ralph Allam, barkeep
Mandy, his mistress

The Blayney Household

Edmund Blayney, journalist
Philippa (Pippa) Blayney, his wife
Cynthia, their daughter
Katie, their daughter
Danielle Darnault, opera singer and agent
Pierre Ducroix, journalist, her husband
Ilia, their daughter

Others

Marco Esquivel, Argentine revolutionary leader
Felicia Esquivel, his wife
Martin Rowely, Esquivel's friend, MP, steam engine developer
William Beardsley, Esquivel's friend, MP
Bobby Derwent, Viscount Pelham, Esquivel's friend (see also Davenport Family)

*Sir Nathaniel Conant, chief magistrate of Bow Street
*Lord Sidmouth, home secretary
Higgins, Bow Street runner
Hopkins, Bow Street patrol

Tristram, Lord Gresham, composer

Lord Warkworth, diplomat

*Lord Palmerston, secretary at war

*Arthur Wellesley, Duke of Wellington, master general of the
ordnance
*Lord Fitzroy Somerset, his secretary

Philip Ledgwood, diplomat
Isabel Fuentes Ledgwood, his wife

For we have heard the chimes at midnight.
　　—Shakespeare, *Henry IV, Part 2,* Act III, scene ii

PROLOGUE

Buenos Aires
February, 1818

Kitty Ashford tightened her fingers on her shawl. The north wind, so sharp in an Argentine summer, tugged at the folds she'd wrapped over her head, and the moon was bright enough that her hair might catch the light. Red blonde was not the most convenient color for a spy.

The wind brought the scent of the water from Wapping, the English nickname for the beach. She could hear the strains of a reel played on an Irish fiddle from one of the grog shops and smell garlic and sour ale. And hints of fish oil, cinnamon, cardamom, cloves.

She scanned the dark line of buildings. He was there, leaning against the side of a shed, blurring into the shadows. Somehow even his distinctive fair hair faded to gray and the lines of his body echoed the lines of the wood. She'd never fail to marvel at his skill. And at other things.

He turned as she approached and took a step forwards, as

though unfolding from the shadows. She saw the quick gleam of his smile and an echoing flash in his eyes.

"I'm sorry," he said, when she was close enough for speech to be safe. "I'm sure it wasn't convenient to get away."

"I'm used to it." She'd had to make an excuse to her husband, but lying to Edward was second nature. "I assume it's important?"

"I'm afraid so." The light shifted, as the wind set the clouds ruffling over the moon. Something leapt in his eyes. "I'm going to have to leave. Tonight."

Her muscles jerked. Like she'd been dealt a blow to the gut. Stupid. She'd known this was coming at some point. "We were right about the leak?"

"Yes. I need to get back with the news. I can't trust it to someone else. And I'm afraid there's no doubt now the League are on to me."

"Of course." Her voice was level. Surprisingly so. She hoped he couldn't detect her erratic breathing. "The only reason you were here was to find a safe place to hide. And now it isn't safe anymore."

"That isn't the only reason I was here. Or at least not the only reason I stayed here."

"Don't, Julien." She took a step back. A board creaked beneath her foot. She should have noted it on her arrival. If she was making such slips on basic spycraft it was probably just as well Julien was leaving. "Your saving grace has always been that you didn't pretend we were anything we weren't or give way to platitudes."

"That wasn't either of those." He took her hand, his fingers steady on her own. "Lie low for a bit, Kitkat. We don't know how much got out and how far it's gone. The League have a long reach, and they may try to use you to get to me. Not to sound overly arrogant, but—"

"They want your services. With good reason." And they might want him for who he was, but she wasn't going to put that into words. Not even here, with seemingly only the wind and spicy air and creaking boards for company. Julien had confessed things to her he hadn't to anyone else. She'd never forget that. Even if she never saw him again.

"They've shown themselves tiresomely stubborn. Like a suitor who won't acknowledge when a lady isn't interested. Whether the lady in question is a cyprian or in her first season, it's a fatal mistake."

She nodded. "I'll be all right. I've been through this in Spain. It comes with the territory."

His fingers tightened over her own. "Tell the boys goodbye. I'd have liked to see them."

Her sons were fond of Julien, despite not knowing his true name. In fact, both Leo and Timothy were rather alarmingly good at seeing through his disguises. "They'll understand. They're both used to changes."

The word hung in the air. Because this was a sea change that would impact their lives for years. Perhaps forever. She'd had her own life disrupted too many times not to know that the polite words about "staying in touch" were just that. Polite.

The realization settled in his eyes. "I'll find a way to write. And we both don't know where we may end up."

"Julien." She drew back without disengaging her hand. "Don't pretend this is something it isn't."

"I'm not pretending anything, Kitkat." He released her hand, but only to pull her into his arms and put his mouth to hers.

For a moment, the world rushed away. As much as it ever could for them. She slid her arms round him, holding him tight. Perhaps too tight. "For once I don't think you had half a mind to who might sneak up behind us," she said when he released her, voice shaking with laughter and other things.

"With you I'm always inclined to lose my head."

"Liar."

She kept her hands at her sides. She was not going to give way to the cliché impulse to touch her hand to her abdomen. She wasn't even sure. And even if she had been, it didn't, couldn't concern him. Especially not now. As well he was leaving before she was sure. Before she could be tempted to tell him.

He bent his head to kiss her again. How provoking of Julien, who was so expert at lying about everything, to be so damnably honest when he kissed.

He held her face between his hands for a moment. "Stay safe, Kitkat."

"My dear. Don't ask the impossible."

Their gazes caught for a moment. "You may have tiresome questions about the gold."

"Answering tiresome questions is rather my stock in trade. I may even be able to track down the gold."

"I have no doubt you can. Send me word when you do. I can share a toast with you across the ocean."

She was not in a mood to think about the ocean that would be between them. "Do you know where the leak came from?" she asked.

"Nothing conclusive."

She put her hands on his chest. Cold as he could be in so many settings, she could feel the warmth of his skin through coat and waistcoat and shirt. Real, vibrant, here, alive. "Have a care, Julien. It's a dangerous time for you to go back."

"It's dangerous to be alive. But somehow I've managed for close to four decades." He took her hand and lifted it to his lips. "I'm sure we'll meet again. I only hope we're on the same side."

She stepped back and drew her shawl round her like armour. "Oh, Julien. What did I say about asking the impossible?"

CHAPTER 1

Seven Dials, London
February, 1821

Malcolm Rannoch slipped through the shadowy crowd. Over a decade of training as a spy told him not to stand out, but there was a limit to what one could do in gentleman's garb in Seven Dials. If he'd had more time he'd have donned a disguise, but he'd been at Brooks's and the summons had been urgent. And his wife was at the theatre and not here to help him.

He skirted a steaming mess that looked to have been dumped from a chamber pot, ducked round two men who had come to fisticuffs, and turned the corner in the warren of seventeenth-century passages and courts and alleys. Only a few streets away from Covent Garden, where his wife was busy with a rehearsal at the Tavistock Theatre, yet a world away. Fewer surprised gazes turned in his direction than he'd have expected. But then he'd passed more than a few men in silk hats and well-cut coats.

Don't be silly, darling. He could hear his wife's voice in his ear.

He turned up the collar of his coat, aware of the heat in his cheeks. Idiot, not to have thought of the obvious excuse. And to be discomfited by it now it occurred to him. Too many years of civilian life were turning him soft. Not that there was anything particularly civilian about scarcely going two months without demands from a former spymaster. One of whom happened to be his father, and his wife's former spymaster. And his own former opponent. The other of whom had been his own spymaster and was far more lethal.

A sailor's shanty cut the air, interlaced with a version of *Over the Hills and Far Away* he knew from nights round the campfire in the Spain. For a moment he was back in the Peninsula. In the uncomfortable early days of marriage, but not yet aware that the woman he'd married to offer her protection was a French spy. And not yet completely disillusioned with spying for his own country. He'd never have thought it then, but life had been so much simpler.

He paused, letting reality settle round him. The air had a chill bite and patches of snow from earlier in the day clung to door-frames and windowsills and hanging signs. A sign of three ladies in gold crowns caught his eye through the greasy lamplight. At last. He slid into the crowd entering and exiting the tavern, climbed the steps, and pushed open the door of the Three Queens.

Heads turned in his direction. It was easier, he realized, when he had Mélanie with him. For one thing, everyone looked at her. Why wouldn't they? In a ball gown or disguised as a cyprian, she dazzled without lifting a finger. And no one questioned what he was about when he had a woman on his arm. Which was disturbing in and of itself. But it was also useful.

But Mélanie was at the Tavistock with their children, rehearsing her new play, and he was on this mission alone. Which happened more and more, of late.

He pushed his way between the knife-scarred tables, over the ale-soaked floorboards, with a careless ease he'd have never felt in a tavern in his own persona. *Of course, dearest.* Again he could hear his wife's voice, could see her smiling at him with familiar irony, walnut-brown ringlets falling round her face. *Life is so much easier when one is playing a role. Why do you think I played one for so long? Why do you think I still do?*

The play's the thing. They lived their lives on that. So did his father and his stepmother and his aunt and uncle and most of their friends. He knew the barkeep was looking at him, but he didn't stop to make eye contact. His summons had been quite clear on where he should go.

A red-haired woman in a clinging green gown brushed against him as he moved to the stairs. "I'm available, guv'nor."

"Sorry." Malcolm paused and smiled at her. Her eyes were green flecked with blue. Not unlike Mélanie's. "I have business to see to."

Her penciled brows snapped together. She turned away with a swish of her green skirts.

He climbed the stairs, aware of more gazes on him. Though not surprised gazes. They assumed, like the disappointed woman in the green dress, that he was on his way upstairs to visit one of the women who worked the tavern. Who, a decade or so ago, might have been the remarkable woman who was now his wife. Which was enough, even now, to nearly stop him in his tracks. And somehow made the thought of being taken for that man even more discomfiting. He wasn't sure whether to be grateful or not that Mélanie wasn't with him. He knew what it cost her to be dragged into her past. But to be dragged into it without her seemed to risk denying that past.

At the top of the stairs, he went to the door his note had indicated, the third one. No different from the other doors with peeling white paint and sagging frames that opened off the landing. He rapped once, then opened the door without waiting for a response.

The smell swamped him at once. Sweet, cloying, choking.

A woman was stretched out on the floorboards, fair hair spread round her, the gray folds of her gown and the black velvet of her cloak tangled round her legs.

A man was bending over her. Tall, wrapped in a loose greatcoat, brown hair ruffled. That was not surprising either. Jeremy Roth had summoned Malcolm, and Malcolm had been quite sure when he received the cryptic missive that it was because of an investigation, probably a murder. Roth was a skilled Bow Street runner, but he was quick to employ Malcolm's and Mélanie's and their friends' assistance when it suited a case.

Malcolm pushed the door to as Roth's head jerked up from contemplation of the victim. "Mel's at the Tavistock," Malcolm said. "But I came as soon as I could."

"Thank you." Roth's voice was unusually husky, his gaze opaque in the greasy light of the tallow candle on the gateleg table by the window.

Malcolm moved forwards. A red stain showed on the woman's chest through the silk of her gown. Her eyes were glazed. He didn't need to feel for a pulse to know she was dead. "How long do you think?" he asked Roth.

"An hour, perhaps. Not much more."

Malcolm looked down at the woman. Her hair was slipping from its pins and tangled round her face, but he could recognize a fashionable crop and the remnants of a Grecian knot. Her complexion was delicate, with the faintest hint of rouge and eye blacking. Her face had the elegant definition of one past the first blush of youth. He had spent enough hours cooling his heels at his wife's modiste's to recognize the quality of the silk and velvet of her clothes, the cashmere lining of the cloak, the elegance of the draped neckline of the gown and the gathers of the sleeves. Her earrings and necklace had the gleam of real gold despite the poor light. "She doesn't look like a woman one would expect to find in Seven Dials." Which would explain why Roth had summoned him. He often wanted Malcolm's and Mélanie's and their friends' assistance with cases involving the beau monde. "You'd like us to assist on the case?" As much of a tragedy as it was, the distraction was not unwelcome, especially with Mélanie busy.

"No," Roth said. His gaze jerked to Malcolm's own. His hands were loose at his sides. He wasn't, Malcolm realized, holding his notebook, which was usually ever-present in investigations. "That is, your assistance would be invaluable. But I won't be able to oversee this case myself."

Malcolm took another step forwards. The Bow Street Public Office was under the auspices of the home office, which meant cases that involved anything to do with the government, espionage, or the royal family were particularly fraught. He didn't recognize the woman, but he might not know. She could be a royal mistress. Or a royal by-blow. Or an agent for any number of people. "Why not?"

Roth looked down at the dead woman again. But though his gaze was fixed on her tangled limbs and still features, for a moment it was as though he was not looking at her in the present but into some hell of his own making. "Because this is my wife."

$\mathcal{M}$alcolm stared at his friend. He had first met Roth in the Peninsula, during the war against Napoleon Bonaparte's forces, when Roth had been a soldier assigned to intelligence missions and Malcolm a diplomatic attaché and agent. They hadn't talked much about their personal lives, but Roth had mentioned a wife at home and a child, and later a second child. Which to Malcolm, at that point determined never to marry, had seemed miraculous and as out of reach as the moon. Later, when Malcolm risked matrimony against all his best instincts, Roth had treated Mélanie with a respect for her talents that it took many much longer to acquire. And the first time Roth had held their son Colin, in their lodgings in Lisbon, he'd shown the ease of one used to babies.

When Malcolm, settled in London as an MP and seemingly free of the intelligence game (which now seemed a joke), had encountered Roth again as a Bow Street runner, Roth had referred to his wife as "gone." He hadn't offered further details and Malcolm hadn't felt the right to pry for them. He knew Roth lived with his sister, who was helping him raise his two sons. Despite Roth's reticence about the beau monde, the Roth family were now frequent guests in Malcolm and Mélanie's home.

"I didn't know she was back," Malcolm said.

Roth met Malcolm's gaze, his own suddenly focused. "And you're wondering if I found her like this or if she was alive when I came into the room."

The words hung hard and still in the air, like raindrops turning to snow. Once Malcolm had confronted a similar question about a dead woman whom he had been found bending over. The person who had found him was his wife. And the dead woman was a lady many—including his wife—had assumed to be his mistress, though in fact she was his half-sister. He still remembered the doubt in Mélanie's eyes, how it had cut him in two, and how he had known he had no right to question her questions.

"I'd never ask that of a friend," Malcolm said.

Jeremy's gaze stayed steady, the gaze of a professional, even in the most personal crisis. "But as an investigator you're too good not to ask it of a suspect. Which is what I am."

"For God's sake, Jeremy." Malcolm took two steps forwards and caught Roth's arm. "Before everything else, my deepest sympathies."

Roth stared up, eyes glazed with confusion.

"Your wife just died." Malcolm pressed Roth into a straight-backed chair. He looked round. There was a bottle of wine on the gateleg table, but he didn't want to disturb anything. Not yet. He strode out the door, called for a glass of gin, brought it back, and put it in Roth's hand.

Roth took a gulp and spoke quickly. "I hadn't heard from Allegra in years. Not since she left. Then I received a note from her this evening, not two hours since, asking me to come here and meet her. I would have thought it was a set-up, save that I'd know her hand anywhere." His voice cracked for a moment. "I found her like this. She was beyond help, though I did everything I could for her." His voice scraped again, like fabric caught on rock. He took another swallow of gin and pushed on. "I realize how improbable that sounds."

"Far too improbable to be anything a man with your skills would have invented," Malcolm said.

"That's one way of looking at it." Roth stared into the glass. The gin was cloudy, though it might be smudges on the glass or the greasy tallow light. "Allegra never seemed content. She could get caught up in moments of fun with the boys, but a part of me always knew she was dissatisfied. Our life wasn't the life she'd dreamt of. Shocking as it was that she disappeared, a part of me wasn't surprised. After all, what else is a woman to do when she's unhappy with her life? Divorce was far out of our reach."

"She didn't just leave her husband. She left her children."

"She must have known I'd have gone after her if she took them." Roth tossed down a swallow of gin. "Perhaps I should be grateful she didn't try to disappear with them."

"Did she leave a note?"

Roth shook his head. He was determinedly not looking away from his wife's body. "She went out to do some shopping one afternoon and never returned. I scoured the streets. I used every source I could find. Shamelessly. I'd have asked you for help, but you were still in Paris."

"I'm sorry we weren't here."

Roth's mouth twisted. "You should perhaps be grateful you weren't pulled into the sorry mess. I was able to trace her as far as the Gloucester Coffee House in Piccadilly. I couldn't find anyone who'd actually seen her on the mail coach. I had a vague description that might mean she'd got into a private carriage seemingly bound for the west country. I had more vague descriptions all the way to Falmouth. The trail ended there."

"She never wrote?"

Roth hesitated, gaze on the glass of gin. "She sent one letter, almost a year after she vanished. She said she was sorry. Sorry to have entangled me in her problems. Sorry to have entangled me in her life at all. She said she'd finally found something that gave her life meaning. That it would be better for the boys to think she was dead and that I should consider myself free."

Malcolm swallowed, hard. He'd had no reason to think it until he knew the truth about Mélanie, but he was now haunted by images of her disappearing. With or without their children. Even after he'd learned the truth, he'd been afraid she might disappear in an effort to protect them. "Did you tell your sons their mother was dead?"

"No." Roth tossed down a quick swallow of gin. "I wasn't going to lie to them and then have them learn the truth later. I said their mother had had to go away and that she loved them but might never be able to come back."

Truth. Challenging. But perhaps easier for children than lies they would recognize as lies. "Did you consider yourself free?"

"Would you?"

"Not entirely."

"Nor I. Though I had no illusions she'd come back. Or that our marriage could continue if it did. I wouldn't be able to continue it, whatever she wanted. But given that I'd never much expected to marry, having a missing wife I was still tied to didn't necessarily impact my life. At least, not as much as one might think."

"Did she write to you again?"

"Not until today." Roth stared into his glass, then seemed to force his gaze to his dead wife.

Malcolm looked at the dead woman, then looked at Roth. It had to be said. "Do you have reason to think she went off with a lover?"

"It seems an obvious assumption," Roth said, as though discussing a victim to whom he had no connection. "I took the wording in her letter to imply that. Some of the descriptions I got on the road to Falmouth included a man with the lady who seemed to be Allegra."

"Though other things could give a life meaning."

"So they could." Roth dragged his gaze back to Malcolm. "I had no evidence Allegra had a lover before she left. Except the growing distance between us. And her increasing absences."

Malcolm looked down at Allegra Roth's body. He noted again the lines of her gown and cloak, the gleam of her jewelry. "A fashionable modiste made this gown and cloak. And that's real gold."

"Yes. All far finer than anything she had when she was married to me." Roth's eyes narrowed, the gaze of an investigator. "I can't imagine she was staying in Seven Dials."

"Have you questioned the tavern staff?"

"Briefly, when I paid the potboy to bring you the letter. I didn't want to rouse their suspicions, but apparently Allegra arrived alone and engaged a private room. They made the obvious assumptions about why she was expecting a gentleman. She wasn't dressed for Seven Dials, but I doubt she's the only fashionable lady to engage a private room here." Roth got to his feet but didn't move closer to his wife's body. "No sign of the weapon."

Malcolm looked round. "Did you—?"

"Search? Yes. So there's no way to prove I didn't take anything. But you'd best look as well, in case I missed anything."

A reticule lay beside her, velvet with a steel clasp, like many Mélanie had. Malcolm unclasped it. An enamel tin of lip rouge, a crystal atomizer of scent, a light jasmine. A silk coin purse. An ivory comb. A stray button.

"Does any of this mean anything to you?" Malcolm asked.

"Only the button." Roth's voice turned rough again. "It's from our eldest son's first shirt. I didn't even know she'd taken it. It makes me wonder—" His face twisted. "I'm going to have to send for Bow Street. They'll turn the investigation over to someone and keep me out of it. I may well be arrested, if not tonight, then soon. No." He put up a hand as Malcolm started to protest. "You know a husband or wife is always the prime suspect, especially if they're found with the body. It won't play well that I summoned you first, but that's why I had to. I needed time to talk. I need you to promise you'll look into this. Learn whatever you can. I know I may be pitting you against the home office—"

"Hardly for the first time."

Roth's gaze locked on his own. "I know what I'm asking."

"You can't imagine I wouldn't help."

"No." Roth held his gaze for a long moment. At their first meeting, Roth had been inclined to dismiss anyone remotely bearing the tang of "gentleman." Roth reached into his greatcoat pocket and pulled out two pieces of paper torn from his notebook. "If I'm arrested before I can go home, this is for Harriet. And this is for the boys."

Malcolm took the papers. "Mélanie once found me over the dead body of the woman she believed to be my mistress. She helped me in the investigation."

"Did she suspect you?"

"She couldn't help but do so. She tried not to let me see it."

"You're doing a good job of that yourself."

Malcolm looked levelly into Roth's gaze. "One can never be sure of what anyone might do. But I know you. Better perhaps than Mélanie knew me at that time. I can't imagine your doing this."

Roth's gaze settled on Malcolm's own. "That may be a failure of your imagination."

"Always possible. But I choose think otherwise."

"You need to keep an open mind. Because more than anything, I want to know what happened." His gaze moved to his dead wife for a fraction of an instant, tense with pain. "Allegra deserves that. My sons need to someday know what happened to their mother. Promise you'll learn the truth, Malcolm. Wherever it takes you."

Malcolm looked into the eyes of the man who had been one of his closest friends for over a decade, for all the secrets on both sides. "I promise."

"Thank you." Simple words that spoke volumes about how far their friendship had come.

Malcolm glanced round the room. "But before you send to Bow Street, let's wait for Julien."

"You've sent for Carfax?" Roth asked.

Still hard for Malcolm to hear Julien Mallinson referred to by the title his uncle, Malcolm's former spymaster, had usurped for a quarter-century. "When I went to get the gin. I want his opinion on the wound to your wife."

Roth met Malcolm's gaze for a moment. He didn't need to ask why. Because in his years of exile, Julien Mallinson, called Julien St. Juste, had not only been a master agent, he'd been a skilled assassin. He'd have an expert view of the manner in which Allegra had been killed, because it had been his stock in trade.

"That was sound," Roth said. "You're thinking better than I am."

"You shouldn't have to think right now." Malcolm looked round the room. "Who brought you the note from your wife?"

"It was left with Alex, the potboy at the Brown Bear. Alex said a young woman in a brown cloak delivered it. He said she was dark-haired, so not Allegra. A maid perhaps. No way to trace her. No way I can think of to trace where Allegra may have been staying. Or with whom."

"She may have taken a hackney here. If not to the tavern, then to Seven Dials. We'll see—"

A kestrel's call sounded on the landing. A bit out of place in a tavern, but an effective signal. Malcolm opened the door to find not only Julien Mallinson, but his wife Kitty. They were dressed as though they'd been dining at home, Julien with a carelessly tied cravat, Kitty wrapped in a brown velvet cloak over a gold silk dress, her red blonde hair loose round her shoulders.

"Thank you," Malcolm said.

Julien nodded. "Of course. What are friends for?"

"Roth's here. Perhaps best you look at the body before we talk more."

"Mélanie's not here?" Kitty asked.

"No, she's at the theatre. Time enough for her to learn about this when we know more."

Julien and Kitty stepped into the room and nodded at Roth without surprise. Like Malcolm at first, they would assume he was here for professional reasons. They moved towards Allegra's body. Then they both went still, almost in the same instant. Looking at a body was a shock, but it was an odd reaction from Julien, who was an expert in such matters, and even from a skilled agent like Kitty.

"Good god." Julien lifted his gaze to Malcolm. "How did you know?"

"Know what?" Malcolm took a step towards them.

"That we knew her."

CHAPTER 3

"*Y*ou *knew* her?" Roth lurched forwards.

"Who is she?" Malcolm said, gaze on Julien and Kitty.

"Alejandra Vargas," Kitty said. "At least, that's the name she used when we knew her."

"You knew her in Spain?" Roth asked.

"No, in the Argentine," Kitty said. "She was a friend."

"What else was she?" Roth asked in an even voice.

"She sang at the theatre," Julien said. "And she was the mistress of Marco Esquivel. One of the leaders of the Argentine revolution against Spanish rule. Their home was a center of revolutionary discussion. People joked that speeches and military plans were drafted on table linens during dinner. And I suspect the jokes were actually true."

"Did you have any notion she was in England?" Malcolm asked.

Julien shook his head. "The last I saw her was three years ago. Kitkat?"

Kitty also shook her head. "The last I saw her was at a party at their house the night before I left the Argentine. It was by far the most diverting place in Buenos Aires. My god." Her gaze fastened on Allegra Roth.

Julien looked from Roth to Malcolm. "Who found her?"

"I did," Roth said. "Because she'd asked me to meet her. Before she was Alejandra Vargas—a name I'd never heard—she was Allegra Wainwright Roth. And she was my wife."

For the second time in the space of a few minutes Julien and Kitty went still. "Always a fatal mistake," Julien said. "Assuming people fit neatly into one category in one's life and don't cross into another. You'd think I, of all people, would be aware of how people can inhabit different spheres and different identities." He touched Roth's arm. "I'm sorry."

Julien didn't express his emotions often. Which perhaps meant that when he did, they sounded even more sincere and not like platitudes.

"You didn't know where she was?" Kitty asked Roth.

"No. I knew she'd made a new life but not where. Or what name she was using. Or anything about her."

Kitty squeezed Roth's hand. "I'm so sorry, Jeremy."

Roth gave a curt nod. "I consider myself trained to expect the unexpected. But not this. For so many weeks, months, years, I expected to see her every day. I'd catch a glimpse of hair her shade, hear a laugh that sounded like hers, see a woman with her gait. It would bring me up short. No matter how long it had been since I'd thought of her, I'd go still, thinking, 'this is it.' But it's been over a year since that happened to me." He drew a hard breath. That was far more than Roth normally confided about himself.

"The past has a way of appearing when least expected," Julien said.

"Yes." Roth held his gaze. "Look at her. I want to know."

Julien gave a quick nod and bent over Allegra's body. "Your colleagues at Bow Street will know I examined her."

"It doesn't matter. Or rather, it's worth the risk. This may be our only chance."

Julien pushed back Allegra's cloak. "Kitkat, do you mind?" he said.

Kitty knelt opposite him and peeled back the torn fabric of the dress. Malcolm moved to stand above with a candle. "A thin blade," Julien said. "Not necessarily the work of someone with experience, but it was a lucky hit in that case. She would have died quickly," he added to Roth.

"Right-handed?" Malcolm said.

"I think so, yes. The cut looks to have come down. So the killer was probably taller than her. Unless they happened to be standing on something, which is unlikely but not impossible."

"Alejandra wasn't particularly tall," Kitty said. "Most men and a number of women are taller."

Julien nodded. "And yes, I'd say either a man or woman could have done this. It depended more on quickness than strength." He picked up Allegra's hand and held it up to the light to look under her nails. "No sign that she scratched or fought back. I'd say she was taken unawares."

"So she knew the killer," Roth said.

"That seems likely," Julien said. "The Alejandra Vargas I knew wouldn't be easy to overpower."

"Nor would the Allegra I knew." Memories shot through Roth's gaze, then were ruthlessly suppressed.

"There's fabric caught on her gown," Kitty said, leaning forwards. "Blue threads, it looks like. Not from her gown or cloak or reticule."

"No." Julien reached for the threads. "Fine cloth. Could have come from a man's clothes or a woman's, but something well made. A coat or a pelisse or a cloak."

"Did you ask the inn staff if they'd seen anyone else come up here?" Malcolm said to Roth.

"Yes. They said not. But they might not have noticed. Or admitted it."

"Whoever it was could have used the window," Kitty said, glancing at it.

Malcolm moved to the window and pushed up the sash. It moved with surprising ease for something set into a cracked ancient frame. And it wasn't latched. Which could or could not be significant. He held up the candle and looked down the side of the building. Melted snow and mud splatters on the wall. Which might have washed away any trace of a man—or woman—climbing in or out. The ground below was a stew of dirty snow, mud, and very likely worse. Too torn up to show footprints. Something moved in the shadows down the building, away from the street. Grunts sounded. A couple engaged in congress against the wall of the tavern. Too hurried to use a room. Or unable to afford one.

Malcolm closed the window. "It's possible. And there must be back stairs from the kitchen. Someone could have got up that way."

"Or the killer could be an inn servant," Julien said. "Do you have any reason to think Alejandra—Allegra—had any connection to this tavern?"

"To Seven Dials?" Roth bit back a laugh of incredulity. "Christ. That's the usual claim of a victim's family. My loved one could have nothing to do with this place or these circumstances. I should know better than most that one can never really claim to know those closest to one. And I can't claim to have known Allegra well for years. If I ever knew her at all."

Kitty sat back on her heels. "I'm not sure I can claim to have known her well, but I knew her more recently than you. And the woman I knew as Alejandra Vargas generally moved in much finer circles. On the other hand, she liked adventure. Which a lot of people seek in Seven Dials."

"She may have been trying to avoid Esquivel's notice," Julien said. "Assuming he came to Britain with her. I haven't heard he's here, but then he could have come quietly. And I don't move in the Argentine expatriate community."

"O'Roarke does, doesn't he?" Roth said.

"He has connections," Malcolm said. His father, Raoul O'Roarke, was engaged with the rebellion brewing in Spain, as Kitty was, but he had connections to revolutionary movements all over the world. In fact, he had once considered going to the Argentine. But perhaps best not to dwell on that, especially as the woman he'd thought of going with was now Malcolm's wife.

"I can't put off sending to Bow Street much longer," Roth said. He held out another paper. "I already wrote. Can you find a messenger?"

Malcolm nodded. Kitty and Julien followed him downstairs to give Roth a moment alone with Allegra. And to give them time to talk.

Malcolm surveyed the taproom and gestured to the potboy, a lad of about twelve (or maybe no more than ten or eleven, being underfed made it hard to tell). He had an alert gaze. And unlike most of those serving, he didn't appear to have been drinking. Malcolm gave him Roth's note with a coin and the promise of more when he returned. The boy's eyes widened at the mention of Bow Street.

"They won't do anything to hurt the Three Queens," Malcolm said. "My word on it." Unless, of course, someone at the Three Queens had murdered Allegra Roth.

The boy considered Malcolm for a long moment, then gave a quick nod, and pocketed the note and coin. Perhaps with more trust than was deserved.

Julien moved to the bar, swiped a bottle of gin, and threw down some coins, then jerked his head towards a table in the corner with a view of the door. "I suspect we could all use it," he said, uncorking the bottle. "God, that was surprisingly appalling. I'm losing my touch."

"You're admitting you're human, darling." Kitty took the bottle from him and downed a swallow. "Alejandra was so vital. How unspeakable for Jeremy."

"Yes." Malcolm accepted the bottle Kitty was holding out.

"Roth's not a killer," Julien said.

"You know better than to say we can be certain anyone isn't a killer." Malcolm took a deeper swallow of gin than he'd intended. It burned straight through him. Not unwelcome.

"With assurance? No," Julien conceded. "We can't be sure of anything. But playing the odds, I don't think you should torture yourself thinking your friend—our friend—may have killed his wife. Among other things, it will distract us from the case at hand. Roth's going to need our help. He's not in a powerful position and I imagine there are more than a few at Bow Street and the home office who would be glad of an excuse to be rid of him."

"Yes, I'm afraid so." Malcolm took another drink of gin and gave the bottle back to Kitty. "What else can you tell me about Alejandra Vargas? That you may not have wanted to say in front of Roth?"

Kitty exchanged a look with Julien. "I'm not sure if it would make Jeremy feel better or worse. But though Alejandra and Esquivel seemed to have a passionate relationship, I'm not sure it was exclusive. I remember once going to the Café de la Victoria with her and some of the other actors after a performance. Alejandra left with one of the actors, and I'm quite sure they were going to his lodgings, not the house she shared with Esquivel."

"Is Esquivel the jealous sort?" Malcolm asked.

"He had—has, I suspect—a temper," Julien said. "They fought a great deal. And I'm quite sure he knew she wasn't faithful. I don't think he was faithful to her."

"They may have been clear that fidelity wasn't part of their arrangement," Kitty said. "It took us a long time to sort out that it was part of ours."

"Yes, but even before that I confess to not being free of jealousy," Julien said. "In fact, I was rather more prey to it, because I was quite sure I wasn't your only interest."

"You're an idiot," Kitty said. "Where on earth would I have found time for other interests? I barely had time for you."

"My point precisely."

"Drink some more gin, Julien."

"Was Esquivel prone to violence?" Malcolm asked.

Julien took a swallow of gin. "He was a soldier. Aren't all soldiers prone to violence?"

"Jeremy was a soldier," Kitty said. "He doesn't strike me as violent. I never heard of Esquivel's attacking anyone. But he strikes me as more unstable than Jeremy. On the other hand, Esquivel's many things, but he's not an agent. So if you're envisioning his storming into the Three Queens and killing Alejandra in a fit of jealousy, I'd have a hard time imagining his doing it without attracting notice."

She shivered. Julien wrapped an arm round her without additional comment. Kitty smiled up at him.

"I think she trusted whoever killed her," Julien said. "So if someone surprised her here, it was someone whom she knew and trusted."

"Or someone she'd planned to meet before she met Jeremy," Kitty said. "Someone else from her past, perhaps?" She looked at Malcolm. "What do you know about her?"

"Little more than you. She left London five years ago. Roth was very open about that. But not about the reasons or their marriage. When I knew him in the Peninsula he didn't talk much about his personal life."

"I doubt you talked a great deal about yours." Julien handed the gin to Malcolm.

"True enough." Malcolm took a swallow of gin. Again it had a welcome fire. He wasn't in the mood for something as subtle as whisky. "But he knew Mélanie. Not that I'd have talked about her if he didn't."

"Precisely," Kitty said.

Julien slouched back in his chair and cast a glance round the room. "Who looks out of place?"

"Gentleman near the door," Kitty said. "Green coat. Too well cut and too new for Rosemary Lane."

"Yes, but he's got a second glass on the table and an anxious eye on the door. I reckon he's left a wife at home and is waiting for a lady. Nothing like Seven Dials for anonymity." Julien's gaze shifted. "Brown coat in the left corner?"

"Journalist," Malcolm said. "Ink on his fingers and paper hidden behind his tankard. If he catches on to this we'll have one more problem." He let his gaze drift round the room. "Lady in blue by the bar? She's not making much of an effort to engage any of the gentlemen."

"That's because she's picked two pockets since we've been here," Kitty said. "I've been watching her."

Malcolm grinned despite everything and shoved the bottle across the table to her. "If—"

He broke off at the creak of the door and a blast of cold air. He turned his head to see a man enter the tavern. Not overly tall, with close-cropped curling brown hair and a compact body. He wore a greatcoat, as Roth was accustomed to do, but his was new, olive drab with two capes and no water stains or signs of wear. Perhaps because of that it hung more stiffly about him. Malcolm had met him at Bow Street and the Brown Bear Tavern, which adjoined the Bow Street Public Office and which the Bow Street officers tended to use as an extension of their official premises.

Malcolm pushed himself to his feet. The man caught his gaze and threaded his way across the tavern to them. "Mr. Rannoch."

"Higgins." Malcolm held out his hand.

Higgins shook Malcolm's hand briefly. "Bow Street are very grateful for your assistance. Naturally. Conant mentioned that Roth would likely bring you in."

"You know Lord and Lady Carfax?" Malcolm sent Julien a

silent apology. Official names were called for, for a number of reasons.

"Higgins." Julien's smile was friendly with just the right degree of hauteur.

"Where's Roth?" Higgins asked.

"Upstairs."

"With the victim?"

"He wanted some time alone with her. He hadn't had a moment to think since he found her." Malcolm hesitated a moment. "I don't believe he's a danger to himself."

"And to anyone else?"

"All other things aside, no one else has gone up," Julien said.

Higgins snorted under his breath. "I imagine Lady Carfax would prefer to remain down here."

"Are you mad, Mr. Higgins?" Kitty said. "Why on earth would I wish to remain in such a setting?"

Kitty was in fact perfectly capable of looking after herself in a tavern, but Higgins appeared to recognize his error. "Then perhaps you will take me up."

Malcolm emptied out half his purse and gave it to the potboy who was lurking behind Higgins. Then the four of them climbed the stairs in a crossfire of interested gazes.

CHAPTER 4

Higgins scanned the room where Allegra Roth's body lay. He was a short man, though he carried himself with an authority that commanded the room. Not unlike Hubert Mallinson, who had been spymaster to Malcolm, Julien, and Kitty. Though Higgins was more self-consciously obvious about it.

Higgins studied Allegra Roth, then turned to her husband. "When did you find her?"

"About two hours ago," Roth said.

Higgins's brows snapped together. "Your message got to Bow Street less than half an hour since. What happened to delay the messenger?"

"I needed time," Roth said.

"Time for what?"

"Time to absorb what happened. She was my wife."

"Damn it, Roth, that's shoddy police work."

"I wasn't thinking like an officer. I was thinking like a husband. Which is why I sent for you. I know full well I can't investigate this."

"Certainly not. And yet you sent for Rannoch."

"He's my friend." Which was perhaps the first time Malcolm had heard Jeremy Roth refer to him that way. "I needed a friend."

"To do what?"

"To help me keep from collapsing," Roth said in an even voice.

"And you needed Lord and Lady Carfax too?"

"I sent for them," Malcolm said.

Higgins fixed him with a level gaze. "Why?"

"I wanted their opinion. They've both investigated with us."

"You wanted their opinion before Bow Street's?"

"We got here more quickly," Kitty said. "We were dining nearby."

Higgins ran his gaze over Kitty's tumbled hair and gold silk gown. "Near Seven Dials?"

"In Seven Dials, actually. We have friends in all parts of London, Mr. Higgins. Surely our eccentricities are well enough known that that doesn't surprise you."

Higgins frowned, opened his mouth as though to protest, then seemed to think better of it. He did not appear to have a great deal of imagination, but he also did not seem a stupid man. He turned back to Allegra Roth. "She was like this when you found her?"

"I didn't do more than check for a pulse," Roth said.

"Nor did I," Malcolm said. Leaving aside Julien's investigation. Julien was leaning against a chair, perfecting the art of saying nothing.

"A good thing. Though of course you'd both say so." Higgins walked round to stare down at Allegra Roth from the top of her head. "It didn't occur to you to reach out to Bow Street when she contacted you, Roth?"

"Why the devil would I reach out to Bow Street?" Roth asked. "She was my wife. However tangled our relations, they were personal, not a matter for public scrutiny."

"Not then, perhaps. But now it rather depends on why your wife was here and why she summoned you. You don't know?"

"I haven't heard from my wife for five years, save for one letter that offered no specific details, until the message calling me here tonight."

Higgins's gaze moved round the room. "And what did you find when you arrived?"

Roth met Higgins's gaze squarely. "My wife, lying dead on the floor. As you see her now. She was plainly beyond help, but I did touch her enough to confirm there was no pulse."

"And then you sent for Rannoch."

"I wanted the benefit of his expertise. He's worked with me on a number of investigations."

"But this isn't your investigation."

"No, it's the murder of my wife. I wanted the opinion of a friend."

"Before the opinion of Bow Street."

"Rannoch and his wife have assisted Bow Street numerous times. They've been thanked by the crown." Leaving aside that the chief magistrate, Sir Nathaniel Conant, and the home secretary, Lord Sidmouth, to whom he reported, frequently didn't trust them. With good reason, Malcolm acknowledged.

"And Rannoch sent for Lord and Lady Carfax."

"I wanted their opinion," Malcolm said.

"Quite a crowd." Higgins's gaze swept the room, pinning each one of them in turn, like butterflies caught for display. "I'm sure I don't need to tell you that from anyone else not so connected, this could be considered interfering with official business."

"And I'm sure we don't need to remind you of our official connections." Julien pushed away from the chair. He might loathe being Lord Carfax, but he'd got quite good at making use of the power the title gave him. "Let's not pretend there's anything normal about any of this."

Higgins glanced down at Allegra again. "You said you hadn't seen her in five years," he said to Roth. "Do you have any idea where she's been?"

Roth shook his head. "I traced her as far as Falmouth. But I don't know for a certainty that she set sail or if so where she embarked to."

He said the words slowly as though to give them all time to think the ramifications through. Without so much as exchanging glances, Malcolm knew Roth, Julien, and Kitty had the same instincts he did. It would be so much simpler to keep Allegra's life in the Argentine secret. To call on Marco Esquivel on their own and learn what they could before anyone else questioned him. But sooner or later Higgins would figure out who Allegra was. He'd likely have them followed if he thought they were concealing information. And when they proved to have lied to him, they would only complicate things for Roth.

Malcolm looked at Julien and Kitty and inclined his head. Julien returned the nod. "But as it happens, my wife and I know a bit more," Julien said. "We'd encountered Mrs. Roth in the Argentine, where she was using the name Alejandra Vargas."

Higgins stared at him. "Are you telling me you and Lady Carfax encountered Mrs. Roth across the Atlantic?"

"We weren't married then and I wasn't Lord Carfax. And we didn't know her as Mrs. Roth. But yes."

"And then she—Mrs. Roth—summoned you here tonight?"

"Oh, no," Kitty said. "Malcolm did that. We told you. He wanted our opinion."

"So it was mere coincidence that you arrived at the murder scene of a woman you'd known under another name."

"One would never believe it in a play, would one?" Kitty said.

"No," Higgins said. "One wouldn't."

"I agree it's preposterous," Julien said. "But any plot I can devise that explains what else we were doing here is even more farfetched. Perhaps Mélanie Rannoch could come up with something more coherent. But if you're too suspicious, you can always arrest us."

Higgins scowled at him. Because of course arresting Earl

Carfax, who was also the nephew of Britain's unofficial head of intelligence and connected to the home secretary who oversaw Bow Street, would rattle more cages than Higgins cared to do. "Of course I take your word, my lord," Higgins said. "And it's far too early in the case to arrest anyone."

Which also made it impossible for him to arrest Roth that night. Julien was excellent at manipulating a situation to his advantage. "I knew at once you were a man of sense," Julien said.

Higgins grunted. "Do you know what brought Mrs. Roth back to England?" he asked.

"From what Lord and Lady Carfax tell me, she appears to have come with her lover," Roth said in the same level voice he'd been using since Higgins's entrance. "A man named Esquivel, who is a leader in the Argentine revolution."

Higgins frowned. Suddenly the domestic drama he was investigating had turned into an international incident, which had a host of repercussions. He looked at Julien and Kitty. "You know this Esquivel?"

"We did, in the Argentine," Julien said. "Neither Kitty nor I have seen him recently."

Higgins swung his gaze to Roth. "You can't tell me you didn't investigate when your wife disappeared."

"Of course I did. I traced her to Falmouth, as I told you. I couldn't leave the country—I had two young children. And then after I received her letter it was plain she did not wish to return. There was little point in pursuing a woman who did not want to be with me."

"You came to see her tonight."

"The mother of my children, with whom I had lived for almost seven years, asked to see me. Of course I came to see her. Our marriage may have been over but our children will always connect us."

"Why do you think she wanted to see you tonight?"

"I should very much like to know. I never got the chance to speak with her."

"Yes, so you said."

"Our life together was over, Higgins. Nothing she might have said to me tonight could have changed that. And from what Lord and Lady Carfax have said, it's clear she had built her own life elsewhere. I can't imagine she wanted to return to me. But she was the mother of my children, whom I once loved very deeply. Whom I had known since childhood." Roth hesitated a fraction of a second, as though aware he'd revealed something. "I want to know what happened to her. I will do anything possible to assist you."

"For the moment, you can best assist us by staying out of the way. I'll need to find this Marco Esquivel, if he is indeed in London. Do you know where he might be?"

"We don't even know for a certainty he's in London," Julien said. "But if he is, I can hazard a good guess where he may be. Would you like us to come with you to talk to him?"

Higgins hesitated. He clearly wanted to run this investigation himself, and he saw them as Roth's allies. On the other hand, he was a good enough investigator to take advantage of help. And he must know if he didn't talk to Esquivel with Julien and Kitty, they would seek out Esquivel on their own. Just as they wanted to be there when he spoke with Esquivel, he wanted to be there when they did.

"Thank you, my lord. Given that you know him, I would be most appreciative. It will be difficult news."

"I quite agree," Kitty said. "Terrible, but better for him to hear it from people he knows."

"Are you sure you wish to be there, Lady Carfax?"

"Quite sure, Mr. Higgins." Kitty smiled at him with complete assurance.

Higgins looked at Roth. "You need to go home and stay out of this."

"I know," Roth said. "It's what I'd say to a victim's spouse. I'm not a fool, contrary to what some believe."

"Believe me, Roth, I think you many things, but I don't think you a fool."

CHAPTER 5

*R*oth stared through the thickening shadows of Longacre. Not so very far from Seven Dials, but a world away. Carriages rattled by, carrying people from Mayfair to their boxes at Covent Garden or Drury Lane or the Tavistock, save that the Tavistock wasn't performing tonight. "You needn't have walked me all the way home," he said. "I'm not going to collapse. Or bolt."

"You're too strong for the first and too sensible for the second," Malcolm said. "But I didn't want you to be alone."

Roth paused and turned to look at him, one half of his face in shadow, the other lit by the glow of a streetlamp. "You're a good fellow, Rannoch."

"I imagine you'll want time alone. But not until—"

"I need to talk to Harriet. And figure out how I'm going to tell the boys. I can't think beyond that just now."

They moved into James Street. Roth stopped again, staring at the dark outline of a lamppost and the murky puddle of light on the paving stones. "She was the mother of my children. But I don't think I really knew her."

"Difficult to know another person. There are many times I've felt I don't know Mélanie."

"But you do now."

Was there the slightest question in Roth's tone? Malcolm couldn't be sure. Just as he couldn't be entirely sure what Roth knew or might have guessed about Mélanie. His wife, whom he had married to protect, who had married him to spy on him for an enemy country, whom he was somehow still married to and still in love with three years after learning the truth. A truth that could still ruin all of them, for all Mélanie had a royal pardon.

"I'm not sure one can ever fully know another person. But we know each other better than when we married."

Roth watched him a moment longer. Mist swirled in the lamplight between them. "People marry for different reasons. And the marriage can go in different directions. You and Mélanie were fortunate."

"Yes. I'm grateful for it every day." Malcolm hesitated a moment, then put a hand on Roth's shoulder. "I'm sorry, Jeremy."

Roth met Malcolm's gaze, his own opaque, though the torment was there, as though behind leaded glass. "I lost her a long time ago."

"There's a difference between that and someone's being truly gone."

"And yet the questions remain. And the secrets."

"You can't—"

"I know. If I poke about in this, I'll rouse Bow Street's suspicions and risk arrest more than I already do, and possibly muck up the investigation because I don't have proper perspective. But could you stay out of it if it were Mélanie?"

"I don't think so. Which is why I'm hoping to hell you can be more sensible than I'd be in such circumstances. We'll update you. Whenever we can."

Roth held his gaze for a long moment. "As much as you can safely share."

"That's how it always is when we work a case."

Roth's gaze continued steady for the space of a heartbeat. Or a rifle shot. "So it is." He looked down Hart Street towards his lodging house.

"Do you want to talk?" Malcolm said. "First?"

"At the moment I want to escape, more than anything."

"It's not cowardly. And I need—"

Roth met his gaze. "To know about Allegra."

"Yes."

They went into a pub at the corner of Hart Street, where Roth was a regular. Malcolm had been there several times with Roth. It could not be more different from the scarred, garish glamour of the Three Queens. Sober, mellowed dark wood, a game of darts in progress in one corner, chess and backgammon on several of the tables. Malcolm ordered two pints of stout to avoid Roth's having to make conversation, and they retreated to a quiet table on a raised section at the back of the pub, though Roth had to exchange words with a few acquaintances on the way.

Roth took a deep drink of stout. "Our parents were friends. That sounds so conventional, doesn't it? Almost like an arranged marriage. But it wasn't that way at all. There wasn't anything conventional about either of our families. My father was a bookseller. I never told you that, did I?"

"No," Malcolm said. Not even when one of their investigations had taken them to a bookseller's.

Roth gave a crooked grin. "I learned early not to talk about personal details. Better for an investigator to be as anonymous as possible. And we mostly associated through my work even if we became friends."

"I'm relieved you'll admit to being friends."

For a moment Roth's grin deepened and they might have been sharing Rioja in a Spanish mud hut instead of stout in a London pub. "I'm not quite so insufferable."

"You're not insufferable in the least. You put up with a lot from your friends."

Roth took another drink, hands curved round the tankard. "My father was Jewish, but he'd left off going to synagogue long before he married Mama. Harriet and I weren't raised as anything in particular. Neither of us was baptized, not so much because our parents were Jewish as because they weren't Christian either."

"Our children weren't baptized either," Malcolm said. He'd been very relieved when he realized Mélanie didn't want them to be. That was before he knew her own father had been a Jewish atheist and her mother had left her family and religion to marry him.

Roth nodded. He might not know Mélanie's history, but he knew Mélanie and Malcom enough now not to be surprised. "Our parents moved in what you'd call bluestocking circles, I suppose. Though certainly not as grand as some. Allegra's mother and step-father were friends of our parents. Her stepfather had a printing business."

Which Roth also hadn't mentioned when a recent investigation had taken them into the printshop where Edmund Blayney published his Radical newspaper. "Stepfather?" Malcolm said. "Who was her father?"

"Her mother's first husband. A Mr. Wainwright." Roth gave another faint smile. "At least that was the story. I remember rumors from when we were quite small that Allegra's mother hadn't been a widow at all, and that Allegra's father was a former lover of her mother's. Someone grand. Allegra rather played into that. But then I think a lot of that was the consequence it gave her. Allegra always wanted to be special. In any case, we all grew up going in and out of each other's houses. Harriet and me and Allegra and her stepsister Cressida. And the children their parents had together, but they were nearly a decade younger."

"Were you childhood sweethearts?"

"Not precisely. Not at all, really. I'll admit I always had a soft spot for her, even when she was putting on airs. And she did flirt with me. But she flirted with a lot of men. She was young and pretty and that was one sort of power open to her. Allegra always liked power. Then, when she seventeen, she disappeared and there were a lot of whispers. At least, that's what Harriet wrote to me. I was in the Peninsula by that time. Harriet knew a bit more than she let on, I think. They were friends, though Allegra always tended to drive Harriet to distraction. Harriet said Allegra had been dropping hints about a fascinating man who was courting her. But Harriet didn't know who it was, or didn't tell me. Then, a year later, I was home on leave and I encountered Allegra in a coffeehouse. Looking back, I think she may have arranged the meeting, but at the time it seemed fortuitous. She told me she'd gone off with Lord Gresham."

"The composer?" Malcolm had met Gresham once or twice and enjoyed his music. Mélanie had talked with Gresham more, but Malcolm knew there were stories that Gresham's romantic exploits rivaled Lord Byron's.

"Yes," Roth said. "They'd gone off to Edinburgh, where Gresham had an opera premiering. The affair had ended and Allegra was back in London alone."

"And didn't want to go home."

"She wasn't sure what her parents would say. Gresham hadn't left her destitute, but the money wouldn't last." Roth shifted in his seat and reached for his tankard. "I know it will seem as though I married her to offer her protection. But that wasn't it. I was in love. If I'm honest, I had been for a long time. Maybe since I was eight." He stared into his tankard, but didn't take a drink. "I thought Allegra was in love too. She may actually have been. We shared a frustration with the world round us. A feeling that perhaps even our Radical parents were too given over to convention."

"And yet you married. Which can seem a very conventional

act." Malcolm studied Roth, who was studying a knothole in the table. "Was Allegra with child?"

Roth looked up and met his gaze. "That wasn't why I loved her. But yes, it's the reason we married quickly when we did. It's so long ago I don't even think about it anymore when I look at Samuel."

"Mélanie was pregnant when I married her. You know that now."

Roth nodded without looking away. Malcolm suspected he was aware of a great deal more. "It was selfish perhaps to marry when I had to return to the Peninsula. Hard for Allegra to be alone with the baby. She was always restless. Odd, that was something we had in common and yet it was what drove us apart. She'd always wanted to be special from the time she was a girl. I told you about her stories about her parentage. Allegra liked the idea of being different. She had dreams—of being an actress or a writer or painter or a singer. But I'm not sure it was the art form that mattered to her so much as the idea of achieving something. We had in common that we were both dissatisfied." Roth stared at his hands for a moment. "I thought that made us kindred spirits. But in the end, she was just as dissatisfied as my wife as she'd been before. And I wasn't there enough to see it getting worse." He stared at the half-timbered beams that overhung their table. "I've wondered since Mélanie started writing. If Allegra would have been happier if she'd had something to pursue."

It was one of the first times Roth had compared their lives. "Surely that would have had to come from her."

"Oh yes. But I could have encouraged it more. I could have noticed more. How the hell could I think she'd be happy living in two rooms? Not the lack of luxury. The lack of scope."

"I missed a lot with Mel. For a long time." And not just that she'd been a French spy. That she was trapped by the role she'd married into.

Roth met his gaze in a rare moment of kinship. "Allegra was depressed after both babies were born. I'm not sure I understood that as well as I might have done. Instead, when I had leave I'd want to be with the boys and she'd want to go out and we'd quarrel. She'd often end up going out with friends and I'd stay with the boys." He took a drink and held the tankard in front of his face. "If I'm honest, I suspected there were other men. I didn't really want to confront it. We were apart. Plenty of men I knew sought consolation. I didn't. But in a way I could understand that she did. When I came back after Waterloo, I thought we could piece things together. I told myself it would take time. But what common ground we'd had seemed gone. It wasn't us against the world anymore. It was us against each other. I was fairly sure she had a lover before she disappeared. But it never occurred to me she'd leave. I thought we'd stumble on as we were, locked in an uncomfortable embrace. I knew she was unhappy. I don't think I realized how desperate she was."

"You had no idea the lover was Esquivel?"

"None. What I said before is true. I traced her as far as Falmouth, but I couldn't learn where she'd sailed. Or even if she had. I had to get back to the boys, but I had contacts making inquiries. Until I got her letter. At that point it was over. Though of course it really couldn't be. I kept wondering if she'd turn up again, the way she had after Gresham."

"Did you want her to come back?"

Roth grimaced. "I couldn't imagine our marriage going back even to the hell it had been. But I'd have wanted the boys to have a relationship with their mother. And—" He glanced away, gaze fixed across the pub, eyes narrowed. He took a drink of stout and looked into his tankard as though it held answers. "I was angry at her half the time. At moments I'd have said I hated her. I'd lost any illusions that we could live together in anything like comfort. But I was still in love with her. At least then."

"What changed?" Malcolm asked.

"I changed." Roth pulled his tankard closer.

Malcolm had an odd sense they'd come to a key point in the discussion, though he couldn't yet be sure how. "In what way?"

Roth took another drink. "You might say I've grown up at last. Let go of illusions from childhood. Allegra haunted me for a long time. She doesn't anymore. But I loved her. And I wouldn't have done her harm."

"Can you think of anyone from her life in England who would?"

"Her stepfather died not long after we married. Her mother remarried and moved to Yorkshire. Took the younger children with her. Allegra didn't keep in close touch, but I heard enough to know they're all settled there." He passed a hand over his face. "I'll have to write to Margaret. Her mother. But the only family Allegra had stayed close to was Cressida. Her stepsister."

"Is she still in London?"

"Oh yes." Roth gave a faint smile. "She lives in Mayfair. I doubt you've ever met her, but I imagine a number of your colleagues have. Cressida Caldwell—the name she uses—is a very successful courtesan. Like Allegra, she wanted to break free of the life she grew up in."

"Were the sisters close?"

"If incessant quarrels comprise closeness, then yes. Though they also shared a certain solidarity against their parents. Cressida brought gifts when the boys were born and Allegra would visit her on occasion. In truth, I think she was jealous. Cressy lived far better than we did. She'd complain about her sister, but also say at least Cressy had managed to carve out life on her own terms. Cressy still visits on occasion and sends presents for the boys' birthdays. We live very different lives, but I've always been fond of her. And however Allegra annoyed her, I can't see Cressida's having anything like a motive to murder her."

"What about others in London?"

"The only ex-lover of hers I know by name is Gresham. Allegra didn't exactly remember him fondly, but she did admit he left her not destitute. I don't know how Gresham felt, but unless a great deal more was going on, it's hard to see a murder motive. I suspect there were others, though. Perhaps before Gresham and almost certainly before Esquivel, while we were still married. But it still would have been far in the past."

"Anyone she might have sought out particularly?"

"Cressy, possibly. She might have been afraid Cressy would tell me. But then Allegra sought me out. I still don't know why. If she wanted to arrange a time to see the boys, the Three Queens was hardly the most sensible choice for the meeting. Though Allegra could always be quixotic. To say the least." He took a slow drink of stout.

"Anything else?" Malcolm asked.

"About Allegra? I'm not sure I ever knew her, but even with the war and her five-year absence I have decades of memories."

"Which you needn't share. Unless there's anything else that could relate to why she might have been killed?"

Roth gave a smile as bitter as the stout. "That's usually my question. And like so many of those I question, I may be missing something. But no."

Malcolm took a drink of stout and nodded. He wouldn't be surprised if Roth was missing something. But what concerned him more was that he was quite sure his friend was holding something back.

"Where do you think Esquivel and Mrs. Roth were staying?" Higgins asked, when he, Julien, and Kitty had left the Three Queens. Queen Street had grown more crowded as the night advanced, the smells of ale, gin, and urine more pronounced in the air. Higgins drew the folds of his greatcoat closer about him. He seemed more uncomfortable than she and Julien, Kitty thought, for all he must be accustomed to all parts of London.

"Most likely Mivart's," Julien said.

Higgins sent him a sharp look. "Why?"

"It's a favorite with foreign visitors who wish to stay for an extended period. Especially if they're plump in the pocket."

It had been too expensive for Kitty when she came to Britain a year and a half ago, but Raoul O'Roarke, Malcolm's father, had made it his London home until he moved into Malcolm's Berkeley Square house. He still hosted a Boxing Day dinner in a private room at the hotel. They had been there with the children not that long ago.

"They won't tell us if he's a guest," Higgins said.

"They'll tell me," Julien said.

Higgins frowned, but did not argue. He knew the world too well.

Julien guided them expertly to the edge of Seven Dials (somehow, however he was dressed, he radiated the air of someone no one would dare assault).

"You didn't bring your carriage to dine with your friends?" Higgins asked, shoulders hunched against the chill air.

"Quicker to walk, with the press of carriages," Julien said. Which was true. Especially as, when they had received Malcolm's crisp but obviously urgent message, bringing the carriage would have meant waiting to have the horses harnessed.

Higgins humphed with the air of one who would never get over the eccentricities of the beau monde, and said little more until they reached the corner of Brook and Davies Streets. The sight of the Mivart's portico brought memories of that Boxing Day dinner less than two months ago. Kitty could almost hear the boys' cries of excitement at the pine and holly in the lobby, and feel Genny wriggling in her arms. Such a different occasion. But the footman at the door recognized them. Higgins had the sense to hang back as Julien asked after their friend Mr. Esquivel. Which wasn't really a lie. Marco Esquivel had been a friend, to the extent either of them had had friends in those days.

However, the footman said that he believed Mr. Esquivel had gone to Covent Garden. Which meant retracing their steps. This time they took a hackney, though they climbed down and walked the last part of the way through the crush round the theatre. Again, she and Julien could help with entrée. They didn't have their box tokens, but an usher recognized them and waved them in. Kitty undid the ties on her cloak. She was wearing a gold silk gown she'd also been wearing the night they'd ended up at an investigation in the mist of Emily Cowper's holiday ball. She'd put it on for a quiet evening with Julien and the children, but with its body-skimming fit and profusion of ruffles it was designed to draw attention. She'd had her husband's in mind, but it worked well for distracting notice from their real motives at the theatre.

The play was a comedy that was imitation Sheridan, though not as good. They found Esquivel in a box with three men who looked to be Argentine expatriates (two were vaguely familiar) and two British men whom Kitty had met once or twice in parliamentary circles. Esquivel looked much as Kitty remembered. Thick dark hair, well-cut profile, a body that looked as though he'd rather be riding or fighting even when lounging in a gilded chair in a box. He stared from Julien to Kitty with a confused gaze.

Not surprisingly. Julien had been in a variety of disguises during their associations and hadn't even been using Julien St. Juste as his name, let alone Julien Mallinson. So Kitty held out her hand and said, "It's Katelina Ashford that was. We haven't seen each other since I left Buenos Aires two years ago."

"Of course." Esquivel pushed himself to his feet and bowed. "Mrs. Ashford. And now you're—"

"Lady Carfax. My husband, Lord Carfax." Which neatly slid past whether or not Esquivel recognized Julien. She flashed an apologetic look round the group. "Could we go somewhere to talk? I'm afraid we have unfortunate news."

Esquivel's brows drew together, but he was used to surprises of all kinds. And still had no notion of the horror of this one, poor man. He excused himself to his friends and accompanied them to the main salon where Higgins was waiting with a glass of brandy he'd had the forethought to procure.

"It's Alejandra," Kitty said.

"You've seen her?" Esquivel asked in surprise.

"Yes, tonight."

Esquivel frowned. "She sent for you? She's at our hotel."

"No. She went out to a tavern. The Three Queens in Seven Dials."

"What on earth would Alejandra—"

"Marco." Kitty touched his arm. She had no experience of this. Someone had once come to tell her her husband had been died, but Edward hadn't meant half to her what she suspected Alejandra meant to Esquivel. "Alejandra was murdered."

Esquivel's eyes went wide. His mouth opened, then closed. "That's impossible."

"I'm afraid not." Julien picked up the brandy and pressed it into Esquivel's hand. "We all saw her. It was undoubtedly Alejandra."

Esquivel stared at him. "You're—"

"Juan Murez," Julien said. "Carlisle Arbuthnot. Francisco Gerrard. Also Juliana Cortez. We met under many guises. But my actual name is Mallinson and I now have the dubious fortune of being Lord Carfax. And the staggering good fortune of being Kitty's husband. Drink some brandy. I can't imagine anything so appalling."

Esquivel lunged as though to strike Julien, then spun away and threw the glass against the wall. It shattered, spattering brandy and shards of crystal against the cream silk wall hangings.

"I'm so sorry," Kitty said.

Esquivel drew a breath that sounded like smashed crystal. "You saw her?"

"We both saw her," Kitty said. "There's no doubt it was Alejandra."

Julien poured another glass of brandy and held it out. Esquivel snatched it and downed half the glass. "What on earth could she have been doing there? Was she meeting you?"

"No," Julien said. "She appears to have had a meeting with her husband."

The glass tilted in Esquivel's fingers. Julien righted it. "You must have known she was married."

"We had no secrets from each other." Esquivel stared into the glass. "That bastard. What did he do to her?"

"He says she was dead when he came into the room," Kitty said. "We believe him."

Esquivel's head jerked up. His gaze pinned her as though he had her pressed against the silk wall hangings. "What were you doing there?"

"Roth sent for us," Kitty said. "That is, he sent for our friend, Malcolm Rannoch, who sent for us."

"You know Alejandra's husband?"

"He's a friend," Kitty said.

"He's what? That—"

"Strains credulity," Julien said. "I know. But it happens to be the truth. I don't know if you know, but Jeremy Roth is a Bow Street runner. He works with Higgins here, who is investigating Alejandra's murder."

Esquivel's gaze went to Higgins. Higgins had been hanging back in the shadows, but now he took a step forwards. "You had no idea your—Mrs. Roth meant to see her husband tonight?"

"Mrs. who? Oh. I see. No. Of course not."

"Why of course, sir? You were in London. Mr. Roth was here. And their children. Surely it had occurred to you she might try to see them?"

"Alejandra said—" Esquivel's throat worked. He tossed down a drink of brandy. "She said it would only tear open old wounds. She almost didn't come on this trip with me because of that. But she thought if she mostly remained at the hotel she could avoid them. Her husband didn't move in the circles I did."

"No," Higgins agreed. "Though it seems he has friends who do."

Esquivel cast a quick look at Kitty and Julien. "We couldn't have known that."

"Where did you think Mrs. Roth was tonight?" Higgins asked.

"I told you. At our hotel. I was invited to the theatre by friends. I felt I should go as we had business to discuss. Alejandra said she had a headache, and in any case she preferred to go about as little as possible."

"She'd written to Roth asking him to meet her," Kitty said. "We saw the letter."

Esquivel stared at her. A protest seemed to die on his lips.

"Difficult to learn the person one lives with has secrets," Julien said. "But not unusual."

"I loved Alejandra. The past was in the past for both of us."

"And yet you'd both come back to the scene of your past," Julien said. "I believe you have a wife here as well."

Esquivel's gaze shot to his face. "What's that to say to—"

"Were you planning to see your wife while you're in Britain?"

"Not that it's any business of yours, but I need to discuss arrangements for our children with her."

"Perhaps Alejandra felt she needed to do the same with her husband."

"Then why wouldn't she tell me?"

"Fear of your reaction, perhaps? Jealousy would be understandable."

Esquivel made an impatient gesture that sent more drops of brandy spattering against the wall hangings. "I had no more reason to be jealous of Roth than Alejandra did to be jealous of my wife."

"Jealousy tends not to be reasonable."

"Whom had Mrs. Roth seen since she'd been in London?" Higgins asked.

"A few friends we'd dined with quietly. The staff at the hotel. That's all."

"That you know of," Higgins said.

"I told you, she didn't have secrets from me. We were open about everything. Including what you might call our indiscretions." He flung that last at Higgins as a challenge.

"That would have been between you and Mrs. Roth, sir," Higgins said. "But since she contacted Roth, we have to consider whom else she may have contacted. I'll need to look through her things—"

"What the devil—"

"They're evidence."

"Quite. I'm not thinking." Esquivel scraped a hand over his hair. "What the hell was she doing in Seven Dials? She knew London. She grew up here. She knew it was a dangerous neighborhood."

"The Alejandra I knew was fearless," Kitty said.

"Yes, she was that." A smile lit Esquivel's eyes for an instant. "But not foolish. Could some madman—"

"It's possible," Julien said. "It's a rough part of town, as you say. But from the look of things, she knew the killer."

Esquivel stared at him. "How—"

"Whoever it was was able to get close. And there was no sign of a struggle. I don't know that this is any comfort, but it happened quickly."

Esquivel glanced away and took another drink of brandy. "I want to see her."

"We've moved her to where a doctor can examine her," Higgins said. "But I can take you."

Esquivel gave a curt nod. "Her husband—Roth—he says he didn't see anything?"

"He says she was dead when he arrived, as Lord and Lady Carfax said."

"And do you also believe him?"

Higgins shifted his weight from one foot to the other. "What I believe doesn't matter at this point. We have very little evidence. Speaking of evidence, I assume you have friends who can vouch that you were at the theatre all evening?"

"Why the devil—" Esquivel stared at Higgins. "You think *I* might have killed her?"

Higgins returned Esquivel's gaze, his own impassive. "Roth himself could tell you the spouse or lover of a victim is always a subject of interest. Which means both Mr. Roth's whereabouts and yours are of interest, sir."

"I loved her, you bastard. She was everything to me. Alejandra was my wife in every way that matters. I'd have married her if I could."

"Why did you come back to England?" Higgins asked.

"I had business. On behalf of my country. Alejandra knew it would be challenging but she wanted to come with me."

"But she didn't want to see her children?" Kitty said.

Esquivel glanced to the side. "She rarely spoke of them. Not—you must believe me—because she did not care. It was a source of great pain that she was separated from them."

"But not, apparently, enough to bring her back," Julien said. "I'm sure Roth wouldn't have kept their children from her."

"I doubt he'd have let her take them to the Argentine."

"Would you have left your life in the Argentine to stay here with Alejandra so she could see her children?" Kitty said.

"I couldn't. One has to think of duty. Your first husband was soldier. You must understand that."

"I understand that duty can mean different things," Kitty said. Edward had had little sense of duty except to the bottle and his mistresses. "More now than I once did. I know that my first duty is to my family. And I can't imagine keeping anyone I loved away from their family."

"Alejandra was not an ordinary woman."

Julien gave a short laugh. "Describe an ordinary woman. I have yet to meet one. And yet family bonds can influence anyone."

Esquivel gave a curt nod. "My own children are in England. I too feel the guilt of being away from them. Alejandra and I both recognized our children were better off where they were. And yet the world looks on her more harshly than me for being away from them."

"I won't argue with you on the unfairness of that," Julien said. "Which doesn't change the fact that children find it hard to have their parents gone."

Esquivel met Julien's gaze, his own hard though not without questions. "I make no excuses for myself. Alejandra wouldn't either. We did what we thought we had to. We were neither of us suited to matrimony, though we both undertook it."

"And yet you said you'd have married her if you could," Higgins said.

"To protect her in the eyes of the world. It would not have been a conventional marriage."

"Neither is Kitty's and mine, if it comes to that," Julien said. "Neither are many I know of."

"Quite, as I learned to say at Cambridge." Esquivel pushed himself away from the wall and looked at Higgins. "I want to see Alejandra. You want to see her things. And distasteful as I find the prospect of your turning them over, I want you to do it piece by piece. I want you to learn who did this to her. So I can make the bastard pay."

CHAPTER 7

"*Y*ou can't expect marriage to completely change a person."

Manon Caret delivered the line with just the right irony with emotional weight beneath. Mélanie Rannoch looked up from the table to the side of the stage where she was sitting with a script before her and a pencil tucked behind her ear. Words could ring true. Perhaps more sharply than the writer intended.

"*Thank god,*" Brandon Ford said. "*Having taken the risk of falling in love, against all prudence and sense, one would scarcely want the person one loved to change.*"

That did sound like Malcolm. In fact, he had said something very similar. Not fair to hear his tones in her head. Brandon was a brilliant actor and she was lucky to have him.

"*You have the best way of putting things, darling,*" Manon said. "*But sometimes people do change.*" Manon looked across the room at Mélanie. "Should that be sharper? I don't mean more cutting—more specific?"

Mélanie frowned. How would she say this to Malcolm? Not that the play was about her and Malcolm, of course. "You're right," she said. "I need to rework that bit."

"A good time for a break." Simon Tanner got to his feet from his chair beside Mélanie. He was a playwright himself and part owner of the Tavistock Theatre, and was staging Mélanie's new play. "Tea."

"Or something stronger," Brandon said.

Simon turned to Mélanie with a grin. "It inevitably sounds different in rehearsal than when one writes it."

"Yes, I know." Mélanie flexed her fingers. "I have a list of lines that don't sound quite natural. But I want to work on this scene in particular."

"It's a key scene. Those often need the most layers. Get some tea. I'm going to use the break to go over notes with Letty and Will. Then maybe we'll run the end of Act II again."

Mélanie moved to the tea table. Normally they had tea in the green room, but for rehearsals a table was set up on the edge of the stage. She poured a cup of tea and splashed some milk into it. Her children, Colin and Jessica, who had been watching from a blanket on the floor in the wings, ran over to her. "It's good," Jessica said, with the confidence of a four-year-old already versed in theatre.

"I hope so," Mélanie said. "It needs to be better."

"You always say that," Colin said. At seven and a half he had remarkably—sometimes frighteningly—keen insight into the adults about him. "Even on the first night."

"But hopefully I'll be more confident on the first night."

"Can we have biscuits?" Jessica eyed the plate on the tea table.

"As long as you leave enough for everyone else."

Jessica grinned, then turned her head at the sound of footsteps from the backstage passage.

"Daddy!" Clutching two biscuits, she ran towards the passage and threw her arms round Malcolm's knees.

"Darling," Mélanie said as her husband scooped up Jessica and walked towards them. "Did you finish at Brooks's early?"

"I left the meeting early, as it happens." Perhaps it was the light slanting from the wings, but his gray eyes seemed darker than usual. "There've been some unexpected developments. Julien and Kitty should be here soon and we can update you."

"Is it an Investigation?" Colin asked.

"I'm afraid so." Malcolm smiled at Jessica as she gave him a bite of biscuit and met Mélanie's gaze over the top of their daughter's head. It was bad. A dozen possible scenarios ran through her head, but she would wait for Kitty and Julien. No sense in alarming the children.

She held out her tea to give Malcolm a sip. "We're nearly through the rehearsal. Which is just as well, because I'm a bit nervous about your seeing the play yet. I have some revising to do tonight."

"It's good," Colin said. "Parts are very funny. And the romance-y bits aren't sick-making."

They moved back to the table where she'd been sitting, with their tea (and at Jessica's insistence, more biscuits). A few minutes later, footsteps announced Julien and Kitty's arrival.

They greeted the children with smiles, but Mélanie caught their concern as well. It had probably been too long without a crisis in their lives. But this one seemed to have both her husband and Julien and Kitty uncharacteristically disturbed.

"I was hoping for a peek backstage," Kitty said. "Perhaps Colin and Jessica would take me?"

Jessica ran to take Kitty's hand. Colin followed them, though he sent a look over his shoulder at his mother. He was going to ask uncomfortable questions tonight.

Mélanie looked from Malcolm to Julien when Kitty left with the children. "What's happened? Don't prevaricate. I knew the minute Malcolm walked in."

Malcolm perched on the edge of the table beside Julien and told her, with the succinctness with which he'd summarize the text of a bill or a diplomatic paper.

Seven years of war, the aftermath of the White Terror, spy

missions and murder investigations, some involving friends and family. And yet Mélanie found herself staring at her husband, her fingers numb on the edge of the table. "How unspeakably awful," she said. "Is Jeremy—"

"I saw him home. I hope he has the sense to stay there. Though I don't think I would, in his place."

"And you sent for Kitty and Julien." Mélanie looked at Julien, who had been quiet while Malcolm told the story, then back at Malcolm. "But you didn't know they knew Allegra Roth then?"

"I needed their opinion. I needed Julien's."

Mélanie's gaze shot to Julien again. Julien looked back, neither pleased nor abashed. "Yes, I can quite see that," she said. "But I wasn't far away from Seven Dials. Why didn't you—"

"You were in the midst of rehearsal, sweetheart." Malcolm's gaze was steady.

"I could have—"

"Left and missed it? You said yourself there's work you need to do, based on what you saw tonight. You wouldn't get that rehearsal back. There'll be plenty of time to investigate later. And you were with the children. I know Manon or Simon could have stayed with them, but why? We had it under control."

"Yes. Of course." God, she was an agent, a mother, a play-wright, and a wife. You'd think she'd be used to the pull of competing loyalties by now.

"I felt the same during the queen's case when I was stuck in Parliament while you lot did the interesting things," Julien said.

"You managed to do a great deal in that investigation," Mélanie said.

"I still cooled my heels far too much listening to details that might be entertaining in a French novel but managed to be damnably dull in court. But you needn't worry, you'll be needed for the long game. We all will."

"Did Jeremy ever talk to you about his wife?" Malcolm asked Mélanie.

"No. He scarcely mentioned her at all."

"I thought he might have talked more to you. You have a way of drawing out confidences."

"Only the smallest comment here and there. An occasional reference to when they'd been married, but mostly comments about her being gone. Harriet doesn't talk about her either. And I didn't want to push. We all have secrets."

"Especially from Roth, among all our friends," Malcolm said.

Jeremy Roth didn't know she had been a Bonapartist spy. At least not officially. Mélanie sometimes wondered if he had worked any of it out. But if he had, he was very discreet. The chief magistrate of Bow Street reported to the home secretary. It would be dangerous for both Roth and her for him to know too much.

"Which makes it a bit ironic that we're going to be wading into the midst of his," Mélanie said. "From what Jeremy says—or what he doesn't say—I think he was once very much in love with his wife."

"That," said Julien, "is mildly obvious. He's scarcely mentioned her to me at all. But I doubt a man like Roth would marry for another reason."

"How did Alejandra feel about the Argentine revolution?" Mélanie asked.

"She appeared to share Esquivel's commitment to it. With a fervor it was hard for me to understand. Recall we are discussing a time when I hesitated to admit I believed in anything. Alejandra and Esquivel's home was a hotbed of discussion. A salon of sorts, but with a distinctly revolutionary bent. And a lot of talk about the Spanish constitution and Paine and Locke and all sorts of people I wouldn't at the time have admitted to having read. Or at least to having paid attention to. The sort I used to accuse you and O'Roarke of droning on about."

"But if you were there, there must have been intelligence intrigues occurring," Mélanie said.

"It was a revolution. Intrigue was everywhere. Especially

among the revolutionaries. They were already breaking into factions. As a detached observer, I found it fascinating. Kitty had allegiances which made it harder for her."

"Say what you will," Malcolm said, "you've always—"

Feet pounded on the floorboards. Colin came running in from the wings. "Someone stabbed Auntie Kitty!"

CHAPTER 8

*J*ulien was across the stage before the words left
Colin's mouth. Malcolm and Mélanie ran close
behind, Colin following them.

Kitty was in the wings, Jessica clinging to her skirts, Manon
winding a bandage round her arm.

"I'm all right," she said quickly. "He ran out of the wings. That
way." She gestured to the stage door.

Julien pressed a kiss to her hair and raced out the door,
Malcolm behind him.

Mélanie exchanged a look with Manon and Kitty, touched
Jessica's hair, smiled at Colin, and ran after Julien and Malcolm.
Out the stage door, into the alley behind the theatre. An alley
where Julien himself had been struck by a would-be assassin's
bullet a year ago. An assassin aiming at a young woman with
secrets.

Mist swirled in the alley. Julien was halfway to the corner.
Mélanie could see a dark form in front of him. Malcolm was a
dozen paces behind. Julien drew back his arm and hurled something. The fleeing man fell to the cobblestones. Julien ran after,
Malcolm close behind. As Julien bent over the fallen man, pulling

him to his feet, a shot rang out. The man collapsed backwards on the cobblestones.

Mélanie got there to find Julien and Malcolm attempting to staunch the blood flowing from the man's chest though the life had already fled from his eyes.

"From the looks of it, I'd hazard he was hired for the job," Julien said.

"Yes. We'll see if Higgins can trace him. And if he was anywhere near the Three Queens tonight." Malcolm scanned the street.

"The shot came from over there." Julien jerked his head towards the shadows down the street. "I saw a blur of movement. The shooter will be gone before we can find him." He was riffling through the man's pockets. "This is what he got Kitty with." He held up a knife. "It's not thin enough to be the weapon that killed Allegra Roth. Which doesn't mean he didn't kill her. But even if he did, there's the question of who hired him. And why."

Julien and Malcolm carried the man back into the alley. Simon came running out of the stage door.

"He's dead," Malcolm said. "We'll have to send for Bow Street. But there's no threat to the theatre."

"Damnation." Simon drew a hard breath. He wasn't an agent, but he had been round Malcolm and Mélanie enough to have been involved in several investigations. "We've kept the doors locked," he said. "Ever since the Thornsby business." Lewis Thornsby had been murdered in the theatre a year ago. Mélanie and the children had found him, and Julien had arrived shortly after. And the murder attempt in which Julien had been shot had been only a few months before that. "What the hell is going on in my theatre?" Simon muttered under his breath. "Tim!" he shouted into the theatre.

Tim, the assistant stage manager, came running out the stage door, followed by Kitty, a bandage wound round her arm, Brandon, Eliza Bentley, the newest actress in the company, Manon carrying Jessica, and Colin, observing the whole with wide eyes. Manon, the mother of three, met Mélanie's gaze. Mélanie understood at once. Impossible to keep the children out of it, and once they'd heard someone had been killed, they might be more frightened by their imaginings if they didn't see. She crossed the alley and took Jessica from Manon's arms. Jessica buried her head in Mélanie's shoulder. Colin took a step closer to her but continued to observe the scene in the alley.

"Will he come back, Mummy?" Jessica asked.

"No, darling."

"Are you going to have to go Investigate?"

"Not right away."

"How the hell did the door get left open?" Simon asked.

"It wasn't," Tim said. "I let everyone in and out for the dinner break, just like we've been doing ever since the Thornsby business. I let Mr. Rannoch and Lord and Lady Carfax in."

"You didn't go out at all tonight?"

Tim shook his head. "Letty and Will brought me a pie and a pint. If I do go out, Jem handles the door. We haven't varied it in over a year. None of us has forgot."

"Then how did he get in here without being seen?" Simon asked.

"He was a professional," Julien said. He'd gone to the door with Malcolm.

Footsteps sounded. Letty Blanchard ran out, closely followed by her husband Will Carmarthen. Letty came to a skidding halt, face suffused with horror. Lewis Thornsby had been in love with her, and though the feelings hadn't been reciprocated, she had been fond of him. And he had been killed because he wanted to marry her.

"I'm sorry," Simon said. "I didn't want you to see this."

"I'd have found out eventually," Letty said. "That would have been just as bad. Anyway, don't worry about me. God how, awful."

Will put an arm round her.

Malcolm and Julien were examining the lock on the stage door by the light of a lantern Malcolm had grabbed from inside the theatre. They exchanged glances in the lantern light. Malcolm nodded. "The lock was picked," Julien said. "You can see fresh scratches. Concerning. But you needn't fear it was an inside job."

"And we can't put off sending to Bow Street much longer," Malcolm said.

CHAPTER 9

The Bow Street runner named Higgins, whom Malcolm had said was investigating Allegra Roth's murder, looked round the Tavistock's green room. Mélanie had Jessica on her lap and Malcolm was beside her holding Colin. Kitty and Julien, Simon, Manon, Will and Letty, Tim, and Brandon were assembled on frayed tapestry sofas and chairs with chipped gilt paint that had once been set pieces. Manon had made strong cups of tea they were all clutching, some with liberal splashes of brandy added.

Higgins, who had declined a cup of tea, sat on a straight-backed chair facing the group. He looked ill at ease in theatrical surroundings. Malcolm had murmured to Mélanie that he had also seemed ill at ease in Seven Dials, which his pristine greatcoat certainly supported. And Mélanie couldn't imagine his being comfortable in Berkeley Square. Which rather made one wonder where he would be comfortable. Not an easy characteristic for a Bow Street runner.

Higgins looked from Malcolm to Julien to Kitty. "This man attacked Lady Carfax?"

"He came out of the wings," Kitty said. "I twisted away and

managed to knee him. But even so, it wasn't a very organized attack. It was very different from the attack on Alejandra—Allegra Roth. A different weapon, and her killer seems to have been someone she knew."

"We don't know for a certainty she didn't know this person," Higgins said. "She was in Seven Dials when she was killed. This man was a denizen of Seven Dials."

"You know who he is?" Mélanie asked.

"I recognized him the moment I arrived," Higgins said. "Eddy Purvis. A thief and ruffian for hire. We'd all taken him into custody at one time or another. He'd also turned informant more than once. Sometimes he had good intelligence to offer. Sometimes he seemed to be playing us." Higgins paused a moment. "He was a particular source of Jeremy Roth's."

"But obviously open to jobs for hire," Malcolm said, ignoring the implications.

"And there's nothing to suggest Alejandra—Allegra Roth frequented Seven Dials," Kitty added.

"No. Not yet. But something made her choose it as a location to speak with her estranged husband. Can you think of any reason someone would attack both you and Mrs. Roth, Lady Carfax?"

Kitty took a sip of her brandy-laced tea. "No."

Higgins grunted. "And yet it strains credulity that they aren't connected."

"I agree," Kitty said. "Which suggests the motive for Alejandra's —Allegra's—murder has to do with her time in the Argentine, when we were acquainted."

"Perhaps." Higgins dug out his notebook. "It's also possible a clever killer wants to give that impression to throw us off the scent. That would explain the rather haphazard attack on you, compared to Mrs. Roth's much more efficient appearing murder."

Which pointed the blame at someone who knew Kitty and Allegra Roth were connected. In other words, Jeremy Roth. Unless the killer was Julien or Malcolm.

"There wouldn't have been much time to arrange that," Kitty said.

"No," Higgins agreed, jotting down notes. "But the attack on you looks to have been hastily set up. And if Eddy Purvis was hired in Seven Dials tonight—"

"I walked Jeremy Roth home," Malcolm said.

Higgins looked up from his notebook with a frown. "I didn't suggest—"

"No, but you're implying it. No sense in pretending we aren't all well aware of that. I was with Roth nonstop from the moment we learned of Allegra Roth's connection to Lord and Lady Carfax to the moment I saw him go into his lodgings."

"You were downstairs in the tavern when I arrived."

"True. But we were within view of the stairs. We saw no one go up or come down in that time. Lord and Lady Carfax can vouch for that."

"But you can't vouch that Roth stayed in his lodgings after you saw him home."

"No. But I left him less than an hour since."

"A lot can be done in an hour. Especially by a man like Roth, who knows the London underworld well. Especially given that the man who attacked Lady Carfax was an informant of his. Of course, I'm the last to wish to cast aspersions on a colleague who has just suffered a hideous bereavement."

"I believe you are the last person who did cast such aspersions," Julien said, voice as smooth as whisky.

Higgins's brows snapped together. "I need to put the pieces together, Lord Carfax. All of you have been involved in investigations. You must know personal considerations can't hold sway."

"Quite," Julien agreed. "They also can't influence one to force the pieces into a place they don't belong, when the entire picture hasn't come into focus."

Higgins returned Julien's regard. "You have quite a way with words, Lord Carfax. I'm not forcing anything. We're gathering up what information we can. But one has to explore possible theories, however uncomfortable. Comes with the job. As civilians, you can back out if your inquiries get too near people you're close to. I can't."

"Someone shot Purvis," Mélanie said. "Are you suggesting that was Roth too?"

"My dear Mrs. Rannoch. As I've said numerous times, I'm not suggesting anything."

"Someone broke into my theatre," Simon said. "And hid here and injured a friend. I would like to know what happened."

"Purvis is dead, Mr. Tanner."

"But as Mrs. Rannoch pointed out, someone shot him. Someone lying in wait with a pistol. Which argues considerable planning and resources."

"I don't believe the threat was directed at the theatre, Mr. Tanner."

"But it occurred here."

"The Tavistock has certainly been the scene of some unusual activity." Higgins frowned at his notebook. "They never caught Lewis Thornsby's killer, did they?"

"No," Letty said.

Because his death had been set in motion by his great-aunt, Lady Shroppington, who was untouchable. But that was one of many things they couldn't say to Higgins.

"And there was the incident the Christmas before," Higgins said. "The night of Mrs. Rannoch's pantomime."

"Actually, it was Mr. Tanner's pantomime," Mélanie said. "I appeared in it, along with Miss Caret."

"And a man was killed in the alley at the end of it."

"He had attempted to attack someone leaving the theatre," Malcolm said. "Lord Carfax was shot in the interchange."

"Lord and Lady Carfax seem to be caught up in a great deal," Higgins said.

"That's always been the story of our lives," Julien agreed, lounging in a corner of a settee beside Kitty.

Higgins tapped his pencil against his notebook. "Difficult to draw a connection between the incidents. Except perhaps the people involved."

Malcolm drew a breath, then closed his mouth. Julien was not so circumspect. "My dear Higgins, are you suggesting the Rannochs and my wife and I bring danger and disruption down upon the Tavistock? If so, you're probably right."

"I wouldn't say that," Simon said.

"No, you're much too kind," Julien returned. "But I do agree that in all three incidents the attackers seem to have followed specific quarries to the Tavistock rather than targeting the theatre."

"Which brings us back to the question of why Lady Carfax was attacked," Higgins said.

"We'd be interested to hear your insights," Julien said, his arm tightening round Kitty.

Higgins flipped to another page in his notebook. "Assuming the motive was connected to the time Lady Carfax and Mrs. Roth spent in the Argentine, can you think of what it might have been?"

Kitty took another sip of tea and settled her cup carefully in its saucer. "No."

Higgins frowned. "Lady Carfax. I understand you have led an adventurous life—"

Kitty raised her brows. "You may speak plainly, Mr. Higgins. But I can't think how any of my adventures could have led anyone to want to murder me. Let alone to want to murder both Alejandra—Mrs. Roth—and me."

Higgins's gaze shifted to Julien. "You were in the Argentine as well."

"I was. I knew Alejandra Vargas, though not as well as Kitty did. I can't think of any reason anyone would have wanted to kill either of them. Or me. Not that anyone appears to be trying to kill me. Yet, at least."

Higgins pushed himself to his feet. "I need to get the body to the examiner. I was there with Mr. Esquivel recently, but he's returned to his hotel. I assume you'll all be available if I need to speak with you further."

"Of course." Simon stood to face Higgins. "We want to understand what happened at our theatre."

"And the threat to my wife," Julien said.

"I'd suggest Lady Carfax remain at home," Higgins said. "But I don't think she'd agree."

"Only a few hours' acquaintance and you already know me so well, Mr. Higgins," Kitty said. "We're going to get on splendidly."

Higgins inclined his head. Though his gaze indicated that he anticipated anything but.

"Dear god." Roth looked across the small sitting room in his lodgings at Mélanie, Malcolm, Julien, and Kitty. "You're all right, Lady Carfax?"

"I'm fine," Kitty said. "And calling me Lady Carfax is a worse wound than the attacker dealt."

Roth gave a faint smile, though it didn't warm his eyes. Mélanie shifted her position on the faded blue velvet settee where she sat beside Malcolm. Roth always held himself close, but she had never seen his gaze as desolate as it was now.

Harriet Roth, sitting on a straight-backed chair beside her brother, pulled the folds of her shawl closer about her shoulders. "Do you think the same man killed Allegra?"

"It seems unlikely, but we can't be sure. When did you last see Purvis?" Malcolm asked Roth.

Roth frowned. His face was ashen, though his eyes were still alert. "A fortnight ago. Perhaps a bit longer. He passed me some information about a warehouse full of contraband brandy. There wasn't as much there as he implied—I suspect he took some for his own use—but it was a good tip."

"Was he a killer?" Julien asked. "I mean, could someone have reasonably engaged him to commit murder?"

Roth met Julien's gaze, his own clear and focused. "I never heard that he had killed anyone. He was involved in a few brawls, but nothing like murder. Which is still extremely rare in London, for all the times we've all stumbled into it. His actions tonight don't make sense."

"So you don't think he would have been hired to kill Allegra?" Malcolm said.

"No." Roth's voice was clipped and precise, the tone of an investigator, not a husband. "I don't think a man like Purvis could have got close enough to Allegra to do what we saw done to her. Not without her struggling."

"Unless they knew each other?" Julien suggested.

Roth frowned again. "I'll grant there was a lot I didn't know about Allegra. She grew up in London and lived here for a quarter-century. She might have known Purvis. But it still strains credulity." He looked at his sister. "In some ways, you knew her better than I did."

Harriet's dark brows were knotted. "Allegra always had secrets. The more so as she got older. But I never heard her mention anyone who sounds remotely like this Purvis."

Julien nodded. "The threads of blue fabric we found on Allegra didn't come from Purvis. At least, not from the clothes we found him in."

"It seems far more likely that someone hired him to make an attempted attack on Lady—Kitty—that was never meant to succeed," Roth said. "And then got rid of him when it looked as though you'd catch him and he might talk. Except that the only person who seemingly would have been able to connect those dots is me. And I didn't engage him."

"The killer could have known to connect the dots," Mélanie said. "If the killer knew about Allegra's association with Kitty. But that still connects the murder to her life in the Argentine."

"And why attack Lady Carfax if they wanted to draw attention away from the Argentine?" Harriet said.

"Possibly to scare her," Roth said.

"Then they don't know me very well," Kitty said.

"Undoubtedly," Roth agreed. "But I suspect it wouldn't be the first time someone misjudged you. Of course, it's possible it really was an attempted attack on you, even by someone other than the person who killed Allegra. Perhaps hastily set up. If you and Julien were seen arriving at the Three Queens, the killer could have panicked and quickly hired someone. They might well have found Purvis if they were looking in Seven Dials."

"Meaning the killer was still in the Three Queens when we arrived?" Kitty said.

"Or had someone watching it. Hiring Purvis may not have been a prudent choice, but in my experience, killers are rarely prudent and often blunder into mistakes as things unravel. And if they were looking for someone to hire quickly and found Purvis, I can see his taking the job. I wouldn't call him a killer, but he also had few scruples about what work he'd undertake for the right price." Roth drew a breath. "Is Higgins—"

"He had to get Purvis's body to the examiner," Malcolm said. "But I'm sure he'll want to talk to you."

Roth grimaced. "Higgins may lack imagination, but he's no fool. I'm sure he's worked out that I'm the likeliest person to have thought to deflect suspicion from myself by having Kitty attacked. And I have a connection to Purvis."

"His thoughts were clearly headed that way," Malcolm said. "I assured him that I saw you home." He looked at Harriet. "I assume Jeremy stayed here?"

Harriet nodded, her blue-gray gaze steady.

Roth glanced towards the door to the rest of the rooms. "I

talked to the boys. I got them settled. They both fell asleep. Truth to tell, they were more confused than anything, I think. Allegra hasn't been part of their lives for so long. Then I needed to talk to Harriet. We'd barely sat down when you called."

Malcolm nodded. "Is there anything else you aren't telling us?"

"You think I'd be stupid enough to do that?"

"Yes," Julien said. "Ask any of the four of us. We've all been stupid when it comes to those we care about."

"Profoundly." Malcolm looked at Roth. "You'd tell us if you'd learned more?"

"Of course," Roth said.

Malcolm held his gaze and nodded.

LAURA O'ROARKE HESITATED in the doorway of the Berkeley Square kitchen. The smell of freshly ground coffee filled the air. Her husband was taking an iron kettle off the range. Not entirely surprising for Raoul to be making coffee in the evening, after the servants were off duty. But he had the full coffee service and an array of cups set out on the deal kitchen table. Mélanie was at the theatre and Malcolm was at Brooks's. And they weren't expecting guests. At least, as far as she knew.

"What's happened?" she asked.

"Simon brought Colin and Jessica home." Raoul poured boiling water over the freshly ground coffee. "While you were upstairs with Clara. He's still in the library with Colin and Jessica, and Emily. He also delivered a note from Malcolm. Apparently, there's been an incident involving Jeremy Roth. They'll be home soon with Kitty and Julien and they want to have a council. I've sent for Harry and Cordelia."

Laura watched as her husband took milk from the cooler and filled the milk jug. "So while we were having a quiet evening at home, our latest investigation started?"

"It appears that way."

"Not entirely unusual for me." Laura had been governess to the Rannoch children before she married Raoul. "But a bit unusual for you." Her spymaster husband was usually the first to know everything.

"As you say." Raoul opened a wooden box beside the coffee service and took out a sugar container with the words "Free-Grown East India Sugar, Not Made by Slaves" on the blue glass. "I'll confess to feeling a bit sidelined, but it's undoubtedly good for me. At my age I should be getting accustomed to the younger generation's taking over."

Laura grinned. "Spare us, darling. No one believes that. Least of all your son. Is Jeremy coming with them?"

"It didn't sound like it."

Disquiet coiled within her. She was very fond of Jeremy. "Then I wonder if it's to do with his wife."

Raoul poured the coffee into Mélanie's silver coffeepot. "What makes you say so?"

"Because I can't imagine what else would sideline him from an investigation."

CHAPTER 10

"You don't think Purvis was really trying to hurt Kitty?" Cordelia Davenport asked. She and her husband Harry had arrived in Berkeley Square just before Mélanie, Malcolm, Kitty, and Julien returned. They and Raoul and Laura had listened to the others' account of the evening with admirable restraint, though Mélanie could see the questions racing through their gazes. So many times, the eight of them, or various combinations of the group, had sat like this at the start of an investigation. In Brussels, when Cordy and Harry had been estranged, and their simply having a civil conversation had seemed touch and go. In Paris, before Malcolm had known she was a French spy, before Malcolm had known Raoul was his father and her spymaster. In London, when Laura had been their children's governess and accused of murder herself. In Italy, all of them in exile and Julien an intruder none of them trusted, least of all her. Back in London, Julien and Kitty living together but not trusting each other.

Kitty blew on her coffee. "It wasn't a very organized attack. So I'm inclined to think not. But whether they were after me or I was a decoy, it does suggest there may be a connection to the Argen-

72

tine. The British have long had an interest in the Argentine." Kitty hesitated a moment. "That's why I was there."

"Because your first husband was sent there?" Laura looked up from refilling the coffee cups.

"Edward was sent there because Carfax—Hubert Mallinson, who, god help me, is now my uncle-in-law—wanted me there." Kitty cast a glance a Malcolm. "Surely you guessed."

"A bit."

"Hubert saw great promise in the Argentine. When it didn't work for the British to take it directly, in '06 and '07, he decided Britain would have a better chance if the Argentine broke away from Spain. Even if Spain happened to be our ally at the time against the French. He was funneling support to the rebels. I was coordinating for him. As I happened to agree with the goals of the rebels, it was an assignment I welcomed. I needed occupation."

Mélanie saw Malcolm's hand clench on the arm of the Queen Anne chair they were sharing. Kitty had needed occupation because his brother, Edgar, had raped her. Partly out of anger over Malcolm's own affair with Kitty.

"I was well-suited for it," Kitty said. "I already knew José de San Martín, who had fought in the Peninsula and was preparing to leave for the Argentine to take part in the revolution. You must have heard the rumors about San Martín."

"That he's a British agent," Raoul said.

"Yes."

"Is he?" Malcolm asked.

Kitty frowned. "I don't know. Truly. He believes in his cause. He's still fighting for it. But then, so do I, and that didn't stop me from being in Hubert Mallinson's employ."

Malcolm turned his gaze to Julien. "Did Hubert send you to the Argentine as well?"

Julien took a deeper drink of coffee. "In a manner of speaking. After Waterloo, it seemed advisable to make myself scarce. France was no longer a place I could conveniently hide from most of the

British. Lines were blurring and breaking down and there was more risk I'd be identified. I already knew the Elsinore League were looking for me. Not to mention I wasn't sure what Uncle Hubert would expect of me if I stayed. So when he wanted someone to make sure a shipment of arms was delivered to the Argentine rebels, it seemed a good option. Hubert found arming the Argentine rebels more complicated after Britain's treaty of alliance with Spain in '14."

"There was a secret clause prohibiting our government from arming and supplying what Spain considered rebel colonies," Malcolm said.

"Quite." Julien nodded. "Of course, a little thing like a treaty wouldn't deter Uncle Hubert. But it did call for more subterfuge. "

"Let me guess. The weapons were supplied by Thurston." A British expatriate they had met in Italy, whose son was now one of their friends.

"Who else? Or rather, of course there are other options, but he was Hubert's main supplier. Still is. So I set sail for the Argentine. I arrived to find another message from Uncle Hubert. He wanted Pablo Diaz out of the way."

"He was one of the revolutionaries?" Mélanie asked. The name was familiar.

"Yes, and though Uncle Hubert sees backing the revolution as a way to replace Spanish influence in the Argentine with British influence, he thought Diaz went too far. I wasn't inclined to go along with what he asked. But I was scouting Diaz's lodgings one night when Kitty jumped me with a knife."

"It was a memorable reunion," Kitty said.

"One I will never forget," Julien agreed. "Few people have got a jump on me like that."

"Pablo Diaz is a friend," Kitty said. "I knew he was in danger. When I recognized Julien—"

"Seeing ruthlessly through my disguise—"

"—I suspected why Hubert had sent him."

"And then you talked?" Malcolm asked.

"Not at first. But when we tangled again—"

"—after I got a blow to the head," Julien said.

"—we finally discussed the situation and worked out that we were on the same side," Kitty said. "We warned Pablo. And Julien protected him. When Carfax—Hubert—sent another assassin after him two months later."

"The beginning of a profitable association," Julien said. "Until—"

"We always knew it would end," Kitty said with a quick smile. "At least then we did."

"Hubert was playing complicated games in the Argentine," Julien said. "Kitty and I were trying to trace some missing gold Hubert had sent to the rebels. In the process, we learned that a colleague from Spain was in trouble. I needed to go back to warn him."

"Julien." Mélanie stared at him. "You're a complete fraud. You were busy being precisely as noble as you always twitted Raoul for being."

"Oh, not nearly that noble." Julien flashed a grin at Raoul. "But I was hardly going to stand by while one of my colleagues was stabbed in the back. There was far too much of that going on after Waterloo."

"You were protecting a revolutionary," Malcolm said.

Julien swung his foot against the leg of the settee. "Yes, all right. I said I didn't admit to allegiances. I didn't mean I didn't have any."

"And you got to know Allegra Roth—Alejandra Vargas—and her lover," Harry said.

Kitty reached for her coffee. "Marco Esquivel came to the Argentine with San Martín and Carlos María de Alvear and others soon after I did. He was dedicated to the revolution, and any romantic relationships he had were transitory. Marco was on a trip back to England—to see his family and negotiate for British support for the rebels—when Julien arrived in the Argentine. Then, a few months later, Marco returned to Buenos Aires with Alejandra. She didn't precisely try to hide the fact that Alejandra Vargas wasn't her real name or that she wasn't Spanish, but she didn't talk about her past. She and Esquivel lived together openly. Some of the hostesses in our set wouldn't accept her—but I did. Which cemented a friendship of sorts."

"What was she like?" Cordelia asked.

"Mercurial. She and Esquivel would sometimes quarrel in public. I remember her storming away from him and going off with another man one Sunday evening when we were all walking along the Alameda. But the passion between them was palpable."

"She wasn't a woman anyone would ever grow bored with," Julien said.

"You liked her," Harry said.

"I did," Julien said. "She had a keen brain and a sharp tongue."

"And she believed in the revolution as much as Esquivel did," Kitty said. "They might quarrel, but their ideals and thoughts were obviously in tune. I remember watching them and thinking I couldn't imagine sharing that with anyone." She cast a quick glance at her husband. "Not then."

"What reasons would someone have had to kill her and attack you?" Malcolm said. "Because if the two are connected, it puts the motive for the attack on Allegra in the Argentine. I know what you said to Higgins, but—"

Kitty and Julien exchanged glances. Julien's hand shot across the settee to encircle Kitty's wrist. "We move in dangerous circles," he said. "Secrets are our currency. And even after a year of marriage, I wouldn't pretend to know half of Kitty's secrets. But I can't think of any I know of that she shared with Alejandra Vargas. Sweetheart?"

Kitty shook her head. "I was gathering information. Some of it perhaps vitally important to those in the Argentine. But I wasn't sharing it with Alejandra. And she wasn't an agent."

An outbreak of laughter came from the other end of the library. Simon had gone home, but Malcolm's secretary Sandy and his wife Bet were playing with the children and the family cat Berowne.

Mélanie waved in response to a wave from Jessica, who was dangling a ribbon for Berowne, then looked back at Kitty. "Any reason Esquivel could see you as an enemy?"

"Esquivel? No. I was more allied with him than with most others in the struggles in Argentine politics. And he adored Alejandra. Though I do agree that can change when someone has a temper. And we don't know that whoever attacked me also killed Alejandra. I've been attacked before."

Including on one memorable night in Hyde Park that had involved all those present. When Kitty had been lying to all of them, including Julien, whom she'd been living with. A situation Mélanie could sympathize with.

"Yes, but not on the same night someone else you knew was murdered," Julien said. "I'm all for keeping an open mind, Kitkat, but sometimes one does have to play the percentages."

"All right," Kitty said. "I admit it strains coincidence that there isn't a connection. And whether the person behind Alejandra's murder and the attack on me was trying to kill both of us or attack me to throw off suspicion, it almost has to be someone who knows about our connection in the Argentine. And unless it's Jeremy—which, being as cold and clear as I can be, I really don't see—it has to be someone we knew in the Argentine."

"Or someone Allegra Roth told about you." Laura set down the coffeepot. "Just because she only wrote one letter to Jeremy doesn't mean she didn't write to others. And just because Esquivel said she was staying quietly at the hotel doesn't mean she didn't go out and talk to others in London after they arrived."

"A good point." Malcolm stretched his legs out and took a drink of coffee. "I learned a bit about her tonight from Roth. Her mother and stepfather ran a Radical press. Her stepsister is a well-known courtesan. At least apparently well known. Cressida Caldwell."

"I've heard of her," Julien said. "Professionally," he added.

"Darling," Kitty said. "With you, professionally could cover a multitude of activities."

"Not in this case," Julien said.

"I need to talk to Roth more about Allegra's connections," Malcolm said. "But tonight wasn't the night for it." He looked at Raoul. "What do you know about Marco Esquivel?"

Raoul, who had been sitting largely in silence after making the coffee and helping serve it, frowned into his cup. "I've met him once or twice."

"In Spain?" Mélanie asked.

"And in London. We met through Alvear."

Mélanie had danced with Carlos María de Alvear on a mission once in Spain during the Peninsular War. He served in the Spanish army, which had been allied with the British. Alvear had left for the Argentine before the end of the war. "I forgot—Alvear came back to England on his way to the Argentine."

"Yes," Raoul said. "He'd spent much of his youth in Britain after he and his father were captured as British prisoners of war in the Anglo-Spanish war. His mother and brothers were killed in the same attack. Carlos's father later married an Irish woman. I'd seen the family off and on through the years. Carlos hosted meetings of a group called the Sociedad de los Caballeros Racionales. The Lodge of the Rational Knights."

"I've heard of them," Malcolm said. "Were they Freemasons?"

"Connected." Raoul took a drink of coffee. "Always hard to tell with these secret societies, and I was on the fringe of this one. They were dedicated to bringing the principles of Enlightenment to South America. I wasn't a member, but they asked me to some meetings, first in Spain, then in London. They wanted me to talk about my experience in Spain and France."

Malcolm regarded his father. "I assume they didn't know—"

"That I was a French agent in Spain?" Raoul said. "No. Which made the situation a bit fraught. I almost didn't accept the invitation. But to decline might have roused suspicions. And I wanted to learn more about them and their plans for South America. Which I supported. I don't have much interest in secret societies, but there's no denying some of them are dedicated to advancing principles I believe in. And given the need to evade government interference, the secret society is convenient. I particularly remember a meeting in London at Francisco Miranda's in '11. San Martín was there that night as well. And Esquivel. Like Alvear, Esquivel had grown up in England after his family were captured by a British ship crossing back to Spain from the Argentine. He went to Eton and Cambridge."

"Of course." Cordelia's fingers went still on the silver net and seafoam taffeta of her skirt. "I knew the name was familiar. I remember Gordon Rowley talking about a friend from South America who'd lived with them and who had gone to Eton and Cambridge with his younger brother."

"With Martin Rowley?" Malcolm asked.

Cordelia nodded, blonde ringlets and aquamarine earrings stirring about her face. She had a nearly encyclopedic knowledge of the beau monde, which often proved useful in their investigations. Malcolm was also connected to seemingly every major aristocratic family in Britain, but Cordy paid more attention. "And of course, now you and Martin are colleagues in Parliament."

Malcolm nodded. "He's supported me on a couple of bills. He allies himself with the Radicals, though he's most focused on the steam engine he's developing. I took the children to see a demonstration. It's quite remarkable. Not surprising perhaps that he and Esquivel were friends—they both have Liberal politics."

"Of course," Kitty said. "I knew two of the men in Esquivel's box looked familiar from some political party. I was too focused on Marco to think about it, but one was Martin Rowley."

"And the other was William Beardsley," Julien said. "Talking of Radicals."

Beardsley, like Rowley, had been elected to Parliament the previous year. Both had been at several late-night sessions in Berkeley Square when Mélanie helped Malcolm and his colleagues polish speeches. But Beardsley was more active than Rowley. He had connections to the Levellers, the Radical group Simon was involved in.

Raoul nodded. "Esquivel has always moved in Radical circles. Shortly after that meeting of the Lodge I attended, he, Alvear, and San Martín all left for the Argentine to take part in the revolution."

"What did you make of Esquivel?" Julien asked. "I'm curious, as one who knew him in different circumstances."

Raoul turned his coffee cup in his hand. "Serious. Competent. A bit impetuous, but he was young. Not yet tempered by the realities of working for change. An idealist. More so perhaps than Carlos Alvear, who later considered a constitutional monarchy."

"I'd agree with that," Kitty said. "Esquivel and Alvear were friends, but by the time Alvear became Supreme Dictator—at all of five-and-twenty—the friendship was frayed. Alvear talked to me about the possibility of a British protectorate in the Argentine. Hubert would have been thrilled, but I did my best to discourage it. When Alvear wrote to Strangford in Brazil asking for British intervention, he and Esquivel had an open falling out. Now Alvear's in exile in Montevideo and Esquivel is at the center of Argentine power."

Raoul leaned forwards to add more coffee to his cup. "It's an exciting time in South America."

"You thought about going there yourself," Malcolm said in an even voice.

Raoul met Malcolm's gaze as he set down the coffeepot. "So I did."

He had considered it when Mélanie was pregnant, though he'd

never got so far as to talk to her about it. A place where they could have had a fresh start. He hadn't wanted to leave the situation in Spain. Or to not see Malcolm again. And he had, according to Julien, started to have a sense of what was happening between Mélanie and Malcolm. Mélanie was inestimably grateful he hadn't asked her to go to South America with him, for a number of reasons. But it was hard not to occasionally wonder what might have been. And she suspected Raoul at times wondered too.

"It would have been an interesting place to be, at an interesting time," Raoul said, settling back on the sofa beside his wife. "But for a number of reasons I'm glad I didn't take myself halfway across the world."

"Esquivel left his family behind," Harry said.

"He was married and a father when I met him," Raoul said. "I remember saying something to him about leaving his young family, at that meeting of the Lodge. And he replied he thought he was better suited to a life of action."

"Once one has children one shouldn't make those choices," Malcolm said.

"No." Raoul met Malcolm's gaze steadily. "I was very aware of being a father myself when I talked to him. And of how much I was away from you. But also that I couldn't imagine being away from you more. Across an ocean. Different people make different choices. I had no right to cast aspersions, but it didn't endear Esquivel to me. At the same time, I admired his dedication to change."

"Did you see him when he came back to Britain after Water-loo?" Laura asked.

"No, I was on the Continent. But I've had news of him. His inclinations remain more Liberal than Alvear's. He's part of the faction among the rebels pushing for a more republican govern-ment. I imagine Kitty knows more."

"There are far more than two factions among the rebels," Kitty said. "In fact, the more they succeeded against the Royalists, the more they seemed to splinter. Something I imagine Raoul appreciates from Ireland and France. And Spain."

"Easier to find consensus in rebelling than in governing," Raoul said.

"Precisely." Kitty added milk to her coffee and stirred it with a thoughtful expression. "Hubert was—and I suspect is—determined to make what he sees as the more stable faction win out. Which of course from Hubert means the least republican."

"Did he ever try to have Esquivel killed?" Cordelia asked. "I mean, you said he wanted Julien to kill someone else—"

"A good question," Julien said. "Not as far as I know. At least, he didn't ask me. But perhaps after the first one he felt he couldn't."

Cordelia clunked her coffee cup down, spattering drops of coffee in the saucer. "Why does Hubert Mallinson end up in the midst of every investigation we undertake? Even one with roots on another continent?"

"Another excellent question," Julien said. "But then my uncle has his fingers in intrigues across the globe. It's interesting, though, that Allegra Roth proves to have been caught in them."

"Perhaps not entirely surprising," Laura said. "Jeremy is an intelligent man who would seek an intelligent wife. And the line between investigation and espionage is narrow and murky. As we all know. Perhaps—"

She broke off as the door opened. Mélanie looked round in surprise to see Miles Addison, Malcolm's valet. Addison was a skilled agent himself, but he and his wife Blanca had been having a quiet evening with their son in their apartment in the mews. Mélanie had assumed he was still there, but he wore a greatcoat.

"I sent word from the Tavistock and asked Addison to make some inquiries," Malcolm said. "Round Hart Street and Covent Garden in general."

He said it easily, but Mélanie went still at the implications.

Julien put it into words. "In case Roth didn't stay home after you left him, as he claims he did?"

"It's a possibility we have to consider," Malcolm said. "Higgins is certainly going to consider it."

Addison shrugged out of his greatcoat and joined them by fire with an ease he would not have shown when Mélanie first joined Malcolm's bachelor household. He hesitated a moment before he spoke. "The barkeep at the Golden Eagle, down the street from Roth's lodgings, reports seeing Roth pass by just after nine-thirty."

CHAPTER 11

or a moment, stillness gripped the library.

"He's sure?" Malcolm asked. "The glass in pub windows tends to be old and thick and smoke-stained. Roth and I were at a different pub in Hart Street earlier in the evening."

"He's sure of the time because the clock had just struck," Addison said in precise tones given the lie by the concern in his eyes. "And he's sure it was Roth because Roth is a local. He made a point of saying he always notes when Roth is nearby. He didn't add that it's because Roth is a Bow Street runner and there might be something illegal going on in the pub, but I got the distinct sense that was true. At the same time, he seems to like Roth. Said he was surprised to see him walk past and not come in."

"So that would give Roth enough time to have hired Purvis." Julien's tone was even more ruthlessly matter-of-fact than Malcolm's or Addison's. "Instead of dancing round the implications, let's confront the obvious. I could possibly see Roth killing his estranged wife in a fit of anger. Though if he'd done so, I think the crime scene would look messier. But I can't see his hiring a ruffian to attack Kitty."

"Even if the attack was meant to be mild and not succeed?" Malcolm turned his own cup in his hands.

"Are you saying you believe it?" Cordelia asked.

"I'm trying to play devil's advocate," Malcolm said. "All my instincts say Roth couldn't have done this. But my instincts have been known to be wrong."

"Notably about your wife," Mélanie said. Because uncomfortable as it was to say it, it was even more uncomfortable not to.

Malcolm met her gaze. His own gaze didn't deny it or make light of it as he once would have done. "Among other things."

"Roth isn't stupid," Kitty said. "Hiring Purvis was a desperate gamble."

"But we've all made desperate gambles," Raoul said. "I don't think he's guilty either," he added, as they all looked at him. "But like Malcolm, I'm doing my best to be objective against all my instincts."

"All right," Laura said. "So he panicked and went out and quickly hired Purvis, not expecting Kitty to be badly hurt but expecting to throw the investigation off the scent by turning everyone's attention to the Argentine. You make a case that that's barely possible. But do you then think Roth was near the Tavistock and shot Purvis? Or hired someone to do it?"

"That strains belief more," Malcolm agreed. "Though theoretically it's possible." He took a deep drink of coffee. "I need to talk to Jeremy about why he left his lodgings tonight, but we also need to trace Allegra Roth's movements since she's been back in London. Where she went, whom she spoke with, who called on her at Mivart's. Whom she may have communicated with. Ideally we need the information more quickly than Bow Street can get it."

"If we all work on it, we can cast a wide net," Harry said. "With all due respect to Bow Street, I think we're more than a match for them."

Mélanie glanced round the library. It was hardly the first time they had all sat together like this at the start of a case, but this was different. Usually, however grim the circumstances, there was the excitement of a new investigation. Tonight, she felt the concern for Jeremy Roth just beneath the surface of the practical comments.

"Do you think they're likely to arrest Jeremy?" Cordelia asked.

"I think some people will push for it," Malcolm said. "They'll need more evidence, but often evidence can be looked at more than one way. They didn't arrest me right away when I found Tatiana in Vienna, but they got to the point where they could. And did. And then there's the mounting pressure to arrest someone as a case goes on. Especially a murder."

"If necessary, we can break him out," Julien said, as easily as if he were discussing moving a planned picnic indoors in case of rain. "Get him and Harriet and the boys to America or Canada or France or wherever they want to start over."

"It hasn't come to that," Malcolm said. "But yes."

Cordelia frowned. "If you're already considering that, then it's serious indeed."

"I thought about breaking Laura out of prison," Raoul said.

Malcolm met his father's gaze. "So did I. But for a number of reasons, I'm glad we didn't have to."

"If I'd never been in prison, who knows how things might have progressed between us," Laura said, smiling at her husband. "Probably far more slowly, given your scruples. We did most of our courting in Newgate. But all things considered, I wouldn't wish it on Jeremy."

"Gordon Rowley and his family should be in town," Cordelia said. "I can ask what Gordon knows about Marco Esquivel. Though we have Justine Lambton arriving to stay with us tomorrow afternoon." Justine, a young classicist, had been entangled in their adventure just before Christmas.

"I'll talk to Danielle Darnault," Mélanie said. "She knows Lord Gresham through performing."

"I can make more inquiries about Mr. Esquivel's movements,"

Addison said.

Malcolm nodded. "After I see Roth, I'll talk to Martin Rowley. He and Esquivel are obviously still in touch."

Raoul picked up the coffeepot and began to refill cups. "Laura and I can go to Mivart's. Between my once making it my London home and the Boxing Day dinners, they know us well."

"Exactly what I was thinking." Laura added milk to her coffee. "I'm sure you want to talk to Esquivel. If you pay a condolence call on him and keep him occupied, that should give me a chance to investigate Allegra Roth's rooms. In the proper disguise. I may not have as much spy experience as some, but one thing being a governess does is train one to blend into the background."

MALCOLM LOOKED at Kitty as she drew her cloak about her. Harry and Cordy had gone home. Julien was helping Laura, Raoul, and Mélanie take the coffee things to the kitchen. "Are you all right, Kit?"

"Of course I am." Kitty's smile was quick. The easy smile of friend who had once been more. A smile that acknowledged the more would always be there, without threatening either of their spouses. "It was the merest graze. Less bad than the knife cut I took in Hyde Park a year ago, and even that wound I was recovering from nicely by the time I married Julien a day later. Considerably less serious than the knife cut I myself dealt Julien last October when I was trying to stop him from killing Alistair Rannoch and sending himself into a spiral that would have been far more concerning than a mere flesh wound." Kitty's fingers tightened on the ties on her cloak. "Don't you start fussing, Malcolm. I have enough of that from Julien. Which is astonishing, because he's the last person in the world one would think would fuss, and he certainly knows I can take care of myself."

"Love makes us vulnerable," Malcolm said. Odd to talk about

love so easily. He and Kitty hadn't talked about it much at all when they'd been lovers.

Kitty's mouth curved in acknowledgement. "There was a time when Julien and I would both have gagged over that. For that matter, there was a time when you wouldn't have talked that way either."

"We've all changed."

Kitty met his gaze. "I know I run risks, Malcolm. Just as you do. But I don't run risks blindly. Once perhaps I did. When you first knew me. When I was angry and had little to live for and thrived on risk. I learned some semblance of caution when I became a parent. But I refuse to live my life in fear. Or to be sidelined."

"I can't imagine Julien would sideline you."

"No, he's at least too sensible for that. Just as I'm too sensible to try to keep him out of danger. Even though it sometimes terrifies me to see the risks he runs."

"Kit." Malcolm hesitated. But it had to be said. Too much was at stake and he needed all the information he could get. "Were there other things you and Allegra—Alejandra shared?"

Kitty dropped her fingers from fussing with the ties on the cloak and regarded him with a faint smile. "Malcolm, are you asking if Alejandra Vargas and I shared a lover?"

Improbably, Malcolm found himself smiling. "Among other things. You don't seem to know of any obvious secret the two of you shared, any obvious reason someone would attack both of you. But I know you enough to wonder if you were holding something back."

Kitty turned away, arms folded beneath the brown velvet folds of the cloak. "I wasn't on a mission that involved taking a lover when I went to the Argentine. And I wasn't in the humor to do so."

Because of what she'd suffered at his brother's hands. He knew what Edgar had done to Kitty. He lived with it every day. But the reminder still hit him like a shock of ice.

Kitty turned, took a quick step forwards, and touched his arm. "Don't dwell on him. He isn't worth it. Suffice it to say, I was focused on healing when I got to the Argentine. I was also pregnant with Leo and then not long after his birth pregnant with Timothy. None of which left much time for dalliance. But there was one man. Philip Ledgwood. I'd known him when he was an attaché in Lisbon. Before you joined the mission."

"I've met him once or twice." Ledgwood was a competent diplomat, though he and Malcolm didn't have much in common. Given that Ledgwood's pursuits mostly seemed to involve sampling the charms of the local women, whether in taverns or brothels or at diplomatic receptions.

Kitty gave a faint smile. "You're not very alike. Philip went to Brazil with Lord Strangford and the Portuguese royal family."

Lord Strangford had helped the Portuguese royal family and court flee to Brazil when the French moved into Lisbon in 1807, though some, like Malcolm's friend Henry Brougham, were of the opinion Strangford hadn't played as key a role as he claimed. The royal family had sailed under the protection of the British navy just ten days before French forces moved in. Strangford hadn't gone all the way to Brazil with the court, but later (to Brougham's horror) he had been sent to Rio as British envoy. The entire court had been reestablished in Brazil, where it still remained, long after Waterloo, governing what was now the United Kingdom of Portugal, Brazil, and the Algarves.

"Unlike Strangford, Philip went all the way to Brazil with the royal family on the first voyage," Kitty said. "He stayed on under Strangford and then Thornton. He was sent to Buenos Aires on a mission while I was there. I wanted to learn about what was happening in the Brazilian court."

"Do you mean Hubert wanted to know?" Malcolm said.

Kitty's mouth twisted in acknowledgement or self-derision. "I was already breaking away from Hubert. Given that I'd been trying to protect someone he wanted to assassinate. But yes, he did. And as you know, our former spymaster is difficult to break away from completely. Since I had a past connected to Philip, it was easy to get close to him. And he was amusing. He was an escape when I needed it and a mission that wasn't too complicated. For a time, we were quite close. But thinking of other moments while he was in Buenos Aires and what I observed at balls and the theatre and military reviews, I think Alejandra may have found him amusing as well."

Malcolm nodded. It wasn't a great surprise. Flirtation and love affairs were inextricably bound up in espionage. "Ledgwood is back in London. I heard it at Brooks's earlier tonight, not long before I got Roth's message that took me to Seven Dials."

"Yes, I heard it as well, a few days since. I had no particular reason to seek him out. Not then. But I will now." Kitty hesitated, hands tightening on the folds of her cloak.

"If it's uncomfortable to see him, for any reason—" Malcolm said.

"Don't be silly. When have you ever known me to shy away from anything because it was uncomfortable? It's just that my entanglement with Philip was after Julien left Buenos Aires. Not that we made any promises when he left. Not that either of us believed in promises. Not that we believed in them when we stumbled back together a year and a half ago. Julien will understand. Rather silly that I feel awkward about telling him."

"Odd how things can change," Malcolm said. "One can realize one has loyalties one wasn't aware of."

Kitty smiled at him, her gaze holding memories of a past that was most definitely past, but still sweet to remember. "You were always loyal, Malcolm. And I don't think you know the meaning of infidelity."

"On the contrary, my dear. I'm a spy and the son of a spy and the husband of a spy. I live with infidelity every day of my life. There are just different ways of defining it."

Kitty took a step forwards and squeezed his hand. "Touché."

CHAPTER 12

Kitty drew the covers over Genny, their two-and-a-half-year-old daughter, sound asleep in her cradle. "It wasn't so long ago, actually."

"No." Julien turned up the lamp on the night table on his side of the bed. "I was a bit shocked to realize it's three years ago that I left Buenos Aires. You'd think Genny would remind us." He caught Kitty's gaze for the briefest moment, smiled at their sleeping daughter, then moved away and lit the lamp on her side of the bed.

"I suspected," Kitty said. "Before you left. I'd been through it twice before."

The lamp flared, spilling golden light across the Axminster rug. Julien turned to look at her over his shoulder. "I didn't ask."

"I know. You never have."

He turned to face her fully. "Were you afraid I'd have stayed if I'd known?"

She glanced down at Genny for a moment, face relaxed in sleep. Julien was so clearly writ in her features, the high cheek-bones, the delicate nose, the full-lipped mouth. Impossible now not to imagine his being her father in every way. She folded her arms across her chest. "I don't think it occurred to me that you would."

"Was I so—"

"We were both different, Julien. You can't claim you wanted to be responsible for anyone."

"I'd never been confronted with the reality that I was."

"I was married to Edward. He was the boys' father. So you—"

Julien drew in and released his breath. She could hear the rasp across the room. "I'm not sure what I'd have done. I'd like to say I wouldn't have left. I can't be sure."

She remembered the night he'd first asked her about Genny. Just after he'd killed Edgar Rannoch to save Malcolm's life. And later that night, the way he'd looked down at Genny. Still later, how he'd held her through the night, both of them shaking from accumulated repercussions. "You had reasons you needed to leave."

He watched her for a moment. His gaze could be so dispassionate and yet could also feel like the brush of fingertips against her skin. "We could have taken the boys and disappeared. I'm quite skilled at disappearing. Would—"

"I'm not sure." Her voice was thick in her throat and to her own ears. "Edward wasn't a conscientious father, but he was their father. In their eyes. But if it was that, or keeping you away from Genny—" She shook her head. "But that's talking as if we were the people we are now. We weren't talking in those terms three years ago. We weren't even—"

"Exclusive. I know. We weren't officially until the day I asked you to marry me, which was damnably stressful."

"We were miles away from that in Buenos Aires."

He raised a brow. "I may not have used the word fidelity, but I knew what you meant to me."

Kitty glanced away instinctively. "I didn't think in terms of anything that lasted. Anything of that nature that lasted. You were always a threat to my sense of order in the world."

"You told me once that you didn't want me to know about Genny because our relationship wouldn't work if I wasn't all in with the children. Which I can understand. You couldn't possibly love anyone who didn't love them. But what the devil made you think I wouldn't be all in?"

"Julien. You didn't want to be tied to anyone."

"I *wasn't* tied to anyone, which isn't precisely the same thing. I'd been questioning my lack of ties for years. Ask Mélanie. I'd even wondered at times about going home. Though I'd have denied it then, if anyone asked." He regarded her for a moment. "I hadn't told anyone who I was until I told you."

"I know. I mean—I know what that meant." Perhaps even more so now, but even at the time he'd told her, she'd known they'd crossed a chasm. A chasm she hadn't then quite been prepared to contemplate. She could see his face that night in the light of a single candle, hear his precise, dispassionate, well-chosen words, taste the caña they'd been drinking.

"Julien—" The words caught in her throat. This seemed a damnable time to say it, yet it needed to be said. There was no better time. And perhaps this was oddly apropos. "I need to talk to Philip Ledgwood. I think he may have been involved with Alejandra. After you left Buenos Aires."

Julien's gaze barely flickered at the change of subject. "So he may have information."

"Yes. And if we're looking for a connection between Alejandra and me, it's possible Philip could provide it."

Julien's eyes narrowed slightly. Then he gave a faint smile. "I believe I promised you last October, when our investigation tangled us with Pendarves, that if we encountered one of your ex-lovers in an investigation, I'd do my best to be equally forbearing."

"Yes, but this was—" She bit back the words. God, when had she become so reticent? When had what had once been a matter of course come to feel like a betrayal?

"After we'd met? No, we'd met before Pendarves and I were

involved. After we'd become lovers? No need to hesitate over that, sweetheart. We hadn't made any promises. We very carefully avoided them. And I certainly assumed there were others."

Just as there must have been for Julien. Which she found she didn't really want to think about at the moment. Which was completely absurd. Until the moment he proposed and she—to her own surprise—accepted, she'd assumed they weren't any more faithful to each other than they'd ever been to anyone else.

Julien crossed to her side, put out a hand, and touched the side of her face with the unexpected tenderness that had taken her breath away from the first. "It doesn't cheapen what was between us."

"No." Even though in some way it now felt that it did. A carefully aged vintage turned to rotgut. Or at the very least *vin ordinaire*.

"It doesn't need to be a fairy tale to be real," Julien said. "And it doesn't change what we are to each other now. Well, as I've said, I'm not sure even infidelity would change that. But I'd much rather not make the experiment." He leaned in and kissed her lightly. "I'm not concerned about your going to see Ledgwood. But after tonight's attack, you need backup."

There was a time she'd have objected, but over a year of marriage and partnership had changed things. "I don't see Philip as dangerous, but yes. I'll accept backup. I need to go in alone to get him to talk. Philip isn't as broadminded as you. He wouldn't talk freely in front of my husband. But you can be outside."

Julien nodded. "I'll bring Davenport as well."

"Honestly, darling. You're going to have half the team involved in this."

"Absolutely." He settled his arms round her. "My wife's safety is at stake."

❦

MÉLANIE CLOSED THE NURSERY DOOR. "Emily regrets missing all the excitement at the theatre. I told her I understood. I regret missing the excitement earlier."

Malcolm tossed his coat over a chair back. "Mel—"

"I know. I won't let the investigation interfere with the play. But this is Jeremy. I couldn't not help. It's all right. I'm used to balancing divided loyalties."

Malcolm was frowning.

"Darling?" she said.

"I trust Jeremy. He's less deceitful than most of us, I think. But he lied about not going out again tonight. And I already suspected he wasn't telling us everything."

"He might instinctively hold things back. He's been through what's probably the worst shock of his life."

Malcolm smoothed the shoulders of the coat. "I'm not sure I ever fully realized."

"What?"

He looked down at his fingers. "Just what a hell it must have been for you to find me looking down at Tania. And to swallow all your questions and lie for me, run with me, work with me to learn the truth. All the time wondering—"

Mélanie met her husband's gaze. For a moment they were in Vienna and she was facing the man she had married to spy on, the man she'd still been spying on, the man she had recently admitted to herself she loved, the man who had not completely told her he loved her. Facing him over the body of the woman she'd been sure was his mistress. "I never really believed it."

"But you had to have wondered. You're too astute not to turn over every possibility."

"All right, yes." The questions had churned at the back of her brain, like glass in a wound. Unthinkable but also unavoidable. "Do you wonder about Jeremy?"

Malcolm undid his shirt cuffs with meticulous care. "A part of me was sure from the moment I walked into the room. But we've seen what people can do. I can't not ask the questions. Jeremy saw that before I did. And we're going to have to face them more as we investigate."

Mélanie perched on the edge of their bed. "Though he never said much about his wife, I knew he was deeply hurt. Bitter. But I never had the sense he was furious with her."

"He was tied to her. To the marriage."

Mélanie reached over to pet Berowne, who was curled up at the foot of the bed. "Jeremy's never given the sense that he found his marriage a burden. We have no indication that he wants to marry anyone else."

"No. But we also don't know why Allegra wanted to talk to him. And if he's lying and didn't find her dead, we don't know what she may have said to him. What she may have demanded. Suppose she'd wanted to take the boys back to the Argentine?"

"Jeremy could have just refused. Husbands have all the power when it comes to custody of children." It had been one of Mélanie's greatest fears before Malcolm learned the truth about her. That their marriage would collapse and Malcolm would keep the children from her.

"It's funny," she said.

"Funny?" her husband asked.

"Ironic." Mélanie linked her hands round her knees. "I risked everything for the mission. I was willing to trade everything, cross every line, sully my soul in every way possible. But that's one line I wouldn't cross."

"Leaving your children."

"Yes. In fact, I'd have crossed just about every line to keep you from taking them from me."

"I'd never have taken them from you."

"I know that now, but I was afraid. You can't blame me."

"No, but I rather wonder how you could have loved me when you thought I might be capable of that."

"I didn't—"

"Know me?" Malcolm moved to the bed and leaned against the bedpost, looking down at her. His dark brown hair fell over his forehead. The candlelight caught the sharp, Celtic lines of his cheekbones and made his eyes look even more deepset than usual. "Yes, that's rather the point. How could you have loved me without knowing me?"

"I did know you. Or at least I knew *you* knew *me*."

"But you thought I wouldn't love the real you."

"Well, you didn't, at first."

Malcolm sat down beside her. "I loved you. I just wasn't sure I could live with you."

"Rather my point."

"For a few hours I wasn't sure. Until I realized that before everything I had to make sure you were safe."

Mélanie straightened her shoulders. "I'm perfectly capable—"

"I know, you can take care of yourself. But I was in rather a better position to protect you from the government I regret having served. I could see the risks to you. We were better positioned to face them if we stayed together. But even before I realized that, even at my angriest, even when I thought we couldn't live under the same roof, I'd never have kept the children from you."

"Did you believe I'd never leave them?"

Malcolm drew a breath. The candle flame flickered in his eyes. "I was blinded by anger at first."

"You thought I might leave."

He let out a rough breath. "I wasn't entirely sure."

"So you didn't know me."

"Perhaps not. And later, I feared you might be so guilt-ridden you'd run to protect all of us."

Mélanie regarded the man whom she had said more than once knew her as no one else had ever done. They could often communicate without even speaking, especially in the midst of a case. But there were so many different ways to know a person. "You still don't know me then, darling," she said. "I wouldn't. I'd abandon everything else first. Including my self-respect. So I've been rather inclined to judge Allegra Roth. She may have been more ruthless than me."

"Or less attached to her children."

"Possibly." Mélanie considered the woman who was still a cipher. Though she had a vivid sense of Allegra's two sons, whom she could see romping in the library with Colin and Jessica and Emily and their other friends' children. Happy children, but she caught the looks occasionally when Jessica or Colin climbed in her lap, or when Emily threw her arms round Laura, or Kitty set up a chessboard for her boys. A longing for something they could perhaps not even remember. Or had never even had. "Not everyone bonds with a child." Some Mayfair mothers she knew cheerfully turned their children over to wet nurses and left them in the country half the year. And barely saw them once a day when they were under the same roof. Was that really so much worse than what Allegra had done? At least she had cut ties and tried to give the children the chance to start over. Built on lies, which Jeremy understandably hadn't been willing to tell.

"Raoul was away from me a lot," Malcolm said. He didn't often talk about Raoul that way, though he did it a bit more easily now. "But he was never gone as much as a year. Rarely close to it. And he wrote. I treasure those letters all the more now. There's a difference between being absent for long stretches and cutting oneself off from one's children. My mother was absent, often even when she was home."

The moments he talked about Arabella were even more revealing than the moments he talked about Raoul. Mélanie reached out and took his hand.

Malcolm squeezed her fingers, though his gaze remained on a point in the past, as though he was studying it like she might a scene in rehearsal that hadn't quite come into focus. "I can imagine Arabella's going off to another country, if the opportunity had presented itself. If she'd thought it would serve her cause."

"Allegra Roth didn't have a cause. At least not that we know of."

"No. But when I think of my mother, I feel I can almost understand Allegra. And when I think of Gelly and me, and even Edgar, I'm furious."

"Good for you."

"For what?"

"For being able to let yourself be furious."

"My darling. Just because I don't express my emotions doesn't mean I don't have them. I can't claim to understand Arabella completely, but I am angry at her. I don't think it gets us closer to understanding who may have had a motive to kill Allegra. It won't be easy. We're going to have to do this without any resources from Bow Street."

"I'm here, Malcolm. I won't leave you to face this alone."

"I'd never think you would. But you aren't going to let this interfere with rehearsals. We have enough of us who can handle this."

That was sensible. Mélanie leaned over to kiss her husband. Because she felt particularly in need of the connection just now. And because she didn't want Malcolm to see how very unsettled she felt.

CHAPTER 13

Roth blew on the steam from his coffee cup. Malcolm had found him pacing the kitchen of his rooms alone, Harriet having taken the boys to the park for exercise. Before raising the question of Roth's activities the night before, Malcolm had suggested they go to a coffee stall in Covent Garden.

"What do you need?" Roth asked as they moved away from the stall. "You wouldn't waste time calling on me in the midst of an investigation if you hadn't learned something."

"Given the nature of this investigation, that's not entirely true." Malcolm took a drink of coffee. It burned his tongue. "I'd have called in any case, to see how you were. But as it happens, I also need to know why you lied about leaving your rooms last night."

Roth froze, his coffee halfway to his lips. "I should have known you'd pursue it."

"Yes," Malcolm said, "you should."

They'd played out similar scenes many times. But it had been the two of them interviewing a suspect, not one of them interviewing the other. They turned of one accord and walked along the piazza, beneath canvas and cloth awnings, past crates of potatoes and onions, paper-screened stalls selling coffee and brown bread, children playing tag, a mother nursing her baby while she tended her stall. The smells of roast potatoes, fresh coffee, and charcoal smoke filled the air.

"I had to send a message to someone," Roth said. "No, not Eddy Purvis. I had to let someone know what had happened to Allegra."

Malcolm curled his fingers round his cup. It warmed his hands through his gloves against the chill air. "Her sister?"

Roth gave a twisted smile. "That would be an easy answer, wouldn't it? But you're going to talk to Cressy and I'm not going to ask her to lie for me. No, a woman who means a great deal to me. We have a system for trading messages through the White Lion. I went there."

Roth had been alone so long. It should not be surprising he had a mistress. Perhaps he'd had others Malcolm had known nothing about. "I assume your mistress will be able to vouch for this? We can be discreet."

Roth paused in the shade of one of the piazza columns. "She has nothing to do with this. And I have no intention of sharing her name."

"Jeremy." Malcolm turned to face his friend. "You can't imagine I'll leave it there. You wouldn't."

"No. But in this case, I can say with absolute certainty that chasing after her will be a dead end. And do her incalculable harm."

"If she's married, we can make sure her husband doesn't find out."

"I didn't say she was married. But if you don't know who she is, you can't do any damage at all."

Malcolm took a step forwards, stumbled over a basket of winter violets, and knocked them onto the paving stones. The young woman tending them looked up at him with indignation. Malcolm muttered an apology and bent to help her scoop the flowers back in their basket. Roth did so as well. Malcolm gave the young woman enough coins to pay for two baskets of flowers before they moved on.

"Jeremy." He took a sip of his cooling coffee. "You asked me to look into what happened to Allegra."

"And my mistress will only be a distraction."

"You can't be sure of that. You know as well as I do one can never be sure where an investigation may go."

Roth turned his head and met Malcolm's gaze, his own hard in the slanting morning sun. "All the more reason to keep her out of it."

"You can't think I'll just let it go."

"No. Unfortunately. But you'll be wasting your time."

Malcolm took a drink of coffee and almost choked on frustration. "And you realize—"

"That the fact that I have a mistress could give me a motive to have wanted to get rid of my wife? Of course. But believe me, marriage between us is out of the question."

DANIELLE DARNAULT WAS in the printshop of the newspaper her journalist husband Pierre Ducroix ran with fellow journalist Edmund Blayney when Mélanie called at the house Danielle and Pierre shared with Edmund and his new wife Pippa. Pippa and Edmund were in the printshop as well, along with their daughters and Danielle's daughter. The smells of grease and printer's ink and coffee filled the air.

"Pierre's out in search of a story," Danielle said, when they had all exchanged greetings and Colin, Jessica, and Emily, who had accompanied Mélanie, had run to talk to the three girls.

"Dare we hope you've come with another story?" Edmund asked, wiping his ink-stained hands on his apron.

"Not yet," Mélanie said. "But if Danielle could help me, it might lead to a story."

Edmund grinned. "Fair enough."

"There's more coffee upstairs," Pippa said.

"Can we stay here?" Colin asked, running over to the press, which fascinated him.

"Absolutely." Edmund flashed a grin at Mélanie.

Danielle untied the voluminous apron she was wearing over her gold-and-cream-striped sarcenet dress. "I quite like the printshop," she said, as she and Mélanie climbed the narrow stairs, "but the ink is the devil to get out of silk or muslin. Or any fabric. I used to tease Pierre about how he had ink stains on all his shirts. It was an excuse to get them off him quickly."

While Danielle poured coffee, Mélanie told her about Allegra Roth. "It isn't out yet that she was Alejandra Vargas. And I don't want to be the source of the information."

Danielle nodded. "I won't tell Edmund or Pierre. Though they wouldn't print it if you asked them not to." She wiped a hand across her forehead. "God. I haven't thought of her in years."

"You knew her?"

"Oh yes. Tristram Gresham slipped over to France secretly when we were working on his *Rosamund* opera. He wanted to see the production and consult with French colleagues. And to visit Paris. He brought Allegra with him." Danielle handed Mélanie a cup of coffee. "I heard her sing at a party once. She had a vivid presence. And a reasonable voice. But not a remarkable one. It wasn't going to carry in a large house. Gresham was besotted. Far more than he'd dream of admitting. She liked to flirt. Which wasn't going to go over well with Tristram. He's a lot of things, but he doesn't play those sorts of games. Particularly not when it's anything to do with work."

"Did you know she was in the Argentine?"

"Theatre's a small world, as you know. I heard second-hand stories about Alejandra Vargas who dazzled Buenos Aires audiences though her voice didn't carry. I pieced together enough to suspect she was Allegra Wainwright. But I hadn't heard she'd married after she and Gresham parted. Poor Jeremy Roth. He doesn't deserve this." Danielle took a sip of coffee, leaning against the deal kitchen table. "I can see his sons playing with Ilia and Cynthia and Katie. I never guessed they were Allegra's children. But there were a few moments she caught my attention. Not her singing so much as other abilities."

"As a courtesan?"

Danielle reached for the milk jug. "As an agent."

Mélanie set down her cup. "Are you saying Allegra was an agent?"

"I'm not sure." Danielle added milk to her coffee and stirred it. "I'm not sure whom she'd have been spying on. Or for whom. But she had the makings of an agent. She was skillful at picking up information. Good at playing a role. It may have all been in the service of advancing her career. But there were times I wondered if it was more. Which made Allegra considerably more interesting."

"You think that's why she went to the Argentine?"

Danielle twisted a strand of her dark hair round her finger. "It would be so much simpler to assume she ran because of a love affair, wouldn't it? Which perhaps is why people are always so ready to jump to that conclusion with women. Most people don't want to think a woman can be complicated. Or have complicated motives. And what better for a spy than to take advantage of people's assumptions?"

Mélanie took a sip of coffee. Nothing like coffee made by a French woman. "That could open a whole new line of questioning. If it proved true."

"I don't have enough evidence to back it up. Perhaps it's my own belief that a clever woman couldn't be preoccupied simply with love affairs." Danielle frowned at an ink smudge on her finger. "You should talk to Tristram, he may know more. I can take you, if you like. He's in London and he's been trying to get me to agree to premiere his new opera. Let me put on a hat and make myself presentable. The children can stay with Edmund and Pippa. They'll be thrilled."

"The children, or Edmund and Pippa?"

Danielle laughed, looking more like a girl than the opera singer who had had half of Europe at her feet while running rings round everyone as a spy. "All of them, actually. Edmund says they're a great help."

~

A PLAINTIVE PIANO melody came from Tristram Gresham's rooms in St. James's Place as Mélanie and Danielle climbed the stairs. Danielle paused on the half landing. "He is good. I could do something with that piece. Modern and free with the emotion, but he doesn't sound like he's trying to copy Beethoven. Which no one can."

When his manservant announced them, Gresham came forwards quickly. He had thick hair the color of birch leaves that flopped over his forehead, giving him the look of an undergraduate. Which was belied by the creases round his eyes and the hollowed-out shadows beneath his cheeks.

The shadows stood out blue-black against his pale skin. A sign of habitual dissipation, perhaps. Or that he hadn't been sleeping well. Mélanie had met him once or twice, at one of Emily Cowper's balls, at a party after one of his performances. He was undoubtedly charming and he wore his charm like armor.

"Ladies. Welcome. I'd like to think that this visit is a sign Danielle is considering being the Liliana in my new opera. But as Mrs. Rannoch is here, I suspect it's to do with last night's events."

"It is," Danielle said. "Though we'll talk about Liliana later. I quite liked what I heard on the stairs."

"New aria for the second act. I heard your voice as I wrote it."

Danielle's strongly marked brows rose. "You're a charming liar, Tristram."

"That's no lie. Any composer would be lucky to have you."

"As I said, charming. But we aren't here to talk about the opera."

Gresham glanced at Mélanie. "I thought someone would come and talk to me. I confess I'm glad it's you."

"You thought a woman would be easier?" Mélanie said.

"I thought a fellow artist would be easier." He scooped a stack of scores off a frayed settee, waved a hand towards it, and moved to the drinks trolley. "We're going to require fortification for this." He poured three measures of brandy and gave glasses to her and Danielle.

"How did you hear?" Mélanie said.

"Talk gets about. I still know people who knew Allegra. Who remembered our involvement. Word got out in the theatre community—there was an incident at the Tavistock last night?— and from there it was a short jump to the opera world."

"You ran off with her." Allegra had been older than Mélanie was when she had become a spy. But it seemed a bit different now she was the mother of a daughter.

"Not precisely." Gresham settled in a chair opposite the settee and took a drink of brandy. "She ran off to become a singer. Her first role was in one of my operas. By the first night, we were lovers. I suppose you could say I seduced her. But you could also make a fair case that she seduced me."

"You were the adult," Danielle said.

"So I was." He frowned into his glass. "Rather more adult than I like to admit. But Allegra made me an offer first."

Which was what Mélanie had done with Raoul. "You could have refused." All things considered, she was glad Raoul hadn't, though she sometimes wondered if he was. She was quite sure he blamed himself. "You could have turned her down."

"So I could." Gresham stretched his legs out, glass cradled in his hands. "Allegra was enchanting. I was besotted."

"You were in love with her?" Mélanie asked.

"I suppose you could say that. If one believes in the term."

"You were definitely besotted," Danielle said.

"I know. I was a fool."

"You didn't think of marrying her?" Mélanie asked.

His gaze widened. "It would never occur to me—"

"To marry your mistress?" Mélanie asked. "Or to marry a girl from her station?"

"To marry at all. I don't believe in it."

"I can understand that. I felt much the same once."

"So did I," Danielle said.

"Of course, it's easier for a man to conduct affairs without contemplating marriage than it is for a woman—a girl—like Allegra," Mélanie added.

Gresham took a drink of brandy, half defensive, half acknowledging. "You have a point. I have enough self-knowledge to admit that, and I'm enough a creature of my world not to let that change my behavior."

"So you left her," Mélanie said.

"Oh no." Gresham set his glass on top of a scribbled-over stack of sheet music on a side table with precision, as though all his concentration was devoted to not sloshing the brandy. "She left me."

That cast a rather different light on the story Jeremy had told Malcolm the previous night. "She left you and came back to London and sought out Jeremy Roth."

"I expect she did, eventually. But she left me for Graham Haverford. I wouldn't promise her the leading role in my new opera, and she was miffed. We had a blazing quarrel. I pointed out that it was nothing to do with her, but Anna Samson could hit a high C. And she couldn't."

"So it was to do with her."

"Artistically. She accused me of having Anna in my bed. Which I didn't. She wasn't my type." He picked up his brandy glass and turned it in his hand, staring into the swirling depths. "I assumed

Allegra would get over it. Even when she stormed out, I assumed she'd be back in the morning. And when she wasn't, I assumed she'd be back the next day. And then the next week. It wasn't until I saw her walking in the Royal Mile with Haverford that I accepted she really had left." He tossed down a quick swallow of brandy. "And then I wondered how I could have been fool enough to care."

Mélanie studied him. Beneath the light voice, the pain was palpable. Like a counterpoint to a simple melody, a counterpoint one later realizes carries all the emotional weight. "Did you see her again?"

"Only once or twice in passing."

"I understood you had provided for her. Was that something you gave her before you separated? Or was that not true?"

"Neither." Gresham took another drink of brandy. "I doubted things would last with Haverford. I didn't want her to be destitute."

"Did you give it to her in person?" Mélanie asked.

Gresham took a drink with studied nonchalance. "No, I had it sent. I had no desire to put us both through an embarrassing and possibly maudlin scene. I wondered if she'd refuse it, but by then things were petering out with Haverford. Allegra has—had—a temper, but was pragmatic."

"And you've always been something of a soft touch," Danielle said. "It may be your saving grace."

"I thought my music was that."

"That too."

"Did you follow what happened to Allegra next?" Mélanie asked.

"You mean her return to London and marriage to the estimable Jeremy Roth? Yes, I heard. I wasn't surprised to find Allegra landing on her feet. Though I didn't give the marriage long. She was restless as an opera singer when she couldn't take center stage. I couldn't imagine her lasting long as a wife and mother, whatever her feelings for her husband. And I'm not sure Allegra was the sort to fall properly in love. She was too preoccupied with herself to give enough thought to someone else to fall in love with them."

Mélanie watched the memories shoot through Gresham's gaze. "You've given her a lot of thought."

"Allegra was—challenging. I told myself I was fortunate to be rid of her, and it's quite true boredom had begun to set in."

"Or so you're telling yourself," Danielle said.

Gresham gave a shrug of acknowledgement. "If it hadn't, it would have done. It always does. I suppose it's not surprising to feel some pique at being left. But beyond that—I can't say I wanted her back a few months on, but I'd be lying if I said I didn't miss her. Allegra was memorable."

Mélanie took a sip from her own nearly untouched glass. "She had her first child soon after she married."

Gresham gave a short laugh. "You're wondering if the boy could be mine? Her affair with Haverford didn't last long, but it lasted long enough to preclude that." He studied his nails for a moment. "I said I don't believe in marriage, but that's one of the reasons I could imagine undertaking it. Not for the morality of the thing—I couldn't care less about that. But because one can't deny the impact on the child of being born a by-blow. It seems Haverford didn't feel the same way. Of course, I think he may have already had a wife." He took another drink of brandy. "Jeremy Roth is to be commended. He seems a decent man."

"He's a very decent man," Danielle said. "He's been very kind to Pierre and me. And Ilia."

Gresham got to his feet, strode to the drinks trolley, refilled his nearly empty glass, and topped off Mélanie's and Danielle's scarcely touched ones. "Poor devil. I imagine Allegra led him a pretty dance."

"Did you follow her life after that?" Mélanie asked.

"You mean did I know she'd disappeared?" Gresham set down

the decanter. "Yes, I heard through sources. She stayed in touch with a few singers I knew."

"So you knew where she went?"

"Not at first. I rather suspected she'd run off to join another opera company. But then I did hear rumors she was singing in Buenos Aires and her lover was Argentine."

"She hadn't contacted you since she'd been back in London?"

Gresham went still. The light from the windows caught him as he stood by the drinks trolley. "I should have known you'd ask. And really, it would be so much easier to say no. But she came to see me the night before last."

"The night before she was killed."

"So I now know." He turned his glass in his hand. The light from the window turned the brandy golden. "It's been more than a decade. But I knew her at once. She was still stunning. Even more so, in fact."

"What did she want?" Mélanie asked.

"Merely for me to put her in touch with some friends in Italy." Gresham returned to his chair and settled into it with almost studied nonchalance. "She was still a singer."

"You think she was considering going to sing in Italy?" Danielle asked.

"She didn't say. But it would be like Allegra to have an escape plan."

"Did you agree to what she asked?" Mélanie said.

"I said I'd write her a letter of introduction. I had little rancor left after so many years."

Mélanie took a sip of brandy. It made sense on the surface. Save that it didn't account for why Gresham had been so reluctant to admit to having seen Allegra at all.

CHAPTER 14

$\mathcal{M}$alcolm found Martin Rowley in the workshop in Isleworth where he had taken Colin, Jessica, and Emily to see the steam engine.

"Rannoch." Rowley came into the office a clerk had shown Malcolm to, his hand extended. He was coatless, waistcoat unbuttoned, shirtsleeves rolled up, fair hair ruffled. Smudges showed on his right cheek and forehead. "Sorry," he said, "we've been working on the new prototype. You may not want to shake hands with me." He wiped his hand on his breeches and then waved a hand towards two chairs by the fire. This room was part of what was left of the original house. Rowley had knocked out walls to convert most of it into a workshop.

"How's the steam engine progressing?" Malcolm asked.

"Better. I'm experimenting with a new type of valve. I hope to be able to try attaching it to a carriage soon. I've set a demonstration up on my property in Devon. Railways are going to change the face of Britain, you know."

"Yes." For better or ill, though there was no stopping progress.

Rowley poured two glasses of Burgundy, gave one to Malcolm, and dropped into a faded tapestry chair across from him, cradling the other. "You didn't come here for idle chatter. Is there committee work I should be doing?"

"Parliamentary committees move notoriously slowly." Malcolm took a drink of Burgundy. "I've just learned you were friends with Marco Esquivel."

"Marco? Oh yes. He and his father were quartered with us when they were prisoners of war. Marco did lessons with me, and later we went to Eton together. My best friend there. One never forgets the friends who get one through one's school years."

"Quite. And while I hope my son has equally strong friendships, I'm determined to spare him the rigors of public school."

"You have a point." Rowley took a drink of Burgundy. "I shall consider that if I ever have children of my own."

"I understand you were with Esquivel last night."

Rowley hesitated, just a fraction of a second, but Malcolm would have sworn the other man was debating how much to reveal.

"Oh yes. We hadn't seen each other in years, but we've written. I admire what he's trying to do in the Argentine tremendously. When I'm at my lowest point over the vicissitudes of persuading Parliament of the benefits of steam engines, I think of Esquivel trying to remake a country. He came round last week and we had a drink and talked about old times. And the changes we're both trying to make. Then he invited me to dinner and the play last night. I almost didn't go. Don't get out much beyond strategy sessions at Brooks's or somewhere more convivial, like your house, these days. But I was glad I went. Though sorry Esquivel had to leave abruptly." Rowley scanned Malcolm's face. "Is that what this is about? Carfax and Lady Carfax came into the box and he left with them, and then he sent word back that he had to leave the theatre. I know the Carfaxes are friends of yours."

"Yes, they are. And we often work together on investigations." Malcolm hesitated but there was no easy way to say it. "Esquivel's mistress was murdered last night."

"Good god." Rowley clunked his glass down, spattering drops of wine on the table.

"Had you ever met her?"

"No. I'd only seen Esquivel twice this visit, as I told you. I doubt Esquivel would have brought her calling. He takes certain forms more seriously than I do. Always did. She wasn't with him last night. Obviously. What—"

"We know very little. She was killed in a tavern in Seven Dials."

"What the devil was she doing in Seven Dials?"

"We aren't sure. But she appears to have been killed by someone she knew. Did Esquivel talk about her?"

"Er—yes, he mentioned her. Mentioned there was a woman he'd been living with in the Argentine who had come to England with him. A bit awkward, because I stood up with him when he married Felicia. I'm their son's godfather. Still remember the wedding and the christening. Not much for such ceremonies, but there was a lot of hope and laughter at both. Odd how much simpler everything seemed in those days." Rowley pulled his glass towards him. "Esquivel said he knew I must think him a reprobate for leaving Felicia. I said, far be it from me to know what went on between a husband and wife. Esquivel said he hadn't been suited to marriage. That it had been a mistake and he was sorry to have locked Felicia into it. But that given he had, they were both trying to make the best of their lives. Then he said he loved his mistress. That he had met her at the wrong time and it wasn't easy, but that she under-stood him as he'd never have thought anyone would." Rowley took a meditative sip of wine. "I confess I thought, lucky bastard to have found that.'"

"I imagine he could use all his friends now."

"Yes." Rowley swirled the wine in his glass. "It's odd, at Cambridge, he was one of my best friends. Truth to tell, I thought Marco and I had little in common these days. Beyond a certain dedication to causes that drove both our lives, but those causes were very different. But then he wanted me involved in the Argentine."

"How?" Malcolm asked.

"Esquivel wants to use one of my steam engines in the mines on land he's acquired in Chile. They constantly need to be able to pump water. Eventually, if my prototype works, he wants to build a railway in the Argentine. There's a broad country to traverse, livestock and all sorts of goods to transport. They'll need railways. Even more than Britain. And Britain will need railways in the Argentine to move goods to ships to send back here. Esquivel's also looking to start a shipping company in Buenos Aires. Suddenly he and I are allies again. I don't know what will come of it, but it was one of the most exciting conversations I've had in a long time."

"That's why he wanted to see you?"

"One of the reasons, at least." Rowley shifted in his chair. "He also wanted to know about Felicia. I've stayed in touch. Called on her and the children. Offered what support I could. Esquivel's parents and sisters are in Spain, and Felicia's parents are both dead. I've known her since we were children. We grew up on neighboring estates. Felicia's an only child. Her parents were keen for her to marry Marco, and I think her father saw him as an heir of sorts, but Felicia's been managing the estate—very competently—handling the investments, raising the children on her own. She's quite brilliant at all of it, but it's a lot to shoulder. I couldn't but take an interest. Marco wanted to know how I thought she'd feel about seeing him."

"Surely he wants to see the children."

"Well, yes. But I think he was—is—afraid of facing Felicia."

"What did you tell him?"

Rowley took a drink of wine. "It won't be easy. I couldn't sugarcoat that. She's got used to being on her own. And she's heard the stories from the Argentine. Their marriage hadn't gone as either of them expected that day we cut the cake from Gunter's.

But I don't think Felicia would be human if she didn't feel abandoned at times. Or feel anger at the idea of being supplanted. Felicia keeps a lot to herself, but she has her pride, and it's been damaged. Marco asked if I'd be willing to act as an intermediary. Which of course I would. But it would be damnably uncomfortable."

"Had you talked to Felicia Esquivel since Esquivel returned?"

Rowley shifted in his chair. "I wrote to her after my first meeting with Marco. Marco and I were supposed to discuss more last night. But we never got a chance to finalize things."

"An awkward situation to be in."

"Yes." Rowley took a drink of Burgundy. "Even before this latest news. As I said, Esquivel and I had drifted apart since Cambridge. Well, literally, with his being across an ocean. And in the focus of our lives. And perhaps because I'd come to see myself as Felicia's ally first. One doesn't want to choose sides in a marriage, but sometimes it's unavoidable. Felicia's the one I've seen, day to day, these past years. It wasn't like that once. Marco and I were allies when we went to Eton. It's a shock of cold water, going off to school after the relative comforts of the nursery and schoolroom. I think Marco always felt a bit like an outsider in England, but at Eton we were both outsiders."

"I know the feeling," Malcolm said. "It was much the same for David Mallinson and me at Harrow."

Rowley nodded. "We made a few more friends at Eton eventually. By the time we got to Cambridge we were a tight circle. We sat in coffeehouses writing things that no one wanted to print. I imagine you know the sort of thing."

"Very well. We had a group like that at Oxford."

"Those people end up being one's closest friends. At least it was that way for us."

"For us too, mostly." Their group at Oxford had once seemed like his family. David, who was a friend again after an estrangement his father had orchestrated over Mélanie. Simon, who always had been and always would be a friend. And Oliver, now married to David's sister, who had been spying on them for Hubert Mallinson. Oliver was still a friend, in a way. But Hubert's interference would always hang over them and the memory of what had seemed a golden time in their lives.

"All of us were a bit given to dreaming, in different ways," Rowley said. "Marco about Argentine revolution—which seemed something of an impossible dream at that point. Me sketching plans for steam engines and locomotives, which also seemed a bit of an impossible dream. At least to everyone I tried to explain them to. Beardsley talking about the franchise and Catholic emancipation."

"I understand Beardsley was at the theatre with you last night."

"Yes, Beardsley's always busy, as I am, though we still find time for a pint every month or so. Marco wants him to invest in the venture in the Argentine as well. He said it would make it like the old days to have us all working together. Of course, it wouldn't be the same without Bobby—"

"Bobby?" Malcolm asked.

"Oh, didn't I mention him? Yes, Bobby Derwent."

"Bobby Derwent," Malcolm said. Good god.

"Yes. He was part of our circle at Eton and Cambridge. A good friend, though we hadn't been as close in recent years. Damnable what happened to him. Do you know him?"

"He was married to my cousin."

Rowley went still. "Oh, god, yes. Judith Dacre-Hammond that was. I'm so sorry. The girl half London was in love with. I danced with her a few times when she was the toast of the season and marveled that someone could be so lovely and also so good-humored. They seemed so happy."

"They were," Malcolm said. Judith, free of the spy game, had had perhaps the simplest love affair of any of them. Until her husband had taken a jump badly and the fairy tale had shattered.

Rowley shook his head. "Odd, Bobby was the only one of us

who wasn't an impossible dreamer. Truth to tell, he always seemed to be looking for something to focus on. But I think he liked the adventure of being round people who were challenging the establishment in different ways. I always thought at some point Bobby would settle on what he wanted to do with his life and astound us all. I still think he might have done, if he'd lived longer."

"Was Bobby close to Marco Esquivel?"

"Oh yes. I think Bobby stayed in touch with Marco more than any of us. Marco had talked to him about investing in his Argentine venture as well. Did he ever mention it?"

"No. I don't recall Bobby's ever mentioning Esquivel."

"Odd. I'd have said Esquivel was one of Bobby's best friends. But then it's odd what people mention and don't mention to their families. I imagine Judith may know more. Though it must be painful to talk about him."

"Judith has shown a lot of resilience." She was quiet these days, talking and laughing at family parties, but more contained than the carefree girl she'd so recently been. "It might do her good to be involved in something." Though Malcolm's impulse had always been to keep Judith out of anything remotely related to espionage and investigation.

Rowley nodded. "Can't imagine what she's been going through. I should perhaps have reached out more." He picked up his glass and frowned at it. "A lot of tragedy to have befallen our Cambridge group. Unconnected, of course. But it makes one think."

CHAPTER 15

Once Mivart's had been the closest Raoul had to a home in London. Perhaps anywhere. Malcolm had confronted him in his room at Mivart's after he learned the truth of Mélanie's spying. Later—remarkably, less than a month later—Raoul had hosted the first of his Boxing Day dinners in a private room at the hotel. Laura had sat next to him that night, by his own design. Partly because he'd wanted to learn more about her. Partly because—well, Laura had intrigued him from the moment he met her.

Laura was presently somewhere in the service passages of the hotel in the dark dress and starched apron of a maid. They had ascertained that Allegra Roth's lady's maid and Esquivel's valet were both downstairs speaking with a Bow Street patrol. So provided Raoul could keep Esquivel engaged, Laura should have ample opportunity to search Allegra Roth's things. There was a time Raoul would have been worried about his wife on a mission such as this. But though she might not have as much experience as the rest of them, her instincts were impeccable. And she had spent years on a mission as a governess spying on her employers.

Raoul rapped at the door. Esquivel opened it, wrapped in a

dressing gown over his shirt and trousers, much as Raoul had once been when he greeted visitors in the hotel.

"O'Roarke." Esquivel extended his hand. "It's been a long time." His face was haggard but he gave a smile of recognition.

"So long, you'd be pardoned for not remembering." Raoul shook Esquivel's hand.

"On the contrary. You made a great impression. You talked about ideas I'd been exposed to, but I'd never heard them pulled together in such a way or to reach such conclusions. You left me more determined than ever to be part of changing my country. It was a timely lesson just before I left for the Argentine."

"I'm flattered if I played any part in shaping your ideas."

"I've followed you," Esquivel said. "We may have been in different countries, but we were fighting the same fight."

Which was true, if one thought in terms of ideas. But ten years ago, Raoul had been working for the French, whom Esquivel had opposed in Spain.

Esquivel waved a hand towards the striped satin chairs by the sitting room's fire. "You made me believe one could change the world."

Raoul settled back in a chair with the same striped satin upholstery as those on which Malcolm had confronted him. For a moment he had a clear image of the book he'd been reading that day draped over the chair arm. It was burned in his memory. "These days I often struggle to convince myself of as much. But I'm pleased if I played any role in convincing you of it."

Esquivel reached for the decanter on the table by the chairs and poured two glasses of port. "You're working in Spain now."

"When I can. I have a family in Britain, which complicates things."

Esquivel handed Raoul a glass. "I remember you had a wife in Ireland."

"So I did." Raoul took the glass. He remembered mentioning Margaret on that long-ago night at the Lodge of the Rational

Knights, picking his way carefully round the tangle of his personal life. "We're divorced. I remarried two years ago and have two young children. I'm away from them too much as it is."

Esquivel took a drink of port and grimaced as though he found it bitter. "I've been away from my own children much of their lives. Difficult to imagine ever living with my wife again. Divorce isn't an option for us—but I can imagine how a person could love again. Though that doesn't seem an option for me now either."

"My commiserations." Raoul had no need to be anything but genuine when he said it. "I can scarcely imagine what you are going through."

"Thank you." Esquivel's mouth twisted. "Alejandra was—I'd never met anyone like her." He shot a look at Raoul. "I took my marriage seriously. I fancied myself in love when we married, though it's also true our families wanted the marriage. It was clear not long after we returned from the wedding journey that we did not have a great deal in common. I won't claim I was faithful all the years we were apart, even before Alejandra. We were separated for years at a time. One doesn't expect—But I wasn't looking for a mistress when I met Alejandra. I didn't think I had the time for a permanent entanglement."

"Is that what Allegra Roth was? An entanglement?"

Esquivel dragged a hand over his face. "God, no. The word is far too simple. Far too transitory. I met her at a lecture on Paine. Not so many streets from here. It was raining and I offered her my umbrella. We ducked into a coffeehouse to avoid the rain. Her suggestion. Most ladies I know wouldn't be seen in a coffeehouse. But Allegra was different. In so many ways. I'd never met a woman with such keen insights into politics."

Raoul settled back in his chair and crossed his legs. "You'd be shocked by most of the women I know, in that case."

"Of course I know there are women who are different. But my mother, my sisters, my wife—they all seemed to inhabit a different sphere. I'd never met anyone like Allegra, as I called her then. I knew I had to see her again. I wasn't even thinking of—well, I was, but I didn't necessarily expect it to go where it did. She was a married woman. Her husband had fought in a war I'd fought in. We met at another lecture, then at a bookseller's. We met to talk. And then we met to do other things." The words tumbled out, as though the story was a way to hold onto his memories of Allegra. "I wouldn't say I anticipated it. But when it happened, it seemed inevitable. I shut my mind to the fact that it had to end when I returned to the Argentine. And then I realized I couldn't bear for it to end. Couldn't imagine going on without her. And Allegra told me that with me she hadn't just found love, she'd found a purpose. After that, we both knew there was no option but for her to leave with me." Esquivel met Raoul's gaze squarely. "I won't pretend I wasn't running off with another man's wife, with the mother of two children. I'd also never claim that the decision was mine and not Allegra's. She controlled her own life. Made her own decisions. She was wilting in England. As I would have, if I'd stayed here. I'd never imagined what it would be like to share my life with someone who thought so like I did. Who shared my ideas and dreams. Whom I could plan with. I couldn't imagine my life without her." He drew a raw breath. "I still can't."

"It's an amazing thing," Raoul said. "To find someone with whom one can share so much." Which didn't mean it justified the damage to those who could be hurt in the process.

"You can't have our goals for the world and live a conventional family life," Esquivel said. "I think you must have realized that before I did. That night at the Lodge meeting, I sensed that you were pitying me for attempting matrimony."

"I'd never presume to pity anyone else's choices. I've made too many bad ones myself. But at that time, I might have agreed with you. Now I'm inclined to wonder if one can fight to change the world without first being loyal to those one is closest to. My son taught me that."

Esquivel's brows drew together. "Your son?"

"Malcolm Rannoch is my son. We don't make a secret of it any longer. I once shared a cause of sorts with his mother. So I can imagine a bit what you found with Allegra." And he'd asked Arabella to run off with him. Though in that case, it had been so they could keep Malcolm with them. He couldn't imagine having gone off with Arabella and leaving Malcolm behind. In fact, one of the reasons he hadn't asked Mélanie to go to South America with him years later was it would have meant leaving Malcolm behind. Well, that and the fact that he'd realized she was already falling in love with Malcolm. And a few other things, like a war that had mattered intensely to him.

"So you were away from him growing up," Esquivel said.

"More than I'd have liked. More than I should have been. Though I managed to see him a fair amount. I was in Britain a good deal, and Spain is closer than the Argentine."

"I think"—Esquivel stared into his glass. "My children will understand when they're grown. Where I was most needed."

"I expect they will, " Raoul said.

Though it might mean they'd decide he'd been most needed at home.

LAURA SLIPPED DOWN the passage at Mivart's. She was wearing a dark wig and a starched cap over her telltale titian hair, and a dark dress and apron that matched the clothing worn by the maids at Mivart's. This was not the first time an investigation had taken them to Mivart's, and they'd found it helpful to have the ensemble on hand.

A lady and gentleman left one of the rooms. Laura moved to the side, as a maid would. The lady was wearing a deep-brimmed bonnet, but Laura thought she recognized the sister of Mrs. Rattisford, who lived on Charles Street off Berkeley Square and occasionally walked her pug in the garden. Laura had met Mrs. Rattisford's sister once or twice. She kept her gaze discreetly averted. Thank goodness for the wig.

The couple moved down the stairs at the end of the passage. Laura continued to the door of the bedroom in the suite Marco Esquivel and Allegra Roth occupied. Fortunately, her husband had taught her to use picklocks and the lock was not a complicated one. After a quick glance up and down the passage, she got the door open and slipped into the room.

It was furnished with the anonymous good taste one expected in an elegant hotel. One trunk stood at the foot of the bed, another beneath the windows on the side of the room. A silver-backed brush and mirror, a crystal scent bottle, tins of rouge and blacking, and a jewel case were arranged on the dressing table, a bit askew, as though Allegra had completed her toilette in a hurry when she left the night before. An adjoining door led to the sitting room. Laura could hear the faint murmur of her husband's flexible tones and an answering deeper voice. Raoul was pitching his voice loud, probably to cover any telltale sound she made.

Laura turned back the lid of the trunk at the foot of the bed, careful not to creak the hinges. Shirts and waistcoats. Esquivel's possessions might yield clues, but time was limited and she needed to focus on Allegra's. She went to the trunk beneath the windows. Shawls and scarves in brilliant cashmere and gauzy silk, and tippets and chemises of fine pin-tucked linen, threaded with ribbon, neatly folded. Out of habit, Laura felt along the inside of the trunk for concealed papers and tapped for a false bottom, though there was no reason to think Allegra would have concealed papers. Still, she'd led a life of mystery.

The wardrobe had an array of gowns, well cut by a Parisian modiste, as Kitty had said of the gown Allegra had been found in last night. The scent of jasmine wafted from them. Allegra's presence remained so vivid when she was gone. It must be unbearable for Esquivel. Whose voice Laura could still hear from next door.

She moved to the dressing table. Strands of fair hair were caught in the silver-backed brush. The jewels in the jewel case were not the most expensive, but good quality—pearls, moonstones, diamond earrings. Nothing appeared to be paste. The drawer held handkerchiefs embroidered with flowers or her initials (A.V., not A.R.) and another jewel case that had bracelets and rings. Laura ran her fingers over the white silk lining on a whim, and felt something. A telltale crinkle. The back of the lid coming loose or—

The silk lining was loose in one corner. It looked like wear. But—

Laura tugged gently at the loose white silk. It peeled back. To reveal papers tucked inside the lining.

A woman like Allegra Roth/Alejandra Vargas would have all sorts of reasons to hide letters. Love letters from a man other than Esquivel, news from home, perhaps mementos of her children. Perhaps a communication with whomever she had been meeting last night.

Laura unfolded the papers. And stood frozen for several seconds staring down at them. Not because of the contents, but because of the form.

They were in code.

~

By prior arrangement, Laura met her husband in a bookseller's two streets over from Mivart's. She'd removed her wig, cap, and apron, and looked more or less herself in her dark dress.

"Nothing unexpected?" Raoul asked, as he met her before a shelf of political philosophy in a back corner.

"Not getting in and out of the hotel." Laura pushed back the volume of John Locke she'd been pretending to examine. "But I found this hidden in one of Allegra's jewel cases." She held out the coded papers.

Raoul stared down at them. "I've never known anyone to use a code for a simple love letter—not unless they were an agent. A lot of intrigues in the Argentine. We know Allegra and Esquivel were deeply involved in politics. And the fact she hid this could suggest it was hidden from Esquivel as well. Poor devil. I'm not sure he was truthful with me about everything, but I don't doubt he's broken up about her death."

"And he may be more broken up when we decode this." Laura tucked her arm through her husband's. Relationships could be fragile. She was aware every day of the wonder of what they had. And of how easily it could be smashed to bits.

$\mathcal{M}$élanie set down her pen. She'd promised to take a new draft of the scene between Fiona and Gideon to Simon at the Tavistock this afternoon. They were going to go through it with Brandon and Manon. If she could get it done in the next hour, she might have time for a council with Malcolm and any of the others who returned before she had to leave for the theatre.

And of course, just as it was hard to sleep when one knew one had to be awake early, it was hard to write when one knew one needed to produce the words quickly. She could grasp the shape of what she wanted with the scene. The details of how to get there eluded her. Gideon and Fiona were both being much too literal. She struck a line through the speech she had just written. It didn't help that she had a gnawing sense that she should be doing something about the investigation. Perhaps—

A rap sounded at the door of her study, and Valentin entered with a look of apology. He knew she was working. He also knew about the investigation. "Forgive me, madam. But Miss Roth has called."

She jumped to her feet far too readily, but really, time away from the scene might help. And she'd been wanting to talk to Harriet Roth.

Valentin had shown Jeremy's sister into the small salon. She was sitting bold upright on one of the chairs wearing a slate-colored gown and bonnet that could pass for mourning, and her chestnut hair was gathered into a simple knot, but as always she radiated quiet, effortless elegance. She sprang to her feet at Mélanie's entrance. "I'm sorry, I know you must be busy—"

"Of course not." Mélanie closed the door. For all Jeremy and Harriet and the boys were frequent guests in Berkeley Square, it was, she realized, the first time Harriet had called alone. "I'm so sorry. I know Allegra had been your friend as well as your sister-in-law."

Harriet's mouth twisted with familiar irony. "There were times when friend was the last thing I'd have called Allegra," she said when they were seated. "And probably the last thing she'd have called me. She thought I was rather dull. But she also liked an audience and we all played her audience at various times. She could be charming. I wasn't as much prey to it as Jeremy, but even I felt her charm. She could charm the boys, when she focused on them. Those are the memories I'm trying to help them hold on to." She shook her head. "I've just been to see Cressida—Allegra's stepsister. Like me, I don't think she'll ever quite forgive Allegra. And like me, I don't think she can fully comprehend that she's gone."

"I know she hadn't written to Jeremy," Mélanie said. "I assume she hadn't written to you either?"

"To ask for news of the boys? That would be a nice thought. But no. Although Jeremy says she'd kept a button from Samuel's baby shirt. That surprised me. Allegra was never given to senti-mentality."

"Everyone can have moments of it."

Valentin returned with a tea tray. Mélanie sensed that Harriet had come to say or ask something specific and couldn't quite come to the point. After all, it was an investigation, and though they were Jeremy's friends, they were also the investigators.

Harriet stirred her tea carefully, took a sip, and set the cup down with a decisive click. "I left the house partly to give Jeremy time with the boys. And because I wanted to see Cressy. But I also wanted to see you. When I came back from my outing with the boys this morning, Jeremy told me that Malcolm had learnt he'd gone out last night."

Mélanie hadn't seen Malcolm since he'd left the house this morning to call on Roth, but if Harriet knew, there was no point in denying it. "Yes."

Harriet took another drink of tea. "I knew. When you called on us last night, and Jeremy said he and I had been talking all evening, I knew he'd gone out."

"He's your brother," Mélanie said. "No one would expect you to call him a liar."

"I told him it was stupid after you left. That you were bound to learn the truth. He said, probably, but he needed to try. Malcolm may not have had a chance to tell you yet, but I know Jeremy told him he went out to send a letter to his mistress. And I can tell you that's true. At least, I know Jeremy does have a mistress. And he was most concerned for her. He wanted her to know what happened to Allegra, and he wanted to keep her out of it. I know there's no reason to believe me when I lied last night, but I wanted to tell you."

"You didn't lie last night," Mélanie said. "You were quiet about Jeremy's lie."

"I hardly think Jeremy would let a witness get away with that. And I did nod agreement."

"Jeremy would understand the impulse to protect family. And for what it's worth, I do believe you." Mélanie reached for her own tea. She shouldn't be surprised that Jeremy had a mistress. There was no reason to expect him to confide in them. And no reason to feel unsettled. She took a sip of tea and wished she'd added honey. "Do you—"

"I don't know her name. I probably wouldn't tell you if I did, that would be Jeremy's choice, but I wouldn't pretend not to know. I wish to god I did know her name so I could ask her to back up Jeremy's story if need be. I wouldn't know about her at all if I hadn't found a note in his coat pocket. Just a scrap of paper setting up a meeting, but it was clear it was a love note. I handed it back to him and he acknowledged the affair but asked me not to ask more." Harriet hesitated. "I can't swear I'd have known if there'd been others. But I can read my brother well. I know the difference between an absence for an investigation and for other reasons. I think she's his first mistress since Allegra." She picked up the milk jug and added more to her tea. "Actually, these past weeks he's seemed the happiest I've seen him in years. That's the terrible thing about this."

She set down the milk jug and drew a breath. Because, like Mélanie, she must know it was terrible and also perhaps significant.

Livia Davenport adjusted the vase of winter violets on the console table. "Do you think Justine will like them?"

"I'm sure she will, darling," Cordelia said. The girls were very excited to be readying the guest bedroom for Justine Lambton's visit. As Cordelia was herself. However adept she'd become at investigations, she wouldn't have been much help watching for assassins as Harry was currently doing. No sense in wasting time feeling sidelined. She had called on Christopher Rowley this morning only to find he was in the country.

"I think she'll like my picture." Drusilla tugged the paperboard pastel she'd drawn to a more central spot on the night table. "It's a statue of the Roman Drusilla."

"One of the Roman Drusillas," Livia said.

Drusilla shrugged with the assurance that she was the most important Drusilla of all. At four and a half she had a strong sense of herself. She tugged the picture again, then spun round and ran to the door. "I hear a carriage. Maybe it's Justine!"

It was early for Justine, but one never knew. Cordelia followed her daughters onto the landing to hear Alec, the footman, in the hall below. It was not Justine. As the girls ran to the stairhead, Alec came hurrying up the stairs. "A Mrs. Esquivel has called, madam."

ALEC HAD SHOWN Felicia Esquivel into the sitting room on the first floor where Cordelia usually received callers. Normally she'd have brought the girls in with her, but she'd explained to them that this wasn't that sort of call.

Felicia Esquivel stood by the windows, back straight, the light behind her. She had smooth, dark blonde hair, a fine-boned face, and clear blue eyes. She was not overly tall, but she carried herself with the assurance. A young woman who still looked little past her first season, with the command of a dowager. "I'm sorry, Lady Cordelia," she said. "I know we haven't been introduced, but I grew up with Martin and Christopher Rowley. Christopher has mentioned you. And this did not seem the time to stand on ceremony."

"I quite agree." Cordelia gestured to the cherry-striped chairs by the fire.

"I know you investigate cases with the Rannochs. I heard they'd taken an interest in the woman who was killed last night." Felicia sank into a chair, back ramrod straight. "My husband's mistress."

"Yes," Cordelia said.

"I don't come to London often." Felicia folded her hands in her lap, her lilac kid gloves in relief against the glossy blue gros-de-Naples of her gown. "There's so much to see to in the country, and I prefer it there. But though Marco is under the impression there is a great deal I do not know, that's not at all the case. I often think he doesn't know me at all."

"You've been apart a great deal, as I understand it."

"Oh yes. We were young when we married. He was the first boy I danced with. He was kind to me, in a way brothers aren't. And of course he had all the allure of being foreign and different from dull English boys. While at the same time being safe, because he'd grown up next door with the Rowleys and was practically one of the family. When Marco proposed, it seemed inevitable." She looked at Cordelia. "You've been married for some years."

"And I made a shocking mull of it at first, and caused a scandal you're too kind to allude to. But we're still together somehow. I love Harry quite desperately." Odd to say that. She wouldn't use those words to most of their friends, or even to Harry. Perhaps especially not to Harry. "I'd be lying if I said it wasn't challenging at times. And it helped that neither of us had expectations when we went into the marriage."

"When I married Marco, I couldn't imagine that we wouldn't live happily ever after. But then it's difficult to imagine anything else at eighteen, isn't it?"

"I imagine it depends on circumstances," Cordelia said. "But I do think life tends to seem simpler at eighteen." Of course, at eighteen she'd been in love with someone else and unable to imagine ever loving another man.

"It did to me. But then Marco went off to fight in Spain, and when he came back to England he was with the Lodge of the Rational Knights and his mind was on the Argentine. And he never seemed to want to talk to me about it. I was curious, actually, but it was as though he'd decided we lived in different worlds. In fact, he was gone so much, I'm not sure we even spent a year living together, if one adds up all the bits and pieces. It dawned on me slowly that this wasn't the fairy tale I'd thought I was getting. At least, not unless the prince was always going off on quests, leaving the princess to raise babies and run the castle. It's not so much that I had a great disillusionment as it slowly fell apart, one bit at a time. Until I realized I had the rather prosaic arrangement one hears about growing up. Except that my husband wasn't just going off to his club, or the races, or fishing in Scotland. When he went to the Argentine, I knew I wouldn't see him for years. But I saw him so little, the separation didn't seem as drastic. And it was easier, in a way, not always wondering when he'd come home. I set about seeing to the property, redoing the house, tending the children. I built a life. I was quite happy. I wasn't naive enough not to realize there must be other women, with him gone for so long. But later, after his visit home after Waterloo, I heard rumors of one woman. Who was central to his life. I hadn't expected that." She folded her arms over her chest and gripped her elbows. "I won't pretend I didn't feel pique. One of the ladies who wrote to me from the Argentine said at least I needn't fear being publicly embarrassed. But the thing was, *I* knew. That he shared himself with her as he never had with me. As perhaps I never even understood enough to want him to share himself with me, not when we were first married. I'm not sure I ever even knew Marco. But I wish I'd had the chance to. When I was the angriest with her, I thought I deserved the chance to. Instead, I was left raising his children and running a house that was supposed to have been ours. Having quite a nice life. But not the life I envisioned." She paused. "I suppose a lot of people at thirty don't have the life they envisioned at eighteen."

"I certainly don't. Sometimes what one has is better. At least for the person one's become. It is, in my case. But that doesn't mean one doesn't regret what one's lost."

"It's more an idea I regret. We were little more than children when we married. It's what we might have become if we'd grown together instead of separately. He's my husband. Whatever life I can build on my own, I'll remain tied to him. Truth to tell, I'm not sure what I'd say if he came to me and said he wanted to start again, to be a proper family. At times I feel we had a lucky escape. But at other times I feel cheated that we didn't have a chance to try."

"And you blamed Allegra Roth."

"I didn't even know her name. In my mind she was That Woman. But yes." Felicia met Cordelia's gaze directly. "In my mind I've called her appalling things. Words I'd never utter in polite company. In any company." She lifted her chin, her gaze steady. "I've imagined doing appalling things to her."

"Many people do, when they're angry at someone."

"Yes. But of course in my case the person in question ended up murdered. I'm hardly the expert you are at murder investigations, but I understand enough to know that makes me a suspect."

"It takes more than that to make someone a suspect."

"Is Marco—he must be devastated."

"I haven't seen him. But I know people who were there when he learned of it."

"Does he have friends with him?"

"I'm not sure about now, but I understand he was with friends at the theatre last night. Including Martin Rowley and William Beardsley."

"They all went to Cambridge together. I'm glad he was with them. I hate to think of his being alone through something like this."

"You hadn't seen him since he's been in England?"

"No. That's why I came to London. I heard he was here and I was determined to speak with him. I saw no reason to simply wait for him to deign to show up. I got to town yesterday. Only to realize that my fantasies of confronting my husband and his mistress were far simpler in Devon than when I actually faced the opportunity to do so. I didn't want a vulgar scene. I even walked by Mivart's, where I thought he was staying, in the hopes of seeing them. Foolish."

"Did you see them?" Cordelia asked.

Felicia Esquivel hesitated a moment. "I saw a woman I thought might be Alejandra Vargas. I saw a print of her once. I said I saw her as The Woman, didn't I? That was true at first. But I learnt her name."

"A natural impulse. What did you do after you saw her outside Mivart's?"

Felicia twisted her hands together. "I followed her. That sounds horrid. But she walked down the street and I found myself moving through the crowd after. She went a few blocks, then went into a coffeehouse."

"Alone?"

"No." Felicia's pale brows drew together. "That is, she went in alone, but I walked by and looked through the windows. She met a gentleman at the back of the coffeehouse. Not anyone I recognized. He looked older than we were—more our parents' generation. Not tall and he wore spectacles. Graying hair. They appeared to be on familiar terms." She paused. "I confess I was pleased. I was wondering if Marco knew and if there was a way I could let him know if not. And yet—I can't precisely say I want Marco back, whatever that means. I'm not even sure what it would look like."

"Did you see more?" Cordelia asked. "Of Allegra Roth and this gentleman?"

"No. Some people left the coffeehouse and seemed to notice me staring and I realized I couldn't stay. I went back to the friends I'm staying with and tried without success to write a letter to Marco."

"What time was it? That you saw Allegra go into the coffeehouse?"

Felicia frowned. "A bit past three, I think." Her blue eyes widened. "What time was Allegra killed?"

"We're not sure precisely, but not long after. What was Allegra wearing?"

"A gray dress. Levantine silk, I think, with black chenille trim on the skirt. And a black cloak with a slate lining. I couldn't help noting she had excellent taste in clothes." Her eyes widened. "You think she went right from the coffeehouse to wherever she was killed?"

"I think it's possible," Cordelia said.

CHAPTER 17

$\mathcal{P}$hilip Ledgwood was staying at the Pulteney in Piccadilly. As fashionable as Mivart's. Rumored to be the most expensive hotel in London. Tsar Alexander and his sister had stayed there during the peace celebrations after Napoleon had been sent to Elba. The concierge was surprised at an unaccompanied lady's calling, but a card embossed with "Countess Carfax" could work wonders. The card was taken up by one of the team of footmen efficient at everything from carrying shopping parcels to ordering carriages to securing theatre boxes, and shortly after, Kitty was shown into Philip Ledgwood's suite.

Warned by the footman, her former lover faced her, with a steady, contained expression. His face was leaner than she remembered, his hair was cropped closer, his brows had less of an ironic tilt. His mouth seemed set in firmer lines. He was dressed fashionably as always, but with an almost studied carelessness, his cravat slightly askew, his coat seemingly carelessly shrugged on.

Questions shimmered in his gaze, but he came forwards, his hand extended. "It's good to see you again. Though difficult to remember to address you as Lady Carfax."

His hand felt the same, firm and steady, though a handshake

was much less personal than the touches they had once exchanged. "Please don't. I'm still not used to it myself. I doubt I ever will be. You always called me Kitty."

At which time they had been far more intimate than now. His gaze said he recognized it, but he merely said, "Kitty then. I haven't had the chance to felicitate you on your marriage."

"Thank you. We're very happy." Odd that something so trite could be so true. "It's remarkable how one's life can change so much."

"So it is." He held out a hand to two figured cream satin armchairs by the fire. "I married over a year ago. I doubt you'd have heard. Isabel Fuentes. Her father was made Barao Fuentes by the regent."

Which probably meant her father was a native Brazilian. Of the many titles given out by the then regent, now King João VI, after the Portuguese court moved to Brazil, by far the majority had gone to those who had come from Portugal with the court. Or to others who had fought against the French and later made their way to Brazil. Those few Brazilians who had been ennobled had been given the lowest-level title of barao.

"I hadn't heard," Kitty said. "My felicitations."

"Thank you." He gave a faint smile. "It came as something of a surprise. Not the wedding, the impulse to marry. I know you will not be offended when I say I had avoided it. In truth, I'd avoided young unmarried girls since I was at university. Far too many risks, to them and to me. I don't know why it was different with Isabel. She's remarkable, of course." The words might be commonplace, but the smile in his eyes was not.

"And perhaps you were at a point in your life when you were ready to get married."

"Perhaps. I hadn't thought of it that way."

"I think it was that way for my husband," Kitty said. "I'm fortunate we were together when he got to that point. I think we might have stayed together regardless, but it wouldn't have been nearly so comfortable."

Philip shook his head. "You never were like other women, Kitty."

"I hope not." Kitty tugged off her gray doeskin gloves. "I hope I'm not like other people. Everyone is unique."

"But some to a greater degree." He smiled for a moment, memories drifting through his gaze, then moved to a pier table and poured two glasses of Madeira. "Isabel and I have a daughter."

"How lovely." Kitty accepted the glass he was holding out. "Children are wonderful."

"I remember how important yours were to you. I confess I didn't fully understand it until our little Bella was born." Philip sat across from her.

"And you came to England to show her to your family?"

"In part." He took a drink of Madeira and settled back against the fringed cushions, covered in a gold that expertly set off the cream without creating too much distraction. "Isabel and Bella are with my parents now. I'm going down to join them as soon as I can wrap up business here. But I'm also in London to meet with Castlereagh. The situation in Portugal is challenging."

A few years ago, a rebellion had broken out in Portugal led by a combination of Liberals and those opposed to British occupation in the wake of the French defeat. Marshall Beresford, head of the British military authority in Portugal, had put down the rebellion and executed the ringleaders. Which had only, as Kitty could have warned him, intensified anti-British sentiments among the Portuguese. Beresford had then gone to Brazil to request more powers from the king in the face of what he saw as Jacobinism among the Portuguese populace. While he was gone, a revolution had broken out, and on his return to Lisbon last year, he'd been forbidden to disembark. The country now teetered precariously, leaving a number of alarming or exciting possibilities, depending on one's perspective. Kitty was inclined to be excited.

"Are the royal family going to return?" she asked Philip.

"It's being discussed." Philip took a drink of Madeira and settled back in a corner of the sofa. Indeed, Kitty knew, the king's return from Brazil was a demand of the revolutionaries, who also wanted a constitutional monarchy. "A great deal has changed in the past fifteen years. Brazil has become an international power. Open trade with the Continent, rather than just with Portugal, has helped that."

Kitty took a sip of Madeira. It took her back to her own time in Lisbon. "And hugely benefited Britain."

"I won't deny that."

Kitty set her glass down. "The British can't run Portugal indefinitely. Or rather, they shouldn't. And I doubt any South American colonies will be content to remain colonies much longer."

"I might have known you'd say that. And I can't disagree." Philip took another drink of Madeira and regarded her. "You didn't come here to debate politics, Kitty. Or to ask after my family. Why are you here?"

Kitty reached for her glass, took a fortifying sip, and set it down again. "It's Alejandra Vargas."

Philip set his own glass down with a clunk. A few drops of Madeira sloshed on the satinwood table. "I'd heard rumors Esquivel was in England. She came with him?"

"She did. And she was murdered yesterday."

It was perhaps a cruel way to deliver the news, but shock could reveal motives. Malcolm had taught her that.

Philip's eyes went wide. "Good god. Brigands?"

"I don't think so. She was at a tavern." No sense in going into where, just now. "When did you last hear from her?"

Philip passed a hand over his face. "Over a year ago. Before my marriage. I haven't been back to Buenos Aires since. And naturally, once I was married it was not a connection I thought it appropriate to pursue."

"But you knew her. Well."

"At one time."

"What enemies did she have?"

"Enemies? You mean someone who would commit murder? Esquivel has enemies, but I can't imagine any of them turning on Alejandra."

"Did she ever talk to you about her past? Before she came to the Argentine?"

"Why should she have talked to me?"

"There's no need to pretend, Philip. It was before you married your Isabel. Given our relationship, you can't imagine it would shock me."

Philip gave a wry smile. "You always said things others wouldn't." He reached for his glass and took a drink, more like a draught of ale than sip of Madeira, as though to steady himself. "Alejandra was fascinated by Brazil. By what was happening there. By the contrast to the Argentine, I think. That's what we talked of —when we weren't engaged in other activities. And the new opera house in Rio, where I think she'd have liked to perform. She didn't talk about her past, except the occasional comment about her childhood—Christmas memories and that sort of thing. I did know she was British. She never really tried to hide that. Is that why she came back here?"

"Esquivel is here, so she came with him. What else she intended, I'm not sure of."

"She had family here still?"

"She had a husband and two sons."

Philip's glass tilted in his fingers. "Good god."

"She never mentioned them, I take it?"

"Can you imagine she would have?"

"I can't imagine not talking about my children. Can you?"

"No." His brows drew together. "Not now I have one. But I can't imagine leaving her either."

"A point. Alejandra seems to have walled off that part of her life. Which I suspect would be the only way one could manage in such circumstances."

"Had she seen her husband since she'd been back in Britain?"

"He found her body."

"Christ." Philip's gaze fastened on Kitty's face. "Found?"

"I'm quite sure he actually did find her. I'm a bit biased because he's a friend. But it's difficult to imagine Jeremy Roth committing murder."

"Roth?"

"That was her name—Allegra Roth. She was born Allegra Wainwright. Her father was a Radical printer."

Philip shook his head. "You think you know someone, and then—"

"Sometimes I think we're so caught up in our own pasts we don't think about other people's." She took a drink of Madeira. It took her back to evenings on the patio of the Café de la Victoria in Buenos Aires. "Did Esquivel know about you and Alejandra?"

"What the devil sort of question is that?"

"I hardly think you were her only other lover. He must have suspected and perhaps known openly."

"He certainly didn't know openly from me. But Alejandra said"—Philip coughed—"she implied they both had other interests."

"Yes, she always said the same to me. Do you think Esquivel was jealous?"

Philip turned his glass in his hand. The light from the windows sparked off the facets in the crystal. "I can't say for a certainty he even knew. And Alejandra certainly implied he wouldn't mind. But there was one evening. A party at Faunch's Hotel. I was only standing with Alejandra and several other people. But I caught Esquivel looking at me. And for a moment I'd have sworn he'd have cheerfully run a sword through me."

"Did Alejandra notice?"

"Oh yes. She looked over at him for a moment and pulled a face. It occurred to me then that she liked making him jealous."

That did not entirely surprise Kitty. "Did you ask her about it?"

"It was hardly the sort of thing—no. We called things off not long after. I returned to Rio, but the affair had run its course, in any case." He shook his head. "God, I can't believe I'm saying these things to you."

"You're saying them to your ex-mistress."

His fingers tightened round the stem of his glass. "Does your husband know you're here?"

"Oh, yes." In fact, he was outside disguised as a crossing sweeper. Harry Davenport was at the other crossing pushing a barrow.

"And he wasn't concerned?"

"Well, a bit, but only about my safety."

"Your *safety?*"

"Someone attacked me last night. Not seriously. That is, they didn't do serious damage. We suspect it may be connected to Alejandra's murder. Which means we're trying to draw connections between the two of us."

"And I'm a connection." Philip stared at her, realization coming into focus in his eyes. "Good god, Kitty, do you think I was behind Alejandra's murder and the attack on you?"

"No. Julien doesn't either. But for a very rational and unconventional man, he is still capable of fussing."

"Understandably. Christ, what is going on?"

"That's precisely what we're trying to determine. You were connected to Alejandra and me. Can you think of reasons someone might have targeted both of us?"

"I told you. I can't imagine Alejandra's having an enemy. Not an enemy who would kill."

"People would say that about most people. But in this case, someone did kill her. And the fact that I was attacked as well points to the motive's having to do with her time in the Argentine."

Philip's brows drew together. His gaze was opaque but Kitty saw the reality settle in its depths. "You know how factions shifted among the Argentine revolutionaries. That hasn't ended since you left. In fact, I think it's intensified. I haven't been to Buenos Aires in a bit, but I get reports. You and Alejandra were both close to key people. I could imagine someone's thinking you had information that would be of use. But how that would lead to their trying to attack—kill—you—"

"They'd have to think we knew something dangerous."

"Alejandra admitted she worried about Esquivel. She didn't talk about him much to me—understandably—but that was one of the things she did say. She admired his commitment but was afraid he was too reckless. I can't see that leading someone to attack her though."

"What about information you shared with her?

"What would I have shared?"

"Comments about the royal family. The queen's intrigues against the king. The latest dispatches from the foreign office. You and I discussed those things. You're an intelligent man, Philip. You didn't turn all that off in the bedchamber."

Philip stared at his hands, then looked up at her. "All right. I probably said more to you than I should have done. It's a relief to talk sometimes and you have a way of getting a fellow to confide. I don't think I said as much to Alejandra, but I did say some. We all lived and breathed politics. It was difficult not to talk. And she was British, so the connection to Britain brought it up."

"Who would that information hurt now?"

Philip drew back in his chair. "It could embarrass people. But I can't see anyone's killing over it. And whatever I revealed, I knew more than I revealed. So if someone was going to try to silence Alejandra and you, why not attack me as well?"

"An excellent point. You should be careful, Philip. Until we get some sort of resolution."

His eyes widened. "You think I'm in danger? That my family are?"

"We have no reason to think so, save that you're connected to a person who was killed and a person who was attacked. And it was before you met your wife."

"But they might think I talked to her as well."

Kitty nodded. "I don't want to panic you. But have a care. Julien has engaged someone to keep an eye on the hotel. And if you give me your parents' direction we can send someone there."

"Is that necessary?"

"I think it's prudent."

Philip nodded. "Thank you. And thank your husband. I hope to meet him one day."

"I'm sure you will." Actually, they had already met, but Julien had been disguised as an Argentine lady, so it was a bit complicated to explain. Kitty picked up her gloves and got to her feet. "And let me know if you remember anything else about Alejandra. Anything at all."

Philip stood, but hesitated instead of moving to the door. "There was one thing."

"Yes? Anything."

"She said it late at night. We'd had quite a bit to drink. I was never sure if she was in earnest or being dramatic. Which Alejandra could be."

"Tell me. And let me be the judge of how important it may be."

Philip hesitated again. "She told me she thought Edward had been murdered."

CHAPTER 18

*K*itty's gloves fell from her nerveless fingertips. "Edward. My husband."

"I'd hardly just say 'Edward' if it were any other Edward."

"Alejandra didn't even know him that well."

"I think she may have known him better than you realized."

"Oh good God." Kitty dropped back into her chair. The wood felt hard beneath the satin. "I suppose that at least shouldn't surprise me. But—what on earth did she think happened to Edward?"

Philip picked up her gloves and handed them to her. "It started with her saying his death had been unexpected. And rather convenient for certain people."

"Which people did she think it was convenient for?"

Philip returned to his chair. "Kitty, as I said, we'd had a lot to drink—"

"Which people?"

Philip's hands settled on the chair arms. "You."

Kitty's fingers froze on the doeskin of her gloves. "Me."

He flushed, but his gaze stayed steady on her face. "It's no secret your marriage wasn't happy. And Alejandra knew your capabilities."

"I was an agent, not an assassin." It was her second husband who was the assassin, but there was no need to go into that just now.

"The line can be blurry. And Alejandra was convinced you were happier with him gone."

"I'd just had a baby when he died."

"Which you always said shouldn't limit what a woman could do."

"Oh, for god's sake, Philip, you can't tell me you—" Kitty stared at her former lover. She could remember his lips on her hair, his arms round her, remember running her own fingers through his hair. "*Do* you? Do you think I killed Edward?"

"Think it? Of course not."

"But you wonder?"

He shifted in his chair. "You hear a possibility raised. It stirs questions. You can't tell me it isn't the same for you."

"I don't go about wondering if people I know murdered their spouse."

"You never wondered about Edward's death?"

Kitty reached for her glass and tossed down a long swallow. "His heart gave out after a fencing match on a hot day. What was there for me to wonder about?"

"You lived a dangerous life. So did he."

"Only in the sense that he was a soldier. Edward was no agent."

Philip watched her. For a moment Kitty had the disconcerting sense that he was the one seeing through her façade. "What is an agent? Someone who undertakes missions. I saw enough of you when we were—together—to see just how skilled you were. But without possessing your level of skill, we were all involved in intrigues. You couldn't be a diplomat or a soldier or anyone involved in public life in the Argentine or Brazil without it."

Kitty's fingers tightened on the fragile stem of her glass. "Are you saying Edward was involved in intrigues I don't know about?"

"Surely you don't doubt that."

"Other than amorous intrigues."

"Intrigues of the amorous variety meld into intrigues of other sorts. Isn't that at least part of what was going on with us?"

Kitty met his gaze. He'd been a charming lover, amusing and surprisingly kind. And she'd been quite sure he didn't have the least idea she slipped out of his arms and went through his papers while he lolled on the pillows or that she scratched over his writing paper with a blank page and a pencil when she had a moment alone at his desk. "That wasn't all of it."

He smiled, a smile that appeared to hold genuine memories. "I'm relieved to hear it."

"But you're saying I didn't know what Edward was really doing?"

"Does any of us know that about another person? Even a spouse we love, much as I love Isabel. Let alone—"

"A spouse who was as much of a stranger as I could contrive to make him." Kitty set down her glass. "What do you know?"

"Very little. Save that Edward was known to boast that your adventures were nothing compared to his."

Which, given her own adventures, was chilling indeed.

It took all Kitty's concentration to keep her feet steady as she left the Pulteney. Her bonnet felt as though it was tilting on her head, though when she put a hand up, the ribbons seemed secure. Perhaps it was her brain that was askew.

Julien fell into place beside her when she was halfway to the corner. He'd returned his crossing sweeper's broom to the crossing sweeper he'd paid to lend it to him. His hair was darkened and he wore a rumpled corduroy coat, but he moved with his customary insouciant gait. "What happened?"

Kitty slid her fingers round her husband's arm despite the incongruous picture they made. "I need to talk."

Julien gave a quick nod and turned in the other direction. Harry, in the guise of a chestnut seller, met them midway down the street, having also returned his barrow to its owner. "There's a coffeehouse round the corner," Julien said. "We're headed there."

"Do you want to go alone?" Harry asked.

Kitty shook her head. "No. This will take all of us."

They moved round the corner through the late morning crowd. The coffeehouse Julien had noted earlier was a quiet one, with sober dark wood and dim lamps, but ladies in coffeehouses were a rare sight, and a lady accompanied by two gentlemen in corduroy and homespun even more so. Julien sauntered to the bar with his usual air of owning the space while Kitty and Harry found a booth at the back with high-backed benches and no one seated on either side. Julien joined them shortly, carrying three steaming mugs of coffee laced with brandy.

Kitty tugged off her gloves with jerky fingers, curled her hands round the mug, and took a fortifying sip. Then she told them what Philip had revealed about Alejandra's comments about Edward.

"Well," Julien said. "This is interesting."

"*Interesting—?*" Kitty stared at her husband.

"Among other things."

"The man I was married to might have been murdered."

"Did you ever wonder if he was?" Julien asked.

"I never questioned his death. He drank too much and he got winded easily. It made sense on the face of it. Edward wasn't an agent. That I know of."

"No, but he lived his life round agents," Harry said.

"That's what Philip said. And he implied Edward might have

been involved in more than I knew." Kitty looked at Harry. "You knew Edward in the Peninsula."

"A bit."

"Was he—"

Harry took a drink of coffee. "I confess I wrote Edward off as a dull fellow who didn't pay enough interest to his wife. I didn't waste a lot of attention on him."

"Neither did I when I could help it," Kitty said.

"He wouldn't be the first dull person to end up murdered," Julien said.

Kitty stared at her current husband, hitherto unvoiced questions clustering in her brain.

"Oh, no, " Julien said. "I was long gone from the Argentine."

"You have a knack for being places you aren't supposed to be."

"And the closest I've ever come to killing anyone who wasn't actively trying to harm me or someone else for personal reasons was when I almost killed Alistair Rannoch last October. And that was a desperate gambit to protect our son. Which I'm glad you prevented."

Kitty continued to watch him. Julien returned her gaze. "He was Leo and Timothy's father," he said. "They may be ours now, but he was their father then. He was even Genny's father officially. He may have been an imperfect father, but I wouldn't have taken him from the children."

Kitty felt as though her face had just cracked. "You're remarkable, Julien."

"I'm a bloody mess who is fortunate to have a wife who prevents me from blundering into idiocy. But I do have a rough sort of standards."

Kitty tightened her grip on her mug to keep her hands steady. "I didn't realize—"

"I always cared about your children. And the fact that I had such an appalling father makes me rather acutely aware of the importance of having better parents in one's life." He studied her in the shadows of the booth. "I never asked you—"

"You can't think I had anything to do with it. Among other things, I was also aware Edward was my children's father. Aside from the fact that I don't believe in murder." She clanked her mug down. "Damn it. When I thought he'd died of natural causes, I could leave him comfortably in the past. But if he was murdered, I have the most aggravating sense that it's my responsibility to figure out by whom and why."

"Among other things, it's a possible motive for why someone would have attacked Allegra Roth and you," Harry said.

"Save that I didn't have the least notion Edward had been murdered, if he was, and Alejandra apparently thought I was behind his death," Kitty said. "So if you're suggesting his killer was trying to tidy up loose ends, they would have been rather wasting their time."

"They might not have realized what either of you knew," Julien said. "Did you know about Edward and Alejandra?"

"No, assuming that it's even true." Kitty pulled her mug closer and took a sip. "Though I certainly didn't track every one of his liaisons."

Julien's gaze shifted over her face. "I also never really asked how you felt—"

Kitty squeezed her eyes shut for a moment. "We were leading such separate lives by the time he died. It mattered to the boys— not as much as one would hope losing a parent would, but it meant something. But for me in some ways it scarcely made a difference that he was gone. While in others, it was a relief. I never put that much energy into being a wife, but even the rudi- mentary pretense I had to keep up was challenging." She stared down into her mug. How had she managed to drink so much of it so quickly? "And yes, I did feel a few qualms of guilt at times for not mourning my children's father. But not many. There was a great freedom in being able to go where I chose and order my life as I chose. I couldn't imagine ever marrying again."

"Yes, so you told me," Julien said. "I'm very fortunate you took the risk." He considered a moment, gaze fixed on a faded, water-stained hunting print on the wall across the room. "If Edward hadn't died, we'd have had to run off. Or have a very uncomfortable affair."

Kitty cast her mind back to several interludes in Buenos Aires. "The affair we had wasn't that uncomfortable."

"We scarcely even got to spend the night together."

"True. That was a pity." She looked at Harry. "Sorry."

"Don't mind me." Harry took a drink of brandy-laced coffee. "I'm used to fading into the woodwork. And Cordy and I've put the rest of you through any number of personal scenes."

Kitty grinned. "You're a good fellow, Harry."

"That sounds like the sort of undergraduate talk I never engaged in. But thank you."

"I don't know that I've ever called anyone a good fellow, Davenport, but it certainly applies to you. And to your wife, if it comes to that." Julien grinned at Harry, then touched Kitty's hand on the table top. "I'm sorry. That you're being pulled into the past."

"It may not be pleasant but it needs to be faced. And there are memories from the Argentine I wouldn't give up for the world."

His gaze darkened in that way that still turned her insides upside down in a manner that wasn't supposed to happen to a sensible woman of thirty-five who was beyond romance. Or theoretically had been beyond it. Theoretically she'd been beyond it at fifteen. "Nor would I," he said. He lifted her hand and kissed her knuckles, but when he drew back his gaze had gone serious. "It sounds as though you believe Alejandra's claims about Edward."

"I think we have to at least consider it. Don't you?"

"He wasn't my husband, but—yes."

Kitty looked at Harry. "You're the outside observer. Do you agree?"

"It certainly needs to be considered. Do you have any theories about why he might have been killed?"

"A jealous husband seems likeliest, given Edward's proclivities. Though it's a bit hard then to tie it to the attacks on Alejandra and me."

"Unless the husband is now in England," Harry suggested.

"And Alejandra worked it out?"

"It's possible," Julien said. "She appears to have been very willing to use what leverage she had on people."

"I suppose it could also have been a cast-off mistress. Who could also now be in Britain. It's hard to think what else Edward would have been involved in. He did seem absorbed in those last weeks and he was out a good deal, but though he was on the edge of a lot, he wasn't caught up in intrigues himself. At least not that I knew of, despite what Philip implied." Kitty saw something flicker across her husband's face. The merest shadow of a response, but still—"Darling? Do you have an idea?"

A simple question to ask her husband. And yet she had the sudden sense she was about to step into a mire. Or a battlefield.

CHAPTER 19

*K*itty heard the quick, almost inaudible stir of his indrawn breath. So rare for Julien to hesitate over anything. Julien had scarcely known Edward. Oh, they'd met a few times. Mostly with Julien in disguise. She'd even seen him dancing with Edward at a ball once, in the guise of an Argentine lady. Which had been amusing. But they'd hardly had an ongoing relationship of any sort.

At least, not that she'd known. Julien had had enough reticence not to frequently refer to the man to whom she'd been married, except for practical questions that involved avoiding his attention.

Harry started to slide out of the bench.

"No," Kitty said. "We need an outside observer more than ever. And you know whatever the truth is, we're all going to have to hear about it." She looked back at her husband. "Julien? Is there more about you and Edward I didn't realize? Oh god." A hitherto unforeseen possibility shot into her mind. "You didn't—"

"Good god, no." Julien's laugh rang reassuringly true. "He wasn't at all my type."

"That wouldn't have stopped you if it was a mission."

"No mission took me near your husband. Not in that way. You were the agent in the family."

"Which is why you seduced me?"

"That came out wrong. And as I recall, you seduced me."

"It was mutual." And had involved a lot of hurried kisses and tugging off clothes. "Tell me about Edward."

Julien folded his arms across his chest. "Your friend Philip Ledgwood seems acute. Edward was perhaps involved in more than you realized."

"What?"

"He made a number of trips to Upper Peru."

That was hardly news. Upper Peru had been the scene of endless fighting between the revolutionaries and Spanish royalists. Edward had gone to gather information on the situation to send on to Whitehall, though from what Kitty had heard he had spent most of his time in taverns and at regimental dinners far from the fighting. "Are you saying those trips were more than they seemed?" she asked.

"On one of them he met a Don Iago Valencia who had found silver on his land but needed more capital to develop a mine. Which was difficult to secure in the midst of the war. Edward invested."

Kitty frowned. "He didn't tell me. But that's hardly surprising. Edward was always interested in a quick way to a fortune. Mostly at the gaming table, but I can imagine his seeing an advantage in silver. As long as he didn't have to do too much work. God, I wasn't a good wife, was I? I always knew that. But the fact that he's dead and he may have been murdered doesn't change who he was."

"No," Julien said. "And the silver mine investments weren't surprising. But he was writing to his family and friends back in England to secure investments. And falsifying information about the mine's production."

Kitty's mind sifted through memories. Edward scrawling

letters. Edward tucking away a ledger she'd assumed recorded gambling debts. "How did you know?"

Julien's gaze settled on her own, steady and a bit removed, as though he'd moved back further than the physical distance on the bench would allow. "This was apparently only one of several silver mines with British investors and dubious production of actual silver. The constant fighting gave an excuse for delays in mine production. It was supposedly a cheap investment now that would be worth a fortune when the wars ended. But eventually there would be questions. It had the potential to be a bubble. Silver mines instead of tulips. That sort of thing can crash and ripple across continents. Uncle Hubert was concerned. He wanted me to look into it."

Simple words that told a story that was anything but. "Hubert had you spying on my husband."

Julien kept his gaze steady on her own. "Yes."

"And it didn't occur to you to tell the woman you were sleeping with? Who happened to be married to the man you were spying on?"

"The key word being married. You'd have had to lie to Edward if you'd known."

"Julien. My love. I lied to Edward every time I left the house to see you. Every time I left your arms and went back to Edward. And that's just about our affair. I lied to Edward every time I didn't tell him about any of the intrigues I was involved in. Using the word intrigue loosely."

"You didn't need one more thing to lie about."

"That's the most ridiculous lot of rubbish." She turned to Harry. "I'd ask you to back me up, but I don't want to drag you into the middle of this."

"You have a point," Harry said. "Though I think we'd all admit to keeping things from our spouses."

"Would you have kept it from Cordy?"

"If I'd been spying on George, say?" Harry didn't shy away from saying the name of his wife's former lover. "That's a bit different. I might have been afraid she'd tell George."

"And you might have been at risk if you'd known about Edward," Julien said quietly.

"Julien." Kitty swung back to her husband. "Are you daring—actually daring—to say you didn't tell me you were spying on Edward because you were protecting me?"

"Possibly."

"My god. And I don't believe it."

"Kitkat." Julien chose his words carefully, an investigator, not a husband. "I wasn't the man I am now. If you'll recall, little more than a year ago I was still feeling my way through how to be a proper partner. And you were lying to me."

"That was different. I was trying to keep my colleagues from being hurt."

"Well, for that matter, this was my mission. Not yours. It's not a good practice to share information about a mission just because one happens to be sleeping with someone. In fact, it's distinctly shoddy spycraft. Davenport can back me up on that."

"As far as it goes," Harry said.

"Is that what we were doing?" Kitty said.

"What?" Julien asked.

"Sleeping together."

"Among other things. Though we got to actually sleep together distressingly infrequently. That's one of the advantages of marriage." He studied her face for a moment, his gaze precise and unyielding. "I wouldn't have used the word love then, though I freely admit now that I was starting to feel it. But we'd made no promises to each other. We trusted each other in a fight. I don't think either of us trusted the other beyond it. Including in the bedchamber."

"I hate it when you're right." She folded her arms. "All right, that was then. What about later? When you admitted you loved me and I was your wife?"

"What was I supposed to say? Your late husband, who is still the legal father of the three children we're raising together, may have been involved in a scheme to commit fraud, though I have no definite proof?"

"At least I'd have had the same information you did."

"To what purpose?"

"I'd have understood Edward better."

"You already had few illusions about him. Would it really have helped to add another negative?"

"Would it have hurt? It's not as though I had an image of Edward to be tarnished."

"Kitty—" Julien paused as though searching through a scattering of possible answers, all breakable as glass. "You were dealing with a lot from the past then."

"You didn't want to tell me about Edward because I was confronting the fact that Edgar Rannoch had raped me and you'd killed him? Julien, I've lived with what Edgar did to me for almost a decade. And in the circumstances, I'm very grateful you killed him."

"You were—"

"Raw. Yes, all right." In fact, she'd collapsed in his arms and he'd held her through the night and he'd been just as raw himself, and if it hadn't happened they might not be where they were now. "But Edward hardly had the power to deal the sort of emotional hurt my past with Edgar could. I could have handled revelations about him."

"I have no doubt you could handle anything you put your mind to, my darling." Julien's gaze moved over her face in the shadows. "I confess part of it may have been that I was afraid you'd react just as you are now. That you wouldn't be happy I'd kept it from you. You were keeping a lot from me at the time. And it seemed a distant hope that I could convince you to marry me."

"Are you saying you were—"

"Oh, I was terrified. Surely you realize that. Terrified you'd never let me in. Terrified even if you did, you'd balk at anything as official—and permanent—as marriage."

"You weren't even sure you wanted to marry me until just before you proposed."

"I wasn't sure what I wanted to do with my life. I knew I wanted you in it. If we hadn't stayed in England, marriage might have been less important. But I think I'd have still wanted it."

"Wanted me officially committed to you?"

"Wanted me officially committed to you."

"Oh." Kitty leaned in and put her hands on his chest. "That's the provoking thing about you, Julien. Just when we're having a proper quarrel you say something completely disarming." She leaned back. "I still think you should have told me."

"I'll admit I should have done."

"I forget."

"What?"

"Now that we're married, and tell each other most things, and live a ridiculously domestic life most of the time, that we're still going to lie to each other."

"I wouldn't say it's inevitable."

"No? Then you're far more naive than Malcolm. I'm quite sure he'd say it's inevitable for him and Mélanie. On both sides. What about you, Harry?"

"If not inevitable, then likely."

"It keeps life interesting," Julien admitted.

"What else are you hiding about my first husband?"

"About Edward? Nothing that I can think of at the moment."

"What about Hubert? You said he was worried about the silver mine scheme. Could he—"

"Could my uncle have been behind your husband's murder?"

"Yes."

Julien considered. "We both know ethics wouldn't have stopped Uncle Hubert if he saw Edward as enough of a threat. I was able to connect Edward to Iago Valencia's mine. I couldn't definitively connect him to any others with British investors. The investments seemed to happen on rumors—someone got a tip from a friend who had it from another friend. We couldn't prove they were all connected, but the similarities were striking. A mine that would yield a fortune when the fighting died down enough to properly put it into production. And given the situation in South America the fighting never did seem to die down enough. I suspected someone was pulling the strings on all of them back in England, but I couldn't discover who. If Uncle Hubert thought getting rid of Edward would stop the silver mine scheme, he might have tried. He didn't ask me to do it, even though I was in place."

"He might not have asked you if he knew about us."

"Possibly. I didn't think Uncle Hubert thought I had morals to that degree, but perhaps I was wrong. If Uncle Hubert had Edward killed, it's difficult to draw a line to Alejandra's murder. Even if she suspected him, I can't see Uncle Hubert's killing her to cover it up. She wouldn't have been able to touch him. Still—I need to talk to our former spymaster. Do you trust me to do it alone?"

Kitty considered her husband. "I think so," she said.

"You didn't know, did you?" Kitty asked Malcolm.

"That Edward might have been murdered? I was in Spain."

Mélanie took a sip of tea. She was long past jealousy of Kitty, but she did recognize there were moments in the past that belonged to Kitty and Malcolm. They were in the Berkeley Square library. She, Malcolm, Kitty, Julien, Harry, and Cordy. Laura and Raoul hadn't returned from Mivart's yet.

"But you were working for Hubert," Kitty said. "Who may have known."

Malcolm leaned forwards on the sofa, gaze intent. "I didn't know, Kit. My word on it."

Kitty gave a quick smile. "That assumes it even is true. But it suggests all sorts of things. And I'm not going to be able to leave it alone."

In the silence that followed, Laura and Raoul came into the library.

"What's happened?" Laura asked, pulling off her gloves. She was still wearing the dark maid's dress she'd worn to Mivart's, though without the apron, cap, and wig.

"It seems my first husband may have been murdered." Kitty looked at Raoul. "Did you know?"

"No." Raoul stopped by the library table, brows raised in genuine shock. "I confess I never thought Ashford was involved in anything of particular consequence."

"Neither did I," Kitty said. "But apparently Julien was spying on him."

"Keeping an eye on him," Julien said. He outlined, quickly and without emotion, what he knew about Edward Ashford and the silver mine scheme.

"Interesting." Raoul took a sip of tea. He was now sitting in one of the Queen Anne chairs with Laura. "Do you think Ashford concocted the scheme on his own?"

"I've been wondering about that," Kitty said. "Edward was more a follower than a leader."

"I don't know the names of anyone else involved," Julien said. "It was difficult to uncover that working from South America. But it seemed clear Ashford wasn't running it on his own. He had support and funding from London. He covered his tracks well enough I couldn't learn more before I left the Argentine."

"Were you able to look at Allegra Roth's things?" Mélanie asked Laura.

"Yes. And while it may not rival this revelation, we found something interesting." Laura drew folded papers from her reticule and held them out. "Apparently Allegra Roth was communicating with at least one person in code."

Malcolm pushed himself to his feet and crossed to look at the papers. He went still as he scanned them. "Much as I don't want to minimize the possibility that Edward Ashford was murdered, this may rival that revelation when it comes to the investigation."

"I know you're good, but don't tell me you can break the code just by looking at it," Laura said.

"No. But I don't need to break it to know how significant it is. I know that code. I invented it. And Hubert Mallinson still uses it to communicate with his agents."

CHAPTER 20

Malcolm and Julien found Hubert Mallinson in Whitehall, leaving the home office.

"I thought you were in the midst of an investigation." Hubert paused, drawing on his gloves. "Don't pretend you aren't looking into the murder of Jeremy Roth's errant wife."

"There'd be no point in doing so, would there?" Malcolm said. "Hardly seems worth the bother. Is that what you were here to meet with Sidmouth about?"

"Why would I be meeting with the home secretary about the murder of the estranged wife of a Bow Street runner?"

Malcolm put a hand on the passage wall, effectively blocking Hubert. "Because she was your agent."

Hubert's gaze narrowed ever so slightly. "Checkmate. Very well done, both of you. Though I wouldn't be surprised if it's your wives who arrived at the truth." He jerked his head towards a door across the passage. "We'd better go in there."

Malcolm followed his former spymaster into the small room. It was crowded with files and ledgers, but there were three chairs. Malcolm tugged one forwards and sat, facing Hubert. Julien leaned against another.

"I might have known you'd be in the midst of this," Malcolm said.

Hubert settled in the third ladder-back chair across from Malcolm and crossed his legs. "You make it sound as though I orchestrated it."

"Did you?"

"Don't be absurd. To what end?"

"Just because I can't think of one doesn't mean one doesn't exist." Malcolm stared at the man who had manipulated his life to a degree he probably did not yet properly fathom. "Did you know your agent was Roth's wife?"

Hubert sat back in his chair and crossed his ankles. "Oh yes. It was interesting when Roth came to my notice in his investigations with you."

"*Interesting?*"

"Don't you find it so?"

"I find the way you play with all of us a number of things."

Hubert pushed up his spectacles. "She was a good agent. I'm sorry she's gone. She could have been of help with what you lot are up to."

Malcolm folded his arms. "Did you have her spying on us?"

"No. She was in the Argentine. But thanks to Roth, she'd have been bound to become involved with all of you. That would have been useful."

"Is that why you brought her back?" Julien asked.

"I didn't bring her back. Esquivel decided to come back."

"Did you convince her to leave Britain with Esquivel?"

"Allegra didn't need convincing. I don't pry into the details of agents' lives—"

"Unless you find them useful," Julien said.

"—but Allegra was eager for escape. That she could wrap it up as working for her country helped her make the break. But didn't cause it."

"In your opinion."

"Well, yes, I don't generally concern myself with the inner workings of my agents' minds." Hubert leaned forwards. "Do you know what the Argentine represents? A market for goods, and as they develop trade of their own—."

"You want to make it a colony," Julien said.

"We don't need to make it a colony. The attempts to move in on them in '06 and '07 were crude mistakes. We had a chance of a British protectorate, but we lost it when Alvear fell from power. What we need are allies. Trading partners. Especially since we've lost our North American colonies."

"So you can control the economy," Malcolm said.

"So we can prosper. And so they can."

"So we have a market for British goods and their goods can fund British production," Julien said.

"It's a wise move." Hubert might say the same, in the same tone, about a peace treaty. Or an assassination.

"And for once it puts you on the side of a revolution," Malcolm said.

"I'm a pragmatist. And this revolution isn't likely to spill over to our shores. Even if people have a distressing habit of going back and forth."

"Napoleon Bonaparte wasn't the only one to dream of empire."

"I have nothing against empires."

"Quite the contrary," Julien said.

"But I should think in this case we find ourselves on the same side."

"There are never only two sides." Malcolm sat back in his chair. "How did you recruit Allegra Roth? Were you suspicious of Roth?"

"Oh no. It was long before she was married." Hubert reached for his coffee cup. "I had Chiltern reach out to her and see if we could turn her."

"Why?" Malcolm had worked with Warren Chiltern. A decent agent, if a bit too dogmatic about following orders. Recruiting likely civilians to spy was a common tactic of Hubert's. But there would need to be a reason he saw the person in question as a prospect.

"She was involved with that fellow Gresham. He was slipping over secretly to France. Even once or twice to Italy."

"He's a composer," Malcolm said. "He wanted to talk to colleagues."

"He also has links to the Carbonari."

"Really? I never heard that. Not that I necessarily would." Malcolm looked at Julien. Julien shook his head.

"You're both better connected to the Italian Radicals than you admit," Hubert said. "Not that you'd tell me if you did know anything about Gresham."

If Gresham had connections to Carbonari, it cast a different light on Allegra's asking Gresham to put her in touch with friends in Italy, as Mélanie had reported. Perhaps she'd wanted to make contact with fellow revolutionaries on Esquivel's behalf. So she could spy on them for Hubert. Malcolm tilted his head back to look at Hubert in dusty light. "Odd. You support the revolutionaries in the Argentine, but oppose them in Italy."

"Not odd at all. The Argentine rebels could help favor British interests. The Carbonari would do the opposite. And the Carbonari are in Italy, which is closer to Britain, so they can spread their ideas more easily to our shores. Just look at your friend Kit Montagu."

"I think Kit spread ideas to the Carbonari as much as the other way round."

"Yes, considering whom he married. Don't look at me like that, Malcolm. I'm aware of Sofia Vincenzo's worth. Brilliant young woman. I can admire her worth while still deploring her ideas."

Malcolm crossed his legs at the ankle. "Your broadmindedness never fails to amaze me, sir. Go on. So Allegra was willing to spy on Gresham?"

"Chiltern thought she was a good prospect, and he was right.

He has good instincts even if he lacks your imagination. Which is a blessing at times. I never need to worry about what he'll do behind my back. The relationship was beginning to cool and Allegra was restless. Or so Chiltern said. And when he approached her, she agreed. She said she wanted to serve her country, but I think she was drawn by the challenge. Which brings a lot of capable women to espionage, now I think of it. Kitty and Mélanie both come to mind. Not to mention Laura O'Roarke."

"Allegra Roth told you she was drawn by the challenge?" Malcolm asked.

"She told Chiltern. Along with some interesting tidbits about Gresham. I won't go into details because they aren't relevant, and there's no sense in sharing things with you that might get back to your Italian Radical friends. She put things capably, according to Chiltern. Then the relationship ended."

"Did you offer her another assignment?"

"What assignment? She was an agent out of convenience, not training. In any case, I scarcely knew her at that point. We gave her something, with our thanks. The next I heard she was married."

"She got married because she was pregnant."

"That was hardly my concern."

"Would you feel the same way if it were Lucinda?" Julien asked.

Hubert's gaze shot to Julien's face at the mention of his youngest child. "Lucinda wouldn't—"

"I wouldn't be so sure of that," Malcolm said. "Lucy is exceptionally capable—it runs in the family—and looking for a scope for her talents."

Hubert's brows drew together. He'd always, in Malcolm's memory, been quick to see his agents as "collateral damage" when anything went wrong. But the loss of his daughter Louisa and the issues his eldest daughter Mary had gone through, as well as the realization that he had another daughter who happened to be Malcolm's sister, had perhaps made him more sensitive to the challenges faced by women. "Allegra seems to have landed well enough."

"Allegra found Jeremy Roth," Malcolm said. "An extraordinarily sensitive and generous man. Who loved her. It may have provided a temporary haven. That doesn't mean the marriage was a success."

"I imagine Roth is happy to have his children."

"That doesn't mean he—and Allegra—might not have been happier in other circumstances."

"It isn't a spymaster's job to see to the happiness of his agents. Even your father, who is far more inclined to dwell on personal matters than he would admit to anyone, would agree with that, I imagine."

This time Malcolm shifted in his chair. "You'll have to ask him sometime. Did you follow up on Allegra's marriage?"

"It scarcely seemed relevant at the time. Roth was a soldier in the Peninsula. He had a bit of an association with Radical causes, and his parents were known for their Radical activities, but not enough for me to ask Allegra to report on them. It was several years before I heard from her again."

"You sought her out?" Julien asked.

"No, she sought me out. Chiltern was in the country, and she said she preferred to deal directly with me. Self-possessed. I admired that. I took her more seriously than I had in the past. Still, I didn't see any particular need for her services. Until she told me a gentleman had been paying court to her."

"Marco Esquivel," Malcolm said.

"Mmm. He'd come to my notice years before. He fought capably for us in the Peninsula. And it was clear he was going to be a force in the Argentine."

"Where he was fighting for your side."

"That doesn't mean I didn't want information on him. You're the one who just said there are more than two sides in everything."

"So you wanted someone to report on what Esquivel was doing? You didn't think of trying to make him your agent himself?" Malcolm asked.

"That would be a bit extreme, wouldn't it?"

"Not necessarily. Is San Martín your agent?"

"No comment. Except that San Martín is brilliant, a credit to his country, and his own man."

"Oh, Uncle Hubert," Julien said. "You needn't speak so like a politician. It's beneath you."

"Esquivel was able at working for his country's independence, but his ideas had a somewhat concerning tendency towards Radicalism. He'd met O'Roarke before he went to the Argentine."

"Yes, Raoul told us," Malcolm said. "Raoul is a force to be reckoned with, but you can't be spying on everyone he ever met with."

"O'Roarke's ability to inspire revolutionaries is nothing short of astounding. But it was more than that. Esquivel ran with a group of young Radicals at Cambridge. Much like you at Oxford. I wanted to keep an eye on him. I wanted a source on the revolution in the Argentine. Allegra Roth was ideally situated to be that source."

"So you asked her to go the Argentine with Esquivel?" Malcolm said.

"Not at first. I suggested it would be helpful if she got close to Esquivel. Eventually she told me Esquivel wanted her to go to the Argentine with him."

As Mélanie must once have told Raoul that Malcolm wanted her to marry him. Though that had been complicated by other things, like her being pregnant. "What did you say?" Malcolm asked.

"That it was her choice. But that information she might gather would be invaluable."

"Did you know she had two children?"

"I knew she had children." Hubert's brows drew together above his spectacles. "I think, though she didn't talk about them a great deal. It was her choice."

"To have children, or to talk about them, or to go to the Argentine?" Julien asked.

"All three, if it comes to that. But she certainly chose to go to the Argentine. A woman—or a man, for that matter—willing to make such a choice was probably not focusing a great deal of attention on their children, in any case."

Malcolm shifted in his chair again. Hubert might have a point. "I know you, Hubert. If you want to pressure an agent you can."

Hubert looked between Malcolm and Julien. "I don't recall any sort of pressure ever working particularly well with either of you. Or with Kitty, for that matter." He adjusted his spectacles. It might have been a trick of the light bouncing off them that made his gaze appear more open than usual. "I'm not unaware of the importance of parental bonds. Despite my past actions. Or perhaps because of them. But Allegra was determined to go to the Argentine. I've rarely seen her so animated as she was when she came to tell me Esquivel had asked her to go with him. She said this was the mission she'd been waiting for her whole life."

"And when she got to the Argentine?" Malcolm asked.

"She sent me reports."

"On Esquivel?"

"Among other things. On the general situation. She and Esquivel were close to the heart of the revolution. She knew all the major players."

"You had Kitty and me in the Argentine as well," Julien pointed out.

"You and Kitty were already slipping beyond my control. Assuming I ever had any sort of control over either of you. And neither of you was sharing the bed of a leader of the revolution. At least, not that I knew."

"No comment," Julien said.

"And Esquivel?" Malcolm said.

"What about him?"

"How did Allegra feel about him?"

Hubert adjusted his other spectacle earpiece. "My dear Malcolm. There may be some spymasters to whom agents confide their personal feelings. I think I need hardly tell you I am not one of them. How Allegra felt about Esquivel was her own business."

"She lived with him and reported to you on him for five years."

"So she did." Hubert's gaze held steady behind the lenses. "Even with my limited sensitivities, I understand this must be an uncomfortable parallel for you."

"I don't know about that. You could say I'm uniquely positioned to understand that she may have been spying on Esquivel and still genuinely cared about him." Malcolm regarded the man who had been his spymaster and Allegra's. "You met with Allegra yesterday."

"Who says so?"

"You were seen with her in a coffeehouse," Malcolm said. Once he'd recognized Allegra's coded papers as Hubert's, it hadn't been hard to guess the identity of the spectacled man Felicia Esquivel had told Cordelia she'd seen with Allegra.

"Sometimes meetings in the open are safer. Sometimes they're a mistake. Yes, she was updating me."

"About Esquivel?"

"He came to Britain to talk to Staples about negotiating a loan for the Argentine government." Robert Staples had been the unofficial British consul in the Argentine, never officially recognized by the government in Buenos Aires but very connected to the British merchant community in the Argentine. "He's apparently also looking for funding to set up his own shipping venture. He's talking to his Cambridge friends Beardsley and Rowley."

"A good commercial venture," Julien said. "You should approve of that."

"It was certainly less alarming than the things they got up to at Cambridge."

"Did Allegra Roth say where she was going when she left the coffeehouse?" Malcolm asked.

"No. And I didn't ask her. But given what we now know, I assume it was to the Three Queens in Seven Dials, to see her husband." Hubert uncrossed and recrossed his legs. "Given that she told me she wished to avoid her husband, I find that interesting. Presumably it was to do with their children. Jeremy Roth's equilibrium impresses me, but he was certainly a much-tried husband."

"I don't think he killed her," Malcolm said.

"You wouldn't."

"I don't either," Julien said.

"I wouldn't expect you to, either," Hubert said.

"We're both endeavoring to keep an open mind," Malcolm said.

Julien kicked his boot toe against the leg of his chair. "I begin to see why the home office take such an interest in this."

"They'd certainly prefer it to be a domestic drama, but we can't be sure it is," Hubert said.

"So they want to blame Roth," Malcolm said.

"Not much help in doing that if we actually have an unravelling international plot on our hands. No matter what Sidmouth might wish, I won't waste my energies trying to convince you not to investigate. And I don't really want to. We need the truth and you're more likely to arrive at it than Bow Street. Especially without Roth, who is possibly their best runner. For all his tendency to strike out on his own. Or perhaps because of it."

"Hubert." Malcolm sat back in his chair. "Did you just ask us to investigate for you?"

"My dear Malcolm. I've long since ceased being under the illusion I could ask either of you to do anything."

"Did Allegra ever indicate she thought Esquivel might be on to her?" Julien said.

"No." Hubert's gaze hardened behind his spectacles. "But if he had done, I'm not sure he'd have been as flexible and broadminded in his thinking as Malcolm was about Mélanie. In fact, one could say he'd have a far stronger motive to have killed her than Roth."

"So one could. Which brings us to another question," Julien said. "Did you have my wife's late husband killed?"

CHAPTER 21

*H*ubert's gaze shot to Julien. "Edward died of heart failure."

"There are theories that it was murder."

"Whose theories?"

"Allegra Roth's, apparently. Or perhaps I should say Alejandra Vargas's. Which makes it particularly interesting."

"Edward Ashford was never of very great interest."

"Ashford was getting investors to sink money into a fraudulent scheme that could have sent ripples from Buenos Aires to London. You told me so yourself when you had me looking into him."

"I didn't tell you to kill him, did I?"

"You didn't tell *me* to kill him. That doesn't mean you didn't hire someone else."

"Why would I hire someone else when I had you in place?"

"Possibly because you thought I wouldn't have followed orders, given my relationship with his wife."

"Malcolm's the one with tiresome scruples, Julien. Not you. At least, not then. I'll own you show them distressingly often, of late."

Julien folded his arms across his chest. "And perhaps also

because if you'd directly ordered me to kill a British officer, you might have been giving me ammunition to use against you. Assuming I tried to come back and reclaim what is laughingly called my heritage."

"Which you did. And as I recall, I stepped aside with remarkably little fuss."

"By then it was the best move to check the Elsinore League. I'm not at all sure you were thinking that way when I was in the Argentine."

Hubert leaned forwards. "If I'd felt we had no choice but to get rid of Edward Ashford, I'd probably have involved you. I didn't think it had gone that far. When Ashford died, the silver mine scheme was beginning to unravel. I think Ashford was being set up to take the blame for it. Once he was dead, whoever else was involved managed to sweep the whole thing under the rug. I'd have stood a better chance of learning the truth with Ashford alive." Hubert frowned. "If Ashford was murdered, it could have all sorts of implications. Do you have any idea who might be behind it?"

"One of our first thoughts was you," Julien said.

"Surely you didn't simply stop there."

"A jealous husband. A spurned mistress. Or someone he'd swindled in the silver mine scheme."

"When you heard Allegra suspected Ashford was murdered, did you hear who she suspected was behind it?"

"Oh yes," Julien said. "She suspected Kitty."

Hubert raised a brow. "Interesting."

"Kitty didn't kill him. Her morals are considerably better than mine. And far better than yours."

"Yes, I wouldn't have thought it of her."

"Did Allegra ever tell you she thought Ashford might have been murdered?"

"No."

"But you had her investigating him," Julien said.

"What makes you think that?"

"You were interested in Ashford. And we heard a rumor he and Allegra were lovers."

"I asked for information on him. How Allegra chose to get it was her own business." Hubert pushed his spectacles up. "Does Kitty know you were spying on Ashford for me?"

"When all this came out, I had to tell her. I probably should have done a long time since. I found reasons not to."

Hubert nodded. "Give it time. With what you have between you, you and Kitty should be fine. I've learnt one can muddle through with far worse."

"Uncle Hubert," Julien said. "Is that the voice of concern?"

"Is that so surprising?"

"Not as much so as it once would have been. Which perhaps is the most astonishing thing of all."

MALCOLM AND JULIEN left the home office in silence, and of one accord turned in to a coffeehouse filled with glossy dark wood and hushed voices. The sort of place where undersecretaries, MPs, and journalists scribbled in notebooks, and deals were made about upcoming votes. They nodded to a few acquaintances, ordered coffees, and folded themselves onto chairs at a table at the back.

"Do you believe him?" Malcolm asked.

"About which part of it?"

"All of it. But mostly that he doesn't know more about Allegra and he wasn't behind Ashford's death."

Julien took a drink of coffee and grimaced as though it was bitter. "I'm not sure he doesn't know more about Allegra, though I tend to think the basic outlines he told us are the truth. My instinct is he wasn't behind Ashford's death, but god knows I could be wrong. I could even be going soft when it comes to my uncle. What a ridiculous thought."

"For someone who prides himself on being without emotion, Hubert has a way of playing on emotions." Malcolm took a drink of coffee. It was strong but not burnt. It should have gone down more easily. "I think Ashford would have had to pose a greater threat than anything we've uncovered so far for Hubert to have killed him. Which isn't to say there couldn't be more to uncover. And if Hubert was behind Ashford's death and Allegra worked it out—"

"It gives Uncle Hubert a motive to be behind Allegra's death." Julien turned his coffee cup in his hand. "Before we knew she was his agent, I didn't think she was much of a threat to him. As an agent, given what she could have known—she might have been." He took another drink of coffee. "I should have added brandy to this." He clunked the cup down. "Kitty isn't going to let this go. She claims Ashford meant nothing to her, and I think it's true, in a way. But he was her children's father and she's too responsible not to pursue it."

"He was a bastard," Malcolm said. The words came out with unusual force. He was also the man Malcolm had betrayed with his wife. "Kitty owed him nothing." He looked down into his coffee. "Though I do confess to a certain amount of guilt where he was concerned."

"More fool you then." Julien met Malcolm's gaze, at once acknowledging their mutual tie to his wife and defusing it of tension. A unique talent Julien had. "Ashford wasn't worthy of it. I wasted no guilt on him. And I don't think Kitty did when we were together. I don't think much of him as a father. In fact, I think distinctly ill of him. But I can now say he meant something to the boys. They may have questions as they grow up. I couldn't look them in the eye knowing we hadn't done everything we could to arrive at the truth. And Kitty takes her responsibilities seriously. Ashford was one of her responsibilities. Whatever she thought of him." He tossed down another draught of coffee. "This is going to rip open old wounds."

"She'll understand your keeping quiet about spying on Ashford," Malcolm said.

"Maybe. Not everyone is quite as understanding in these matters are you are, Rannoch."

"It's practicality. One knows what one values and doesn't want to lose it."

"Oh, if it comes to value I'm lost."

"Don't talk rot, Julien. You know what Kitty thinks of you."

"Mmm. If she thinks too much, I'm rather afraid of where her thoughts will take her. She managed to trust me enough to marry me. I'm worried about what I've done with that trust."

"We all know we have other loyalties in our work. I was a bit slow to get the point. But I finally did."

"You're a bloody saint, Rannoch. Not that I believe in saints."

"I'm a pragmatist who recognizes what's important. Kitty will too."

"Kitty doesn't like to lose."

The memory of his last, horrible quarrel with Kitty echoed in Malcolm's head. She had indeed not liked losing. And it had destroyed what was between them. Which, given who they both were, would probably not have survived in any case. He had no doubt that they were both happier where they were now, and what regrets he'd had had been erased by their current friendship.

Still. It was not a pleasant memory.

Julien turned his cup in his hand, watching Malcolm. Seeing more than was intended, as he had a way of doing. "Quite. I adore my wife. I believe in what is between us. In a way I never thought I'd be able to do. But though I may be late to even believing in relationships, I recognize that any relationship is a precarious balancing act. And ours is perhaps more finely balanced than most."

Malcolm reached for his own cup and stared into it. "Perhaps the trick is recognizing the balance is fragile and not panicking when it's overset."

"So you don't worry yourself?"

"My dear fellow. I worry every day. Every day is a balancing act, as you said. I don't doubt my feelings for my wife. I don't doubt hers for me. I do doubt where the future could land us. Though perhaps less than I used to."

Julien frowned into the depths of his coffee. "I was stupid. Uncle Hubert couldn't threaten me with much at that point. I didn't need to take his orders. I resisted the assassination he wanted me to carry out when I got to Buenos Aires. I should have resisted spying on Ashford. Especially because he was Kitty's husband."

"Perhaps that was why," Malcolm said.

"You mean I had a grudge against Ashford because he was Kitty's husband?"

"No, I don't think you're so petty. But knowing you, I do think perhaps you may have been alarmed by your developing feelings for her. And I can see your responding by not letting personal feelings interfere with spycraft."

"Damn it, Rannoch, I hate it when you're right. That's possible." Julien took a drink of coffee.

"And Hubert still had a hold on you. You went to great lengths after you came back from the Argentine to get the papers Hubert had." Now that Malcolm knew who Julien really was, he could begin to piece the timeline together. "You never let yourself appear rattled, but knowing what I know now, I think that effort was singularly important."

"As I recall, I've appeared more than a bit rattled several times where Kitty was concerned, and more than once in front of you." Julien slumped back in his chair, nursing the coffee. "Getting those papers back did give me freedom. A freedom I needed to have a life with Kitty, now I think about it, though I wouldn't have put it that way then. And it helped others escape Uncle Hubert. If

I'd known he had that evidence to use against me, it would have been dangerous to get too close to Kitty and the children. But I still shouldn't have followed his orders about spying on Ashford. Kitty has a right to be angry."

"Kitty understands compromise."

Julien met Malcolm's gaze, blue eyes agate hard. "Spycraft broke the two of you."

"But we didn't have what you have."

"You're putting a lot of faith in what we have."

"That's because I've seen it."

For a moment, Julien's eyes were raw and roiling as water when a sheet of ice has cracked. Then he gave a crooked smile. "You're a hopeless romantic, Rannoch."

"Mel's the romantic in the family. I'm much more inclined to pragmatism."

"In theory. As I think you'd say yourself, watch your hands." Julien pushed himself back from the table. "We have work to do. However Kitty feels about me, she's going to need my help. The investigation is going to dredge things up. She may speak lightly about Ashford, but he put her through a lot. A lot I'd have liked to spare her."

"Talking like a romantic."

"Oh, I'll freely admit Kitty makes me a romantic. At least, I'll admit it to you. Kitty's likely to run screaming in the opposite direction if I admit it to her. But you suffer from the same disease. Fortunately, none of us lets it interfere with completing an investigation. I have inquiries to make at the Three Queens."

"And I should see William Beardsley," Malcolm said.

"I like Beardsley," Julien said. "He has the courage to stand up for himself. And he's the sort who drives Uncle Hubert mad."

"Precisely."

"All of which leaves a larger question."

"Do we tell Esquivel about Allegra?" Malcolm asked.

"It might be a good way to gauge if he knew already."

"And better we break the news than Bow Street do. Higgins isn't a fool. He's likely to work it out eventually."

"So this is our chance to see his reaction. You don't let a chance like that pass by. Poor devil."

"Yes." Malcolm tossed down the last of his coffee. "But I'm not the one to tell him. Raoul is."

CHAPTER 22

"Hubert is very interested in Esquivel," Malcolm said as Raoul shrugged on his greatcoat. Malcolm had found his father in Berkeley Square, and Raoul had agreed it made sense for him to talk to Esquivel.

"Not surprising." Raoul settled the coat over his shoulders. "Hubert casts a wide eye when it comes to advancing Britain's interests."

"He doesn't seem as afraid of revolution in the Argentine."

"Given that the revolution removes the influences of Spain and Portugal? No. And he may believe ideas don't travel that far. In which I'd argue he's mistaken."

Malcolm followed his father from the library to the hall. "Is Esquivel that important?"

"He's intelligent. And he's outlasted Alvear. He'll be part of the new nation that's forged."

"There's a lot of excitement in the sound of that."

"And a lot of the same infighting and compromising one finds in a country that's centuries old."

"So it makes sense Hubert engaged Allegra to spy for him. On Esquivel."

Raoul turned back, one hand on the front door, and met Malcolm's gaze. "This has to have resonance."

Damn. Better to have said as little as possible. "Even if Esquivel can come to terms with Allegra, she's gone. It makes me realize how fortunate I am."

"Because you still have Mélanie?"

"Inestimably. But also because we had the chance to confront the past." The words tumbled out almost unbidden. "Because I got to see her for the person she was, knowing the truth of her past and her motives. Esquivel is left with questions and shadows. The woman he loved is dead and he won't even have her memory because she isn't the person he thought she was. He doesn't have a chance to get to know the real Allegra." Malcolm drew a breath that scraped his throat. "Don't tell Mel I said that."

"I'd never tell Mélanie something you said." Raoul touched his shoulder, and then went out the door to deliver a blow from which Marco Esquivel would find it hard to recover.

Unless of course he already knew.

RAOUL CLIMBED the steps at Mivart's again. Once, the knowledge that he'd made unforgivable compromises had been a bite he'd lived with daily. An ache beneath the surface, so ever-present one got used to not letting it affect daily life. Like Harry Davenport's injured arm. Most of the time a casual observer wouldn't even know Davenport lived with an injury. But then he'd make a sudden movement or sit too long in one position and a flash in his eyes would reveal the pain he lived with daily. Raoul suspected Harry couldn't imagine his life without that ache.

So one simply got in the habit of not dwelling on it. Of not letting it interfere with one's daily actions or choices.

But in recent years, the ache he had learned to live with had begun to recede. Malcolm and Mélanie were happy, happy enough he could at times ignore what he'd done to both of them. Malcolm accepted him as his father and perhaps even more amazingly, as a friend. Mélanie was forging her own life. Raoul had found Laura and was managing to balance marriage and being a spymaster. They had young children, which had a way of focusing one's mind on the present and making the future seem full of promise. He was living a life that was more content than anything he'd known in the past thirty years.

Until something like a murder victim proving to have been spying on her lover for five years brought it back. Because the news he was about to share with Marco Esquivel would unleash the same pain he had brought down on his own son three years ago.

He found Esquivel in the restaurant, finishing a hasty meal. He'd been out making arrangements for Allegra's funeral, he said, though they had to wait for the inquest. When Raoul said he had news, Esquivel made no objection to returning to his suite.

Once there, he listened to Raoul in thunderous silence.

"You can't seriously expect me to believe this nonsense."

"I can imagine how difficult it is," Raoul said. He could see the banked devastation in Malcolm's eyes when Malcolm had confronted him in a similar sitting room in this same hotel just after learning about Mélanie. Which in turn was shortly after Malcolm had learned Raoul was his father.

"Because it's absurd." Esquivel strode across the sitting room. "I've lived with Allegra for five years. We discussed my work. We shared the same vision. She believed in it as much as I did."

"I imagine she convinced herself of that much of the time," Raoul said. "It's what an agent has to do under deep cover." It was what he'd done, on shorter assignments. It was what Mélanie had told him she'd done in the years before Malcolm learned the truth.

"She wasn't under deep cover. We were in love."

"The two are not mutually exclusive," Raoul returned.

"Don't be an idiot, O'Roarke. If she'd gone into the relationship to spy on me, stayed in it to spy on me, it would have all been a game. You don't think I could have told if the woman I shared my life and my bed and my innermost thoughts with was playing a game with me for five years?"

It had been five for Malcolm and Mélanie. Almost to the date of their fifth wedding anniversary. Though it had been less than two before Mélanie told Raoul she was in love with Malcolm. And yet she'd continued to spy on him. And if Raoul hadn't pushed her to, he certainly hadn't stopped her. "I think a number of people can be deceived in that regard," Raoul said. "And I think the lines become blurry."

"For whom?"

"For everyone. But particularly for the spy." So blurry that by Waterloo, it had begun to seriously damage Mélanie's health.

"Damn it, O'Roarke. You're an agent. A bloody spymaster. You must have set up missions like this. Are you telling me you could live a lie for five years with someone you were gathering information on, someone you disagreed with, and that you could genuinely care for the person even while you were rifling through their papers and reporting their private conversations?"

"Could I do it?" Raoul asked. "Perhaps. I'm good at compartmentalizing, though that level of mission would take an extraordinary amount of skill. But I know agents who could." Mélanie. Julien. Kitty. Malcolm's sister Gisèle. Probably Laura. "And I do think it's possible to fall in love in the midst of the deception."

Esquivel spun away and slammed his hand down on the satinwood table. "I knew Allegra. You can't tell me I didn't."

"I'm not telling you anything of the sort. After so much time together, I can't imagine you didn't know her."

"What the hell do you call—"

"I'm not sure we ever fully know another person," Raoul said. "We know bits and pieces. More with those we're closest to."

Memories twisted through Esquivel's gaze. "I was as close to her as one can be—"

"And she probably lost herself in what she shared with you. But I'm afraid we've seen papers she wrote to her spymaster confirming her work."

The realization slammed home in Esquivel's gaze.

"I don't think she could have carried on for so long if it wasn't genuine," Raoul said.

"Genuine?" Esquivel's voice cracked and bounced off the ceiling. "It was lies, through and through. If what you're telling me is true. And god help me, it sounds as though it is."

Raoul looked into Esquivel's eyes. He recognized that torment. But he also knew what had got Malcolm through it. "Tell me you've never lied to someone you genuinely cared about."

"I—Not on this level."

"But it's the idea," Raoul said. "I imagine for weeks, months at a time she lost herself in caring for you and the life you had together. She didn't even think about her mission." He saw Mélanie, waiting to meet him behind an aisle of books in a lending library, dropping into a seat at the back of a café. Seeming to physically transform from a political wife to an agent as she drew off her gloves.

"I loved her."

"I suspect she loved you," Raoul said in a quiet voice. "And for your sake, I hope you can let yourself love her again."

"Love her? It seems I didn't even know her."

"She may have been more herself with you than with anyone."

Esquivel spun away, then turned back to Raoul. "Does this have to do with why she was killed? Did some source kill her? Someone on her own side?"

"I don't know," Raoul said. "But it opens up a number of possibilities."

"Because I want to know. Whoever killed her, I want to know. And I want them held to account. Whatever she did to me, I owe that much to what we shared. Even if it was a fairy tale."

~

"Rannoch." William Beardsley set down his copy of the *Morning Chronicle* as Malcolm came into the sitting room at Brooks's. "Thank god, a friendly face. Everyone looks at me as an interloper here. Of course, I am an interloper here. Wouldn't have joined except there were one too many times people wanted to draft bills here and I had to have someone else bring me in. Rather felt as though I were capitulating."

"Sometimes one has to meet others on their own territory," Malcolm said.

"You mean the enemy?"

Malcolm moved to the chair across from Beardsley. Covered in a fine velvet, but well worn. Brooks's still had one foot in the last century. As did the Whig party, some might say. "I'd hardly call the Whigs the enemy."

"No, that's plainly the Tories. Still, I sometimes wonder if I've got so far inside the system I've forgot what's wrong with it."

Malcolm glanced at a print on the wall, riders sending their hunters over a fence in ardent pursuit of a hapless fox. "I worry about the same thing myself. But as long as you can ask the question, I rather think you haven't."

Beardsley nodded. "What brought you here, Rannoch? Do you want my support for a new bill? If it's yours, you need hardly ask."

Malcolm sat back in the chair worn smooth by decades of Whig politicians. "I'm grateful. And I'll undoubtedly take you up on that. But that's not it this time. I'm here because I've learned you were at Cambridge with Marco Esquivel."

Beardsley's eyes narrowed slightly. "He was one of my best friends. What of it?"

"You were at the theatre with him last night."

"Yes, he had to leave early. I've been expecting to hear from him all day."

"His mistress was murdered last night."

Beardsley jerked straight. "Good god. I had no idea."

"Had he mentioned Alejandra Vargas?"

Beardsley shifted in his chair. "We met for dinner a week since. At a coffeehouse in Westminster, the Gray Horse. I hadn't seen him in years before that. He said he needed to see Felicia—his wife—while he was in Britain, and it would be awkward. I said something about absences being difficult, and Esquivel said yes, and then added there was another lady in the Argentine he was very attached to. I said at least she was far away, and Esquivel said she'd accompanied him to England. I said I wasn't married, but plenty of men had wives and mistresses in London at the same time, so obviously they could juggle it. Tried to keep it equable. But it was hard, because I'd been at his wedding to Felicia. They seemed—happy. You know. It seemed to be a love match."

"Did you say anything about that?"

"In a roundabout sort of way. I mentioned I'd seen Felicia and the children a few times since Marco had left Britain. Rowley makes even more of an effort to keep up, but then he's the eldest's godfather and he's known Felicia since they were children. Esquivel said he'd never meant to hurt Felicia, but people changed. I gathered this woman, the one in the Argentine, means —meant—a lot to him."

"I think she still does, though she's no longer alive." Or had until Raoul broke the news that she'd been spying on him.

"Poor devil." Beardsley shook his head. "Esquivel was always committed to the cause. He said that once he got to the Argentine it was clear how much had to change. That his work was there and everything here seemed rather frivolous. He said he thought I'd understand because I was committed to a cause myself. He also said Felicia would never be able to understand. Which I'm not sure was giving Felicia enough credit, but it wasn't my place to say so. So I asked if his mistress did, and he said yes. She was integral to his work. That he couldn't imagine it without her." Beardsley stared at a nick in the wood of his chair arm. "Do you know—was whoever killed her trying to get at Esquivel?"

"It doesn't seem so. She had a history in England herself. If Esquivel was part of the motive, she clearly seems to have been the target."

"Should I reach out to him? I imagine he could use a friend."

"I'm sure he could. I gather a group of you were close at Cambridge."

"Yes, Rowley and Esquivel and poor Bobby Derwent. Talking of tragedies." Beardsley looked at Malcolm. "Wasn't he—"

"Married to my cousin, yes."

"I'd lost touch with Bobby a bit—he didn't have much interest in politics for all he married into a political family, and I was a bit too Radical for him even in our student days. But I still saw him from time to time. He and Rowley and I would sometimes meet up in Cambridge. Go back to our favorite haunts. I was going to suggest that to Esquivel, but it seemed wrong somehow, with Bobby gone. Wouldn't be the same. I mean, it's never the same, but without Bobby we couldn't even properly recapture the memories."

"I haven't had the misfortune to lose any of my university friends, but sometimes the memories can be out of reach. For any number of reasons." Such as one of those friends having proved to have been spying on the others for Hubert Mallinson. Who had also employed Allegra Roth. "Rowley said Bobby was in touch with Esquivel," Malcolm said.

"Oh, yes. Maybe more than any of us. Bobby had invested in this shipping venture Marco wanted to start. Marco wanted all of us to invest. I don't have enough blunt to invest in anything. But at the theatre last night I found myself saying I'd see what I could do.

That's Marco for you. He made it seem so compelling I wanted to be part of it. He made investing seem like part of remaking the world."

"So Esquivel isn't just working for a revolution. He was planning a commercial empire."

"I think he sees the commercial empire as necessary to make the Argentine its own country. Of course, who controls the commerce rather impacts that. Right now most Argentine goods are transported in foreign vessels. If some in Britain have their way, the Argentine will become an unofficial British colony, if it has its own government or not."

"In fact, that would be more easily accomplished if the Argentine has its own government instead of being someone else's colony."

"Precisely. Esquivel doesn't want the Argentine to be an unofficial British colony. Nor do I. I don't think he'll ever forgive Alvear for considering a British protectorate. He also wasn't very happy with San Martín over the proposal to crown a noble from the Inca empire as king, even of a constitutional monarchy." Beardsley stared across the room at the logs sparking in the fire. "You said Esquivel's mistress had a history in Britain. She was British?"

"Yes." Malcolm hesitated, but it was no longer a secret, and information could bring help. "Her name was originally Allegra Wainwright, then Allegra Roth."

"Good god." Beardsley's head jerked up. "Any relation to Jeremy Roth?"

"She was his wife." Malcolm regarded Beardsley. "You know Roth?"

"Of course. He's a Leveller."

The Radical group started by one of Malcolm's closest university friends. That deeply involved another of his closest friends and many who had become his friends.

"Oh." Beardsley stared at him. "You didn't know. I'm an idiot."

"No. I needed to know. Now."

Beardsley's gaze locked on Malcolm's own. The gaze of someone who has perhaps blundered into something he shouldn't. "What will you do?"

"As my son says, Investigate."

CHAPTER 23

"*D*avenport. Haven't seen you in an age."

The voice stopped Harry in the entry hall of the Classicists' Society. He had ducked in quickly to drop off some notes he'd promised a colleague. He turned to smile at Gerry Schofield. Difficult not to smile at Gerry, who had something of the air of an eager puppy. "Schofield. It's been too long."

"I imagine you've had a lot going on—"

"We're in the midst of an investigation, as it happens. But that doesn't mean I can't talk for a few minutes. In fact, I'd relish the break." Harry opened the door onto a sitting room that was generally empty—it was small and the fireplace usually smoked. The fireplace was indeed puffing smoke today and the room was empty. Harry strode through the smoke to the drinks table, poured two glasses of sherry, and gave one to Gerry.

Gerry clinked his glass to Harry's with the air of one still awkward about such rituals. "It's good to see you, Davenport. Sorry I haven't been round the Classicists' Society. It's been—challenging—at home."

"I imagine it was an uncomfortable holiday season," Harry said. Their investigation just before Christmas had ended with Gerry's father revealed to his family as a French agent, and with Gerry's sister ending her betrothal.

"To say the least. Mama kept asking about Marianne's broken engagement and berating her for letting Thornsby slip through her fingers. Mama's words. Marianne just kept saying it wouldn't have worked. Mama said then it would be up to Sophy to make an alliance for the family. Sophy said Mama should know better than to wish for the moon. Then she—Sophy—told Papa she didn't want any presents from him this year. Or ever. Because of where his money had come from. Marianne convinced her to at least go through the motions of Christmas for Sally's and Billy's sake and said she didn't have to actually keep the presents. She could put them in Marianne's room. Sophy said that was a shocking compromise, but she went along with it and we sort of limped through the holidays. Sophy dumped all her presents in Marianne's room before Christmas dinner. Marianne went off to stay with Charlotte Wilcox and her family after Boxing Day. Never so wished I had an invitation to stay with friends in my life."

"You're always welcome to visit us."

Gerry's eyes widened. "Very good of you. I couldn't impose—"

"You wouldn't be," Harry said. He might have said it anyway, but it happened to be true.

Gerry gave an abashed smile. "The thing is, I don't know how to look at Father. I mean, he stood up to Lady Shroppington to protect Justine's father. That helped me make sense of it for a bit. But when we all really thought about it, everything he has, everything he is, is built on a lie. Which means everything we have is." Gerry looked down at the glass in his hand and then at the shiny toes of his shoes.

Harry took a drink of sherry. "Not to excuse it. But if you search the history of most fortunes, they're built on some quite intolerable behavior. I can't claim to be particularly proud of Davenports past. There was a tobacco plantation in Virginia that makes me cringe, and a venture in India that looks like straightforward pillaging. Repudiating your fortune won't resolve anything. But this might be reason to think through what you do with it."

"Help the poor, you mean?"

"Among other things. I've made a number of what I see as more positive investments with the fortune I am remarkably lucky to have. Try to make the world a better place than you found it. People are complicated. Good people can do quite appalling things. And appalling people can do unexpectedly good things. And good and appalling are relative terms."

"So you wouldn't repudiate him if he were your father?"

"I don't know what it is to be your age and have a father. I have Uncle Archie, who's more a father to me than my biological father ever was. I'm beyond grateful that I have him. I don't think repudiating your father would resolve anything."

Gerry nodded and kicked his foot against the chair leg. "Sophy thinks Mama should know. But none of us can bring ourselves to tell her."

Harry settled back on the frayed tapestry settee. "You might suggest to your father that your mother should know."

Gerry's eyes widened. "Do you think he'd tell her?"

"I haven't the least idea. But he might." Harry watched Gerry for a moment. "He'll always be your father. Not casting him out of your life doesn't mean you forgive him. And there are people working in our country's interests who have probably done things that are more unforgivable." Such as Hubert Mallinson, whose surviving children were on speaking terms with him though they were all well aware of his activities. And not comfortable with them.

Gerry's eyes widened. "More unforgivable than selling information—"

"I suppose it depends on how one defines unforgivable. Which lines one can't imagine crossing."

Gerry nodded. "It changes things. For all of us. I don't think any of us feels as inclined to do what's expected of us. Well, Sophy never did in any case. As exasperating as my sister can be, I think she may be the most sensible of us."

Having met Sophy Schofield, Harry was inclined to agree. "The fact that you can say so indicates a great deal about your own sense." Harry took another drink of sherry. "Have you heard from Miss Lambton since she went back to Cambridge?"

A quick, almost abashed smile crossed Gerry's face. "She wrote to tell me she'd got back safely. And that her father was well. She wrote again with New Year's greetings. She said you'd invited her for a longer visit."

"We like her. And we promised to take her to a Classicists' Society lecture. She's due to arrive at our house this afternoon, as it happens. I'm sure she'll be happy to see you again while you're still in town."

Gerry's eyes lit up like candles. "I hope—Justine's capital."

Never had the word capital sounded so romantic. Gerry was years younger than Harry had been when he'd tumbled into love with disastrous results. At least, initially disastrous. "You're very young. But she's not the sort of girl one would like to lose for want of expressing oneself."

"It's not a question of—I don't think that's what Justine wants."

"I don't know that she's interested in marriage in general. I think you may be a different case. Speaking as a disinterested observer."

Gerry colored. "You must know—I mean, she's far above my touch, but it's difficult to think of anyone else."

"That's an interesting use of above my touch."

"I mean, she has ten times my understanding."

Harry leaned forwards and clapped Gerry on the shoulder. "You have a good sense of priorities, Gerald. Why don't you come back to Hill Street with me? I suspect nothing would make Justine happier than to have you there when she arrives."

Gerry sat back, sherry glass tilting in his fingers. "Oh no, I couldn't. Wouldn't want to intrude."

"You wouldn't be intruding in the least. You'd be making Justine's arrival far more convivial than if she simply found Cordy and the girls and me when she arrived." Harry tossed down the last of his sherry. "I may be more used to judging the motives and emotions of those in the first century than today, but some things are universal."

~

Simon turned from adjusting a candle sconce on the canvas wall of the set on the stage of the Tavistock Theatre. "Sorry, didn't hear you come in."

"Didn't mean to startle you," Malcolm said. "I used Mélanie's key. I thought she might still be here."

"She and the children left for Berkeley Square about half an hour ago."

Malcolm moved out of the wings onto the boards of the stage. "Do you normally do this?"

"What? The set? Sometimes. Don't you do things at home you'd normally leave to the staff? A theatre is much more democratic than a Mayfair house. Perhaps even your Mayfair house. Or mine." Simon jumped off the stepladder he'd been standing on. "What brings you here?"

It had been in this same theatre, on this same stage, that Malcolm had confronted his wife about her being a spy for the French, and the mission that had been their marriage. The scent of dust and the glow of rehearsal lamps would never fail to take him back to that moment. "Jeremy Roth is a Leveller."

The glow from the lamp on the stage shot through Simon's eyes. "Roth told you?"

"No, William Beardsley did."

"Why the devil—"

"He was friends with Marco Esquivel. Allegra Roth's lover. At Cambridge. So much seems to go back to university."

"So it does."

Simon leaned against the stepladder, arms folded across his chest. "Roth's in a difficult situation. We know his politics. But he works for Bow Street, which are under the auspices of the home office. It was up to him to decide who should know about his involvement in a political group that skirts the law."

"Of course. But I wouldn't—"

The lamplight bounced off Simon's eyes, dark and hard as obsidian. "You're an MP. You've often said or implied that there are things Kit and I are involved in you'd as lief not know. I've kept things from David for the same reason. What Roth said to you was his own decision."

"Of course. That's true for all of us when it comes to everything. But you can't think that I—"

"I told you. It wasn't my decision. My god, Malcolm. You know I trust you. But there's plenty you haven't told me. For good reasons."

Including the truth about Mélanie, until Hubert Mallinson had forced it into the open. Simon had understood at once. David had not, which had nearly destroyed both his friendship with Malcolm and his relationship with Simon.

"Roth's walking a delicate line," Simon said. "Much more so than the rest of us. Most of the Levellers aren't dependent on employment for their sustenance. Or that of their family. And then there's the fact that you're connected to Hubert."

"I *used* to be connected to Hubert."

"It's difficult to extricate oneself, as we both know."

"For that matter, you're connected to Hubert. He's your father-in-law, to all intents and purposes."

Simon gave a short laugh. "I never thought to say as much. But we may be at the point where even he sees it that way. Still, he hardly confides in me."

"You think he confides in me?"

"In a way. You may be the closest he has to a confidant."

"You can't think I don't protect my friends."

"Of course not. And I doubt Roth thinks you don't. But perhaps he didn't want to put you in that position."

Malcolm moved across the stage, where the dusty light fell more clearly across Simon's face. "So I assume Roth knows Beardsley?"

"Is that important?"

"Given that Beardsley was close to Esquivel, and Allegra was Esquivel's mistress? Yes."

"They know each other. Given that Roth didn't know about his wife and Esquivel until after she was killed, it's hard to see how it's important."

"Roth *said* he didn't know about Allegra and Esquivel until after she was killed."

"You don't believe him?" Simon's gaze sharpened.

"At the moment I'm finding it hard to know what to believe. About any of it." Malcolm watched Simon for a moment in the shifting light, thinking back to the far more makeshift stage at Oxford where they'd performed *Henry IV Part 1*. "They were all friends at Cambridge—Esquivel, Beardsley, Rowley—and Bobby Derwent, apparently."

Recognition flashed in Simon's gaze. "I didn't know Beardsley knew Bobby. Not that there's any particular reason it should have come up. Beardsley wouldn't necessarily realize I knew Bobby, and I can't claim to have known him well. I'm sorry if this drags Judith into it."

"So am I, though she might welcome the distraction. But mostly it made me think about university friends. About all of us at Oxford. It sounds as though they had much the same bond. And like us, they both stayed close and drifted apart."

"That's inevitable. Our lives pull us different ways. But the bond is still there. More for us than for many. Difficult, I would think, with Esquivel across an ocean."

"Yes. Though apparently he was in touch with all of them. He was planning a shipping venture and he had Bobby and Rowley and perhaps Beardsley investing in it."

Simon frowned. "The Argentine is going to be important. They'll need commerce. Though one hopes it won't lead to more exploitation of the same people who were exploited by the colonial powers. But better the Argentines build their own infrastructure than that the British do."

"Which is what Hubert would like."

"Quite. But it's difficult to see how any of that could connect to Allegra Roth's murder."

Malcolm considered for a moment, then decided to risk it. No particular need to keep it secret. "Allegra was an agent for Hubert."

Simon let out a whistle. "When—"

"Since before her marriage. Hubert claims he wasn't getting information on Roth. Of course, that was before I knew Roth was a Leveller."

"The Levellers didn't exist when Allegra married Roth."

"But Jeremy's politics were the same."

"You already knew Jeremy's politics. The question is if Hubert did." Simon braced his hands on the stepladder. "Am I going to have to deal with David's father being accused of murder? Again?"

"This is nothing like Miranda Spencer." In that case, Hubert had been found in the murdered woman's room and had been arrested. "If Hubert was involved, he'll be too far away from it to be implicated."

"That's cold comfort."

"We don't have any evidence to tie him to it."

"You don't have any evidence to tie anyone to it."

"Not yet."

Simon turned his head to the side. The rehearsal lamp caught his grimace. "I like him, you know. That's the hell of it I'm not sure when I started to, but I'm quite fond of him. The last thing I want is to see him accused of something like this. Though I know he's perfectly capable of doing it."

"I don't want to see him accused either."

Simon turned back and pinned Malcolm with his gaze. "But you may find yourself doing the accusing."

"I may."

～

COLIN, Jessica, and Emily raced up the stairs of the Berkeley Square portico. They were very proud of their ability to let themselves in, so they tumbled into the entrance hall without ringing for Valentin.

"What is it, Uncle Julien?" Mélanie heard Colin ask as she followed them through the door.

Julien was in the hall, by the console table for calling cards, frowning at a slip of paper he held in his hand. Bet Trenor stood near him, arms folded, gaze fixed on Julien with concern.

Mélanie closed the door behind her. "What is it?"

Julien looked up, flashed a grin at the children, and then met her gaze. "I called back here to see if anyone had updates to share and found a message from Robby. He sent it to Carfax House and Kitty sent it on here when she went back to Carfax House to look through Ashford's papers. Bet and I are a bit worried."

Robby, Bet's brother, had grown up in near Seven Dials himself and gone to work for Julien, first as an agent, then as a groom.

"No cause for panic, though," Julien added, as the three children fastened anxious gazes on him.

Bet held out a hand to the children. "Let's go in the library. Mrs. Erskine made scones and I put a plate in there."

The promise of the scones, and the smell when they opened the library door, distracted the children to a degree. They settled on the hearth rug with the scones and Berowne and Bet, though Colin looked at Mélanie over his shoulder.

"Robby Simcox traced a hired carriage driver who drove Allegra the day before she was killed," Julien said to Mélanie as they stood by the library table, pretending to nibble scones. "He took her to an address outside the city and waited half an hour for her."

"How far outside the city?" Mélanie asked.

"Richmond." Julien held out a slip of paper, brows uncharacteristically drawn.

Pelham Lodge.

Mélanie stared at the letters in Robby Simcox's careful, recently learned lettering. "But that's—" She let the words dangle. Such an obvious reaction. But for a moment she was robbed of speech.

"Yes," Julien said.

A villa belonging to Malcolm's cousin Judith. Since her marriage to the recently deceased Viscount Pelham, they'd divided their time between Pelham Lodge and his larger estate in Kent. In a family of agents, they were all used to finding connections to family and friends in investigations. Judith's mother Frances had married a former agent, who also happened to be Harry's uncle. Judith's elder sister Aline had helped them break codes in more than one investigation. But Judith, a happy diamond of the first water in her season, a happy bride and mother soon after, had never been more than on the very fringe of spy intrigues. And while her family history wouldn't have made it surprising for her to be drawn into the intrigues of the Elsinore League, there was nothing that should connect her to Allegra Roth, who had been born in Radical circles, become an opera singer, married a Bow Street runner, and then run off to the Argentine.

Julien took in her reaction. "I know."

"Allegra didn't know us," Mélanie said. "She shouldn't have known we were connected to Jeremy. So how on earth she'd have got to Judith, who would have been a child when Allegra left London—We need to talk to Judith. She came up to London this morning. Fanny sent me a note. Better for Malcolm to talk to her, but we shouldn't wait. Come with me?"

Julien nodded.

CHAPTER 24

"I know I can't ask what you've learnt," Roth said. "But have you learnt anything?"

"A number of things." Malcolm dug his hands into his greatcoat pockets against the chill. They had walked to the terrace off Somerset Place, where they were accustomed to go to talk. They had paced this worn stone during other investigations, discussing someone else's nightmare. "Some of which I can share. For instance, I had no idea you were one of the Levellers."

Roth's head lifted. His gaze caught and settled on Malcolm's own. "Ah. I should have known that might come out, I suppose."

"William Beardsley is a friend of Esquivel's. He mentioned it."

"Good god."

"You didn't know?"

"How could I have known? Esquivel's name would have meant nothing to me even if Beardsley had mentioned him. Which he didn't. I like Beardsley, but I can't claim to know him well. There's quite a gap between an MP and a Bow Street runner."

"I'm an MP."

"Yes, you are."

"It didn't occur to you to—"

"What? Tell you I was part of an organization you do your best to know as little about as possible?"

Malcolm glanced at the roiling gray of the river. "I wouldn't say that. I talk about them with Simon. With Kit. With Roger Smythe, more recently."

"But you're clear there are things you don't want to know."

"If the law is being broken, it's better for me not to know it. I would imagine that's something we share."

"It's a challenge for a Bow Street runner," Roth admitted. "But at a certain point I get tired of being quiet. And unlike you, I can't speak out in Parliament. I knew I was taking a risk. I didn't want to involve my friends."

"You were worried about me?"

"I didn't want to put you in an awkward situation. We both have enough to contend with."

The wind tugged Malcolm's greatcoat. He caught the folds to still them. "We're on the same side."

"We believe in the same things. But we come from different worlds. We'll never work for change in the same way. We'll never face the same challenges."

That sounded like something Mélanie might have once said, though he couldn't say as much to Roth. Talking of secrets that hung between them. "That's true of most of my friends. God knows there's a lot about Julien that's very different from me."

"But you still come from the same world."

"You seem far more focused on different worlds than the rest of us."

"Perhaps because the impact is greater. An aristocrat can go out for an evening in Seven Dials with little consequence, so long as he takes care of his purse."

"And so long as he is a not a lady."

"Fair enough. But someone at my level risks more in Mayfair than you do in Seven Dials. Unless I'm there as part of my employment. If I'm not there for work, I'm more aware of the sidelong glances. I've seen them when I call in Berkeley Square."

The flat statement hit like a shock of river water. "God, Roth. I don't—"

"Think about it? No, of course you don't. You don't get the looks. There's no reason for you to notice. You're broadminded and benevolent for crossing class lines. We're social climbers."

"No one who knows you could possibly—"

"That's just the problem. They don't know me. Or Harriet or the boys. They just know people who were born in Somers Town and live in Covent Garden are dining in Berkeley Square."

"I'm sorry."

"You needn't be. You're good friends to all of us. It's not your job to fix the situation."

"If not, then whose? What else should someone born to privilege do? Especially someone with a seat in the House of Commons."

"Which keeps you from getting too close to the Levellers."

"You're the one who said you couldn't confide things in me."

"Given your position, yes."

"Are you saying being in Parliament blinds me to the real issues facing the country?"

"Nothing of the sort. There's a lot of good you can do. But we've chosen different ways to fight. We have to, given where we started in life. I'd never say one is more valid than the other. In fact, there's probably a great deal you can accomplish that I can't."

Malcolm stopped, one hand on the crumbling balustrade. "The House of Commons can be a bubble. One can get so focused on the debate with the opposition that one loses track of the real arguments going on outside Westminster. Being a Radical in the House doesn't mean being a Radical in the real world."

"Fair enough," Roth said. "But you can accomplish more with one victory on a watered-down bill that the Levellers excoriate as a hopeless comprise than those of us on the outside can with the most eloquent and succinct articles." His gaze narrowed. "You must have realized that yourself. You used to write those same articles."

"Yes." When he'd scribbled pamphlets in Oxford coffeehouses with Simon and David and Oliver. "And then I decided the whole thing was hopeless and went to work for Hubert Mallinson, for which I'll never forgive myself. But I did somewhat recover my senses."

"You care about Hubert Mallinson."

"I—"

"Don't deny it, Malcolm. I'd think less well of you. I can respect the fact that you care about him. So does Julien. So does your father."

Malcolm drew in and released his breath. The damp wind freshened the air but the stench from the river was still there. "I don't trust Hubert. I question everything he says and does, as I'm sure Julien and Raoul do. But yes. I do have some affection for him."

"I'm impressed. By the admission."

Malcolm looked out at the boats on the river. Smaller vessels ferried goods down the Thames. Goods that had come from across the sea. "It seemed simpler," Malcolm said. "When we were all at Oxford, dreaming in coffeehouses and scribbling pamphlets. And it sounds as though it was the same for Esquivel and his friends."

"Beardsley?"

"And Rowley. And Bobby Derwent."

"Judith's husband?"

Malcolm forgot sometimes that Roth had got to know Judith at countless family parties at their house. "Yes. I didn't realize they'd known each other until today. I don't suppose Bobby ever came to Leveller events?"

"Not to my knowledge. He and Judith appeared to move in very different circles. Even from yours in Berkeley Square."

"Well, yes. They weren't agents."

Roth nodded. "A difference indeed."

Justine Lambton emerged from the carriage Harry and Cordelia had sent to Cambridge for her, bonnet bouncing back on her shoulders, strands of brown hair tumbling down about her ears, cobalt blue pelisse creased from travel. All of which might be owed to the large, brown paper–wrapped parcel clutched in her arms, Harry thought, observing from the steps with Cordelia and their daughters. Justine stepped carefully down onto the cobblestones and flashed a smile of gratitude at the footman as he steadied her.

"Justine!" Livia and Drusilla tumbled down the steps to greet the new arrival, who had become a firm friend on her previous visit, their new puppy Cleo running after them.

Justine bent to hug them, one armed, keeping control of the paper-wrapped parcel. "Do you mind?" she asked, surrendering it to Harry. "I'd never forgive myself if something happened to it. I so need your opinion."

"Of course." Harry took the parcel and knew at once what he held. Marble. Old marble, if his instincts were at all right. Carved.

"It was sent to Papa." Justine looked up from hugging Livia and Drusilla. "I'll tell you more when we're inside. Oh, what a sweet dog!" She bent to pet Cleo, who was jumping up on her pelisse.

"We got her for Christmas," Drusilla said. "She sleeps in my bed. Well, sometimes in Livia's."

Harry followed Justine and the girls and puppy up the steps, cradling the parcel much as he would one of his daughters. Justine hugged Cordelia, then stopped short at the sight of Gerry, who was standing in the shadows just behind Cordy.

"I saw Schofield at the Classicists' Society today," Harry said. "Thought you'd like to see each other."

"Of course." Justine smiled with both friendship and determination. "I'm so glad. And I'd like your opinion about my discovery too."

"Didn't want to intrude." Gerry shifted his weight from one booted foot to another. "But it's good to see you."

"You couldn't intrude. And I'm so glad you're still in London. I need all the classical minds I can get."

Gerry grinned. It said a lot about his devotion to classical studies that he wasn't disappointed it was his opinion as a scholar that Justine wanted.

It was a quarter hour or so before they were settled in the library with refreshments and Livia and Drusilla playing with Cleo by the fire. Justine tossed down a swallow of tea, then got to her feet and tugged loose the brown paper wrapping on her parcel, which sat in state on the library table. It fell away to reveal the bust of a woman. Small, first century, head turned to one side. The marble shimmered in the light from the windows. The shadows left her eyes cloaked in mystery.

"It's Agrippina," Justine said. "The first one, Caligula's mother, not his sister who married Claudius and was Nero's mother."

"I thought so," Harry said. "I've seen other likenesses of her."

"It was lost when Napoleon went into Rome," Justine said. "Father had tried to trace it because it was one he had studied particularly when he was in Italy before the wars. Then it suddenly showed up in a crate of things in Cambridge last week."

"Not wholly surprising," Harry said. "A lot of art treasures disappeared during the wars—into government and private hands."

"Yes, but this crate had come from the Argentine."

Harry's teacup tilted in his fingers. "You're sure?"

"Oh, yes. I know who sent it. He used to be a student of Papa's. Marco Esquivel."

CHAPTER 25

*J*ustine looked from Harry to Cordelia as they both struggled not to send their teacups clattering to the carpet. "What is it? Do you know Marco Esquivel?"

"We haven't met Mr. Esquivel," Cordy said. "But we've heard a good deal about him since last night. We were called into an investigation, and sadly the victim was his mistress."

"Good heavens," Justine said. "How horrible. I did know Mr. Esquivel was in London. I was hoping to see him. Did his mistress come with him?"

"Yes," Harry said, "but she was British, as it happens. We learned Esquivel went to Cambridge, but we hadn't heard he read classics."

"Oh yes. There was a whole group of them who came to Papa for tutoring and who were all friends. Mr. Esquivel, Martin Rowley, William Beardsley, and Bobby Derwent. Sometimes they'd all come together and stay afterwards and talk in our parlor or kitchen. I liked to sit in because they had quite intelligent things to say."

"Unlike some of us," Gerry said.

"No!" Justine gave him a quick smile. "Well, not like you. But they were an interesting group. They'd talk about politics as well. Especially Mr. Beardsley and Mr. Esquivel. About how they wanted to change both their countries. Mostly I have my head so deep in the past I don't think about the present. They were good about bringing out the parallels. That the past can be a guide to the present, in a way."

"So it can," Harry said. "In some ways, that's my reason for studying it."

Justine flashed a smile at him. "Mr. Rowley was always sketching some scientific invention. Mr. Derwent—Lord Pelham later—liked to say outrageous things, but he often seemed more interested in gossip. It was so tragic he died so young. Mr. Esquivel taught me some Spanish. After he went back to the Argentine, we followed his career closely."

"Did he write to your father?" Harry asked.

"Occasionally. I remember poring over those letters because the Argentine seemed so intriguing, and then tracing the path he'd sailed on the globe in Papa's study."

"What did he say when he sent your father the bust?" Cordelia asked.

"Simply that he knew it would be safe in Papa's hands. He said he'd be in London and would come down to Cambridge and explain more. As I was coming to see you, I wanted to show you the bust and to get an answer from Mr. Esquivel in person. But in the circumstances—"

"In the circumstances," Harry said, "we most definitely need to ask him about the bust."

Justine's eyes widened. "But surely you can't think a bust that's almost two thousand years old has anything to do with Mr. Esquivel's mistress being murdered."

"It's difficult to see how it might," Harry agreed. "But at the moment, anything to do with Esquivel and his mistress Alejandra Vargas and their life in the Argentine is of interest."

Justine set down her teacup. "Mr. Esquivel was—he is —married."

"Yes," Cordelia said. "Had you met his wife?"

"He brought her to see us once, just after they married. I was quite young. She was very kind. She complimented me on our parlor, though it must have looked so shabby compared to what she was used to. I can still see her and Mr. Esquivel sitting together on the settee. They seemed so happy."

"I imagine they were, then," Harry said.

"They'd been living apart, of course, since he went back to the Argentine. I did notice he didn't mention her as much in his letters, or when he visited us when he was in England after Waterlo. Sometimes he'd talk about the children." Justine looked at Harry. "Have you seen him? Since his mistress was killed?"

"No, but Julien and Kitty did. It seems they knew him in the Argentine."

"And Mr. Rowley and Mr. Beardsley—?"

"They were with him last night. Apparently he wanted them to invest in a shipping venture and to use Rowley's steam engine in his mines."

"But surely that doesn't have anything to do with why this woman—"

"She went by the name Alejandra Vargas, but her name was Allegra Roth."

"With why she was murdered?"

"Difficult to say, at this point. But there seem to be ties to the Argentine."

Cordelia leaned forwards to refill the teacups. "Mélanie and Malcolm asked us to Berkeley Square tonight. Which I think is a very good thing."

～

"WHAT A LOVELY SURPRISE." Judith came into the hall as her mother's footman was ushering Mélanie, Julien, Colin, Jessica, and Emily through the doorway of the house in South Audley Street. She wore a simple blue round gown, and her toddler daughter Serena and toddler half-brother and sister, Philip and Francesca, were clustered round her.

"Just the thing," Judith said, as the children ran over to hug the new arrivals. "I've been running out of games. Mama's taken Chloe to a dress fitting and Archie's at a committee meeting in Westminster."

Becky, the twins' nurse, appeared and took the children up to the nursery. Judith took Mélanie and Julien into a salon on the ground floor, off the library, done up in her mother's favorite shades of lavender. It was in the first fashion, and yet timeless, with the same instinctive elegance Judith seemed to have inherited from her mother. An elegance she wore lightly, even when attired for a simple day at home.

Judith looked from Mélanie to Julien. "Not that I'm not delighted to see you, but given that Malcolm and Kitty aren't here —and Leo, Timothy, and Genny—I think this isn't just a family call? Is anything wrong? Is it Gelly?"

Malcolm's sister Gisèle, who had grown up with Judith like a sister, had sought Judith's refuge during her intrigues with the Elsinore League. That was the closest Judith had come to their investigations. Though even then she'd been careful not to ask too many questions.

"Gisèle's fine," Mélanie said. At least as far as she knew. "She and Andrew were happily enjoying Scotland and chasing Ian round Dunmykel in their last letter."

"Not that Gelly doesn't have the resources for all sorts of adventures," said Julien, who had trained Gisèle in spycraft. "But I think she's enjoying a break from them for the moment."

They paused while the footman brought in tea and wine and biscuits and arranged them on the satinwood sofa table.

"Sherry or tea?" Judith said in a bright voice. She had had that tone from girlhood, though it sounded a bit more forced these days. Her hair, tumbling down her back and caught back with a blue ribbon, was as bright a gold as ever, and her eyes the same clear blue, but there were shadows round them that hadn't been there a year ago. She had led a charmed life for much of her two-and-twenty years, pretty, accomplished, well-dowered, seemingly happy with the life of a young lady in the beau monde. She'd seemed to relish her first season, and before long had been in love and happily married to an eligible man. Such a contrast to the paths so many in the family had taken to marriage and family life.

And then, after less than two years of marriage, not long after the birth of their daughter, Bobby Derwent had taken a jump badly, fallen from his horse, and been carried back to the house with a broken neck. Mélanie still recalled the stark horror on Frances's face when she had rushed to her daughter's side. Judith had seemed to draw inwards afterwards, though she still came to family parties with Serena, and smiled and laughed as she always had.

"We're in the midst of a new investigation," Mélanie said, accepting a glass of sherry from Judith. "A woman was killed in a Seven Dials tavern last night. She was Jeremy Roth's wife, though she'd been gone from England for years."

Judith's glass tilted in her fingers. "Good god. How horrible for Jeremy. And the children. I knew his wife was gone from England, but not the details. Do you know where she'd been? And why she'd come back?"

"She'd been in the Argentine," Mélanie said. "Using the name Alejandra Vargas. But we just had a report that she called at your house two days ago. The day before she was killed."

Judith went still. Her back was as straight as when she had walked about with a book on her head as the young teenager Mélanie had first known. She set her glass down with meticulous care, as though the smallest waver of her hand might shatter the crystal, and her life with it. "I might have known. Part of me did know the moment you arrived. But I had myself convinced it was something different. Idiotic of me."

Mélanie stared into Judith's cornflower blue eyes. The eyes of the girl she had first met at fifteen. The eyes that had shone at her wedding. Had smiled down at her baby daughter. Had laughed at countless holiday parties. Which were suddenly shadowed with secrets.

Beside Mélanie, Julien was still relaxed into his chair, but she felt his stillness. It was he who said, "Allegra Roth called on you?"

"Yes. As you already know." Judith reached for her glass, tossed down a quick sip, set it down again.

"Had you met before?" Mélanie asked.

"No. But she wanted to talk to me."

"So she knew of you," Julien said.

"Yes." Judith took another drink of sherry. "Oh, the devil. It's like tearing off a bandage. Better to do it in one jerk. She wanted to talk to me about Jeremy. She wanted to talk to me because I'm her husband's lover."

CHAPTER 26

Mélanie stared at Judith, trying to picture her and Jeremy Roth together. They'd both been at countless parties in Berkeley Square and at Cordy and Harry's, at Fanny and Archie's, at Carfax House. An image shot into her mind. Judith on the window seat with Serena in her lap at Fanny's last autumn. Jeremy picking up a stuffed kitten Serena had dropped. Judith smiling up at him in thanks. But surely she'd seen a score of similar exchanges between Jeremy and so many other people in the family.

Julien sat back in his chair. "Always fatal. To see people in certain groups and not imagine connections. I am quite caught out."

Judith's mouth curled in a bleak smile. "In other circumstances, I might be pleased to hear that. I grew up being quite accustomed to being the last one in the family to learn secrets. If I ever learned them at all." She raised her carefully plucked brows and turned her gaze to Mélanie. "It shouldn't be so surprising. We met at your house. We've met dozens of times at your house. We've spoken together quite openly."

More images shot through Mélanie's mind, fragments flooding

back. Jeremy bringing Judith a cup of coffee. Jeremy picking up Serena when she stumbled. Judith admiring Samuel's drawing. And along with those images, a sense that there were a host more she'd missed. "Yes, but you never seemed—"

"Well, naturally. We weren't keen to have everyone know." Judith tilted her head to one side. Now that the words were out, self-possession settled over her. She had never looked more like her mother. "I suppose you think you should be able to see through that." She glanced from Mélanie to Julien. "But honestly, just because I'm practically the only person in the family who isn't an agent doesn't mean I'm not capable of deception. Look at what Mama managed for years before she married Archie. Well, I suppose a lot of her affairs weren't secret, but the one with Alistair certainly was. And I'm not sure everyone knew about her and Archie before they became betrothed. I don't know why everyone's so shocked—do you think me too frivolous to interest a man like Jeremy?"

"Of course not," Mélanie said.

Judith spread her fingers over her figured sarcenet skirt. "I shouldn't have minded it being public for myself, but you see what it could do to Jeremy. In his work. The scandal for his children. Well, I was concerned for Serena too, if it comes to that. I knew you'd all worry and there was no point."

"Had you and Jeremy talked about the future?" Mélanie asked.

"We hadn't had time. It was so new. Whenever we even got close to that, it seemed he assumed things had to end, so that was the last place I wanted to venture. Because, quite honestly, I couldn't bear for it to end." Judith swallowed. "I was in love with Bobby. At least, I thought it was love, and it may really have been, but it was already wearing a bit thin when he died. It was almost too easy. We never had to work for it or at it."

"Do you think love should be hard?" Julien asked.

"No—not necessarily. But if it comes too easily, how does one know it's real? What I have with Jeremy is something one could give up everything for."

"You don't mean that," Mélanie said.

"Haven't you been in love enough to give up everything?"

Everything? She'd given up her cause, her work, turned her back on her comrades. But—"Not to give up my children. And I like to think there's some core of myself I'd hold on to."

Judith folded her arms. "Well, no. I wouldn't give up Serena. I suppose that's what Allegra did. I can't quite fathom it."

"I can't quite fathom Allegra Roth either. But I think it was far more complicated than that she gave up her children because she was madly in love."

"What did she want when she came to see you?" Julien asked. "And how did she know about an affair your family had woefully failed to notice?"

Judith folded her arms. "She didn't tell me how she knew. That troubled me, because we'd been so careful. She wanted to know what it meant. What we intended. I suppose you could say she wanted to know what my intentions were when it came to Jeremy."

"What did you say?" Julien asked.

"That I wanted to be with him. But that I was having a damnably hard time convincing Jeremy of that. Allegra laughed and said Jeremy had a surprising tendency to give way to middle class morality, despite his background. I must have looked anxious, because then she added that I needn't worry, she didn't want Jeremy back, and even if she did it was far too late for it. They'd never been suited, and whatever chance they'd had had been over years ago. I was horribly relieved. Though at the same time, I couldn't but wonder if Jeremy felt the same way she did." Judith looked down at her fingers against the pale blue of her sleeves. "I don't think he's over her. Not as much as she appeared to be over him. Not as much as I'm over Bobby, oddly enough.

Poor Bobby. He deserves to be mourned more. But I think he'd want me to be happy."

"I'm sure he would," Mélanie said. "What else did Allegra say?"

Judith tugged at a ribbon on her sleeve. "She asked if I'd seen the boys. I said I had a bit, but only at parties. That Jeremy had never brought them to see me and they didn't know about us. She asked if they seemed well. I said they did and that she must miss them dreadfully. She got an odd look on her face. She said she did, at times, but she hadn't been very good at being a mother. That she could go weeks on end without thinking about them, which perhaps proved it. That the boys were better off without her. I must have looked shocked at that. I said I couldn't imagine children being better off without their parents. She said surely that depended on the parents. She hadn't the patience or temperament for parenthood. I must say perhaps she had a point. I don't think Aunt Arabella did either. Mama says she wasn't suited to being a parent for a long time. But Mama changed. And I don't think she'd have ever thought any of us were better off without her." Judith stared at her fingers. "I liked Allegra, in a way. But listening to her, I also couldn't help but be horribly angry. Because I can tell how much it still hurts Jeremy that she left. And it must hurt the boys. And even if I'm not particularly special to them, they can't but be special to me. Because they're Jeremy's. And who couldn't love them?"

"I hope they never doubt they're loved," Julien said. "It's a common reaction when one loses a parent, for any reason."

"Jeremy would never ask me to leave Serena. He's too worried about Serena as it is. I think it's partly because of Allegra." Judith's brows drew together. "I'm not sure I know the core of myself enough to try to hold on to it. But I think I'm more myself with Jeremy than I ever have been."

"I remember thinking that about Malcolm," Mélanie said.

"When?"

"When I realized I loved him." On the beach at Dunmykel. Before she'd stopped spying on him.

"So you understand."

"I understand love can make one think of turning one's life round."

"That's what I meant. I could walk away from all of"—she gestured round the salon with its cameo friezes and watered silk hangings and giltwood furniture—"this. And don't tell me it's because I don't know what it is to be poor. We wouldn't be poor. I have my own portion. It's rather insulting if everyone thinks I couldn't bear to be out of society, when the rest of you have been happily out of society for years."

"Years is a bit of an exaggeration," Mélanie said.

"You know what I mean. Just because I learned how to play the game, no one thinks I can be happy without it like everyone else. Gelly's been running round England doing god knows what for over two years. She and Andrew pop up with Ian at odd times of night needing a bed and food, and I pretend I'm too naive to ask questions. It's rather insulting. But then Gelly's always been convinced of her own cleverness."

"What does Jeremy say?"

"About Gelly?"

"About your giving everything up."

Judith hugged her elbows. "He said it was impossible. But that was because we couldn't marry. I never saw why that was an insuperable barrier—look at Laura and Raoul, and you can't tell me any of you wouldn't cheerfully live together if you couldn't marry. But it's amazing how a man who calls himself a Radical can be so conventional when it comes to the woman he loves. Only now we could marry. So it's quite different."

"Quite," Julien said.

Judith's gaze shot to his face. "Oh god. You think one of us killed her."

"Think you did?" Julien said. "No."

"But we both have a motive. So you wonder. You can't not wonder." She looked the most mature she had in the entire interview, even more like her mother. "I do understand."

"Investigations raise challenges," Mélanie said. "This isn't the first time one has touched on our friends and family. Jeremy asked us to look into it."

"Of course. Better you than Bow Street. I mean, they'll have their reasons for not seeing things to his advantage. I keep hoping the murder of a Bow Street runner's errant wife won't cause that much attention. Even if she was the mistress of an Argentine revolutionary."

"I'm afraid it's a bit more complicated," Julien said. "Allegra was a British agent."

Judith stared at him for a moment, then started to laugh. "I'm sorry," she said between gasps. "It shouldn't be funny—but what other response is there to one more spy in our circles. Was she—"

"She was working for Uncle Hubert. He admitted it."

"Was she spying on Jeremy?"

"Not explicitly."

"But she went off with Esquivel to spy on him?"

"Apparently," Julien said. "It doesn't mean she didn't develop feelings for him."

"She seems to have been looking for something to give her life focus," Mélanie said. "Apparently she always wanted to believe she stood out. She thought her father wasn't really her mother's first husband but someone powerful and mysterious. We have no notion if that was true—"

For some reason, at that Judith went still. "Does Jeremy know that?"

"He told Malcolm," Mélanie said.

Judith's gaze hardened. "That explains a lot."

CHAPTER 27

"Odd," Malcolm said. "You'd think at this point I'd be used to my family's surprising me."

"I'm so sorry, darling." Mélanie had told Malcolm as soon as they returned to Berkeley Square. Julien had gone back to Carfax House to see what Kitty had discovered. Mélanie and Malcolm, were talking in the library while the children played lottery tickets. "But when I heard from Julien, all I could think was that we should talk to Judith as soon as possible."

"Of course." Malcolm dug his shoulder into the paneling. They were both standing, too keyed to sit. "That was the obvious next step in the investigation."

"Yes, but she's your cousin."

Malcolm met her gaze, his own level and direct. "She's your cousin too."

Mélanie gripped her husband's hand. On her first visit to England, when they'd stayed with Frances and she'd first met Judith, she hadn't been able to imagine how she could ever feel like a proper part of Malcolm's family.

"I didn't see this," she said.

"I didn't see it either. Not remotely."

"Yes, but—" She thought of countless dinners, evenings. Holiday gatherings this past year. Times Judith and Roth had dined at her table, talked in the library where they stood now. She had an image of Roth turning the pages of Judith's music when she sat at the pianoforte one night. She hadn't thought anything of it. "I'm good at reading nuances between people. My work as a spy depended on it. My writing is built on it. It never occurred to me Roth and Judith could be more than casual friends who saw each other at our house. I wonder why."

"They hid it well."

"Yes, but I'm rather afraid a part of me just didn't consider it. Because I had Judith in one category and Jeremy in another."

"Jeremy's married."

"And estranged from his wife. And Judith is a widow." Mélanie bent to pet Berowne, who was winding against the scalloped hem of her gown. "But I'm afraid it didn't occur to me that Judith would fall in love with a Bow Street runner or that Roth would fall in love with a duke's granddaughter. After everything we've been through. After the marriage we've built from backgrounds that are almost diametrically opposed. After everything we've seen from our friends. Breakfasting with Sandy and Bet almost every morning. How could I be so blinded by prejudice?"

"Judith's always been—conventional."

"I imagine Benedict Smythe was as well, before Nerezza. Sandy always struck me as conventional before I stumbled into a room in St. Giles and found him with Bet. I'm afraid much of the time when it comes to Judith, we were so busy trying to make sure we kept things from her that it didn't occur to us she might be keeping things from us." A ripple of laughter came from the lottery tickets game. Mélanie smiled at the children. They could be so clear-sighted. "I don't like to think of myself as someone who generalizes and makes assumptions."

"Nor do I. Nor do any of our friends. And yet I'm quite sure we all missed it. I think even Fanny did. I doubt she'll be pleased with herself. Though perhaps more philosophical than we are."

Berowne had caught a claw in the barège silk. Mélanie disentangled him from the cherry-colored fabric and watched him scamper off to join the children. "To own the truth, I've thought a dozen times that Jeremy would be happier with a partner. I wondered about Lisette a few times—they've always seemed to get on." She turned and leaned her shoulders against the bookshelf behind her. "I'll confess I even wondered about Laura—before Raoul, obviously. Laura has a head for detection and common sense, and she and Jeremy always got on well. The thing is, I never thought of Judith." Mélanie stared at her husband in the cool wintry light streaming in from Berkeley Square. "Darling, I'm afraid I'm the most horrible snob."

"My love." Malcolm's eyes lit with laughter. "That's the last thing you are. I'd never have thought of Judith and Roth either. I probably wasn't giving Judith enough credit. I'm still inclined to think of her as my headstrong little cousin who liked to wear one of her mother's tiaras round the house and pretend she was a princess."

"And I still think of her as the fifteen-year-old I met when you first brought me to England."

"And Jeremy has a hard enough time being friends with people who live in Mayfair, let alone falling in love with one of them."

"But then, one doesn't always fall in love with convenient people."

"Very true. Or you'd never have fallen in love with me."

"It's not quite the same thing. That's spies and opposite sides."

Malcolm turned to face her directly. "Tell me as a committed republican you don't look askance at the way the beau monde live."

The liveried footman hurrying to the carriage door on their arrival at Fanny's that first visit to London. Their first arrival at Dunmykel, with the staff drawn up to greet them. It wasn't until that trip that she'd fully grasped the scale Malcolm lived on. "Sometimes. You do as well, sometimes. Other times I'm all too happy being caught up in that life."

"Or feel trapped in it."

"On occasion. But I've learned to play the game. Jeremy holds himself aloof. I can't see that changing even if he and Judith—"

"Married? Is that likely?"

"According to Judith, she's considering it. But it wasn't even possible until—"

"Allegra's murder. One of the arguments against Jeremy as a suspect was that he didn't seem concerned about the status of his marriage. This gives him a motive. And it gives Judith a motive as well."

Mélanie's gaze jerked to her husband's face. "I can't—"

"No, I can't imagine it, either. But we're going to have to consider possibilities outside our imagination. We didn't think of them as a couple before either." Malcolm shook his head. His eyes were serious but there was a bemused twist to his mouth.

"What?" Mélanie said.

"I'm imagining Jeremy and Judith at our dining table."

"Can you see it?"

"Almost. It's coming into focus. Can you?"

"I think so. I have to adjust my view. But then, that's rather the story of my life."

Malcolm smiled, then went serious. "Of course, that assumes that's what they both want. And that we get through this investigation without damaging it if they do." He took a step towards the door. "I need to talk to Jeremy."

"And say what?"

"And ask him for answers. Surely that's clear."

"Yes." Mélanie moved after him and gripped his arms. "But don't fall into the trap of thinking you need to defend Judith's honor."

"When have I ever fallen into any sort of trap like that? When have I ever used the word honor?"

"On occasion."

"Fair enough. Not in association with the women in my family. Judith is her own person. And an adult, much as I'm inclined to remember her as a child. It's not up to me to do anything but welcome into the family anyone she chooses to love. Believe me?"

"Actually, yes. I'm just not sure Jeremy will."

Malcolm grimaced. "We'll see."

"I was going to call on Allegra's stepsister, Cressida Caldwell," Mélanie said. "But in light of this—"

"No," Malcolm said. "We need to know what Miss Caldwell has to say about Allegra. And for better or worse, I think Roth's more likely to talk to me alone."

THE ASSEMBLED crowd in the White Lion were similar to last night's. Some of the regulars were undoubtedly the same, like the stout man with the ink-stained cuffs and the red-haired man scribbling in a notebook. The sip of stout Malcolm had taken had the same bite. Pungent and earthy. But so much had changed.

Malcolm stared at Roth across the expanse of ale-stained table. "You never thought of confiding in me?"

Roth curled his hands round his pint. "And say what?"

"That you're in love with my cousin." Malcolm enunciated each word with precision.

Roth took the words like the rifle fire they were. "And you'd have said?"

"That I wish you well."

Roth gave a rough laugh. "A Bow Street runner in love with a viscount's widow—"

"For god's sake, you can't think that would have mattered."

"Christ, Malcolm." Roth slammed his hand down on the table.

The sound reverberated between them, with echoes of moments when social class had separated them, from the Peninsula to Mayfair. "You write more eloquently than anyone I know—except possibly your wife—about injustice. You're friends with thieves and whores, and with your own valet, which is probably harder than any of the others. But some lines can't be crossed."

"What do you call Sandy and Bet?"

"Remarkable." Roth sat back in his chair. "I've wondered at what's developed between them and how it's seemed to work. How they've withstood challenges I thought would crush them. I was ready to try to come up with an alternative for Bet a score of times. When I first learned about her, when Trenor's parents started to interfere. I was sure there would be a moment when they'd break."

"So was I, truth to tell."

Roth's gaze settled on Malcolm's own. "Well then."

"But they didn't break. Sandy stood up for what was possible. Bet didn't let qualms get in her way."

"But this is different." Roth's voice was as hard as the flat of a blade. "Sandy could stand up and cross that line. It's amazing that he did, but easier for them than—Judith—"

"Careful, Roth. I think you just said a man can marry outside his social sphere and a woman can't. You'd best not repeat anything of the sort in front of Mel. Or Laura or Kitty or Cordy, or any of the women of our circle. Including Judith. Who has as much backbone as Sandy, I'd say."

"I'm talking about the realities of our world. Women like Judith don't—and I couldn't offer her marriage in any case."

"If you thought marriage was so impossible, that rather takes away the murder motive."

"What the hell—"

"Just being practical. But if you're talking about my own reaction or Mélanie's, Raoul and Laura lived together in our household for over a year before they could marry."

Roth dragged his pint closer. "Raoul's as dedicated a revolutionary as I know, but he was also born to aristocracy. I don't deny what they went through, but the rules are different."

"Since when are you one to talk about rules?"

"I may not like the rules. I may think they're idiocy. But I can't deny the world we live in." Roth tossed down a drink of stout.

"Are you sure you aren't the one who can't bear the thought of crossing class lines yourself?" Malcolm said.

Roth clunked his tankard down, spattering stout on the scarred wood. "What the devil—"

"You've never thought well of the beau monde. That's been clear from the first. You were quite forbearing when you decided you'd put up with Mélanie and me."

"Malcolm—"

"I imagine it was a shock to find yourself in love with an aristocrat."

Roth slumped against the high back of the bench and folded his arms. "Don't talk rot."

Malcolm took a drink of stout. "Tell me there's no truth to it."

Roth grimaced and stared at the splashed stout on the scarred table. "Even if there is, what matters now is keeping Judith out of this."

"My dear fellow. Her lover's wife was murdered. There's no keeping her out of it."

Roth's gaze shot to Malcolm's face. "No one has to know—"

"You know better than that. And you told me to pursue every lead."

Roth stared at him, face washed white. "My god. You can't suspect Judith?"

Malcolm kept his gaze steady, though inchoate images cut his brain. Remembrance of betrayals past. "I don't have enough evidence to do so. But I have to consider everyone. Tell me you wouldn't in the same circumstances."

Roth wiped a trail of stout off the side of the tankard.

"Mélanie suspected me," Malcolm said in a quiet voice. "And we survived."

Roth's gaze fastened on the table, though he seemed to be seeing into a future hell. "Judith and I—"

"I have no idea what Judith wants, but given her family and fortune she could marry a Bow Street runner with ease and be damned to what society thinks."

"I can't marry her. I'm about to be arrested."

"That is the crux of the problem."

Roth stared at him, as he had in the early days of their acquaintance, when he'd been taking Malcolm's measure. "This has to make you wonder."

"About what?"

"About me. I lied to you about this. I managed to keep it from you—"

"—yes, that's impressive—"

"—and so you have to be wondering what else I might be hiding."

Malcolm met his friend's gaze. His wife. His father. His sister. His former mistress. One of his best friends. He should be used to surprises. "Doesn't one always wonder in an investigation? There have to have been moments you've wondered all sorts of things about us."

"Quite," Roth said.

The door of the pub opened. It had been opening and closing the entire time they were talking, but Malcolm was aware of footsteps moving towards them. He saw a woman in a pale pink pelisse approaching, went instinctively still, and then froze as he recognized his cousin.

"Oh good," Judith said, stopping beside the table. "It's probably as well I've found you together."

Roth half-pushed himself out of his chair, then went still. He knew the dangers of a public scene. "Judith, for god's sake, you can't be here."

"Why not?" Judith slid onto the bench beside Roth. "Mélanie goes to pubs. This has to be less scandalous than my going to your lodgings. Or your coming to see me. You must admit we need to talk."

"At the moment we need to stay as far away from each other as possible."

"Because I'm a danger to you? I suppose it might seem that way—"

"Judith, I'm trying to protect you."

"I think you should worry about protecting yourself, Jeremy. I'm trying to protect you. I think Malcolm is too." Judith met Malcolm's gaze. "Mélanie and Julien came to see me. So I assume by now you know everything and Jeremy knows you do."

Malcolm looked at the cousin he used to carry round on his shoulders. "If by everything you mean your relationship, then yes. As I was telling him, I wish you both well."

"That's good to hear," Judith said. "But at the moment I'm more worried about Jeremy. Is he about to be arrested?"

"I don't believe imminently. I'm not in Bow Street's confidence in this case."

Judith inclined her head. Pink silk roses drooped over the crown of her bonnet. "I understand Jeremy and I are both suspects, but I hope you'll tell us what you can."

"Judith!" Roth said.

"Jeremy, it's quite obvious. I'll own I didn't see it at first—I was contending with a lot. But though Mélanie and Julien didn't say it outright, I can quite see it. Allegra was a bar to our being together. She came to see me. Did Malcolm tell you that?"

"I hadn't got the details yet."

Judith reached for his hand. "I'm sorry. For you and the boys. This is beastly. I wanted to come to you as soon as I got your message last night, but I was afraid it would only make things worse."

Roth held himself still but notably didn't attempt to withdraw his hand from Judith's clasp.

Judith looked at Malcolm. "Can you give us a moment to talk? If Jeremy feels better having a chaperon, perhaps you could stay nearby?"

"Of course."

"Rannoch—" Roth said.

"I know when two people need to talk," Malcolm said, getting to his feet. "I've had enough private conversations with my wife during balls."

CHAPTER 28

Judith looked at her lover. Who was at least consenting for her to hold his hand, but didn't look as though he'd consent to much else. "How are the boys?"

"Shocked." Jeremy's gaze was focused inwards on a place she couldn't touch. "But Allegra was a blurry memory to them. It's a shock that's she's gone, and horrifying, but they can't precisely miss her when she's been gone so long. Still, it means something that they'll never see her again."

"To you too." Judith saw the memories cluster in his gaze. Allegra's return and death had pulled him into a part of his life that went back to before she'd known him. He'd be living there for a long time. What they shared, however strong it felt, was so recent. He and Allegra had lived together for seven years. And apparently he'd known her far longer.

"I learned she was your childhood friend as well as your wife," Judith said.

"Yes." Jeremy passed a hand over his face. "We grew up together. I supposed I didn't—I'd hardly have talked to you about her."

"It's all right. I didn't talk to you about Bobby. At least, not that much."

"Judith—" Jeremy reached for his tankard, then set it down. "I've done you a great wrong. I should never have pulled you into this."

"You didn't pull me into anything. At least, not anything I didn't want to be in. And as I recall, I did most of the pulling." Judith studied his face. For a few sweet weeks, when they were together they'd seemed to be in their own world. Now he seemed to have moved miles apart from her, for all they were pressed close together on the bench. "Are you saying you regret it?"

"Regret it?" Jeremy's voice rose, then he brought it under control. "How could I? But I regret what I've tangled you in. It was so obvious from the first there was no way for this to end happily."

He might as well have splashed the contents of his tankard in her face. "Why are you so focused on its having to end at all?"

"Because there's no way for it to continue." His gaze had hardened, like the thick glass of the pub windows when the lamps were extinguished.

Memories shot through her. Jeremy's smile. Jeremy's laugh. Jeremy touching her, taking her hand, his eyes laughing into her own across the pillow. Moments that were indelibly carved into her memory. Julien's words at the end of his visit with Mélanie echoed in her head. "Julien said Allegra always believed her father wasn't her mother's first husband."

"What?" Jeremy asked. "Oh, yes. Especially when we were children. I have no idea if it was true. But I think she liked that it gave her consequence."

"That's what Julien said." Judith drew back a little on the bench. "You've probably heard that I was the same. I mean, in my case, I do think it's true. Cedric's the only one of us Papa actually fathered in the biological sense. But I used to like to make up stories about who my father really was."

"Understandable." Jeremy's gaze had softened slightly, but she could tell he was confused at where she was headed.

Judith drew back a fraction more and straightened her shoulders. She could feel the pull on the seams of her pelisse. "You think I'm like her, don't you? Looking for distraction, thinking myself special because my father is someone mysterious. And you think like her I'll get restless and leave you the moment we settle into domesticity."

The glass in Jeremy's gaze cracked to reveal a roiling tumult. "Judith—"

"Can you tell me you aren't afraid of that?"

"Afraid I'll trap you in a life where you aren't happy? My darling, of course I am. You're far too young—"

"I'm older than Allegra was when you married her. I'm not madly seeking sensation. I thought Bobby and I would settle into a comfortable marriage, and then it turned out marriage wasn't as comfortable as either of us expected. But that was Bobby and me, not marriage in general. I only met Allegra once, but that was enough for me to tell that I'm not like her at all. And what I learned about her from Julien and Mélanie just confirmed it. But I don't think you realize how different we are." Judith regarded Roth, the intense eyes, the mouth that could kiss so tenderly. The gaze she had thought saw her so clearly, in a way it seemed Bobby never had. "In fact, I'm starting to wonder if you fell in love with me because I seemed so like Allegra. I can imagine that. It must have been horribly painful to lose her. I mean, lose her the first time. When she ran off."

"Judith—"

"But I'm not a replacement. If that's what you wanted, you don't know me."

"Judith." Jeremy lunged forwards on the bench and gripped her shoulders. "My god, is that what you think? Can you believe I don't see you? That I don't recognize the amazing woman you are?"

His face was inches away. It would be so easy to lean in and pull him into a kiss, damn anyone in the pub who might be watching. Her back was to them and she'd long stopped caring for her reputation. All she'd have to do was edge forwards a fraction of an inch and the conversation would be ended. But the questions wouldn't go away. "What am I supposed to think, from the way you were just talking? You don't treat me like a woman. You treat me like a child who needs to be protected."

"Because I don't want to drag you into a life you'll regret. Because I know I have nothing to offer you."

"If you think you have nothing to offer me, Jeremy, you don't know me at all."

Jeremy released her shoulders and drew back on the bench. "Judith, you know the life I live. Or rather, you know all too little about it. I could not in honor—"

"For heaven's sake, Jeremy, you don't even believe in honor. Any more than Mélanie does."

"I don't believe in high-flown conceptions of honor that tend to be used to support aristocratic positions. I do know that I could not in good conscience drag the woman I love into a life away from the world she'd grown up in."

"I'm relieved you acknowledge I'm a woman." And that he'd said he loved her. Those words sang through her. "But what if the woman you loved didn't care?"

"My sweet, you don't really understand the life we're talking about. You've scarcely been exposed to it."

It was true she'd never been to his lodgings. He'd never wanted to meet there for fear of scandal, and she could hardly expose his sons to their affair. But it was not as though she'd never called on anyone outside Mayfair. "I understand it's too soon to think of the future. You need time to mourn Allegra. The boys need time. I'm probably hopelessly in the way right now."

"I didn't say—"

"But when it comes to our future, when we're ready to have a future, you're hardly poor, Jeremy. Besides, I have enough money for both of us. And it's not as though the people who matter to me would cast us off. I don't care about Almack's—which even you must realize doesn't matter much after one marries, and even before that doesn't matter that much to some of us. I never went often because Mama couldn't abide it. I don't care about being invited to the Esterhazys' or the Lievens' or Sally Jersey's or even Emily Cowper's, though I can't imagine Emily wouldn't invite us. She'd be delighted to have you to show off."

Jeremy looked away. "Don't."

"I don't know that it's any worse than a woman's being shown off, but I'd never ask you to do it. You have to know that."

"My love." Jeremy dragged his gaze back to her face. She had the horrible sense he was looking at a memory. "It's difficult to know what either of us would think or feel in five years. Let alone ten or twenty. I couldn't bear the thought of your looking round and realizing you were trapped."

"You don't trust me."

"It's not a question of trust."

"You do think I'm like Allegra." She cast a glance across the pub. Malcolm was nursing a tankard, pretending to be focused on a dart game underway, though she had no doubt he was aware of them. She couldn't delay much longer. But really, there wasn't much more left that could be said. "If you want to replay your life with Allegra, Jeremy, you'll have to find another woman to do it with. Because I'm not her. If you're in love with her, you're in love with a memory. You aren't in love with me. You don't know me at all."

He stared at her. They were no longer touching, but she felt the wrench of loss. "You can't believe that, Judith."

"What else am I supposed to believe?"

Cressida Caldwell lived in a neat house in Jermyn Street, small but exquisitely proportioned, from the blue-painted window moldings and Ionic portico to the shiny red front door and the airy entrance hall, filled with yellow and peach roses that had to be hothouse at this season but still managed to fill the air with a fragrant scent.

A footman took Mélanie's card with well-masked surprise and conducted her up a winding staircase with a polished walnut rail to a sitting room done up in shades of yellow and red. Vibrant but not garish. His mistress, he said, would be with her shortly.

About five minutes later, judging by the gilt clock on the tasteful white mantel, the door opened and Cressida Caldwell stepped into the room. She may have been tending to her toilette before receiving her guest, but Mélanie suspected Cressida Caldwell liked to make entrances. It was a trick she'd employed herself on more than one occasion.

Cressida Caldwell was tall and slender with dark hair arranged in a Grecian knot and artful ringlets that spilled over her ears and down her neck, tawny skin, and arresting green eyes. She wore a wrapping gown of ruby merino over a muslin slip that was cut lower than most afternoon gowns without quite being scandalous.

"My apologies for keeping you waiting, Mrs. Rannoch." Miss Caldwell closed the door behind her with a graceful turn of her wrist. "I was with my son, and it took a bit to extricate myself from a mock battle. Toy soldiers against wooden animals."

So much for calculated entrances. Or at least wholly calculated entrances. "Who won?" Mélanie asked.

"The animals. I think he prefers them to soldiers."

"My son does as well," Mélanie said. "He's seven."

Cressida Caldwell hesitated a moment. She did not appear to be a woman who shared personal information easily. "Mine is five." She studied Mélanie with an appraising gaze. "I'd heard you were unusual, Mrs. Rannoch, but I didn't grasp your daring. Ladies from Mayfair don't call on me."

"You're a lady from Mayfair yourself."

"I live in Mayfair. But I'm not a lady." Miss Caldwell waved a hand towards a sofa and settee set at right angles and covered in a yellow and red striped fabric that echoed the colors in the floral wallpaper.

"I write plays," Mélanie said, moving to the settee. "I appear on stage myself on occasion." Not to mention that she'd once been employed in a brothel. "My husband's father—who wasn't his mother's husband—is divorced and lives with us along with his second wife. Which limits the places we're invited as a household. To put it mildly. If I gave a damn about social position, I'd live my life very differently. Fortunately, my husband doesn't care about it either."

Miss Caldwell smiled as she sat on the sofa at right angles to Mélanie. "I very much enjoyed your first play and I look forward to the next. And I was fortunate to be in the audience at the Tavistock the night you appeared in the Christmas pantomime. You are magnetic on stage. But you can't deny the gulf between us."

"That's a matter of perception." And of how well one could conceal one's past.

"We live in a world governed by perception."

The footman returned with a tea tray—silver with Wedgwood cups, milk and lemon, a plate of biscuits. The refreshments of any call in a Mayfair drawing room. When the footman had withdrawn, Cressida Caldwell reached for the teapot and poured two cups of tea with a steady hand. "Jeremy and Harriet both said you or your husband would come to talk to me. I was sure it would be your husband, because in calling here he'd only risk the sort of mild scandal that gives a gentleman a bit of caché. But I see now that I misjudged. You both thought it would be easier for me to talk to you? Or that you could get more information out of me? Or perhaps you didn't want to expose your husband to my charms. Though looking at you, I doubt that last. A woman like you doesn't need to worry. In any case, whatever the explanation, you are far more formidable than I anticipated. And perhaps kinder." She handed a cup of tea to Mélanie.

"I'm sorry about your stepsister," Mélanie said.

"Thank you." Cressida Caldwell settled back in the corner of the sofa and took a careful sip of tea. "I've been remembering her as a girl ever since I heard. I wouldn't say Allegra and I were ever close. There was always too much rivalry. Though we were allies at times, against our parents. A common enemy can make for a united front."

"How old were you when your parents married?"

"Allegra was five. I was six. I was used to being an only child. My mother died when I was born. My father met her when he went to India to write about the evils of colonialism. Which apparently didn't extend to his thinking he should marry my Indian mother when he got her with child. Still, he looked after me and brought me back to England with him, for which I should be grateful. Allegra always held it over me that she was legitimate. While at the same time throwing out hints that her actual father wasn't her mother's late husband at all but some mysterious and powerful person, which somehow made her special. Allegra saw herself as the princess. On good days I was her lady-in-waiting. More often I was a pesky peasant. The one thing we had in common was we were both determined to break out of our world."

Miss Caldwell leaned forwards, added some milk to her tea, stirred it thoughtfully. "When I tell people who my father was, they think I must have grown up with so much freedom as the daughter of a Radical freethinker. But it was just as stultifying as the life of most girls. I grant we were better educated. But we were still expected to go into what seemed like dull respectability. To marry someone—albeit another freethinker—and manage a household without quite enough to pay the butcher or the baker— and raise a passel of children. Allegra escaped first. She had her voice. She ran off to be a singer. A few months later I simply ran off with a viscount's younger son. A year later I was a duke's mistress. And Allegra seemed to have sunk into the domesticity we'd both been trying so hard to avoid."

Mélanie took a sip of tea. It was fragrant with spices. Cardamom, ginger, cinnamon, a hint of nutmeg. The sort of tea Laura, who had grown up in India, liked to brew. "You must have known Jeremy Roth growing up."

"Oh yes. I always liked him. And his parents, who were a good deal less restrictive than ours were. I'd hang round the bookshop and browse through books and pamphlets I'd never be allowed to read at home. Jeremy's father gave me freedom to explore. Jeremy was as eager to escape as we were. He'd often pull some of the most intriguing books for me to read." She settled her cup in its saucer. "I felt sorry for Jeremy when I heard he was marrying Allegra."

"Why sorry?"

"Because I had a sense of what Allegra had always meant to him. More, I think, than he'd admit to anyone, including perhaps himself. I remember the way he used to look at her while she was playing the piano or pouring tea. Or sometimes when he was dancing with her himself. Like she was something rare and precious and forever out of reach. And even if I was exaggerating his feelings, I knew Jeremy would take marriage seriously. I couldn't imagine Allegra taking any relationship seriously. At least, not one that offered her so few advantages."

Mélanie set her cup on its saucer. The light from the window shot through the translucent porcelain, warming the brick-red flowers painted on the cup. "There can be advantages in a relationship that offers emotional support. I didn't realize that myself when I married." An admission she wasn't used to making, but she was less reticent these days, and something about Cressida Caldwell invited plain speaking.

An odd look crossed Cressida Caldwell's face. As though she'd been about to laugh off Mélanie's comment with a brittle quip, and then caught herself up short. Almost against her will. "If you've found that, you're a fortunate woman, Mrs. Rannoch. But I can imagine a woman finding such a haven in Jeremy Roth. Allegra wasn't the sort to care for intangible advantages though. And I don't think she found fulfillment in motherhood. I couldn't imagine finding fulfillment in motherhood myself at the time. It makes a bit more sense to me since my son was born. But even though I can't imagine my life without him, it doesn't change the other things I want from life."

"No," Mélanie agreed. "And I wouldn't want it to, for myself or for my children." She took another sip of tea. "So you weren't surprised when your stepsister disappeared?"

Miss Caldwell's exquisitely arched brows drew together. "I wasn't surprised the marriage broke up. I didn't see them as a family often, but Allegra was obviously restless. She wanted to do great things with her life. I don't know that she wanted to sing so much as that she wanted the notoriety being a singer gave her. She came to see me, once, when Vincent—my son—was born. I was basking in the glow of having a small human who needed me so much, and even though I felt a bit pulled to pieces—literally and figuratively—she said she was surprised to see me so content. She said she'd been in low spirits after both the boys were born. And that the births were so close together it was only lately she'd begun to feel like herself again."

"That happens to some women after they give birth." Isobel, Hubert's daughter who was married to Malcolm's Oxford friend Oliver, had talked about being given to the blue devils for months after all three of her children were born. "Though for many it passes, thankfully. I was fortunate not to go through it." As she'd been fortunate to have two easy childbirths. Which perhaps balanced some of the other challenges of her life and marriage.

"I think it did for Allegra, but she was already restless. At one point she said she was sorry for her sons because they didn't have more stability. So I wasn't surprised she left Jeremy, and not even that surprised that she left the boys. She needed protection when she married Jeremy, but once she'd gathered up her reserves she was going to go looking for adventure again. I was a bit surprised she seemed to disappear completely though."

"You didn't have any idea of where she'd gone?"

Miss Caldwell hesitated and reached for the teapot. Mélanie saw the calculation in the other woman's eyes as she refilled the cups. The risk of sharing information set against the possibility that the information would come out anyway. And perhaps the idea that shared information might help find the person who had killed her stepsister. "Jeremy came to see me once, not long after Allegra disappeared, to ask me if I'd heard anything from her. Which I hadn't, then. But later I got a letter. Saying she was safe and not to hate her, that it was better this way for Jeremy and the children. That she finally knew what she was meant to do with her life."

"Now you know where she went, do you think it was because she was working for Argentine independence?"

"I'm not sure." Miss Caldwell turned her cup on its saucer. "I don't think she was the type to lose herself in a cause. Though she might have fancied herself as the heroine of a revolution." Miss Caldwell took a sip of tea. "I sent word to Jeremy when I heard from her. He called and I showed him the letter. He said he'd heard from Allegra as well, with similar information. That seemed to end it, and there was little more we could do. He sounded resigned. But he looked—unsettled. More than that. Haunted. As though Allegra wasn't as much in the past as he'd like her to be. And perhaps never would be."

"You and Jeremy have stayed good friends."

"In a way." Miss Caldwell leaned her elbow on the sofa arm and rested her chin in her hand, easy elegance in every line of her body. "I've always liked him, and I think he likes me. Though he completely disapproves of the way I live. Oh, not on moral grounds. I could be a whore in Seven Dials and while he might worry about me, he wouldn't disapprove in the least. But Jeremy's never had any sympathy for the aristocracy. And while I'm hardly an aristocrat, I live off aristocrats. And I live a life of luxury that nine-tenths of the population—at least nine-tenths, as Jeremy would say—couldn't imagine. I can see him toting up the value of the furniture and wall-hangings whenever he comes into my house and imagining how many mouths that could feed."

"Yes," Mélanie said. "He does the same when he comes to our house in Berkeley Square. But he has accepted us. At least to a degree."

"To a very great degree. He talks of you as friends. Some of the best friends he has. Though he also said this investigation might strain your friendship to the breaking point."

"Do you know what he meant by that?"

Cressida Caldwell chewed on her lower lip. "That it would be hard for him to face the truth of what you uncovered. Or hard for you to face it?"

Mélanie's throat tightened. But Cressida Caldwell was a window onto a part of Jeremy they didn't know. "Do you think—"

Miss Caldwell's gaze locked on Mélanie's own. Hard as emeralds and as inscrutable as the sea. "That Jeremy could have killed Allegra? If anyone could drive him to murder, I imagine Allegra could. Because he loved her, and love can so easily turn to anger. And because Allegra was the sort who could drive just about anyone over the edge. But can I imagine the Jeremy I grew up with murdering anyone, let alone someone he loved? No. Take that as you will. I'm not an investigator."

"But you do need to be able to judge people."

"Because gentlemen can turn violent in the bedchamber? Or elsewhere? Very true. But then so can husbands. And a wife doesn't have the option of throwing her husband out and telling the servants to bolt the doors."

"No." Mélanie could hear Kitty saying in a light teasing voice that belied the truth that she wouldn't have married again without trusting the man in question completely. Mélanie herself hadn't thought nearly enough about Malcolm before she married him. Save that she'd been sure she could escape if she needed to. And perhaps underneath that she'd understood the person he was.

Cressida Caldwell turned her teacup in her hand. "I don't allow a gentleman into my home unless I feel I can trust him. Especially now that I have a child. And I certainly don't enter a lasting liaison unless I feel quite certain. It would never occur to me to become romantically entangled with Jeremy Roth, for any number of reasons. Not the least of which is that he rather seems like a brother. But when it comes to trust, he certainly passes my test."

Mélanie held Cressida Caldwell's gaze. "That's saying a lot."

"Assuming you trust me."

"When it comes to those instincts, I do."

"But one can never be sure."

"No."

"It's a finely tuned thing," Cressida Caldwell said. "Taking a man to one's bed. Engaging him as a protector. You don't seem as shocked as I'd have expected, so I'm speaking freely. More freely than I perhaps should. I gave up on marriage as an option before I was even old enough to truly consider it. I wanted a more adventurous life. I wanted to live here." She glanced round her sitting room. "Not in rooms in Somers Town that fit into two of the smaller rooms in this house. I've found I enjoy being a mother, but I didn't want to spend my days hanging out the washing and trying to make a mutton chop last a week. And even without the trappings of my life, I can't imagine giving a man that sort of control. Far easier to treat love as a game."

Mélanie laughed. "What do you think love is on the Marriage Mart? At least for many in the beau monde. And even for those for whom it starts as something genuine, it doesn't always last." Judith's face this afternoon danced before her eyes.

"You're fortunate then."

"What makes you say so?"

"I've seen you and your husband. In your box at the Tavistock and Drury Lane and Covent Garden. Aside from the fact that you actually watch the play or opera, what's noticeable is the way you look at each other. Particularly the way your husband looks at you."

"Many people think I married him for his money and we have a passionless marriage."

"Many people are fools. In my profession one learns to recognize real passion. And love. Though I wouldn't have admitted love existed until..."

She let the words trail off, half covered by a rough breath. "Until?" Mélanie said.

Cressida Caldwell stared into her teacup for a moment, her gaze clouded. Then she gave a rueful smile. "It's nothing. I let myself be impetuous recently. With an ardent gentleman who has nothing to offer except the exuberance of his feelings and a good leg and a good—many other things. Not to mention a quick wit.

He got a friend to bring him to one of my parties. Normally I'd have sent his sort packing, for his own sake as much as mine. But he was persistent. And I was in need of diversion. Or perhaps of something deeper. I have little patience with Jeremy when he says this life is empty—I mean, one can say it is, but so is life in a great many places—but I can't deny there are moments I long for something that isn't about calculation and transaction and a careful exchange of passion for security. In any case, I gave way against all my instincts, and I've let it go on far too long." She glanced at a vase of violets on an escritoire in the corner. The wrong color for the room and beginning to wilt, but still vibrant. Not from a hothouse. "He can't keep me, and in his life he's going to need a proper wife at some point. For the sake of my pride, I really should extricate myself before he decides he has to extricate himself first."

Mélanie watched Cressida Caldwell. Her eyes had warmed in a way they hadn't for the entire interview. "Perhaps you don't wish to extricate yourself."

Miss Caldwell shook her head. "I may have allowed myself to get a bit foolish. Everyone needs that at some point in their life, and I was too focused on surviving as a teenager to lose my heart. I never was a Juliet. But I'm not entirely lost to sense. I know what we can and can't be to each other. And a failed love doesn't mean a star-crossed ending. After all, every love affair ends at some point. I need to find a graceful way out of it. Love has a damnable way of interfering with one's freedom."

"Do you feel as though you aren't free with him?" Mélanie asked.

"No." Cressida Caldwell paused a moment, as though surprised. It looked like much the same surprise Mélanie recalled feeling on the beach at Dunmykel Bay when she'd realized she loved Malcolm. "He's rather remarkably good at not making demands. He's less jealous than some protectors who should know the game better. But my feelings for him interfere with my freedom. And in the end, I have to be able to make my own choices. Or what has become of my life?"

"I can understand wanting freedom."

Cressida Caldwell lifted a brow. "Even happily married?"

"There are different types of freedom. My husband doesn't make demands." Emotionally or otherwise. "But it's taken a while to work out what I needed to do to be myself."

"That you can even talk about being yourself is rather remarkable, to my mind." Cressida Caldwell watched her for a moment. "I'll own a part of me envies you, Mrs. Rannoch. You appear to have found a remarkable balance with your husband. And to have given up less of your freedom than most. But I can't imagine giving up enough of myself to indulge in a prolonged love affair without material advantage. Even without the practical exigencies that go against us."

"And your stepsister? Did she feel the same?"

Miss Caldwell gave a brief laugh. "Allegra wasn't ever the sort to lose herself in love. Even before we both ran off, her flirtations were about what the gentleman in question could do for her. If she found herself in the Argentine, I don't think it was for love of Marco Esquivel. Poor devil."

"And yet you seem to have fallen in love, perhaps for the first time, after many years," Mélanie said.

Cressida Caldwell froze for a moment, then laughed. "Is that what I've done? Yes, I suppose I have. I just admitted to it, which was not a wise thing to do in many ways. So perhaps I'm wrong about Allegra. Perhaps she did at last fall deeply in love. But if she was capable of caring on that level, I don't think she'd have—left her children."

"A point. But love can take different forms. Men leave their children. For years. To go to war. To go to another country. Marco Esquivel did."

"So he did. I don't think the better of him for it. I simply find it hard to imagine a person's being able to love outside themself and

—" Miss Caldwell shook her head. "I probably sound the most dreadful sister. But the truth is, I've grieved for Allegra since Jeremy broke the news, more than I'd have thought possible. She was my past. She shared more of it than my younger half-brothers and sisters, because we were both there from the start. And so many of our struggles were the same. I don't know that Allegra loved me, because I'm still not sure she was capable of loving anyone. But I loved her."

Mélanie added more milk to her tea and stirred it carefully. "I had a sister." It was not something she normally admitted to. It was not part of her cover story. It could get her into trouble. But the words came to her lips and seemed important to say. "I lost her a very long time ago. When we were quite young. But I'll never forget her. She'll always be a part of me."

Miss Caldwell met Mélanie's gaze. Her eyes showed an understanding that was dangerously acute. "I'm sorry. And I imagine it will be the same for me."

"When did you last see your stepsister?"

Cressida Caldwell's fingers froze on the handle of her cup. Again, calculation flashed in her eyes, the weighing of risk and benefit, danger and perhaps duty. "All my instincts scream to deny it. But you'd undoubtedly learn the truth in any case. You're obviously very good at what you do. And I do want to learn what happened to Allegra. I owe her that much." Miss Caldwell set her teacup down with care, though drops of tea sloshed into the saucer. "Allegra came to see me three days ago. It was the first time I'd seen her since she left England."

The visit was not wholly a surprise, though the admission was. Often when someone admitted something so readily in an investigation, it was because they were concealing something greater. "What did she want?"

Miss Caldwell flashed a quick smile. "You're very astute, Mrs. Rannoch. Of course, if Allegra called on me it was because she wanted something, not out of sisterly feeling. It was even like that when we both lived in London. Though in fact, all she wanted was my opinion on how Jeremy would react if she reached out to him. I said it would depend on what she wanted from him."

"Did she tell you what that was?"

Miss Caldwell took a sip of tea. "No."

For the first time in the interview, Mélanie was quite sure Cressida Caldwell had lied to her.

CHAPTER 30

*J*udith looked at her mother across a tea table laden with Frances Davenport's Spode china. Judith had come to London first thing this morning in response to the message she'd received from Jeremy late the previous night. Even before Mélanie and Julien had confronted her with the truth, she'd known she wanted to be close to the unfolding events. And, though she wasn't going to admit it to Frances and was barely prepared to admit it to herself, she wanted her mother. But she hadn't told Frances the reasons for her visit until she'd returned from her confrontation with Jeremy at the pub.

"Are you shocked, Mama?" she asked.

Frances set down the teapot with a delicate flick of her wrist and handed Judith a cup of tea. Mechlin lace fell back from her wrist and her sapphire ring flashed in the lamplight. "Of course not. I hope you didn't go into this to shock me."

"Don't be silly." Judith accepted the tea and took a sip. Mama's signature blend, specially ordered from Fortnum's. "I'm not a child."

"My darling. One's children are always children. You'll learn that when Serena is older."

Judith set down her tea and squeezed a wedge of lemon into it. She normally took it with milk, but she wanted something different today. Something with more bite. "I never felt any particular need to shock you. I wouldn't have known how to begin to do so. That's not what—this isn't about that. I wasn't looking for—I wasn't looking for anything. I suppose I was lonely. Bobby was gone and everyone else seemed to share secrets, even if they were very busy not talking about them. Sometimes the things not being said at family gatherings echoed more loudly than the things being said. Especially last autumn. I said something like that to Jeremy. He'd come across the room because Serena was upset, and we started talking once he jollied her out of it. He said he never knew half the Rannochs' secrets either. I said, 'Oh, but you're one of them.' And he said, 'Not really, not even when I'm in the midst of an investigation.' I must have frowned, because he said there were secrets, and secrets, and it wouldn't be safe for Malcolm and Mélanie to share their most intimate secrets with him. I said I was simply on the outskirts of everything, and he said it was all a matter of perspective. Then we got to talking, and by the end of the party it felt as though we'd known each other for years. I don't think anyone else even noticed us talking, or noticed that we talked at the next family party. Really every-thing between us started in full view of everyone. But I don't think anyone was paying us enough heed to think it remarkable."

Frances set down her cup with the faintest clatter. Mama was free-spirited, but she did everything with remarkable control. That seemed to characterize how her generation had carried on their love affairs. "My darling. Are you saying I've ignored you?"

"No." Judith picked up a silver spoon and stirred her tea. A lemon seed floated to the top. "Perhaps a bit. I know I'm grown up—"

"But I've been busy with the babies and Archie, and I don't think one is ever grown up enough not to need one's parents. At least not if one has a decent relationship with them."

Judith spooned the lemon seed onto the saucer. "Part of me was relieved not to have interference. And part of me was quite proud of my subterfuge."

"You should be."

Judith looked up and met her mother's gaze. "But I suppose—you have to admit with everything going on—the investigations and Malcolm and Mélanie's leaving for Italy, and Gelly's disappearing and then popping in and out mysteriously, and your marrying Archie—no one's taken a lot of interest in me. Which I should understand."

Frances settled back among the violet and lavender sofa cushions, fingers curled round her teacup. "No one should be asked to be comfortable with their family's not showing a lot of interest in them. I think the truth is everyone was relieved you seemed so happy."

"You mean because I had a 'normal' life?"

"I'm not sure what 'normal' is. And I'm not sure I'd like it if I saw it. But by the standards of this family, you certainly appeared to be navigating life more easily than many."

"I thought I had what I wanted with Bobby. But I don't think I did. Not really. We were both restless. I'm not saying—I wouldn't have betrayed him. I don't think I would have. That is, I'm not judging—"

"Sweetheart, you have every right to judge me." Frances took a sip of tea. "I try not to have a great many expectations for my children, but I'm quite pleased to be making the mistakes I made."

Judith choked on her tea. "I never thought I could measure up to you, you know."

"In what? I've hardly made a success of much. Except I hope my marriage to Archie, and my parenting in more recent years."

"You live life on your own terms. You don't care what people think of you. And you can own any room you walk into."

"I spent far too much of my life caring what people thought of me. And do you want to own any room you walk into? You certainly could."

"No. Not really. I enjoyed being called an Incomparable, but it gets a bit dull. It all got a bit dull."

"Including your marriage."

Judith squeezed another wedge of lemon into her tea. "Yes."

"And what you found with Jeremy Roth—is that more real?"

"I thought it was." Judith gulped down a swallow of tea and grimaced as the lemon bit her in the throat. "But now I'm not sure of anything. I think Jeremy may still be in love with Allegra—his wife. I think he may have seen me as like her. Which I'm not at all. I can't imagine being so careless and heedless of people's feelings. But I'm not sure what was between us was real at all. And yet—I can't bear what's happening to him."

Frances set down her teacup and leaned across the sofa table to grip Judith's hand. "Jeremy Roth always struck me as having a very keen understanding. I may have been woefully blind to what was happening between the two of you, but I can't imagine his falling in love with a woman and not seeing her for who she was."

"Oh, Mama. Aren't you always saying love makes fools of us all? Can you say you've seen all your lovers clearly?"

"Oh, not in the least. Well, many of them, but I made severe mistakes with a few. But I do think I saw the two I actually fell in love with quite clearly. For good or ill."

Judith studied her mother. One of the two, she was quite sure, was her mother's current husband, Archie Davenport. She wasn't sure about the other. Save that she was quite sure it wasn't her putative father, George Dacre-Hammond.

Frances's smile said she saw a great deal. "I'd also say, from what I've observed, Jeremy Roth sees people rather more clearly than I do."

Judith squeezed her mother's hand, then picked up her cup and spoon and stirred her tea. She felt a desperate need to be doing something with her hands. "What would you think if Jeremy and I—" She couldn't quite say it.

"If you married?" Frances said in a serene voice. "I try not to have expectations for my children, as I said, but I can't imagine I'd be anything but delighted to see my daughter marry the man she loved."

"That's what I thought. But Jeremy doesn't see it that way. He's a dreadful snob in some ways."

Frances smiled. "There are different types of snobbery. I can see Jeremy's being too proud to live on his wife."

"But that's silly. He believes fortune isn't distributed equally enough. We'd only be helping along the redistribution."

"Oh, my darling. It's one thing to believe in principles. It's another to sacrifice one's pride."

"Why should a man's pride matter more than a woman's? Women marry men with a greater fortune all the time."

"But the world looks differently at men who do. And it seems even Jeremy Roth isn't deaf to the world's opinion."

"It's rot." Judith set down her cup and folded her arms across her chest. "I'll have to work out a way to persuade him of that." She chewed on her nail. "Which I suppose means I haven't given up on us quite yet."

Frances reached for her cup with a faint smile. "That's the most promising thing I've heard all afternoon."

"Do you mean you want—"

"Dearest, I want you to be happy." Frances took a sip of tea. "That's all I've ever wanted for you."

"Malcolm." Sandy Trenor's voice stopped Malcolm as he started up the stairs to dress for dinner.

Malcolm turned back to look at his secretary. Sandy was standing a few steps from the open study door, a sheaf of papers in one hand, a pencil in the other. "Do you need me to sign something?"

"What? Oh no. I was just wondering if there was anything—that is, I know you're in the midst of the investigation and there's not much I can do. Not an investigator. But I've always liked Roth. Must be beastly for him. God, that doesn't say it by half, does it?"

"It makes your point." Malcolm crossed the hall towards Sandy. "And yes, it's hell. You're doing a lot by keeping up with the parliamentary issues so I can focus on the investigation."

"Glad to do it."

"Sandy," Malcolm said, as Sandy turned back towards the study.

"Yes?" Sandy's gaze was bright with the urge to be of help.

Malcolm searched for the right words. "I know it hasn't been easy. What you and Bet have been through. You're to be commended."

"Oh. Thank you. Yes, it's been a bit of a muddle. But I can't imagine doing any differently. I mean, I love her, so obviously I'm going to do whatever it takes for us to be together. That's what one does when one's in love."

"Quite so. Or one should."

"Should have done it sooner," Sandy said. "It's this damn world we live in. I didn't think about it in the right way. Marriage, I mean. Certain things just didn't occur to me. That was foolish. More than foolish. It was wrong. I have a hard time thinking back on my actions, frankly. Or my lack of actions."

"You did the right thing when it mattered."

"I hope Bet understands. I mean, she does, she understands everything. She'd forgive anything. But she shouldn't have to. I know she still worries about my parents, but she shouldn't. Not her fault that they're being unreasonable."

"She doesn't like that you're separated from them."

Sandy's gaze hardened. "That's their choice. But it's one more challenge for her. And it's not easy, living in this world. I don't mean Berkeley Square," he added quickly. "We love being here. I mean, being an outsider."

"No. I don't think it's easy for Roth either."

"I suppose not. But it's a bit different, being a friend, rather than marrying into this world. He goes back and forth in a way. Visits, doesn't live in it."

"An apt way of putting it."

"Can't imagine a man like Roth—I mean, I used to think he always thought I was an idle fribble, truth to tell. That I wasn't worthy of Bet. And he was probably right."

Sandy's insights sometimes took Malcolm by surprise. "If he ever thought that, I don't think he does anymore."

"I hope not." Sandy scanned Malcolm's face. "Is there something more about Roth?"

Judith's secrets might soon be all too public, but for now they weren't Malcolm's to share. Though he was going to have to tell the rest of the investigative team tonight. "Merely my concern about what the investigation may do to him and his family. Along with losing his wife."

"Can't imagine—I mean, I can imagine a Mayfair marriage falling apart like that. One like my parents have. But one thinks someone like Roth would marry for—er—love—not issues about estates and alliances and things."

"Marriage is complicated for everyone. And love doesn't always last."

Sandy's eyes fastened on Malcolm's face. For a moment it was as though Malcolm had told Jessica happily-ever-afters in fairy tales might not be real. "Surely if it's real, it lasts."

"Define real. Something can be real while it lasts, but still not endure." What he'd felt for Kitty had been intensely real while it lasted. Not that it no longer existed, but it was different.

"But surely you and Mélanie—"

"No. I can't imagine my feelings for her changing." Which left aside what circumstances could do to the state of their relationship. He was no longer as anxious about that as he had once been. But the concern still lingered. Sharpened at times, in ways he wouldn't admit to anyone. "Relationships aren't static," he said to Sandy. "They inevitably change with time."

"For the worse?"

"Not always. Sometimes by far for the better. Mélanie's and mine has. Which doesn't mean there still aren't challenges." Malcolm clapped a hand on Sandy's shoulder. "You and Bet have had a number of challenges at the start. That should help you weather a lot."

Whether he'd ever get to the point where he could say that to Roth and Judith was another question entirely.

$\mathcal{M}$alcolm smoothed his hastily tied cravat and shrugged on a black cassimere coat. As he tugged at his shirt cuffs beneath the coat sleeves, a movement caught his eye in the looking glass. Addison, standing in the dressing room doorway.

Malcolm turned to smile at his valet. "Just a family dinner, so I thought I could handle things myself. I hope my neckcloth doesn't set you over the edge."

"On the contrary, sir. You're improving." Addison adjusted one of the folds round Malcolm's neck. "I just came in to say that I'll go back to the Three Queens tonight. I think it may take several visits to get the staff to really talk to me. I know Lord Carfax has been trying as well."

"Thank you." Malcolm glanced in the looking glass. The cravat looked remarkably better with Addison's simple adjustments, the folds crisper, the lines more precise. "Thanks to you and Julien, we have a comprehensive list of the Three Queens staff. I think you have better luck there than I would."

Addison smoothed Malcolm's coat over his shoulders. "It's difficult to imagine anyone's having better luck than you, sir. Or rather, greater skill. But it's possible I have certain insights into Jeremy's world that you don't."

Malcolm caught Addison's gaze in the looking glass. "I didn't realize you called him Jeremy."

Addison gave a faint smile. "He told me he'd stop visiting the house if I continued to call him Mr. Roth. It was Roth on its own, or Jeremy. He said Roth made him think of what Sir Nathaniel calls him."

"And he calls you Miles?"

"In general."

Malcolm turned his head to study the man who in many ways had been his closest companion since he started at Oxford. Longer than his wife. "I don't suppose you'd consider calling me Malcolm?"

"That would be singularly odd, sir."

"Unlike the rest of life in this household, which is so very normal?"

"Some rules can be broken. Others are more challenging."

"Because of what? If we broke them, you wouldn't want to be a valet at all? I could understand that."

Addison took a step back and then turned to face Malcolm, leaning against the dressing table, hands braced behind him. "I've always enjoyed being a valet. But I confess if I hadn't become your valet and learned to become an agent, I'd have grown bored. It's a remarkable life and I'm grateful to you for including me in it."

"I'm grateful to you for putting up with us." Malcolm watched Addison a moment longer. "You're one of the most important people in my life, Addison."

"Thank you, sir. I need hardly say the same applies in reverse."

"It's all a ridiculous charade, you know. Masters and servants."

"That charade supplies my livelihood. I know you're capable of dressing yourself, but I hope I'm not going to lose my employment in the name of principle."

"Don't be an idiot, Addison."

"Thank you, sir."

"I don't suppose you'd consider calling me Rannoch."

"What difference would that make?"

"It's a bit more on a par with Addison. We'd be equal."

"We're not equal, sir. Not in this world or any world you can even come close to imagining remaking."

"Define equal."

"Among other things, I can't vote."

"If we succeed, you'll be able to. Sooner than Mélanie or Blanca."

"A palpable hit."

"Roth calls me Malcolm on occasion."

"He doesn't work for you. I imagine it's challenging for him, though."

"He looks at us with a much more jaundiced eye than you do."

"You and Mrs. Rannoch provide employment for a number of people. On very fair terms. It may not be an ideal situation, but given the world we live in it's to be commended."

Which was more or less how Malcolm viewed things, with less emphasis on the 'commendable.' But the words still had a bite. "You'll dine with us now."

"Yes, that was a challenge. But Blanca persuaded me. My wife has quite a way with words."

Addison was one of the first of Malcolm's friends who had known the truth about Mélanie. At the same time, he had learned the truth about the woman he himself loved. "I don't know how I'd have got through those days three years ago without you, Addison."

"Nor I without you, sir."

Malcolm tugged at his cravat. "You could just be an agent, you know. Stop being a valet. I'd pay you the same salary."

Addison reached out and adjusted a fold of the cravat that Malcolm had disturbed. An almost imperceptible touch that somehow made the whole thing fall in more symmetrical folds. "I rather like being a valet. And with all due respect, sir, while you can manage without me, your attire is more harmonious when you have my assistance. I imagine Mélanie would tell you the importance of proper costume."

"I imagine she would. What did you just call her?"

Addison smiled. "A slip. But you know she does rather object to Mrs. Rannoch. And I've got used to what my wife calls her. Marriage has a way of changing one."

"So it does."

RAOUL GREETED Kitty and the children at the door in Berkeley Square. The boys and Genny ran into the library to find Colin, Emily, Jessica, and Clara. "Malcolm, Mélanie, and Laura should be down soon," Raoul said as he and Kitty followed more slowly.

"Julien said he'd meet us here." Kitty dropped her cloak and reticule on the library table. Her husband, still inclined to fuss, had insisted she and the children take the carriage the short distance to Berkeley Square. "He came back to Carfax House, but then he went out again to make more inquiries. We haven't had a chance to fully compare notes."

"Neither have the rest of us. We can catch up when every-one's here." Raoul had moved to the drinks trolley. He added whisky to his glass, then poured one for Kitty and handed it to her.

"Thank you." Kitty accepted the glass and moved to one of the Queen Anne chairs. "There's been a lot to digest today. In truth, I don't think I've even begun to process all of it."

Raoul sat in the other Queen Anne chair. "I didn't know Ashford well. But I saw enough to say with fair certainty that you don't owe him anything."

Kitty tossed down a drink of whisky. The Rannoch malt tasted rougher than usual. "If your first wife had been murdered when you were estranged, wouldn't you have felt compelled to learn what happened to her?"

Acknowledgement glinted in Raoul's gaze. "Caught. I wouldn't have been able to let it go. But I feel a certain amount of guilt where Margaret is concerned."

"You think only men feel guilt about marriage?"

"No, but I was older than Margaret and felt I should have realized what we had wasn't sustainable."

"I was a bit younger than Edward, but arguably more mature than he was and certainly saw that what we had wasn't sustainable. Not that we ever had very much. And if I hadn't been an agent, if it hadn't seemed a good idea to get close to British troops, I probably wouldn't have married him. I can't say I took advantage of Edward precisely. And I can't say I didn't give him what he deserved, because I'm not sure what he deserved. But it certainly wasn't what a marriage should be. I didn't have a clue what a marriage *could* be then." She took another drink, fingers not quite steady. "But it means something. Living together all those years, however separately one lives. Sharing things, however imperfectly."

Raoul met her gaze, unexpected kinship in his own. "Yes," he said. "It does. Whatever happened to Ashford, we'll all do our best to help you learn the truth. And we'll all understand. I venture to say your current husband most of all."

"Oh, Julien understands everything." Including how damaging lies could be. "Julien will be all right. We'll be all right. We've both always known we'd end up lying to each other. It shouldn't be such a shock to me that he lied to me in the past." Kitty took a sip of whisky and watched as Raoul curled his fingers round his own glass. Perhaps it was a trick of the candlelight, but his face looked sharper-boned and more shadowed than usual, his eyes deeper set. "It must be a burden."

"What?" Raoul asked.

Kitty settled back against the sofa cushions and took another sip of whisky. "They all admire you. But it's more than that. You've molded them. Their ideals. What it means to be an agent."

Raoul turned his glass in his hand. "Malcolm and Mélanie?"

"Undoubtedly. But also my husband. He wouldn't admit it. But you've molded him far more than Hubert Mallinson has."

Raoul gave a faint laugh. "By giving him something to react against?"

"Now you're sounding like Julien." Kitty curled her feet up on the sofa. "He may not have admitted he was paying attention when you met him. When you were still fighting for the ideals of a revolution that had almost killed you. When he was trying to make everyone believe he was a cold-blooded assassin. But he was listening. That's why there's still a core of him left."

Raoul shifted in his chair. "There was always a core of Julien that believed in humanity."

"Yes. I quite agree. But without you he might have lost it."

Raoul took a drink of whisky. "Julien has found his way back to ideals he never wanted to admit he hadn't abandoned, as much as he tried to make everyone believe to the contrary. Don't mistake that for any sort of influence I may have had."

"You made him believe things could be possible. Change. A better world. Progress. Against all evidence to the contrary. Because you believed and kept on fighting."

"Against all evidence to the contrary."

"What could be more inspiring?"

"Put like that, Don Quixote would be the most inspiring of all."

"Which he is, in a way." Kitty took another drink of whisky. She'd first had it in Spain, but it was in Britain she'd truly come to appreciate it. It was so bound up in the life they all shared. A family she'd never admitted—never known—she wanted. "But you actually accomplish things."

"At times."

"Don't overdo the false modesty. You're a force to be reckoned with, Raoul O'Roarke. It's part of why Hubert Mallinson finds you so dangerous. You inspire people."

He regarded her over the rim of his glass. "But you appear to have a bit more perspective."

"It's different. I like you. I admire you. But I was an adult when I met you. And I use the word advisedly. I won't claim to have had more maturity than the others. But in some ways, I was more fully formed."

"So you can see through me."

"I don't think any of us can see through the others, do you? I might have done better if I'd had your example when I was younger." Kitty watched him for a moment. "You should give yourself credit for what you've done for all of them."

"Or blame myself."

"None of them are the worse because of you. I'm quite sure of that. And you can't tell me you don't worry about all of them." She watched him a moment longer. "Julien was a boy when he met you. A rather dangerous boy capable of very dangerous things. But still. He needed an example that something else was possible. Something and someone to hang on to."

"Have you said that to Julien?"

"Not in so many words. You have an amazing power, Raoul. And you still inspire the younger generation. I think you inspired Marco Esquivel."

"I'm not sure how helpful it was if I did. I don't think I'm what sent him off to the Argentine, but I don't think I helped matters."

"You think he should have stayed?"

"Does that surprise you? I wasn't exactly the greatest success as a father, but I wouldn't have gone that far away for that long. I'm not sure I'd have put it that way then. I would now. Speaking as a father who's still gone more than I should be."

Kitty smiled. "Malcolm's right. You're a fraud. You didn't change when you married. You revealed yourself."

"Surely both are possible. I'm not the man I was. Thank god."

"But you never were the man you showed to the world."

He sat back. "Is any of us, truly? We show different parts of ourselves to different people in our lives. I'll own I felt more than I let on. I also didn't act on my feelings as much as I should have done. And much of the time my motives were a muddle."

"Dear god. So were mine." Kitty curled her hands round her glass. "Perhaps that's the worst of Edward's death's being tangled in all this. It forces me to confront who I was and what I did."

"We make choices," Raoul said. "The best choices we can at the time. Or, at least, it's folly to refine upon them."

Kitty looked at him, understanding with the clarity of the crystal glass in her hand, just what he meant to her husband and Malcolm and Mélanie. "Thank you."

He gave a crooked smile. "On the contrary. I owe you my thanks. My bones are aching considerably less than when we sat down to talk."

Kitty found herself smiling in return. "What are friends for?"

MÉLANIE LEANED FORWARDS to pour more coffee. They had spent dinner hearing Justine Lambton's account of the bust of Agrippina that Marco Esquivel had sent to her father and were now catching up on everyone's investigations of the afternoon. They still had more questions than answers.

"Esquivel met Beardsley and Rowley and an Argentine expatriate named Alvarez at Goring's in Henrietta Street at seven," Raoul said, glancing at his notes. "Several of the staff at Goring's vouch for the time. From there they went to Covent Garden, where they arrived fashionably late and met two more friends, Flores and Varela."

"So Esquivel would have had time to go to the Three Queens and kill Allegra," Malcolm said.

Raoul nodded. "Though he'd have been gone before Kitty and

Julien arrived, so it's more problematic that he hired Purvis. And he couldn't have shot Purvis—he was with Higgins by then."

"You made more progress than I did," Julien said. "And I hope Addison does better than I did at the Three Queens. I went twice today, once disguised as a costermonger, the other time as a cyprian. I'm quite sure no one saw through either disguise, but they're so very close mouthed about the whole incident I can't but think there's more to uncover. I did find some drops of dried blood on the back stairs down to the kitchen. I'm quite sure the killer left that way. And possibly came up that way as well."

"Wouldn't the killer have been terribly bloody?" Cordelia asked. "I mean, he or she would have been in the midst of a crowd once they got outside—"

"They might not have been that bloody," Julien said. "It was a precise hit with a thin blade like—" He bit back the words.

"Like George," Cordy said.

"Yes. And if the killer was wearing a greatcoat or cloak or pelisse, they might have removed it before the murder and then put it back on after to cover any blood on their clothing."

"That would mean the killer knew Allegra Roth," Malcom said. "Which fits with how close they got without a struggle."

"It may have been the murder weapon that dripped on the stairs," Julien said. "I suspect the killer discarded it shortly after. Addison and I both searched round the Three Queens, and I'm sure Higgins had his men do the same. But in Seven Dials someone likely snatched it up to sell before Allegra Roth was even found."

Kitty blew on her coffee. "I'm well served for not taking Edward seriously enough. It never occurred to me to look through his papers after he died. But I did keep them—I thought there might be something the boys would want someday. I looked through them this afternoon. I know he kept ledgers, but I didn't find those. Either he destroyed them before he died or someone managed to take them. But I found a draft of a letter, I'm not sure to whom, saying he felt as though he was being left to take the blame. It wasn't clear that he was referring to the silver mine scheme, but putting it together with what Julien says I suspect so. There's no date, but from where it was in his writing box I think it was from not long before he died."

"That fits," Julien said. "Even by the time I left the Argentine the scheme was starting to unravel."

"It's interesting," Kitty said, "but it doesn't really provide a murder motive unless his associates thought it would be easier to blame him if he were dead. Perhaps—"

She broke off as the door opened and Valentin stepped into the room.

"A Mr. Esquivel has called."

It was the first time Mélanie had seen Marco Esquivel. Tall, dark haired, well-cut features, strong brows. He was not precisely her type, but she could see what must have attracted Allegra. He had an air of command, even as he hesitated just inside the library door. "I'm sorry. I didn't mean to interrupt when you were entertaining. And I know I have not been introduced to many of you. But I received a note from Miss Lambton saying she would be here this evening."

"You aren't interrupting." Mélanie got to her feet. "Nothing we do just now is unconnected to the investigation into Alejandra Vargas's death. And Miss Lambton is particularly eager to speak with you."

"Mr. Esquivel." Justine got to her feet as well. "I don't know that you remember me—"

"How could I forget you, Miss Lambton?" Esquivel bowed. "Though you were rather less tall at our last meeting."

Justine smiled. "It's good to see you. I know that sounds odd with everything that's happened. I'm so sorry—"

"Thank you," Esquivel said. "And it's good to see you too." He gave a smile, genuine but a bit strained about the edges.

"I met the Rannochs and the Davenports and everyone else at

the holidays," Justine said when Raoul had made formal introductions and they were all seated. "And I was already planning to come to London and stay with the Davenports. So of course I brought the bust to show them." She looked at Harry and Cordy. "They're both classicists."

"Yes. I wasn't thinking of that aspect." Esquivel nodded at Harry and Cordy. "I've heard about your work. I still follow classics journals when I can."

"The bust is an amazing piece," Harry said. "How did you come across it?"

Esquivel accepted a cup of coffee from Mélanie and steadied it on its saucer, as though weighing his words. "It's no secret we're in need of funding. We being those involved in the revolution. But Britain's treaty with Spain a few years ago forbids your country from supplying us with weapons."

"Which certain elements in Britain have managed to supply you with anyway," Julien said, quite as if he hadn't been involved in the supplying.

Esquivel nodded. "We also need funds to purchase the weapons and other things. It can be difficult to transfer money abroad. Some of our—friends—have sent valuable goods instead. As you must know, a number of art treasures made their way into various hands during the war."

"I saw some of that at Vitoria," Harry said.

"So did I," Julien said.

Mélanie set down her coffee. She had no idea what Julien had been doing at Vitoria, what side he'd been on, or whom he'd been spying for. Julien sent her an *I'll tell you later* look.

"I imagine sending art treasures as currency was particularly appealing to those connected to the British government who couldn't arm you directly," Malcolm said.

Esquivel met his gaze. "Precisely. You're an MP, Rannoch. You'll appreciate that I don't wish to say more."

"It's all right," Julien said. "We already know. My uncle was arming you. I helped facilitate shipments. So did Kitty."

Esquivel drew in and released his breath. "Your uncle was Alejandra's spymaster. I didn't realize he was yours as well."

"And mine," Malcolm said. "Though we all broke away from him. Hubert Mallinson has a way of getting his hooks in people."

"But you're all too intelligent not to have gone to work for him of your own free will," Esquivel said.

"Define free will," Julien said. "What one enters into with Uncle Hubert may be very different from the situation one subsequently finds oneself in."

Esquivel's jaw tightened. "I didn't come here to debate Alejandra's actions. Or to ask for excuses for them."

"This is the first I've heard of Hubert Mallinson's sending art treasures to fund arms purchases," Kitty said. "But it's like Hubert to be creative."

"I saw the bust in a shipment of valuables that had been sent to a colleague," Esquivel. "I recognized it as one Mr. Lambton had talked about. I wanted to get it in his hands. He instilled enough love of antiquities in me that I didn't want to leave it to serve as a bargaining chip."

Harry turned his cup in his hands. "I'm generally a pragmatist when it comes to your uncle, Julien. But using that bust as currency may be one of the most objectionable things I've heard of his doing."

"Considering Uncle Hubert's lack of appreciation for human life, I suppose his lack of appreciation for works of art shouldn't be surprising," Julien said. "But I confess it still brings me up short." He looked at Esquivel. "If—"

He broke off as the door opened and Valentin came back into the room. "Mr. Roth."

CHAPTER 32

Roth hesitated on the library threshold, a mirror of Esquivel a short time before.

"Come in, Jeremy," Mélanie said. This was either going to be good for the investigation or turn her library into a battlefield. Or both. "Mr. Esquivel just called to share some information."

"Esquivel." Roth took two measured steps forwards and inclined his head. "I suppose it was inevitable that we meet."

"Roth." Esquivel got to his feet to face Roth. "It seems we have something in common. Alejandra deceived both of us."

Roth moved to a straight-backed chair. "Allegra never made a secret of the fact that she wasn't happy in our marriage, so I'm not sure you could say she deceived me. Though it's true she wasn't open about your affair."

"Which surely was a betrayal."

"Of sorts." Roth seated himself. "Though I understand the two of you were open about such matters."

"It's not—" Esquivel looked round as though aware he was the only one in the room standing. He returned to his chair. Mélanie gave Roth a cup of coffee.

Roth accepted the coffee with a smile. "Harder, I would think, to be spied on. I should say I'm sorry for you, and I am in a way. Though I confess I'm less charitable about Allegra's having left our children."

"Are you saying you'd have let her take them to the Argentine?"

"No. Would you have stayed in Britain with her?"

"That would have been impossible. And presumably Alejandra would not have wished to do so, considering that she was spying on me and my work."

"You have a point there." Roth took a drink of coffee. "It seems neither of us knew her. I couldn't have explained why she left, and it seems you didn't know the real reason either."

Esquivel inclined his head, shoulders held at a military angle. "I admit you have a right to call me to account."

Roth laughed, though the sound was not a pleasant one. "My class don't use violence to settle disagreements."

Esquivel's gaze locked on Roth's. "Not in that way, perhaps."

For a moment swords might have clashed between the two men. "If you mean I had a motive to have killed Allegra, then I have to admit you're correct," Roth said. "I'd probably suspect myself first, were I investigating the case from the outside. The only person with an equally strong motive would be you."

"As you say." Esquivel set down his coffee cup. "Mrs. Rannoch, I should not impose on your hospitality longer. I imagine Mr. Roth has things to discuss with you."

"Marco," Kitty said. "Before you go. Did Alejandra ever suggest to you that there might have been anything odd about Edward's death?"

"Edward's—your husband's?" Esquivel asked.

"Yes. I spoke with Philip Ledgwood today and he mentioned that Alejandra suspected Edward had been murdered."

Esquivel dropped back into his chair.

"You needn't worry about speaking in front of this company," Kitty said. "Including Jeremy. As I was attacked last night, it's possible there's a connection to Allegra's murder. And in any case, as you can imagine, I'm interested in what happened to my husband. Or perhaps you wouldn't think it, based on our relationship, but I am."

Esquivel picked up his coffee and stared into the cup. "Allegra was shocked by the news of Ashford's death. I still remember the moment we heard. We were dressing for dinner when she received the message."

"From whom?"

"I assumed it came from you."

Kitty shook her head. "I was too busy dealing with the repercussions to be sending word to anyone."

Esquivel gave a slow nod. "Alejandra kept saying it didn't make sense. It's a shock, of course. Someone young suddenly dropping dead. But it does happen. I pointed that out. Alejandra said it was suspicious. She was—close to Ashford."

"They were lovers," Kitty said. "I didn't know until today, but it scarcely matters, and it seems you knew."

Esquivel gave a curt nod.

"Was it a heart ailment?" Roth asked. He looked from Kitty to Esquivel. "Forgive me. But investigating suspicious deaths is my stock in trade."

"The doctor who attended him believed so," Kitty said. "Edward had no history of a heart condition, but he drank heavily and he was fencing when he died."

"Had he eaten or drunk anything within hours of his death?"

"Probably. Edward drank fairly constantly. I hadn't seen him since the day before. By the time I was summoned, he was dead."

Roth looked at Esquivel. "Had Allegra—Alejandra—seen him more recently?"

Esquivel frowned. "Possibly. We'd been out separately the night before."

"Did she say whom she suspected?"

Esquivel reached for his coffee, as though for delay.

"She told Philip she suspected me," Kitty said.

Esquivel choked on a drink of coffee. "She was upset by a friend's death. She may have pointed out that your marriage had not been happy."

"Hardly a surprising insight. Did you consider who might have been behind it?"

"I was convinced Alejandra was being overly imaginative. Which led us to quarrel. Even granted the intrigues of the Argentine, it was hard to imagine Ashford's being murdered."

"According to Philip Ledgwood and my current husband, Edward was more involved in those intrigues than I realized."

Esquivel's gaze flashed to Julien.

"You must have heard about the silver mine," Julien said.

"Rumors," Esquivel said. "I had more substantial concerns."

"Did Alejandra talk about the silver mine?" Kitty asked.

"Not to me." Esquivel set down his cup. "Surely you don't think this has to do with why Alejandra was killed."

"Kitty was attacked the night Alejandra was killed," Julien said. "Edward Ashford is a link between them."

"But Alejandra thought—"

"That I was behind Edward's death," Kitty said. "Yes, that's rather a conundrum. Unless you think I had Alejandra killed because she was on to me, and then set up the attack on myself for cover. Of course, Alejandra said she suspected me some time ago. It's possible she'd learned something new."

"If she did, she didn't tell me. But then, as I've learned, I didn't know Alejandra at all. So god knows what other secrets she was keeping." Esquivel set down his coffee cup. "Mrs. Rannoch. Thank you again for your hospitality."

JUSTINE AND GERRY got to their feet in the silence after Esquivel left, and moved to the far end of the library to join the charades Sandy and Bet were organizing with the children.

Laura looked at Roth. "Do you want any of the rest of us to leave? Before you talk about what brought you here?"

Roth met her gaze and gave a faint smile. "Thank you. But no. That is—" He looked round the group. "I assume you all know about Judith?"

"It's part of the investigation," Malcolm said in an even voice.

Roth inclined his head. "And you're all working on it. I quite understand the need to share information. Which is why I came to share this." He took a gulp from his coffee cup. He seemed at a loss for what to do with his hands without his habitual notebook and pencil. "I need hardly state that Higgins and I are far from friends. But I still have friends at Bow Street. Hopkins—you know him, he's a patrol who often works cases with me—came to see me tonight. A risk, but he has the excuse that he was checking on how Harriet and the boys and I are doing. Which he did. But he wanted to speak with me in private." Roth took another drink of coffee. "Apparently Higgins learnt about Judith and me. Which I should have known would happen. And the home office are concerned. Because of who Judith is."

The words settled over the room for a moment, with implications no one quite wanted to voice.

"Fanny has always stood out in society," Raoul said, which was true, though also a cover for other things he left unsaid. "Unfortunate to draw more attention to the case, but I imagine Bow Street and the home office will want to keep Judith out of it. At times, the impulse to protect the aristocracy can be helpful."

Roth nodded. "I hope so. It's best for Judith and me to have as little contact as possible, but I hope you can get word to her to warn her."

"We will," Malcolm said. "She's staying at Fanny's."

Roth grimaced. "I wish to god she was as far out of this as possible."

"The women in this family have a way of not wanting to stay out of things," Mélanie said.

"I know that full well," Roth said. "But Judith's not—"

"I'm not sure any of us can say what Judith is at this point," Malcolm said. "Save that she's a great deal that none of us realized."

KITTY LOOKED AT ROTH. The others had joined the charades game. He had stayed to answer some questions from her about Edward's death, though no detail she could offer had been conclusive of anything. She was fairly new to knowing Roth, compared to others in the group. But in her year and a half in Britain she'd come to appreciate his quick thinking and loyalty. He also had a tough outer shell. Which just now must be particularly battered. She knew something about both herself. "It seems we have something in common," she said.

"A deceased spouse?"

"Who may have been murdered. And left us with more questions than answers. Harder, of course, if one desperately loves them. But if one doesn't, there's all the guilt of not having loved them. All the questions about what the relationship meant. And if one feels relief at being free—I don't know that you do, but I did— that makes the guilt worse." She glanced towards the charades game. Timothy had a silk hat on and a bugle in one hand. "And then, if they're the parent of your children, that adds another whole layer."

Roth met her gaze. Behind the habitual defenses, she saw a spark of kinship and relief. "I thought I was free of her," he said. "But I think a part of me always wondered if she'd come back someday."

Kitty nodded. "You were left in an unbearable situation. But regardless, I think if your spouse died violently—which it now seems Edward did—there's the sense that one should learn what happened. I'd have sworn I didn't owe Edward anything, but I think I do owe him that. I owe the boys that. I confess I find it quite tiresome of Edward to have managed to interfere with my life again. Here I am focusing on him when I thought I was free."

"You have a remarkable way of putting things, Kitty."

"Better that than to dwell on it, don't you think? Or to pretend to feelings I don't have. I may feel I owe Edward something, but I find him just as provoking as ever. Though I'm beginning to suspect he may have been cleverer than I credited. What that says about my powers of perception is rather lowering, considering I lived with him for so long."

"But you just said you led separate lives."

"Touché. I'm not sure that lets me off the hook though. I was still his wife. I couldn't really avoid him."

Roth looked into the fire flickering in the polished iron grate. "I wasn't sure I knew Allegra when we were married. I was even less sure when she left. And now I find myself wondering if I knew her at all."

"Everyone has different sides to them. I can't come close to seeing all the sides of Julien. Though I do think I understand him as few do."

Roth looked up and caught her gaze with a smile. "What the two of you have is remarkable."

"It's worth it. As much of a risk as it was. And honestly, now I wonder at myself for being afraid of the risk. The risk was botching it and hurting each other, but we were both going to be hurt if we didn't try at all." She smoothed her chestnut velvet skirt. "I'm sorry. I'm sure you're tired of happy married couples trying to give you advice."

"Not that." His smile was surprisingly open and yet at the same time remote. "But you all have a tendency to draw false parallels."

"Everyone's different," Kitty said. "I used to think that about Malcolm and Mélanie, and Harry and Cordelia, and Laura and Raoul. Just because domesticity worked for them—even Raoul, who once seemed to epitomize being alone—didn't mean it would work for Julien and me. And of course, the fact that it works for them isn't why it works for us. And doesn't mean it would work for you."

"The situations are quite different."

"Oh, very. Julien was worried about being arrested, and didn't even have a legal identity. We thought we might have to flee the country. Which, come to think of it, was rather less terrifying than moving into Carfax House." She picked up her coffee and took a drink. "I do understand your qualms, Jeremy."

He regarded her with the look of one who knew the game she was playing. "I don't discount how daunting it must have been. But no one could doubt your right to be Countess Carfax."

"Believe me, many did. Because I'm Spanish. Because I was the widow of an untitled army officer. Because I lived in lodgings in Carnaby Street. Because Julien lived with me, though not everyone knows that. Julien would say people doubt his right too, for any number of reasons, but chiefly because his mother was the daughter of a slave. But the fact that his father was a Mallinson tends to trump that."

"As birth does."

"But given that none of us believes in birth determining fortune, why should that matter?"

"Because we don't live in the world we'd like to create. Allegra once told me she didn't believe in marriage, and I said I wasn't sure I did either. But it wasn't going to be good for her child—our child—to have parents who weren't married."

"An excellent point. But who exactly are you afraid of now? I don't think the views of the denizens of Mayfair matter a lot to you."

Roth shifted in his chair. "I'm afraid for Judith. She'd be giving up a lot."

"What, precisely?" Kitty glanced at the charades again. Sandy was sitting on the floor with his arm round Bet, who had Genny in her lap. "It's not like she's Sandy, who had his parents cut him off—though he doesn't seem to regret it. Judith wouldn't lose her fortune."

"She's scarcely more than a girl. She wanted something different from her marriage. When she decides she wants something different again, and gets restless—"

"You're afraid she's like Allegra."

"Judith accused me of that. No. She's more aware of others' feelings than Allegra ever was. So it would be much harder for her to be in a relationship that made her unhappy. To realize she'd closed off her options in life."

"Why should marriage necessarily do that? Unless you think a woman's only options are whom she chooses as a husband?"

To his credit, Jeremy didn't argue. He settled back in his chair. "A point. My sister would clout me. So would Judith, I suspect. But you can't deny marriage is one major option for a woman or a man."

"So you'd be closing off your options as well."

"I'm older. More than half again her age."

"So it wouldn't bother you? Moving into a world you despise."

Jeremy frowned. "I never said I despised it."

"Not in so many words. But even though we all lamentably missed so much about you and Judith, I wouldn't be much of an agent if I couldn't read faces. You're very forbearing, but I know what you think of Mayfair."

"You make me sound a conceited prig."

"On the contrary. I've thought it myself. I never moved in what anyone would call society until I married Edward. I was living with a guerrillero band as a teenager. I didn't experience Mayfair until a year and a half ago, when I brought the children to London. It's a bewildering world, and from some angles, quite appalling. But many of my favorite people grew up in it. Yours too, I think. And it has its compensations."

"That's not—You know what people would say of me."

"Jeremy Roth. Since when do you of all people care what people think?"

He looked up and caught her gaze. "We're all susceptible."

"Ah. I can't argue with you there. The remarks behind the fans bother me more than I'd ever admit to Julien."

"It's not just what people say. Our whole lives have been different. It's a whole vocabulary of what matters, what's familiar, what one cares about."

"I'll grant that. Julien despises hunting, but he has a whole lexicon about it I can't understand. You're tough though. I have no doubt you could handle it."

"It's Judith I'm worried about."

"I gather that," Kitty said. "But surely the woman you fell in love with is equal to it?"

Jeremy drew in his breath, but before he could respond, Genny came hurtling across the room and held her arms up to Kitty. "Hold you."

Kitty scooped her daughter into her lap. Genny's favorite phrase was singularly apt. She couldn't say which of them needed to be held more.

CHAPTER 33

Frances closed the door to the night nursery where Francesca and Philip were asleep. She'd already tucked Chloe in, though she'd probably have to go in in another half hour and tell Chloe to douse her candle and stop reading. She wouldn't go down the passage to Judith's room, the room that had been hers from girlhood. But she had a feeling Judith's troubled face when they'd said goodnight would haunt her dreams. "I'm a fraud, Archie."

She was turned to the door, but she heard her husband's soft laugh. "You're the furthest thing I can imagine from a fraud, my love."

Frances turned round and met Archie's blue gaze. "I scoff at the idea of fairy tales. Even when I fell in love with you, I'd have said we were lucky to be in a real relationship instead of some sort of happily-ever-after nonsense. But I wanted that for Judith. The fairy tale and all that goes with it. Or at least I was happy that she seemed to have found it. That she of all my children had seemed to transition seamlessly from adolescence into adulthood and fallen genuinely in love, without broken hearts or traumatic secrets or anyone spying on anyone. I never even quite thought I had that when I married Dacre-Hammond. But everything that seemed so dull to me as a girl seemed so perfect when my daughter had it."

"I think it's perfectly reasonable to want one's children to find happiness without trauma in getting to the happiness," Archie said. "I wouldn't trade the life I have for anything, but I rather hope Chloe and Philip and Francesca find love before fifty. And I'm sure Harry and Cordelia hope Livia and Drusilla don't go through what they did."

"No, of course not." Frances moved into the bedchamber that had been hers for so many years. She hadn't shared it with anyone, including her first husband, until she'd taken the risk of marrying Archie. Against all sense and reason and all the supposedly hard-fought lessons of the first five-and-forty years of her life. "But I keep thinking that if I hadn't been so busy being pleased things had worked out so perfectly for at least one of my children, I'd have noticed the cracks in Judith's marriage sooner. Because, even for people who don't make the spectacular mistakes I did, life isn't a fairy tale. It's far more complicated and interesting. Look at Allie and Geoff. Their romance was free of the angst that's troubled so many of our friends, but no one would call it a fairy tale."

"I'm not sure why we can't call it a fairy tale," Archie said. "Except that they're both too interesting to be a prince and princess. If that's the only difference, who would want a fairy tale?" He studied her for a moment in the shifting candlelight. His gaze was soft and yet piercing in that way it could be. "It's hell watching one's children in pain. I remember when Harry and Cordy were separated. It was far harder on me than I'll ever admit to either of them. One of the worst times of my life. But they came out of it happier. Judith may as well. She may discover she has interests far beyond those of a fairy-tale princess whose life bored her."

Frances managed a smile. "Are you saying I underestimated her?"

"Possibly. She's always struck me as more like you than you perhaps credited. And she's already shown surprising mettle."

"She has." Frances frowned. "I'd never have thought of Jeremy Roth for her. But perhaps I didn't know her at all."

"Oh, I think you know all your children very well. But children can surprise one. That's part of the fun of being a parent."

Frances felt herself smile. She went up to Archie and put her hands on his chest. "You're very wise, Archie. Why didn't I find you earlier?"

"You did. You just didn't think I was interesting enough."

"I thought you were in love with my sister."

He slid his arms round her. "The perils of good cover."

"And I think I hadn't grown up enough," Fanny said. "It's not just finding the right person. It's finding the right person at the right time. You didn't think I was interesting enough before either."

"Hardly that." He brought a hand up to cup her cheek. "You didn't show an interest in me. And I knew about—"

"Alistair and me."

"Well, yes. That was a deterrent. All things considered, as well for us that I thought he was dead when we started our affair, even though he wasn't."

They could talk about it now. Her love for Malcolm's putative father, who had caused so many problems and who was still a threat. Talk, and even almost laugh. That must be an improvement. Even if she could feel the strain beneath the laughter. Even if her insides were twisting into knots beneath the linen of her nightdress and the silk brocade of her dressing gown.

"He's gone now," she said.

Archie looked down at her, his gaze at once open and armored. "He'll never really be gone, my darling. But that doesn't matter."

"It doesn't matter to me. But—"

"Alistair will always matter to you." He pressed a kiss to her forehead. "It's all right, Fanny. I can live with it. Now. I was a bit of an idiot for a while. Jealous idiocy is possible at any age."

"You weren't at all an idiot, Archie." Fanny swallowed, realizing she'd never quite addressed it. "You were—quite amazing."

"I don't think I trusted my wife enough. I don't think I trusted what was between us. Because while I may not believe in fairy tales, I do believe in love. And I believe one can go through something and come out stronger on the other side."

"Is that what we've done? That sounds if not like a fairy tale, rather like something out of a play."

Archie bent his head to kiss her. "I've always believed there's a great deal of truth in fiction."

KITTY SMOOTHED the blankets over Genny. She managed to hold her fingers steady as she did so, so she didn't jerk the soft merino, a gift from Lady Frances, who had a surprising love of knitting. She wasn't as confident she managed to keep Genny from sensing the tension in her fingers. But she'd long since given up even trying to keep the children from sensing her tension. It would do more harm than good. Or perhaps that was an excuse.

She turned from the cradle and strode across the bedroom. "I should have seen it."

"What Ashford was involved in?" Julien closed the door of the boys' room. He'd had it ajar ever since they'd tucked them in, listening to them settle.

"I keep remembering when we decided to go to the Argentine. I was so focused on what I needed to do. What I wanted."

"You needed to leave Spain."

"I needed to get away because Edgar Rannoch had raped me and left me pregnant, and I couldn't bear to be near Malcolm, who'd been my lover and would think the child was his. Unless I told him the truth and ruined his relationship with his brother. No sense in wrapping plain facts up in clean linen."

"Which you never try to do." Julien leaned against the nursery door, watching her.

"But I couldn't say any of that to Edward." Kitty stopped beside her dressing table. She remembered her discussion with Edward about going to the Argentine, by her dressing table in their lodgings in Lisbon, in another bedroom that they hadn't shared, though sharing her bed with Edward that night had been part of the price she'd paid for persuading him. "So I had to focus on convincing him we should go to the Argentine. Trying to make him think it was his idea." She folded her arms, gripping her elbows. "I was so focused on making him think it was his idea, that it never occurred to me it might have been his idea in the first place."

"You think Edward was already plotting the silver mine scheme then?"

"What do you think? You seem to know more about my husband than I did."

Julien moved away from the door and leaned against the bedpost, closer but not within touching distance. "Edward was far more of a player than I suspected before Uncle Hubert tasked me with looking into him. Edward always struck me as an opportunist, but he also seems to have been more forward thinking than we thought. And I always suspected he was involved in more than the one mine, and the scheme wasn't his alone, which seems clear from the letter you found today. So it's possible he was planning it before you left Lisbon."

"And I played into his hands."

"You needed to leave for your sanity. If Edward was determined to go to the Argentine, you wouldn't have been able to dissuade him." Julien moved to the cradle and smoothed the blanket over Genny. "And if you hadn't gone, we wouldn't have Genny."

"No." Kitty chewed her nail. "I know it's folly to refine upon the past. But I think in retrospect Edward agreed too easily. And if he already had the plan in mind, I don't think it was his alone." Kitty loosed her hands and pushed her hair back from her face. "I'm sorry. But I need to know."

"I understand."

"I wish to hell I did. I wanted to leave Edward in the past. But I can't let go of the fact that I should have known what was going on, and—"

"Protected him?"

"All right, yes." Kitty dragged her fingers through her side curls, sending two hairpins tumbling to the floor. "He was an idiot. But at that time, we were family."

"He didn't do much to protect you."

"I didn't want him to. And he wasn't capable of it. He might have challenged Edgar to duel after the fact, if he'd known the truth, but that would hardly have improved the situation." She bent down and scooped up the hairpins. "I'm the one who should have seen what was going on and ensured Edward was safe."

"So you could have divorced him," Julien said. "I mean, you'd have had to, for us to be together."

She tossed the hairpins on her dressing table. "I wouldn't have let him be killed so we could be together."

"No. Nor would I, tempting as it would have been. But I wouldn't say you owed him anything."

"I missed something, and the father of my children is dead." She looked at Julien quickly. "You're their father. But Edward—"

"Was. It's all right."

"If I'd known—"

"You mean, if I'd told you what he was involved in."

"No. Yes. You couldn't have known. But it might have helped."

"From what I knew, I didn't see Edward's activities leading to anything violent. Which means I missed obvious clues too. You have a right to be angry at me."

"It wouldn't help anything for me to be angry at you."

"That's never stopped anyone from being angry."

Kitty spun away and drummed her fingers on the polished walnut of her dressing table. "How would you have done it?"

"Done what?"

"Murdered Edward."

"I didn't—"

"I know, but if you had. If he was murdered, he must have been poisoned, mustn't he?"

"Yes," Julien said, in an easy voice that was somehow like frayed rope. "I can't say how I would have done it, but based on what I've heard, if he was murdered, I suspect it was foxglove. Which Geoff would tell us can be a handy medicine, but with the right dosage can bring on a heart attack. Difficult to prove. Even though Edward was young, a doctor would be much more likely to think it was natural causes."

Kitty nodded. "How long—"

"It works slowly. He might have ingested it a couple of hours before."

"I'd been to a concert at The Philharmonics the night before. I'm not sure where he was. He came home after I did, and left before I got up. At this point, at this distance, it's impossible to know whom he might have seen before he went to the fencing academy. He could have stopped at a café or a tavern or the British Commercial Subscription Room. A servant could have been bribed to put it in his coffee at home, even. Though I trusted our staff."

"Most likely someone was paid to do it. Even if we could determine who did it, it won't tell us who was behind it."

Kitty nodded. "I need to learn what happened. I can't promise that will solve it. But it will give me back a measure of control. Because that's what started all this. Our going to the Argentine.

My losing control. Having it ripped from me. In the worst way possible." She pressed her hands to her face for a moment, then dragged them away from her eyes and looked at her husband. "I told myself I'd put it behind me. That it was a horror many women suffered and I had to get on with my life. And I did get on with my life. But it's not behind me."

Julien hesitated a moment, then closed the distance between them and put his hands on her shoulders. Lightly. Just brushing the velvet of her gown. "You're the strongest person I know. And whatever you need to do to get through this, I'm here. I always will be."

Kitty nodded, and put her hands over his own.

MALCOLM CLOSED THE NURSERY DOOR. "Investigations tend to keep them up all night along with the rest of us."

"They can sleep later tomorrow at least. Although they're more likely to come bounding in asking what we're Investigating." Mélanie moved to her dressing table and unfastened one of her garnet earrings. "Malcolm." She looked through the soft glow of candle and lamplight at her husband. The topic none of them had quite ventured to broach in front of Roth hung between them. Given their family, it shouldn't be hard to ask. "Judith's father—"

Malcolm moved to the bed and began to undo his shirt cuffs. He'd already removed his coat before they looked in on the children. "Has Aunt Frances said anything to you?"

"No." Mélanie unhooked the second earring without looking away from her husband. "But Allie once said when Judith was younger she liked to give herself airs and claim her father was royal."

Malcolm grimaced, gaze fastened on a button. "According to Aunt Frances, Judith was correct. Though Fanny didn't want to admit it to her."

"Did she say which royal?"

"No."

"But Frances was—"

"Rumored to be connected with at least three of them."

"So Judith's father could be—"

Malcolm released the button. "The king. Quite."

Mélanie bent down to pick up Berowne before he could climb the pomegranate terry velvet of her gown. "Odd. It sounds more official than saying Prince of Wales." She settled Berowne against her shoulder and pressed her face into his fur. "I imagine the king has a number of children." Including, if rumor was correct, her fellow playwright George Lamb, the brother of her friend Emily Cowper. "But if she's his child, and the home office know about her and Roth, and that's entangled in the murder investigation—"

Malcolm tugged at the folds of his cravat. "Quite. I need to talk to Frances."

CHAPTER 34

"I still can't believe we never noticed anything about Roth and Judith." Cordelia turned to look at her husband in the privacy of their bedchamber. They had put the girls to bed and said goodnight to Justine, and finally had a moment to talk alone.

"Always a good reminder of what the best agent can miss." Harry moved to the armchair by the fire.

Cordelia pulled a pin from her hair. "There's plenty all of you get as agents that I miss. But I rather pride myself at being good at noting personal feelings. Especially romantic intrigues." She pulled out another pin. "They used to be my forte." They could joke about that now. Better to joke about it.

"Sometimes one doesn't see what one isn't looking for."

Cordelia pulled out another handful of pins and shook her hair out. "I can quite see it now, though. Judith was bored. She won't be bored with Jeremy."

"I hope they both have the chance to put that to the test," Harry said. But he was frowning and Cordelia didn't think it was about Roth and Judith, however concerning their situation was.

"Darling?" Cordelia asked. "What is it? Something about the case?"

"No." Harry gave her a quick smile. "That is, there's plenty to be concerned about over the case. But I was remembering how Gerry talked to me about his father this afternoon. About how it's hard to forgive him. I'm the last to want to make things easier for Theodore Schofield. But I couldn't but be aware that I was quick to forgive Archie for being a spy."

"It's a bit different." Cordelia moved to the armchair and dropped into her husband's lap. "Theodore Schofield sold British secrets for money and then used his inside knowledge from his spying to make still more money. Archie was acting out of principle. And he wasn't paid for it."

Harry's arms tightened round her. "So it's the motive that matters?"

"I think it makes a difference, don't you? A rather crucial difference. And are you going to blame Archie because he was born in Britain, but not blame Raoul because he was born in Ireland, or Mélanie because she was born in France? I know loyalty to one's country is supposed to mean something, but surely so does loyalty to principles."

"Which brings us back to Malcolm and me, who acted against our principles in the service of our country. I'd say we fare rather worse than Archie in the equation."

"You and Malcolm both stopped. That's what matters." She looked down at the tangle of their dressing gowns, hers rose, his paisley. "Look at Julien. I somehow suspect Theodore Schofield worried about his ethics less than any of you. Including Julien."

"And yet in the end Schofield stood up for his friend."

"People constantly surprise one. And that should give Gerry and his sisters some reason to hold on to their relationship with their father."

"I hope so. For their sake, if not Schofield's. I can't help but think—"

He broke off, suddenly taut. A second later Cordelia heard it too. Creaks. Footsteps. Sounds that weren't supposed to be in their house.

❧

Harry gripped his wife's arm. "Library or study. Check on the girls."

Cordelia ran to the nursery while he raced into the passage and down the stairs, dressing gown flapping round him, bare feet thudding on the floorboards. A crash sounded from the study. Halfway down the last flight he vaulted over the stair rail onto the tiled floor of the hall, caught himself in a crouch, and raced to the study in time to see a figure bent over the desk. As Harry lunged, the intruder ran to the open study window and dropped through.

Harry sprang through the window after the intruder, raced along the side of the house, and vaulted over the area railing into Hill Street. Snow dusted his shoulders and crunched under his bare feet. He dodged into the street to avoid three young men in crooked silk hats who had just stumbled out of a hackney. The fleeing man was almost at the corner, but another carriage had pulled up and a couple had descended. Lord and Lady Faversham. The man ran full tilt between them, knocking Lord Faversham against the area railings of their house. His hat went flying. He slumped on the paving stones. Lady Faversham screamed.

"Are you all right, sir?" Harry stopped and helped Lord Faversham to his feet. His quarry was out of sight round the corner.

"Quite, Davenport, thank you." Faversham, who was well past eighty, straightened his shoulders.

"Who on earth was that man?" Lady Faversham asked.

"I'm not sure." Harry retrieved Lord Faversham's hat, shook off the snow, and returned it to him. "But he broke into our house."

"Good heavens," Lady Faversham said. "Are Cordelia and the children all right?"

"Yes. And our guest and the servants, I think."

"What was the miscreant after?" Lord Faversham asked.

"That," Harry said, "is what I'd very much like to know."

"NOTHING MISSING," Cordelia said, when she and Harry and Justine, who had awoken as well, were in the study and she had poured him a large whisky. "But the Agrippina bust was on the edge of the desk. He definitely moved it."

Harry took a drink of whisky. "I think he was looking at it when I came in. We're fortunate he didn't try to run with it."

"But why?" Justine asked. "I mean, I know it's valuable, but why would a thief target it? How would the thief even know I'd brought it?"

"An excellent question." Harry took a deep swallow of whisky and moved to the desk. Cordelia and Justine had repositioned the bust safely back in the middle. "He seemed to be examining it when I came in. If he'd wanted to take it, you'd think he'd have grabbed it and run before I could get downstairs. We heard him quickly, but there'd still have been time. Cordy, can you hold the lamp?"

Cordelia picked up the desk lamp and held it over the bust. Justine followed her to the desk. Harry turned the bust round in the lamplight and then paused. "There."

"Yes, I know," Justine said. "There's a crack in the marble. Not unusual in a bust so old. It was there when we got it, so the attempted thief didn't do that."

"No." Harry pulled open a desk drawer that held oddments of the spy variety, such as picklocks, and pulled out a pair of tweezers, made from the thinnest metal imaginable. Cordelia found them useful for repairing particularly delicate jewelry. "I'll be careful," he said to Justine, and then slid the tweezers into the crack.

Cordelia angled the lamplight over the crack. Harry felt about for a few seconds and then very slowly drew out a folded paper.

"Good heavens." Justine stared down at the paper on the desktop. "That's not any language I can imagine. It's a code, isn't it?"

"Yes," Harry said. "And not an obvious one. I think we're going to need Judith's sister Allie to break it."

CHAPTER 35

There was a time when Malcolm wouldn't have found his aunt Frances outside her bedchamber before noon. The birth of her twins had changed things a bit. He found the family finishing breakfast. Archie, Frances, Chloe, the twins, and Judith and Serena. Malcolm met Judith's gaze and assured her he had no news, but needed a word with Fanny. Anxiety flashed in Judith's eyes, but she nodded, and she, Archie, and Chloe took the twins and Serena into the library while Frances poured Malcolm a cup of coffee.

"You know Judith's going to ask me questions about whatever it is you want to talk to me about," Frances said, handing Malcolm his coffee.

"Yes." Malcolm accepted the cup and settled into a chair. "You'll have to decide how much you want to tell her." He took a drink of coffee. "Roth came to see us last night. Bow Street know about him and Judith. And apparently the home office are concerned." Malcolm set down his cup and regarded his aunt. Hadn't they just had this conversation? Or a similar one. "Aunt Frances—It wouldn't be any of my business. But—"

Fanny's gaze was clear as Highland water. "You want to know who Judith's father is."

"At this point, I need to know."

Her mouth twisted, perhaps with acknowledgement, perhaps with memory. Her gaze went to the breakfast parlor windows, the outside world of Mayfair filtered by the gauzy muslin sub-curtains. "He was more appealing then, though he certainly wasn't my type. But I suppose even I wasn't immune to the allure of titles. At least then. And one can't deny there isn't a more significant title. Though I must say lately I've felt I owed an apology to his wife. I didn't think much about the marriage tie in those days, and I'd have said when a marriage was effectively over and both partners were free to go their own way, it shouldn't matter. But really she wasn't free at all, and what she went through was quite appalling."

"So Judith's father—"

"Is the present King of England." Fanny turned her gaze back to Malcolm, steady and unruffled as a loch on a windless day. "It sounds rather more official when one puts it like that, doesn't it?"

Malcolm saw the then prince regent in a room in this house on the night Fanny had persuaded him to grant Mélanie and Raoul pardons for actions of which he didn't (Malcolm profoundly hoped) know the full extent. Malcolm had already been more than half convinced Fanny had been the prince's mistress. But he hadn't been sure about Judith. "Does the king know? That Judith is his daughter?"

"I never told him. But though he isn't possessed of a keen understanding, one assumes he can count."

The things an investigation could make one discuss with family members. "But you weren't—"

"Exclusive? Not precisely. But the timing suggests it was him. And I don't believe he knew there were others at the time. I didn't make him any promises, but he has a difficult time seeing the world about him. I don't think he'd have liked to be second. Or third or fourth."

"Does Judith know?"

Frances's brows, the delicate, arched brows Judith had inherited, drew together. "I think she must have heard something growing up, because she always liked to claim her father was royal. But I never admitted it to her. I didn't like the idea of her putting on airs."

"But if someone knew—"

"He has other children. Probably more than we are aware of."

"But with Judith suddenly connected to a Bow Street runner—"

Frances shook her head, sending her side curls stirring. For a moment she reminded him of Judith—or eleven-year-old Chloe—while at the same time he couldn't discount the worldly wisdom in her gaze. "Malcolm, do you seriously think the king would interfere? Would even know what is going on? He certainly wouldn't have known about the affair, given that none of us did— my daughter is far more discreet than I am myself."

"He may have heard of the investigation into Allegra Roth's murder. Sidmouth knows."

"Possibly. But Prinny—the king—is one of the most self-absorbed people I've ever met. And I've met a number of self-absorbed people."

"Anything's possible. But I wasn't thinking of the king so much as some of his ministers and advisors."

"Malcolm, are you suggesting a royal functionary had Jeremy Roth's wife murdered because Roth was having an affair with the king's illegitimate daughter?"

"No. Put like that it's preposterous. But once the murder had happened, I can imagine someone's taking an interest because Roth was involved with the king's illegitimate daughter. And perhaps seeing this as a convenient way to break up what they saw as an unfortunate entanglement."

Frances's brows drew together again. "If it weren't for unfortunate entanglements, Judith wouldn't be here."

"Roth's a Bow Street runner. And a Radical. And Jewish."

"Malcolm. No one would—"

"It makes him that much more of an outsider. And he's been uncomfortably close to a number of secrets."

Frances looked at her hands. "I liked Bobby. I was happy when Judith chose him because she was in love and they were happy and that's what one wants for one's children. But later—I confess there were moments I suspected something was missing. I think this is different, though."

"One can never be sure," Malcolm said. "But yes. I think it is. Which isn't to say it will be easy. Or last."

"You're supposed to be a romantic."

"That's my wife. I know my good fortune in having blundered into happiness. That doesn't mean I believe it's easy to find. Or that I don't question what I have."

Frances reached out across the table and touched his face. "Oh my dear. Do sometimes try to enjoy what you have."

"Believe me, Aunt Frances, I do."

"And don't let your questions interfere with your enjoying it. Do you think I don't question what I have with Archie? That I don't worry about the future? But that makes it all the more miraculous. That's all the more reason to hold on to what we have in the present."

"Roth's going to have a harder time believing this can work than Judith."

"Undoubtedly. Snobbery can cut both ways. Long before I knew about his affair with Judith, I realized how impossibly frivolous we must seem to him. Really, he's remarkably forbearing." She looked at Malcolm for a moment. "You don't think—"

"That he might have killed Allegra? I can't let myself think at all. And I can't be sure of anything."

∼

BLANCA WATCHED her son Pedro run over to join Colin, Jessica, Emily, and Clara in the Berkeley Square garden, then walked over to sit beside Mélanie on one of the benches. "It's good to be investigating again."

"The challenge," Mélanie agreed. She'd rather regretted not going with Malcolm to talk to Frances, but it was a talk he needed to have with his aunt alone, and she had more revisions to work on. The sun had broken through the clouds, so she'd seized the moment to get the children outside, despite the cold. Snow lingered on the ground and they were making a snowman.

Mélanie folded her gloved hands round her pencil on top of the script in her lap.

"It's always a tangle, but usually I don't mind much," Blanca said. "That is, I can keep on going and not dwell on the unpleasantness. Miles dwells on it more. He doesn't admit it, but he does. But this case—" She wrinkled her nose. "It's harder than most."

"Knowing people involved makes it hard."

"We always know people involved. But somehow this time—I like Jeremy, I like him a lot, but I've liked other people we've known caught up in cases." Blanca shrugged, casting off her qualms as she had been casting off challenges from when she first became a spy. From when she and Mélanie went undercover, lying to the men they were both involved with. Or at least, Blanca had been involved with Addison not long after Mélanie married Malcolm. "This may be nothing. It doesn't obviously seem connected. But Jessica said you and Julien went to see Judith yesterday. I'm guessing that was to do with the case."

Normally Mélanie was completely open with Blanca in an investigation, but Judith and Roth's relationship was delicate ground. "It was," she said.

Blanca nodded. "I'm friends with Mary, Judith's nursemaid. She came to town with Judith and Serena yesterday. Mary called round this morning. Judith had sent her on an errand and she stopped to have a cup of tea. Mary's not one to gossip. I think she suspects Judith may have a lover, but she didn't say so. Not in so many words. She's very fond of Judith, who treats all the staff well. But she did say she'd swear someone had been in the study recently in the Richmond house. It's upstairs, next to the bedchamber that was Bobby's. They had separate bedchambers."

"Many couples in the beau monde do. Most, in fact."

"I know. But most of your friends don't. I mean—"

A cry of glee came from the children. Emily launched a snowball at Colin. Mélanie smiled. "The staffs talk. I quite understand."

"Not about that. Well—"

"It's why Malcolm went on sleeping with me after he learnt the truth." Mélanie had never admitted that to anyone else, probably never would admit it to anyone else. "He knew if he didn't, the staff would know something had changed and wonder, and someone would say something to a friend and word would get back to Hubert. Or he was afraid it would."

"Did he say so?" Blanca asked.

"Not in so many words. But knowing Malcolm, I'm quite sure it's the truth. He went undercover pretending to still be happily married, because that seemed the only way to keep us safe."

"And then you were happily married again."

"Eventually. Miraculously." Assuming the word happy could ever be so easily used. She looked across the garden. Colin tossed a snowball back at Emily. Emily caught it in her gloved hand. "Undercover one can start to believe the truth of the cover. I should be grateful for that."

Blanca shot a look at her. "Feelings undercover can be real."

"Yes. We know that better than anyone."

Blanca watched Pedro scoop up snow and toss it at Jessica, who giggled and threw a handful back. "Apparently the study isn't used much since Bobby died, but Serena likes to go in there and play with the lion bookends. Mary said one day she was quite sure the pen and pen knife on the desk weren't exactly as they'd been left. Another day she thought the writing box had moved. She's observant. The thing is, from what she said, I think she suspected a man who might have been there to see Judith." Blanca hesitated. The snowball fight had stopped. Emily helped Clara pick up a snowball and add it to the snowman. "Not that Judith shouldn't have a lover. It's been more than a year. But I couldn't but wonder if this is connected to everything else."

"Yes," Mélanie watched Jessica tuck a stick arm into the snowman's side. Amazing what a difference a small detail could make. "I think it very likely is."

MALCOLM SETTLED himself at the table on the raised platform at the back of the White Lion, where he and Roth had talked before. He'd asked Roth to meet him here so he could update Roth on his talk with Frances. Normally it would be something for Roth and Judith to discuss, but any contact between them was risky, and with the home office involved, Roth needed to know.

A stir of movement caught his attention, but when he looked up it wasn't Roth approaching through the crowd. It was Higgins.

"Mr. Rannoch." Higgins covered the remaining distance to Malcolm's table. "I was hoping I'd find you here."

"Please sit down," Malcolm said. Because there wasn't really an alternative. And because if Higgins wanted to talk to him, he wanted to talk to Higgins.

Higgins settled himself in the chair across from Malcolm. "I know you're investigating, Mr. Rannoch. No sense in either of us pretending that isn't the case. I've been told by official channels to let you do as you please. I don't begrudge you. You have a skill for it, obviously. And Roth's a friend of yours. Difficult to be personally connected. But also hard to stay away. I do recognize that. I also thought you might be interested in a bit of information I came across."

Malcolm inclined his head, wary of what he might be asked for in recompense. "Anything relating to the case is obviously of interest. We aren't in competition."

"Of course not. Though it's different, of course. I'm beholden to bring the perpetrator to justice." Higgins paused for a moment, expression studiously neutral, though the very pause let the implication that Malcolm might not bring the perpetrator to justice linger in the air. Higgins tapped his fingers on the table. "Roth said that he engaged someone to make inquiries about Allegra Roth after she disappeared. One of my patrols tracked down the man in question."

It was a shock of cold water he should have seen coming. He couldn't control his expression quickly enough.

"Didn't think of that, did you?" Higgins said. "Not surprising. Roth's a friend of yours. Of course you'd trust what he said. I have to take a different tack." The slats creaked as he shifted in his chair. "The man he engaged is named Timmons. Formerly employed by Bow Street. Makes more money now on private cases. He confirmed that Roth had traced Allegra—Mrs. Roth—to Falmouth, as he told us last night. And that he couldn't find a further trail, couldn't even be sure she'd left the country. He couldn't leave himself, because of his children."

"All of which he told us."

"Yes. But Timmons wasn't tied to England. He was able to travel and had a number of sources abroad. He said it was challenging, but he was eventually able to place Allegra Roth on a ship bound for the Argentine."

Again, it shouldn't be a surprise. Roth was good. He wouldn't have given up. And his instinct was to hold secrets close, even from friends. Malcolm could understand that. But damn it, hadn't Jeremy realized this would come out? "Did Timmons say he told Roth?" Malcolm asked.

"Oh yes. He gave Roth the name of Allegra Roth's lover. According to Timmons, Roth was getting regular reports from a source in the Argentine. And Roth had Timmons looking into Esquivel here, though Timmons said Roth seemed to want to do most of that himself. Though he did say Roth was very interested in Esquivel's life in Britain, especially his time at Cambridge and the friendships he'd formed there."

Malcolm took a drink from the tankard of porter on the table before him. This time he managed to school his features. The friendships Esquivel had formed at Cambridge. Martin Rowley. William Beardsley. And Bobby Derwent. Whose widow Roth had tumbled into an affair with.

Malcolm had still been struggling with how Roth had fallen in love with Judith, and even more how he'd risked an affair. But if the affair had been cover for an investigation, it made a great deal more sense.

Roth had gone into the relationship to spy on Judith.

CHAPTER 36

$\mathcal{M}$alcolm stared at Roth across the same table at which he'd spoken with Higgins. "You've been lying to me from the start."

"I haven't told you everything. Just as you frequently haven't told me everything in investigations."

"You knew Allegra had run off with Marco Esquivel."

"Yes." Roth drew a breath. "I traced her to Falmouth, as I said. But I found an inn where a woman matching her description had stayed with a man looking like Esquivel. I'd already had suspicions about their affair before she ran off. I knew she had a lover. I was jealous enough to make inquiries and identify him. I didn't think it would last. It wasn't her first affair, and I didn't expect it to be her last. I didn't let myself expend a huge amount of energy on it. Not until she disappeared. But then my suspicions about Esquivel helped me trace her. I engaged a former runner named Timmons to make further inquiries. He got a reliable report of Esquivel's boarding the ship for the Argentine with a lady. It took over a year, but through Timmons I got reports of the singer Alejandra Vargas who was Marco Esquivel's mistress. I was quite sure it was Allegra."

"My compliments," Malcolm said. "Your shock and confusion last night appeared genuine."

"I may not have been an agent on your level, but I have acquired basic skills."

"I know your skills, and I was a fool not to credit them. If Mélanie disappeared, I wouldn't stop at tracing her to Falmouth. I should have known you wouldn't stop either. But then I didn't want to see it."

"Always a fatal mistake," Roth said.

"Yes, so it is." Malcolm scoured Roth's face. After Higgins left and before Roth arrived, Blanca had come to see him at the White Lion, bringing information that only confirmed the suspicions he'd formed based on Higgins's revelations. "That day last autumn when you went over to help Serena, when you and Judith both say you began to talk and began to see each other as more than friends—did you approach Judith because you'd learned Bobby was close to Marco Esquivel?"

Something flinched in the depths of Roth's eyes, but he kept his gaze steady. "Judith means an incalculable amount to me. But yes, I knew. And yes, that's why I first let go my reticence and let myself talk to Judith. Whom I had noticed from the first time I saw her in Berkeley Square."

Malcolm tightened his grip on his tankard, regarding his comrade from the Peninsula, the man who had saved his life and whose life he had saved, his investigative partner, the man with whom he shared secrets, the man from whom he was still concealing secrets. "I'm trying, Jeremy. My every instinct from the first has been that you couldn't have done this. But you have to stop lying to me."

"So that you can prove my innocence?"

"So that I can learn who killed your wife, as you so eloquently told me you wanted to do. Unless that isn't what you want at all."

Roth's gaze clashed with Malcolm's own. They might have

been back on the field in the Peninsula, sabres in hand. Save that Roth, not an officer, had never carried a sabre. And neither had Malcolm, a civilian. "Are you accusing me of killing Allegra?"

"I don't know who killed Allegra. But given the lies you've told, I'm questioning what you really want out of this investigation."

"You must know it's never as simple as wanting one thing. I want to learn who killed Allegra. And to achieve what we rather laughably call justice for what was done to her. I want to protect Judith. I want to keep myself out of Newgate and avoid the hangman's noose. Because I want to be there for my children. And because I enjoy my life enough I don't want to part with it."

"I'm relieved to hear you say so. But you aren't doing a very good job of it. You've got even the people on your side asking questions. I'm not saying to be honest with Bow Street and Higgins, but for god's sake be honest with us."

"Because you've always been honest with me?"

The sabres clashed again. Unvoiced secrets danced in the air between them. Half-formed suspicions about what Roth might know, might guess, shifted in the air like images in cannon smoke. "I want to save you, Jeremy."

"And you want the truth."

"Isn't that the point of an investigation?"

"That depends on who's running it, as I soon learnt when I began my employment. Do you still believe I'm innocent?"

"I want to believe you are."

Roth held Malcolm's gaze for a long time. The sabres were down, but the field between them stretched longer. "You must know by now that you can't always see the truth. Even about those closest to you."

It was the closest Roth had come to admitting he knew the truth about Mélanie. Which opened a whole range of possibilities of what Roth might do as the investigation progressed.

"You went through Bobby's things."

Roth's gaze flickered with the question of how Malcolm knew, but he didn't ask. "Yes."

"What did you learn?"

"Esquivel had been writing to his friends about starting a shipping company in the Argentine. Bobby was investing and he wanted Beardsley and Rowley to invest . He was talking to Rowley about using his steam engines in mines in Chile and possibly starting a railway in the future. I don't think Judith knew anything about it. Though not necessarily because of any secrecy. I don't think she and Bobby talked a great deal."

"No, nor do I."

"But Esquivel talked to Allegra. That was clear from Esquivel's letters to Bobby." Roth raked a hand through his hair. "I don't even know what I wanted when I looked through Bobby's papers. I had no illusions that Allegra would come back. I didn't want her back. I told myself I needed to be sure she was safe. Which was true. But I think I also needed to understand why she'd left. Why did I have questions about something so obvious? Our marriage hadn't worked. But we'd attempted to build a life together—"

"I understand," Malcolm said.

Roth shot a look at him.

"Despite everything else, I understand that. She was your children's mother. That made her part of your family forever, no matter what. You're too conscientious not to have cared. I'm not saying that excuses your deceiving Judith, that it excuses your going through Bobby's papers, however you got into the house. But I do understand the impulse."

"You're remarkable, Rannoch."

"I didn't say I forgave anything."

"I didn't ask you to forgive anything." Roth pushed back his chair. "I'd like to tell Judith myself. I know it's not best for us to be seen together—"

"Bow Street and the home office already know. And yes, of

course she should hear it from you. But it's probably safer to have her meet you in Berkeley Square. No one would look askance at either of you calling there."

"Sensible. Assuming she'll agree to talk to me. She wasn't very happy with me when we left yesterday."

"She'll talk to you."

"And then you'll question her."

"It's an investigation, Jeremy."

JUDITH STARED across the small salon in Berkeley Square at the man she loved. The man she'd thought she loved. She'd been shocked when her mother's footman had brought her a note from Jeremy asking her to meet him in Berkeley Square. Shocked and hopeful. Until she arrived and saw his guarded expression. It was the only safe place they could meet, he'd said. No one would think of their both calling on Malcolm and Mélanie, and no one would think they'd come to see each other. Even then she'd put his wary delivery down to his qualms and the awkwardness of their being in her cousin's house as acknowledged lovers. He wanted to talk to her. After her ultimatum at the White Lion. That had to mean something.

And then Jeremy had begun to talk. And her life unraveled in ways she would not have thought possible.

"I was always surprised you spoke to me at that party," Judith said when Jeremy finished speaking. "Because often as you came to family parties, you always hung back from those not involved in investigations. As though you could be friends with people you already associated with, but held the rest of us at bay. I thought you'd think I was too frivolous—"

"Judith—"

"Or above your touch somehow. Which is silly. Or maybe not.

I grew up with plenty of people who thought I was above their touch and plenty who thought they were above mine. That's life in Mayfair. I thought it was Serena and our both being parents that broke through your reserve. But that wasn't it at all, was it?" Judith heard her voice crack. She dragged it back under her control. "You came over deliberately. Because you'd learned Bobby had been close to Marco Esquivel. As much as you try to stay out of the beau monde, you're an investigator. And suddenly I was an object in your investigation."

"Judith, for god's sake—"

"Can you deny it? Was there any other reason you approached me that day?"

Jeremy drew a breath that grated like ungreased wheels on granite. "Yes, I'd learned Bobby had been friends with Esquivel. Yes, I couldn't but be curious about what you might know. I was on my way to talk to you when Serena dropped her toy. I came over to help."

"And to see what I had to say about Bobby."

"Yes." Roth met her gaze without flinching. His gaze was steady, even kind, but the gaze of a distant acquaintance, not her lover. "I wanted to hear what you had to say about Bobby. I wanted to know more about Bobby's connections to Marco Esquivel. I wanted to unravel what had happened to Allegra."

"Because you're still in love with her." There it was. The same realization that had ripped her insides apart in the White Lion yesterday.

"Because she's the mother of my children. Because we made promises to each other. Because I felt I'd let her down."

"And getting close to Bobby's widow was a good way to learn more. And atone for your mistakes."

"No." He took a half step forwards. "Your being Bobby's widow may have got me across the room and across my reticence that day. It didn't get me beyond that. My god, you know what's between us—"

"I thought I did." Judith folded her arms over her chest. "I know what I felt for you. I know what it meant to me. What it still means. But I'm questioning every one of your motives. Every conversation we had. The first brush of our fingers. The first kiss. When I took you into my bed—"

"Judith—"

"Bobby's bedchamber was next to mine." Her fingers bit into her arms through the taffeta of her sleeves . "Can you tell me you didn't use that? Did you ever go through Bobby's things?"

His expression was answer enough. Judith spun away. "I'm such a fool. I grew up in a family of spies. I thought I was immune to all that. I thought I lived my life on different terms. More boring perhaps, but more honest. I never thought I was being spied on, especially in the most intimate moments of my life."

"Judith—" Jeremy's voice was rough and yet somehow stripped to a sort of honesty. As though in that instant, he had stopped trying to protect her. Perhaps for the first time. Assuming he'd ever really been trying to protect her at all.

Judith turned back to look at him. She couldn't let her guard down. She never would with him again. But she wanted to hear what he had to say.

"You grew up among spies," Jeremy said. "You've seen them. You've heard them talk. You must know spy missions don't negate feelings. That it's possible to be on a mission, and to meet some-one, even become lovers with someone, on a mission and still care for them."

"Is that what I was? A mission?"

"Of course not."

"But learning about Bobby was a mission." She swallowed, forced herself to think, forced herself to view her family not as the child on the outside but as one of their number. "I believe spies have feelings. I can see Malcolm or Mélanie or Raoul or Kitty or Julien caring about someone they lied to to uncover information. Feeling guilty about what they'd done. I think even Julien might feel guilty. But I can't see them falling in love so deeply they felt they'd found the other half of themselves. The way I did with you. They all have that. But it's with another spy. Not with someone they spied on."

"Sometimes spies spy on each other."

"I'm not a spy. I'm a person caught in a web I thought I'd managed to stay out of." Judith stared at the man she had loved in a way she hadn't thought possible. "The irony is if you'd just come to me and told me Bobby had been friends with the man who'd run off with your wife, I'd have told you anything I could. I'd have let you look through any of Bobby's things you wanted. I always liked you. I liked the boys. You wouldn't have had to go to the trouble of seduction."

"It wasn't trouble." His gaze wasn't guarded now. It sliced her in two. "And I don't think it was seduction."

"No, I'll grant you that. If anything, I seduced you. I'm sorry. Perhaps you never meant to be caught in that net. And I pulled you into it. Instead of its being a simple mission."

"Judith." He put out a hand, then let it fall. "I can't justify myself. It's insulting to us both for me to try to do so. Believe what you will of me. But what I felt—what I feel—for you had nothing to do with a mission or with Bobby or Allegra. It was something I've never known before in my life and don't expect to ever know again. And though I'll never forgive myself for what I've put you through, for myself it was worth it."

Judith stared into his eyes. They had always seemed so free of artifice. That was one of the first things that had drawn her to him. He didn't play the drawing room games she had grown up with at balls and Almack's, on Rotten Row, in the galleries at Somerset House, in boxes at the theatre. And he didn't play the spy games that seemed to put so many of the people in her family in a state of constant turmoil. That made her question who they were (sometimes literally, recalling certain moments she'd seen them in disguise). Jeremy was himself and had seen her as herself. Not a diamond of the first water. Not the daughter of the scandalous Fanny Dacre-Hammond who might be a royal by-blow. Not the widow of a young sprig of the ton. Not a future Mayfair hostess.

Or so it had seemed. Everything between them, a love built on the bedrock of reality, had been an illusion, built on shifting sands.

"How can you possibly say that, Jeremy? How can you possibly know that or anything else? You obviously don't know me or you wouldn't be attempting any of this. And I begin to wonder if you know yourself."

Jeremy stood there watching her. Brown hair ruffled. Coat creased. Cravat askew. She'd never before noticed how ridiculously delicate the spindly legs on the chairs were. Or how gleaming and impractical the ivory watered silk that covered them. She'd always loved this room. Emulated it when she decorated the villa in Richmond. Suddenly it felt wrong. Or she felt wrong.

"I knew it had to end, Judith," Jeremy said. "I should probably be happy to see your feelings for me die, because it had to happen at some point. And I should probably be glad to leave you thinking the worst of me. I'm not proud of myself. I can't defend my actions. But somehow I can't bear to see what was between us tainted."

From his tone and gaze, one would swear he believed it. And she believed him. That was the hell of it. "What was between us was an illusion, Jeremy. It didn't even exist. Let's stop pretending."

"I understand you'll never trust me again. I imagine you think—"

"That you killed Allegra?" She hadn't let herself consider it, but now looking at him, the man she had thought she knew so well, the man she realized she didn't know at all, the answer was obvious. "No. I can't imagine it. Which perhaps shows just what a fool I am. And yet—"

She crossed to him and took his hands, though a few moments before she'd have sworn she'd never touch him again. "I don't expect we'll see each other again after the next few days. But whatever I can do to help you prove your innocence and learn the truth, tell me. Because much as I can't bear all of this, I can't bear the thought of your being imprisoned." Or worse. "If what was between us means anything, it means that."

He looked down at her, face white with shock. "I can't ask you—"

"You're not asking me. I'm telling you. And if you owe me nothing else, you owe it to me to listen. You need to do everything you can to clear your name. Which means telling Malcolm and Mélanie and the others everything, no matter how much it hurts. They can't save you if they don't know. And you can't save yourself. You're too hemmed in on all sides. You need to learn the truth. To save yourself. To give the boys an answer. And because whatever you feel for Allegra, you need some sort of closure."

"I am letting them help. I summoned Malcolm and asked for his help at the start."

"And lied to him."

"I couldn't tell him—"

"That we were lovers? Or that you were spying on me?"

"Both."

"You can't have those qualms now. You can't have any qualms. Or pride. And you have to let me help."

"You can't—"

"I can't do anything? That's rather lowering. I may not be an agent, but I was born into a family of agents. I grew up in it. I have some skills. I'm not claiming I can do this on my own, but I can help. You owe it to me to let me at least do that much."

A slow smile crossed Roth's face. "Judith. My darling. I've

never been able to—would never have attempted to—control anything you did."

"Well, then." Judith put her hands on his chest. "That's the most sensible thing you've said all day, Jeremy Roth. Now you need to do the hardest thing of all."

"What?"

"Go home and stay put and let the rest of us handle this."

CHAPTER 37

*J*udith found Mélanie in her study. Pencil scratching over a manuscript stack, hair slipping from its pins, sleeves of her gold-striped moss green sarcenet gown pushed up. Still impossibly lovely, just as she'd been the moment she'd got out of the carriage when she first arrived at Judith's mother's house. How did she do it? She'd more than half walked away from the beau monde and she was still better attuned to surviving in it than Judith, who'd been born to it.

Mélanie set her pencil down on the polished walnut writing desk and looked at Judith. Two more strands of dark hair slipped artfully beside her face. Her gaze told Judith all she needed to know. "You knew?"

Mélanie adjusted the manuscript pages before her. Judith could see the names of characters. Script pages from the new play. "We learned today. Jeremy wanted to tell you himself. He asked Malcolm. Was that the wrong decision?"

Judith pulled a straight-backed chair closer to the desk. It was simpler wood than the chairs in the small salon and had a surprisingly comfortable cushion. It occurred to her that Mélanie had done this room for herself while the small salon was for guests.

"No. I needed to hear it from Jeremy. I might not have believed it otherwise. I'd have insisted on talking to him and hearing it from him, and I'd have called anyone else who tried to tell me a liar."

"I'm sorry," Mélanie said. Judith had seen that same look in her eyes when she talked to her children, though she had no doubt Mélanie was talking to her as an adult.

"You're an agent. At least, you've been one." Judith was still not entirely sure of the parameters of her cousin's wife's life, but she knew it had been adventurous. Was adventurous. "I know you have to pretend things. Even to people you like. But you couldn't genuinely love someone and lie to them, could you?"

A host of emotions flickered across Mélanie's face. "Oh, darling. We all tell different lies to different people in our lives, don't we?"

"Yes, but not on the same scale."

"Is it the scale? Or the fact that one can compartmentalize? Care for someone deeply in most of your life and yet at times other loyalties take hold?"

Judith felt herself frown. She wanted to ask if Mélanie could do that to Malcolm, yet it somehow didn't seem right. "But it all began with a lie."

"Where a relationship begins doesn't necessarily dictate what it becomes."

Judith sat back in her chair. "Are you on Jeremy's side?"

"By no means. I don't agree with what he did to you, and you have every right not to see him again if you don't wish to."

"What if I do wish to see him again?"

"That's up to you. I'd certainly say people can do outrageous things without being bad people. In fact, I don't really think there's such a thing as bad people, though I do agree some actions are unforgivable. But most of us are very fortunate that a great many actions are forgivable, one way and another."

"I'm not sure if it's even a question of forgiving. If I even have a right to, in a sense. I'm not sure what he is to me. I know I'm furious with him. I think perhaps I always will be. But I also know I'm terrified of what this investigation may do to him. I can't walk away, at least not until I know he's safe."

"You have plenty of time to decide what more you want."

"I'm not sure what more is even possible. I may even believe him when he says he genuinely cared for me. But he was obviously still obsessed with Allegra. I was already afraid he fell in love with me because he thought I was like her. Now I know if it weren't for wanting more information about her, he'd never even have tried to get close to me. How can he possibly care for me or even know me if he's still in love with her?"

"My dear. It's entirely possible for someone to love two people at once. It's also possible to be determined to ferret out the truth about a lost love for all sorts of reasons other than love."

"But I don't think Jeremy really knew me. Knows me. Oddly, I think I know him better than he knows me, for all he was lying to me."

"Which could argue that at least some of what you fell in love with is real."

"Maybe."

"Did you think he knew you when you were together?"

"Yes. That's just it. He seemed to understand me as Bobby never had. The real me, not the person I was in society. Not even the person most of my family sees." She stared at her hands. "I didn't know."

"About Jeremy?"

"No. Well, yes, I didn't know any of that. But I didn't know about Bobby. About his investing in this shipping venture in the Argentine. I didn't even know he had a friend named Marco Esquivel. Well, I did know he had a friend from Cambridge named Marco, who was in the Argentine. He'd come up every so often in Bobby's university stories. Along with Martin Rowley and William Beardsley. But Bobby didn't talk about university much. I'm starting to wonder what we did talk about. I didn't know he was writing to Marco Esquivel. And he certainly never told me he was investing in a shipping venture. Jeremy knew more about my husband than I did."

"Couples talk about different things."

"Can you honestly tell me Malcolm wouldn't tell you something like that? I can't imagine Archie's not telling Mama. Or Raoul's not telling Laura, or Geoff's not telling Allie, or any of our close friends. The truth is, after the first few months, Bobby and I spent less and less time together. Part of it was what was expected of us. Bobby went to his club, went out with his friends, I paid calls and went to china and silk warehouses because we were doing up the house, and went to my modiste. And we went out in the evening, and sat beside other people at dinner, and danced with other people." Judith studied Mélanie, thinking of the quick communication she saw between her and Malcolm, the way they seemed to have a whole conversation sometimes just in the meeting of their gazes. "Investigating must give you and Malcolm something to talk about. You have a whole life together because you're agents."

Mélanie gave a laugh that was unexpectedly sharp. "That's true."

"And you talk about politics. Bobby didn't seem to have any interest like that. We could have talked about the Argentine. I'd have been quite interested, I think. I wonder if Bobby thought it would bore me. Or if he wanted to keep it to himself. I wasn't a very great success as a wife."

"It takes two people to make a marriage work, dearest."

"Everyone always seemed to think ours was working."

"Sometimes people see what they want to see."

"I don't remember ever quarreling with Bobby. It was just that there was a lack of"—Judith frowned, struggling for the right words—"a lack of everything I see between you and Malcolm, and Mama and Archie, and all your other friends. Until I met you and saw you with Malcolm, I didn't really know that was possible. I certainly didn't see it between my parents."

"When you met me, Malcolm and I still had a lot to work out. It isn't easy to learn to share your life with another person. And Malcolm and I got married rather abruptly."

"But you were trying to share your lives. You were—interacting. It sounds so simple, but it's amazing how one can share a house and barely interact at all, beyond a superficial level. I wonder if Bobby thought I was superficial."

"I very much doubt he thought anything of the sort. You were at the very beginning of your marriage. You didn't have a chance to see what it might grow into."

"I hope it would have grown into something. I hope I wasn't a fool who made a dreadful mistake. I wasn't unhappy, but I was restless. I wonder if that's how it was for Mama. If that's how her affairs started. Not that I—I mean, I didn't even consider. I don't think Bobby did—that is, I didn't used to think it. Now—I'm not sure what I know about him. I need to look through his papers. Perhaps I should be grateful to Jeremy for teaching me something about my husband. In some ways, Bobby's as much of a cipher to me as Allegra must be to Jeremy." Judith started to push herself to her feet, then looked at Mélanie. "Do you think Jeremy will be arrested?"

"I don't know." Mélanie's gaze was steady and honest, for which Judith was intensely grateful. "Bow Street are under a lot of pressure to resolve things. But also to find answers. Hubert wants that as well. Assuming, of course, that Hubert isn't behind this. We're doing everything we can to find the truth."

Judith studied Mélanie's face, reading the things that she wasn't saying, like the notes she could see in between the lines of dialogue in the script on Mélanie's writing desk. "And you can't really be sure Jeremy is innocent, can you?"

Mélanie drew in and released her breath. "Difficult to be sure of anything. Not entirely."

"I do see that. You have to make yourself ask that question. Especially when someone proves to be keeping secrets. And you still have to ask those questions about me. I mean, just because what was between Jeremy and me wasn't real, doesn't mean I didn't think it was. Didn't have every reason to want Jeremy to be free so we could be together. Because a part of me can't let go of that. Even now. Even though I know it's an illusion."

AFTER HE DELIVERED the coded paper from the bust of Agrippina to Aline Blackwell, Harry found Fitzroy Somerset in the ordnance office in Pall Mall. "Davenport." Fitzroy greeted him with the same easy smile he'd managed to keep in place in mud huts and leaky bivouacs from the Peninsula to Belgium. He'd been Wellington's military secretary then and was his secretary now that Wellington was master-general of the ordnance. "I thought you'd be busy helping Malcolm in his latest investigation."

"You've heard?"

"There are rumors. You know how quickly rumors spread. There's a connection to the Argentine, I understand."

"Yes. That's why I'm here, actually." Harry moved to a chair. "Have you ever heard any rumors about Edward Ashford's death?"

"Ashford?" Fitzroy's fair brows drew together. "What's he got to do with this?"

"He knew the murder victim, Allegra Roth, who was called Alejandra Vargas then, in Buenos Aires."

"And you think Ashford has something to do with why she was killed?"

"Miss Vargas apparently believed Ashford was murdered."

Surprise crossed Fitzroy's face. But not the shock Harry expected.

"Kit—Lady Carfax is naturally concerned," Harry said.

Fitzroy tended to overestimate the fragility of women. For

once that could be helpful. "Never had much use for Ashford, I confess. What he put his wife through was appalling. And she appeared to have ten times his understanding."

"More like twenty."

Fitzroy grimaced. "We had to sweep Ashford's involvements with married local women under the carpet more than once. He had a knack for choosing the wives of our Portuguese and Spanish allies, whose husbands were less than complacent. I once had to spend a very uncomfortable afternoon convincing a conde not to challenge Ashford to a duel. It was a distinct relief when he went off to the Argentine."

"So that was an effort to get rid of him?"

Fitzroy shifted his left arm. Like Harry, he had been injured in the war, but Fitzroy had lost his right arm entirely. "No. Oddly, Ashford was pushing for it. Wellington said good riddance and he wished he'd thought of it sooner, except he wouldn't have wished Ashford on the Argentines. I never could understand how Ashford didn't have more appreciation of his own wife. Glad she seems happy with Carfax—odd calling him that."

"It is. And she is. Very much so." Harry stretched his legs out. "How did Ashford last as long as he did?"

"What do you mean? He hadn't actually done anything to get himself cashiered."

"No, but Wellington doesn't suffer fools gladly. He's good at arranging a quiet transfer."

"Well, by the Peninsula we needed everyone we could get. Though I always wondered—"

"What?" Harry asked.

Fitzroy picked up his pen and turned it over. "It may be a fancy, but I always had the sense Ashford had friends in Whitehall. We've seen enough of those. Promoted when they shouldn't be."

"The Ashford family aren't particularly powerful."

"No. It wasn't his father. Ashford had an uncle in the diplomatic service, but he died before Ashford went to the Argentine. As I said, I may be wrong."

"And when you heard he'd died?"

"Wellington said he was shocked it hadn't happened sooner. When we heard it was his heart, Wellington's first comment was that he must have been with a mistress."

"There was never any discussion that it might not have been natural causes?"

Fitzroy frowned down at his desktop. He shifted some papers on the ink blotter. "Not that I heard directly. But I did once over-hear Wellington and Castlereagh muttering about it. I was in the passage outside Castlereagh's office. Palmerston was there too. Difficult not to listen. We couldn't hear much, but I did hear Wellington say they'd be wiser not to ask questions."

MALCOLM FOUND Marco Esquivel in Jackson's Boxing Academy. He and his sparring partner, William Beardsley, had just stepped out of the ring.

"I miss activity," Esquivel said, a towel draped round his neck. "There's much less sitting about in the Argentine. And lately I confess I find the sitting about insupportable."

"Understandable," Malcolm said.

The three of them repaired across the street to a pub. Beard-sley came along as a matter of course, which wasn't a bad thing considering the subject matter. He might be more tangled in the investigation than Malcom had realized at first.

"You didn't tell us last night that you'd hidden a coded paper in the bust of Agrippina," Malcom said, when they were seated at a table with pints in front of them.

Esquivel's shocked gaze was answer enough, even before he said, "What?"

"Someone broke into the Davenports' house last night and

tried to steal the bust. Harry examined it and found a coded paper tucked in a crack in the marble."

Beardsley was looking at Esquivel. "You don't mean the bust of Agrippina that Mr. Lambton used to talk about?"

"Yes." Esquivel pushed his pint between his hands on the table. "It ended up in the Argentine. It's a long story. But I never hid anything in it."

Malcolm believed that. Probably. "So who might have done?"

"I can't—" Esquivel's gaze froze. "Alejandra asked me what had happened to the bust after we got to London. She seemed distressed when I said I'd sent it to Lambton. I didn't think much of it. But now that I know she was a spy—what did this paper say?"

"I don't know. It's a complex code. Davenport's taking it to someone to decode it."

"You think it has to do with why Alejandra—"

"I'm not sure what it has to do with. But anything to do with Alejandra is potentially connected to the case." Malcolm took a drink of porter. It was a long time since he'd paid so many visits to pubs in two days. "I've also realized you were more in touch with Bobby Derwent than I knew."

"Bobby? Oh yes. He was one of us. At Cambridge." Esquivel took a deep drink of porter. "You knew him?"

"He was married to my cousin."

"God. I'm sorry."

"She had no notion Bobby had invested in your shipping company."

"Yes, he was the first to commit. Very excited about it. He was planning a trip to the Argentine when he died."

Beardsley shot a look at Esquivel. "Bobby was going out to the Argentine?"

"We'd talked about it." Esquivel turned his tankard on the table. "Truth to tell, Bobby was the one who was eager for it." He cast a quick look at Malcolm. "I think he was restless at home."

"His wife would agree with you," Malcolm said. "Though I don't think she realized he was planning to leave the country." That was going to be another shock to Judith.

Beardsley stared at Esquivel. "Surely you wouldn't have asked Bobby to—"

"What?" Esquivel swung his gaze to his friend. "Leave his family, as I did?"

"It was your fight," Beardsley said. "Not that—"

"You'd have done it?"

"We all make different choices. I suppose it seems different to me now that—"

"What? Don't tell me you're thinking of leaving your mysterious beautiful mistress and marrying yourself."

"None of your damned business." Beardsley took a drink of porter. "I'm just surprised Bobby was playing that deep."

"Bobby was more involved in the shipping venture," Esquivel said. "More even than Rowley, and you haven't fully committed."

"He had more money to invest," Beardsley said.

"That's true." Esquivel took another drink. "Though lately I'd begun to wonder—" He broke off.

"What?" Malcolm said.

Esquivel turned his tankard, swirling the porter. "Some information I'd shared with Bobby in those last months got to the wrong places. I'd begun to wonder if I could trust him at all."

CHAPTER 38

Cressida Caldwell looked from Mélanie to Kitty. "I'm sorry. I seem to have called at a bad time."

"If it's to do with the case, there can't be a bad time," Mélanie said as Miss Caldwell stepped into the Berkeley Square library.

"And I realize it's problematic for me to call on you."

"After our talk yesterday, you can hardly think that matters to me. I don't believe you know Lady Carfax?"

"Miss Caldwell." Kitty inclined her head. She had brought the children round to Berkeley Square. Julien was off making inquiries among former agents who might have heard rumors about Edward Ashford, and though Kitty had agreed he could do it better without her, she clearly felt sidelined.

"I won't waste your time on pleasantries," Miss Caldwell said when they were seated. "But I've been trying to remember anything Allegra said to me that could connect to this. You said she was killed in Seven Dials."

"Yes," Mélanie said. "In a tavern. The Three Queens."

Miss Caldwell's elegant brows drew together. "I don't know anything about the Three Queens. But there was a man Allegra used to visit. Before she ran off with Gresham. And later, after she married Jeremy. I don't know that she saw him on this visit to London. She didn't mention him when I saw her. But I wouldn't be surprised. Whatever was between them, it endured."

"What was his name?" Kitty asked.

"Ralph Allen. No, that's not quite it. I used to think that, but later I realized—it's Allam. Ralph Allam."

Mélanie got to her feet and went to the library table.

"You've heard of him?" Miss Caldwell asked.

Mélanie flipped through the papers on the table. "He's on the list Lady Carfax's husband and our friend Addison compiled of the staff at the Three Queens. He's a barkeep there."

Miss Caldwell's eyes widened in surprise. "You think Allegra went there to see him?"

"She summoned Jeremy to meet her there," Mélanie said. "But it may give us a clue as to why she chose it. What else do you know about Ralph Allam?"

"Very little. Allegra was always secretive about him. And when she did mention him, she'd laugh as though there was some secret about him. Allegra was always drawn to danger." Miss Caldwell looked from Mélanie to Kitty. "Will you—"

"We can take care of ourselves," Kitty said.

"I don't doubt it," Miss Caldwell got to her feet. "I won't keep you. Much better for you to get on with the investigation."

After she'd seen Miss Caldwell from the house, Mélanie returned to the list of the Three Queens staff. "We need to go back to the Three Queens."

"Yes." Kitty was already on her feet.

Mélanie fingered the paper. She'd told Malcolm more than once that being a mother made her more cautious. And it was true. In theory, at least. "We could wait for Malcolm and Julien."

"We could." Kitty lifted her shawl from the chair back she'd tossed it over. "But who knows how long either of them will be. Or Raoul and Laura, for that matter." They were out trying to trace Allegra Roth's movements. "We risk letting the trail grow cold. Or Higgins getting to him first. I don't think Julien or Malcolm would wait for us in those circumstances, do you?"

"No." Mélanie set down the papers. "Put like that, there's no question."

"Besides"—Kitty wrapped the shawl round her and threw one end over her shoulder—"I think we may be better suited to getting information in a Seven Dials tavern than Malcolm and Julien are. There are times it's helpful to be a woman in an investigation. Not that Julien isn't very capable of being one when he puts his mind to it." She looked down at the shawl. "Can you lend me some things? We're not going to do well in our current guise."

"Already ahead of you," Mélanie said, moving to the door.

Mélanie gathered up her velvet and lace skirts to avoid the snow and muck in the street. The dress, purple velvet with braid on the sleeves and a lilac lace overskirt, was one she kept for occasions such as this. The black velvet cloak, tied at a haphazard angle over it, had seen better days, though it could still be used in her normal life. The melting snow leaked through the worn soles of her half boots, a pair she'd had since the Peninsula. One heel was lower than the other. An effective persona could make for uncomfortable walking.

Kitty, wearing another pair of her boots that were a size too small, was negotiating the slushy paving without seeming difficulty. She had a feathered hat tugged at a rakish angle over her disheveled hair and wore a frayed green velvet spencer over a tattered black spangled sarcenet. She'd brought her own shawl for added warmth, but was letting it slip off her shoulders to display her costume.

"For a playwright," Mélanie said, "I forget how uncomfortable costumes can be."

"Liberating, in a way," Kitty said. "No one's looking askance at us for being out without a maid or footman. Or without a carriage. Or being in this part of town at all. I'll take that over the questionable offers we've had to fend off."

"Quite," Mélanie said. "God, I never used that word before I met Malcolm."

"I know, it's one of his favorites."

"Not doing well at being in character." Mélanie flashed a flirtatious smile at a man in a spotted neckcloth who was lounging in a tavern doorway.

"It's a mental jump," Kitty said.

Mélanie coughed. Despite the chill bite, the air was thick with the smells of tallow candles, gin, ale, rot, unwashed bodies, emptied chamber pots. All crammed between close-set buildings. There had been a time in her life those smells had not been unfamiliar. She glanced at the grimy wall of a gin shop. Two men and three women lounged on the rotting steps, drinking gin despite the weather. A child about Colin's age picked his way past them, a gin boat balanced in both hands with the care Colin would give to a first edition, or one of Harry and Cordy's potsherds. "Malcom told me this was supposed to be a fashionable quarter when it was laid out over a hundred years ago. It never caught on. Now even the sundial itself is gone." Seven Dials took its name from the sundial that had stood at its heart. The sundial had had six faces, the column being the seventh "dial." It had been taken down fifty years ago and resurrected in Weybridge last year as a memorial to the Duchess of York. Peering through the crowd, Mélanie could imagine townhouses spilling off the central star-shaped juncture of streets where the sundial had stood, though the maze of alleys and courts about it now was nothing like Mayfair.

"Neighborhoods can come down in society just as people can," Kitty said. "Or I suppose go up."

Mélanie lifted her velvet skirt to show a few inches of tattered-stocking-covered ankles. Because it was the sort of thing her character would do with an appreciative gentleman in view. "It's almost half my life ago that I worked in a place like the Three Queens." She angled a smile at a man on the other side of the street. "Not now, love. I'm on my way to a job." She looked back at Kitty. "I learnt a lot from it. I wouldn't be the person I am now without it. Which I suppose I should be grateful for, as I quite like who I am now. But at times I don't care for the memories." She kept the images at bay, but they picked at her senses. Like pecking birds. But much worse. She quite liked birds. "I hate that I was ever that powerless."

"Powerless? From what I know, you survived. When many wouldn't have—figuratively, or perhaps literally. That's a triumph."

"I'm not sure I would have, if Raoul hadn't given me a reason to go on."

"There's a power in turning the tables and using one's wiles to get information," Kitty said. "But it reminds me of things I'd as soon forget. Times it wasn't a matter of getting information, but simply of enduring the life I was in. Times I didn't have a choice." She tugged at the brim of her hat and flashed a smile at a man in a patched coat and jaunty cravat crossing the street in front of them. "I haven't ever quite told Julien that. I don't want him ever to put his arms round me and wonder—"

"Quite," Mélanie said. She took two more steps in silence. "It bothers me more now I have a daughter. Now she's old enough to talk and notice things. There are things I took for granted in my own life that I don't want her ever to go through."

Kitty nodded, sending a lock of hair swinging in front of her face with artful abandon. "Not that I don't think about it with the boys. But I do more with Genny. I don't want her to accept the things that I did as a normal part of life. And not just the outrageous things. I don't want her to accept even a casual touch she doesn't want. I don't want her to marry unless she loves the person and trusts him. And I want her to leave if he crosses certain lines. Which I realize is easier said than done. But there are things no woman—no person—should put up with. Things I put up with from Edward. Things I didn't even question putting up with. Because that was life. And I had no understanding of what marriage could be."

"I never thought of it as anything but a trap," Mélanie said.

"I suppose I did too, in a way. A trap I fell into." Kitty lifted her skirt away from a puddle of melting snow. "I wonder if Allegra Roth felt the same way."

THE THREE QUEENS was half full at this relatively early hour. Two men were bent over a dice game in one corner. Three more were playing darts in another. Several flirtations were underway, and a handful of women, milling about the bar or moving between tables, appeared to be looking for more. A crossfire of appraising glances shot over Mélanie and Kitty as they came in. They were competition for the slim pickings available.

Mélanie and Kitty paused for a moment to take in the room and let their presence be felt, then sauntered up to the bar and asked for Ralph Allam. The barkeep, a stout middle-aged man with a jagged scar on one cheek, said Allam wasn't working today, and he couldn't say where he might be found. Undeterred, Mélanie and Kitty ordered gin and retreated to a table with a good view of the tavern.

"Different barkeep than the night before last," Kitty murmured over her glass of gin. "Can't be sure if the other was Ralph Allam."

"'Blue dress," Mélanie murmured, taking a sip from her own glass that was more of an invisible, pretend sip, just touching the gin to her lips. "Left by the dartboard. Watching us."

"Doesn't look jealous," Kitty said.

The woman was slight and fair-haired, with a pointed chin and sharp green eyes. Mélanie met the other woman's gaze and inclined her head. Not too much. Not enough to scare her off. She remembered all too well how one viewed strangers from those long-ago days in the brothel in Spain. The cautious appraisal before trusting anyone, even for the most casual interaction. The instinct that at first blush no one was to be trusted. That it was better to remain in one's shell than to take any risk. Sharing one's body made it harder to share anything else.

Mélanie turned back to Kitty with the bright smile of a friend sharing casual conversation. "Give it five minutes."

In fact, it was two before the woman in blue appeared at their table. Girl might have been a more accurate term. Despite the shadows round her eyes, Mélanie suspected she was little more than twenty. Her cheeks were rouged, her eyes darkened with blacking. Her blue gros-de-Naples gown had had its cuffs turned more than once, and the lace and ribbon added at the neck covered a tear and a tea stain. But Mélanie could see the design of a skilled modiste in the lines of the gown. Lines from the time she herself had first come to Britain, over five years ago. A Mayfair ballgown that had made its way to the second-hand clothes sellers in Rosemary Lane, remade more than once along the way.

Even when she reached their table, the woman hesitated. "Heard you asking about Ralph Allam."

"Oh yes. Do you know him?" Mélanie asked.

"He's the barkeep here. One of the barkeeps."

"But not working today," Kitty said. "And no one seems to know where to find him. Is he a friend of yours?"

"Oh no." The girl's brows rose at the word friend. "No one— that is, I can't really afford to have friends."

"I know just what you mean." Kitty leaned forwards, elbows on the table. "Molly's too shy to say it"—she cast a glance at Mélanie —"but we need to find him as soon as possible. Before he spends it all."

"All?" the girl asked, attention caught despite her qualms.

"Half a week of Molly's earnings. He made off with them. I told Molly to be careful, but she has a soft spot for a pretty face and a story of a hardened man who wants to reform." Kitty poked Mélanie in the ribs.

"He was kind," Mélanie said with indignation. "And he does have the nicest eyes."

"Hrmph." Kitty rolled her eyes at the girl in blue. "She's a hopeless case."

The girl in blue grabbed an empty chair from another table, scraped it over the floorboards, and sat beside them. "So if you find Ralph"—she leaned forwards over the table, voice pitched low—"you'll make him pay you back."

"That's the plan," Kitty said. "Trust me, I won't let Molly back down."

"I'm sure it was a misunderstanding," Mélanie said. "But I do need to get the money back."

"Good," the girl said. "He deserves it. Never known him to make off with money, but he's broken enough hearts. And I know what it's like to lose wages." She cast a quick glance round the room.

Kitty pushed her glass across the table in a gesture of camaraderie.

The girl in blue snatched it up and took a sip. "Haven't seen Ralph since he was supposed to meet me four nights ago and didn't show up. But when he's not working, he frequents the Blue Dragon. In Queen Street. Says he can't relax where he works."

Kitty snorted. "I know the feeling. Trust me, Molly doesn't have any future designs on him. I won't let her."

Mélanie opened her eyes wide. "I wouldn't—"

"Famous last words," Kitty muttered. "You're the most hopeless romantic I've ever met."

"I don't have any designs on him either," the girl in blue said. "Glad to have made my escape." She turned to Mélanie, the mask dropped, for the first time. "Have a care. Ralph's not just a barkeep. The things he deals in—I don't want to know about them, and you don't either."

"We'll be careful," Kitty said. "And thanks for the warning."

"Intriguing," Kitty said to Mélanie when they were outside.

"Very." Mélanie lifted her skirt to veer round a suspicious-looking pile of slops someone had dumped on top of a patch of slushy snow. "Though I'm still recovering from being cast as a hopeless romantic."

"You're a good enough actress to carry it off." Kitty automatically slapped away a hand reaching for her reticule. "And you're far closer to it than I am."

"I've seen the way you look at Julien."

Kitty flashed a grin at her. "Caught. Though some might describe that as lunacy."

A group of children were playing catch with a bundle of scraps tied to make a ball at the juncture of Queen Street. One of them dodged the game to reach for Kitty's reticule. This time she pressed some coins into his hand.

Dust motes danced in the lamplight as they stepped into the Blue Dragon. The air smelt the same as at the Three Queens—sour ale, cheap gin, cheaper wine, fried drippings, tallow candles. It was less crowded than the Three Queens but with a similar clientele. Dice, cards, darts. Amorous encounters being set up.

As Mélanie and Kitty threaded their way between the rickety tables, the door thudded open behind them, letting in a rush of cold air. The new arrival, a man in a bottle-green corduroy coat, strode towards a man with sleek dark hair and a spotted neck-cloth who was lounging alone at a table, nursing a pint. Corduroy Jacket lunged and grabbed the dark-haired man by the lapels. "What the bloody hell are you doing being late?"

The dark-haired man kicked Corduroy Jacket, knocking the table over and sending the pint flying in a stream of ale and shattered glass. Corduroy Jacket stumbled backwards, skidded on the ale-soaked floorboards, and fell, pulling the dark-haired man down with him. Dark-Haired Man aimed a blow at Corduroy Jacket's chin, then scrambled to his feet. One of the dart players turned, dart in hand, and threw, aiming the dart at Dark-Haired Man's head. Dark-Haired Man ducked. The dart whistled past, burying itself in the paneling.

Dark-Haired Man ran, upending another table and two chairs. Dart Player chased after, two darts in hand. Of one accord, Mélanie and Kitty followed. Screams went up. Someone shouted a wager. Dark-Haired Man raced past the bar. Dart Player loosed another dart. It caught Dark-Haired Man's coat as he stumbled through a door. Mélanie and Kitty followed him into the smells of grease and coal and frying meat and potatoes. A girl in an apron by the range screamed. Kitty stuck out a foot, tripping Corduroy Jacket as he followed them into the kitchen. Mélanie snatched a rolling pin from a flour-covered table.

"Sorry, we'll pay for it," she shouted as she and Kitty ran through another door and down a winding set of stairs down which Dark-Haired Man and Dart Player had run.

The smell of damp rose to meet them. Mélanie grabbed the stair rail as her uneven half-boots skidded on the worn steps. The rail cracked in her hand. Kitty caught her arm before she could tumble headlong down the stairs.

They emerged in a low-ceilinged unlit passage. Thudding footfalls ahead indicated Dark-Haired Man and Dart Player. Mélanie and Kitty ran after them over damp, rocky, uneven ground, through puddles and the stench of fetid water.

A crash sounded ahead. They rounded a bend in the passage to see two figures pummeling each other on the floor. Dim light spilled into the passage from ahead. Enough to distinguish Dart Player, who was on top, fist drawn back, and Dark-Haired Man, struggling to get a purchase on Dart Player's arm.

Mélanie swung the rolling pin and brought it down on Dart Player's head. Dart Player slumped to the ground. Dark-Haired Man pushed himself to his knees.

Mélanie held out a hand. "Ralph Allam, I presume?"

CHAPTER 39

$\mathcal{D}$ark-Haired Man glared at her in the shadows. "Who's asking?"

"Given the service we've just rendered, I think you'd be wise to talk to us." Kitty had stepped ahead to block Allam's route down the passage. "We want information about Allegra Roth."

Mélanie was prepared for Allam to run again, but he accepted her hand, got to his feet, and jerked his head down the passage. "Dawkins will wake up soon. Need to make ourselves scarce."

He led the way down the passage to a sort of cellar. The light came from a lantern hanging from a hook on the rock wall. It revealed shelves stacked with crates, bottles, and casks.

"There's a cellar below each of the taverns facing where the sundial was," Allam said. "And passages connecting them. Handy."

He led the way up another set of stairs, into another kitchen, where they were eyed with only mild surprise, and out a back door into a narrow alley, then across a court and through a set of passages to the third Seven Dials tavern they'd been in in the past hour. Five minutes later they were sitting at a gateleg table in a small back room in the Queen's Lace, a bottle of gin and three glasses on the table.

"I owe you my thanks," Allam said. "Never let it be said I don't honor those who help me. Spot of bother over a business transaction." He picked up the gin bottle, then froze, reached over his shoulder, and tugged the dart from his coat. "Didn't know that was still there. Clever bastard, Dawkins. He's the one who threw the dart. Works with Hillyard, the chap in the corduroy jacket. Surprised Hillyard didn't chase after us too."

"He did," Kitty said. "I tripped him."

"Ah." Allam flashed a grin at her. "My thanks, ma'am." He poured three glasses of gin and took a drink from his own glass. "What do you know about Allegra?"

Mélanie curled her hands round her glass. "We're investigating her murder."

He didn't look as surprised as she'd have expected. "Clear you weren't ordinary morts. I heard there was a posh crew looking into Allegra's death. I've been waiting for someone to show up ever since I got the news. Which wasn't until today. Been out of town. Sooner talk to you lot than Bow Street."

"Accommodating of you." Kitty untied her shawl, which she'd wrapped round her shoulders to keep it out of the way during the chase.

"I want to learn what happened to her."

"You'd known Allegra a long time," Mélanie said.

"She wasn't more than sixteen when we met. Before she ran off with Gresham. You know about him?"

"I spoke with him yesterday," Mélanie said.

Allam cast a glance at the peeling wallpaper and chipped moldings. "Allegra always liked Seven Dials. She said the world came alive here. Course, it was easier for her to like it when she could leave."

"How did you meet?" Kitty asked.

"She came looking for me."

Kitty raised a brow. "An usual way for a love affair to start."

"Love affair?" Allam threw himself back in his chair with a

laugh. "You've got the shoe on the wrong foot. Allegra wasn't my mort. She was my sister."

Mélanie cast a quick glance at Kitty. "But you didn't grow up together?"

"God no. I didn't know she existed until that day she wandered into the Three Queens. She was tough even then, but one glance said she didn't belong here. Sixteen-year-olds in Seven Dials look years older than she did." For a moment his face softened with what might have been affection.

Mélanie had learned to turn on the illusion of youth as a spy, but she'd left youth behind long before her sixteenth birthday. "What did you say to her?"

"Usually I'm wary of people asking for me," Allam said, "but in her case I thought I should say yes before someone else took advantage of her." He met their gazes, his own at once hard and abashed. "Just because I make my trade in Seven Dials doesn't mean I'm entirely without feelings."

"We never said you were," Kitty said.

"I took her to a table in a corner and got her the mildest ale we pour. Didn't want to take her to a private room and risk all sorts of talk. Just wanted to find out how she knew my name and figure out how to get her home. That's when she said she thought she was my sister. I just stared at her as if she'd gone mad. Even madder than I'd thought she was for coming to Seven Dials in the first place. My mum worked at the Three Queens. I had two sisters who died of a fever, and my mum died when I was eight giving birth to a third who didn't survive. Nowhere for Allegra to fit in. I said as much, and she said it wasn't our mother. It was our father. She'd always been sure her father wasn't her mother's first husband, and now she knew who he was, and she'd been digging and she thought he was my father too." Allam took a drink of gin and frowned into his glass. "That caught me. I mean, it was possible. Never knew who my father was. But my mum said he was a gentleman who had her in keeping for a while. Was never sure if that was just a pretty story to cover my being made in a night's trade or if it was truth. My mum told a lot of fairy stories. But I couldn't deny it was possible. And I couldn't deny I was curious. Though I thought it was a bit odd Allegra was so eager to prove she was born on the wrong side of the blanket. Allegra just laughed and said our father was a much more interesting father than her official father. At that point, I had to ask her who this paragon was."

"And she told you?" Mélanie asked.

"Lord Warkworth." He watched the words take effect on their faces. "I didn't even know who he was then. But I've learned he's quite a nob."

Mélanie had met the Earl of Warkworth. The first time on her first trip to Britain, in 1814, when Napoleon had been on Elba. She'd sat next to him at a long dinner for the Tsar of Russia. In between the endless toasts, he'd been politely flirtatious. Her main memory of that night was sipping champagne and focusing all her attention on the need to smile over the wreckage of the last remnants of the Revolution. She'd nearly thrown up at a toast to the restored Bourbon king. An image of Colin clutching a white Royalist flag Fanny had bought him in Hyde Park had hovered before her eyes.

But Warkworth had been kind. Malcolm had later told her Warkworth was a seasoned diplomat. He hadn't been posted to the Peninsula or France. In fact, she thought he'd been sent to South America. Which had been mildly interesting then and suddenly was of keen interest.

"Warkworth spent time in Brazil and paid a visit to Buenos Aires while I was there," Kitty said, looking at Allam. "I don't know if he saw Allegra, but she was there then too. Have you met him?"

"No." Allam made the curt word as final as a door slammed shut. "Wouldn't be interested in me." He dragged the toe of his boot over the floorboards. "Part of me liked the idea of looking the man who fathered me in the face. But another knew he'd dismiss me. And that's not a pleasant thought. Being denied by one's father."

"No," Mélanie said.

"Did Allegra meet him?" Kitty asked. "I can't remember if they saw each other in Buenos Aires, but before?"

"Eventually. And then she kept saying the fact that we were his children made us special." He gave a wry smile. "Funny. I've learned her mother and stepfather thought everyone was born equal. I even read some pamphlets she brought me." He looked from Kitty to Mélanie. "My mum taught me to read. She wasn't from Seven Dials. Didn't like to talk about her past, but her parents were farmers on some grand estate. Warkworth's, I think now, or maybe one of his friends'. Anyway, I learned to read. I like to read."

"So do a lot of us," Mélanie said. "And having taught my children, I'm constantly amazed at the wonder of mastering the skill."

Allam grunted in acknowledgement. "A lot of sense in those pamphlets. But Allegra was awfully focused on birth making her special. That first day, I told her I was glad we'd met, but she had to get home. Walked her out of Seven Dials and scrounged up enough to pay for a hackney. But she insisted we set up a way to trade messages before she left. After that, she'd sneak out to visit me. Once or twice she met a man at the Three Queens. Wasn't best pleased, but figured it was better she was having assignations where I was about to keep an eye on things. Then she told me she was going to run off and join an opera company. Made a certain sense. She had a lovely voice. Sang for me sometimes. Didn't see her for ages after that. She wrote once or twice. Then suddenly she was back, saying opera hadn't worked and her protector had left her. As had her next protector. Well, they do, don't they? And not long after, she told me she was marrying. A Bow Street runner." He shook his head. "Never thought I'd have a family connection to Bow Street, even if it's on the wrong side of the blanket. But she said she'd known him from childhood, and he was someone she could trust."

"Did you know she was with child when she married?" Mélanie asked.

Allam shifted in his chair. "Know that, do you?"

"And so does her husband," Mélanie said. "It doesn't change the way he feels about his son."

Allam nodded. "I knew. She said she didn't have a choice but to marry, at that point. And that this Roth would be a good father. She said she'd always liked him. That he was interesting. But I don't think she found being his wife very interesting. Being *a* wife, that is. Allegra always wanted drama."

"She went on visiting you?" Kitty asked.

"Oh, aye. She'd slip away, from time to time. More often, as time went on. Sometimes she'd—"

"Meet a man here?" Mélanie asked.

He met her gaze squarely. "Sometimes. I don't think fidelity was in Allegra's makeup."

"I didn't used to think it was in mine," Mélanie said.

"Your husband must be a remarkable man."

"He is. But I'm the one who changed."

"He's a lucky devil, if you'll pardon my saying so, ma'am."

"Thank you." Mélanie tightened her fingers on her glass because she needed to grip something. "But I'm the one who's fortunate."

"Did Allegra tell you she was planning to leave England?" Kitty asked.

"Allam's fingers tightened on his own glass. "She told me. She looked happier than I'd seen her in years. I was worried about the boys—losing my mum wasn't easy on me. But she said Roth was a better father than she was a mother. And our father hadn't seen us at all. Though I didn't count that a virtue in him, as I told her."

"Did she say where she was going?" Mélanie asked.

"The Argentine. She said it meant silver. I laughed and said then she'd make her fortune. She got an odd look and said perhaps she would, but that wasn't why she was going. She was going because she'd found something that would make her life worth living. I laughed again and said I couldn't imagine what would make a life worth living. Except getting through to the next day." He frowned into his gin. "Course, that was before I met Mandy."

"Blonde?" Kitty said. "Green eyes? Works at the Three Queens?"

"Aye." Allam shot a glance at her. "She sent you to me?"

"Mmm." Kitty regarded him. "She's not best pleased with you."

"Got scared," Allam said. "Afraid of pulling her into a mess. Like Allegra. Afraid of how it would change my life. Which is barmy, because what's so special about my life? I never had illusions about that. Not like Allegra." He took another drink. "Allegra wrote once or twice from the Argentine. Said she had the life she'd always wanted. She felt a world away. Which she was. Never thought I'd see her again. Then suddenly, last week, she walked back into the Three Queens. She wanted to talk in a private room this time. Said she was here with her lover and didn't want her husband to know."

"What else did she say?" Mélanie asked.

Allam picked up the bottle of gin and refilled their glasses. He'd finished his, but it seemed as much prevarication as desire for another drink. He swirled the glass in his hand and took a deep swallow. "That it was good to see me, but she wasn't back for long and couldn't afford to get entangled with her old life. That was Allegra. Never the sentimental sort. She had people she needed to meet with, and she couldn't do it at her hotel or anywhere her lover might know. He wouldn't understand."

"Why?" Kitty asked.

"She didn't say. But given that one of the people she needed to talk to was her husband, I can hazard a guess."

"Did she say she needed to talk to her husband?" Mélanie asked.

"Not then. Asked if he'd come looking for me or I'd heard anything about him. Which I hadn't. I did say didn't she want to see her boys? Sentimental of me, I suppose, but damn it, I'd want to if they were mine. Damn lucky she has children, if you ask me. But she said it was better not to. It was only later she told me she was going to have to talk to her husband, and she'd better do it at the Three Queens. She said she needed his advice."

"That's an odd way of putting it," Mélanie said.

"Yes, that's what I thought."

"What else did she want you to do?" Kitty asked.

Allam shifted in his chair. "She had a job for me."

"She wanted you to steal something?" Mélanie asked.

He flashed a look at her.

"It's that or that she wanted you to tend bar. And somehow I think she'd have turned to the staff at Mivart's for entertaining."

He gave a short laugh. "You're right at that."

He hesitated again.

"We're not working with Bow Street," Mélanie said. "We want the truth of what happened to your sister. But we have no cause to turn you in."

He grunted. "What people have cause to do has a way of changing."

"You saw me bash a man over the head," Mélanie said.

"Like anyone would believe me if I turned you in. Like I could without betraying myself. Still, I seem to have thrown my lot in with you lot. And we at least have a goal in common." He took another drink of gin. "Allegra wanted me to break in and nab something for her."

"We're spies," Kitty said. "We aren't shocked by break-ins. Where did she want you to break in?"

"House in Cambridge. Some tutor there. Nab some paper hidden in a damned classical statue thing. She gave me money to pay for the stage. But when I got there and made inquiries, I learned this tutor's daughter had left for London with a parcel that sounded a lot like the marble. Bound for Mayfair. Hill Street."

"You're good at gathering intelligence," Kitty said.

"Part of doing a job well. So I headed back to town. Got in last night. Hadn't heard about Allegra. I went to this house in Hill Street and broke in to get the marble—or rather, the paper in the marble. Only I got chased out before I could snatch it." He looked from Mélanie to Kitty taking in their reaction. "Does that mean something?"

"It's the home of friends of ours," Mélanie said. "One of our friends chased you into the street."

"Your friend's quick on his feet. I only got away because some nobs blundered between us."

"Why did Allegra want the paper?" Mélanie asked.

"She didn't say. But she said it could be the key to her future. Mine too. Not that I believed that. She said I'd be handsomely rewarded, if so. But that isn't why I did it. I did it because she's Allegra. And then after I escaped back to Seven Dials, I learned she was dead." He looked from Mélanie to Kitty. "What was in the paper?"

"It's in code," Mélanie said. "I can't promise we'll tell you what's in it when it's decoded, but I can promise we'll do everything we can to learn what happened to her."

"Fair enough." He looked between them again. "I know Roth's your friend. And Allegra didn't seem afraid of him. I said we had a goal in common. And we do. But if Roth killed her, we won't anymore. Because I think you'll want to protect your friend. And I want Allegra avenged."

"We have no reason to think Jeremy Roth killed Allegra," Mélanie said.

"He was found with her body," Allam said. "And he was her husband."

"And spouses are always suspect." Mélanie saw no point in not confronting that. "We realize that. But we don't think he's guilty. And until such time as we learn differently, I hope we can be allies."

Allam sat back in his chair and stretched his legs out, glass clutched in front of him. "Talking to you, aren't I?"

Kitty took a drink of gin. "You said Allegra wanted to meet people at the Three Queens. Whom else did she meet there besides Jeremy Roth?"

"Don't know for a certainty." Allam took a drink from his own glass. "I just set it up that she could have the use of a room. I think she preferred it when I wasn't there so she didn't feel anyone was watching what she did. She never quite got past the days when she was sixteen and I was a concerned elder brother. God, talk about a role I never thought I'd play."

"We all play unexpected roles," Mélanie said. "I never thought I'd be a mother. You have no idea who else she met?"

"Well, there was one night I was working the bar. And I wasn't really surprised to see them, given what I'd seen in the past. I think he still felt for her too. But Ledgwood was always hard to read."

"Philip Ledgwood?" Kitty had gone still as ice.

"Aye. You know him?"

"Yes. And I knew Allegra knew him. But I thought they met in the Argentine."

"Oh no. They met in London. Used to rendezvous at the Three Queens. Talk about times I felt like a concerned brother. Never trusted him."

"Nor did I," Kitty said, knuckles white on her glass. "But it seems I wasn't nearly suspicious enough." She tossed down the last of the gin and clunked the glass down. "I need to talk to Philip."

"He's a friend of yours?" Allam asked.

"At this point I'm not sure what he is."

CHAPTER 40

*H*arry put up a hand to anchor his hat as a gust of wind threatened to yank it off. "I left the code with Allie. She'll make faster work of it than any of us."

Malcolm nodded. Harry had found him in the pub with Esquivel, and they were walking home along Old Bond Street.

"Fitzroy didn't know anything conclusive about Ashford. But he'd heard rumors about Ashford's death." Harry described his talk with Fitzroy as they threaded their way round dirty patches of snow, between the crowds hurrying in and out of shops. At least Bond Street was less of a crush than in more clement weather. "It sounds as though Ashford has protection from White-hall. Horse Guards, perhaps. We can ask Kitty, though I suspect she won't know."

"So do I. But it could relate to what Ashford was doing in the Argentine. Which could relate to Allegra Roth's death." Malcolm stared at the gray sky. They'd had a bit of sun in the morning, but now clouds were massing. "What do you think?" he asked.

Harry swung his gaze round. "About Ashford or Allegra Roth?"

"About Roth. About his story. Which keeps changing."

Harry, being Harry, didn't shy away from difficult facts that might interfere with his preferred thesis. "You mean, do I think he murdered his wife?"

"Yes." A relief in a way to actually say it, though his throat hurt.

"I don't," Harry said, in the voice of a detached scholar. "Though I recognize my biases. And I'm less convinced he's innocent than I was two days ago."

"So am I." Malcolm watched a haberdasher's sign swinging in the wind. It was coming off one of its hinges. "Every instinct tells me the man I've known for a decade couldn't have done it. But I'm always saying one can never be sure of what anyone might be capable of, in the right circumstances." The sign creaked, as though it couldn't decide where to settle. "And there's no denying I haven't shown myself the best judge of knowing when people I'm close to are lying to me."

They moved past a gentleman in a padded coat and a young woman, probably a lady's maid, arms full of shopping parcels, stopping to flirt despite the weather. "It's all right, you know," Harry said.

A landau clattered past. When the noise died down, Malcolm turned his head to meet his friend's gaze full on. "That I haven't shown myself the best judge of my loved ones?"

Harry's gaze was steady and open. "That this couldn't but remind you of some uncomfortable situations in your own past."

"Oh well." The admission came more easily now. But even with Harry, he felt his defenses settle round him, a familiar cloak that had long been essential to his ability to live his life equably. "It's not as though I ever forget those. But there's no sense dwelling on them."

"No. And you do an admirable job of pushing forwards. But the feelings are still there, I think, and one ignores them at one's peril." They turned down Grafton Street. "I know," Harry said, the words precise and yet rough as sandpaper. "Because that's how it was for me when George Chase reentered our lives."

Malcolm stopped walking and turned to face Harry. Last

October must have been hell for his friend. He'd known that at the time, and yet— "We never talked about it much."

"Oh, we did at first. You got me out of the Palace of Westminster so I could talk."

That had been one of their franker talks. There was an amazing amount they said to each other. More than Malcolm said to most people. But also an amazing amount they didn't put into words. "Mostly you were worried about what Cordelia was going through."

"Well, she was the one whose former lover had been murdered. I can't say I felt any grief for George Chase. But it was a reminder of his impact on our lives."

A curricle trundled past, yellow wheels sending up a spray of water from puddles of melting snow. They started walking again. "I had as good a motive to be behind Chase's death as Roth does to be behind Allegra's," Harry said as they followed the bend in Grafton Street. "Maybe better. Roth once loved Allegra. I never felt anything but contempt for Chase. And he threatened my life and my children's lives more than Allegra threatened Roth, I think. Did you suspect me?"

"I knew you couldn't have killed him yourself because you were with me."

"But I could have engaged someone else to do it."

"I'll admit I forced myself to examine the possibility," Malcolm said. Which was true. "But it goes against everything I know about you. And that would have been a calculated act. I can't see Roth committing calculated murder. I can perhaps imagine him killing in a fit of rage. I can see just about anyone killing in a fit of rage, with the right trigger." They turned down Hay Hill. "On the other hand, given that he was spying on Judith, and concealed his affair with her so well, I'm not sure what to think when it comes to what he may have been capable of plotting."

Harry was silent for what Simon and Mélanie would call a

beat. "Someone can be on a mission and have an ulterior motive, and still feel genuine emotions."

Snow crunched beneath Malcolm's boot. For a moment he felt he was standing on a sheet of glass. But this was Harry, and there were things he could only say to Harry. "I forget. For days at a time. Weeks at a time. Most of the time, honestly. At first it was a conscious act. The only way we could get through this was for no one to suspect anything had changed between Mélanie and me. Almost from the moment I learned the truth about her, as soon as the first anger faded, I was bloody terrified the truth would come out and she'd be accused of treason. Any sign of a breach between us risked questions and the whole thing unraveling. My wife's being arrested. A jailbreak and a midnight flight and our children traumatized. So I had to act as though nothing had changed. To everyone. Our family and friends, our staff. Even to you and Cordy, at that point. And to do that, I had to play the role of someone for whom nothing had changed. I know you and Cordy weren't entirely convinced—"

"We knew something had changed. But not what. You were bloody brilliant."

"Not that. But I'm a good enough agent I could lose myself in the role. And I was enough in love with my wife it wasn't hard to lose myself. But Mel accused me recently of playing a role those first months, and in a way, I was. Then we learned Hubert knew the truth and we fled to Italy and had the leisure to face a number of things. And then we came back, and she and Raoul were pardoned. And somehow it wasn't a role anymore."

They had reached Berkeley Square. Of one accord they stopped, leaning against the black metal railing of the square garden. Malcolm drew a breath of the damp, cold air. He hadn't said this much about his tangled relationship with his wife to anyone in a long time. "As I said, I genuinely go weeks without thinking about it at all. But every so often, I'll look at her and it hits me. She lied to me. For five years. Every day. Every night.

Every minute. So expertly that I missed all the clues I should have caught as a competent agent. What does that say about me? And what does it say about now, when I think I know her better than I know myself? How can I really be sure? Of her. Of anything. And then there are times I look at Raoul. Times when I'm not worrying he's going to get himself killed, or being bloody stunned at his brilliance, which is most of the time. It's odd. I sometimes worry Mel wouldn't be with me if it weren't for the past. If it weren't for the children. I don't doubt Raoul loves me. I don't doubt he always has. Not anymore. But I was completely taken in by him as well. And Laura lived with us and spied on us, and we only learned the truth because she was caught up in a murder investigation. So I'm surrounded every day by people who lied to me very effectively. For that matter, I didn't guess Julien was actually someone I'd grown up with for almost two years."

"You didn't see him constantly for those two years. And you were very young the last time you saw him."

"Even so. I'd be an idiot if I didn't question my judgment. If I didn't question my judgment of Roth now. You're an idiot if you aren't questioning it."

"I'm undoubtedly an idiot. But I am questioning it. So that makes you question your judgment of other things?"

"I suppose. Yes. I'm frustrated with Jeremy for not telling us the full truth from the start. Which I'm not sure he is. I'm frustrated with Mélanie, and Raoul, and Laura, and even Julien for not telling me the truth. Even though I understand their reasons perfectly well. Even though in their position I might well do the same. But at times, I feel an impossible idiot."

"You're anything but an idiot, Rannoch."

"At a charitable analysis, I could be called lacking in insight." Malcolm glanced at the plane trees in the square. Their branches formed a sodden tangle. Impossible to imagine separating them. "I'll look at Mélanie. With everything we share. With the understanding between us now, which I think is remarkable. And I'll think, what else am I missing? What else is a mirage? And then she'll smile at me and I'll be certain I understand everything. But one can never truly understand a person on that level. Not fully. Not completely. That would be a shocking invasion of privacy, as Mel says."

Harry's gaze moved to the trees as well. "I believe Cordy loves me. Honestly believe it, which I don't think I did for a long time. Even when we were back together. A part of me still thought it was her attempt at atonement. Or that she loved me, but it was the sort of love that developed because we had a child together. It's different now. I didn't fully realize that until George Chase came back into our lives. Which brought old hurts to the fore, but also revealed how things had changed. Even so, there are moments—" His gaze fastened on a branch, bare of leaves, not yet showing any hint of spring. "It's always there in the background. Like my arm. Much of the time I don't notice it. Because it actually doesn't hurt, or because I'm so used to the pain it's just a part of my daily life. But then I'll try to do something and my arm doesn't work as it should, and I'll remember again. I'm not the person I was. Which isn't wholly a bad thing. But I used to blame myself for the times I remembered George, for the times I remembered what Cordy and I had done to each other. I don't blame myself anymore. I think it's more dangerous to deny it and let it fester."

That was also perhaps the longest speech Harry had made about his personal feelings and marriage in a very long time. If ever.

Malcolm touched his friend's arm. Lightly. "We're both fortunate. Beyond fortunate, to have what we have. But I don't think I'll ever fully trust my instincts again. Mélanie taught me that. And though I know she regrets that I can't trust as easily, it may not be a bad lesson to have learned. Just now, Esquivel told me he suspected Bobby of leaking information. I can't begin to think what to make of that. The truth is, people can surprise you for good or ill. And I can't be at all certain that isn't what's happening with Jeremy Roth."

"Which brings up another question," Harry said. "We talked about getting him out of prison if he's arrested, assuming he's innocent. And I'm quite confident we could do it. What are you going to do if we're convinced he's guilty?"

Malcolm's gloved fingers tightened on the railing. The air seemed to have chilled. It cut his lungs. "Allegra Roth deserves justice. But you know how I feel about capital punishment. I'm not sure I could stand by and watch a friend hang. So I don't know."

Harry nodded. "Nor do I."

CHAPTER 41

"Y ou lied." Kitty was surprised at the intensity in her own voice. She was used to lies. She was particularly used to them from people who had shared her bed. Including Julien. She had never had any illusions he didn't lie to her, and recent events had driven the point home like a dagger thrust. And Malcolm. Their relationship had ended because he lied to achieve the outcome he wanted. An outcome she could now admit had been better than the one she had been seeking. And yet, Philip's lies—and the fact that she had accepted them— cut. She had liked him. When had she started letting herself like people? It made life so much more complicated.

She stared at Philip across his sitting room at Mivart's. Once again, she had guards outside. Mélanie was downstairs in the lobby, and Malcolm and Harry, who had been in Berkeley Square when she and Mélanie returned, were in the street. "You saw Allegra Roth recently. At the Three Queens in Seven Dials. Don't deny it."

"I won't." Philip's gaze was a wasteland in his white face. "You obviously have proof. I shouldn't have denied seeing her to begin with. But you have a family. Can you imagine the impulse to protect them at all costs?"

"Yes. Telling lies doesn't usually help."

"Kitty. You can't tell me you, of all people, don't see the dangers in telling the truth. I thought spies built their lives on lies."

That was truer than she cared to admit just now. "Not lies that can unravel so easily. Allegra asked you to come to the Three Queens."

"She did. Not the night she murdered. And not for the reasons you might think. Not for the reasons I imagine the tavern staff assumed. She needed my help. We were better friends than I let on."

"And for longer. You didn't meet in the Argentine. You met in London. You seemed far too comfortable with each other when you first seemingly 'met.' I should have noticed it then."

"We met in Covent Garden when she was still Allegra Wainwright. I'd been sent back from Brazil with dispatches."

"And you were lovers then."

"No sense in denying it. She was as enchanting then as she was later. I was as lost then as I was later."

"It was after she'd run off with Tristram Gresham."

"Yes. She was in London on her own."

"So you're the father of her eldest child, not Graham Haverford?"

"What?" Philip shook his head. "No. Allegra and I were involved then, but the affair wasn't a serious one—"

"That's never stopped anyone from conceiving a child."

"She was quite clear that I wasn't. Haverford wasn't either. She wasn't with child when she left Edinburgh and came back to London. But I wasn't her only lover here. In fact, I met her because I was bringing her messages from her current lover."

The time in Allegra Roth's life that was a blank. The time Samuel had been conceived. And yet—Kitty regarded the man who had once seemed determined to give Don Giovanni a run for his money. "You were carrying messages for another man."

"Who happened to be my superior."

"At what?"

"Diplomacy." Philip spun away, then turned back to her. "It was Lord Warkworth. My mentor in the diplomatic service. I know you and Rannoch probably think I didn't take my work seriously, and perhaps compared to you, I didn't, but I owed Warkworth a lot. When he entrusted something to me in the greatest secrecy, I took it seriously. Even if it involved his mistress."

"Did he say Allegra was his mistress?"

"Not in so many words. But he was most determined to maintain secrecy. Odd for a man in his position. Many are more inclined to flaunt their mistresses. Perhaps it was for Allegra's sake, though she scarcely had a position to maintain either. Perhaps it was to do with his relationship with his wife. I understand that better now that I'm a husband. But it still struck me as odd."

"So Warkworth never said he was the father of Allegra's child?"

Philip frowned. "No. As I said, he never admitted he was her lover. I do know he was relieved when she married Jeremy Roth. He said it was the best thing for her. I can't imagine why else he was in secret communication with her."

"I profoundly hope he wasn't her lover. Because he was her father."

Philip's eyes widened.

"Neither of them ever told you?"

"Can you imagine if they had, I'd have thought they were lovers?"

"It's been known to happen. But I think in this case, Allegra's parentage may explain the secrecy. Not that all men keep illegitimate children so secret."

Philip frowned. "I can see—it makes sense of his attitude towards her. And perhaps hers towards him. Had she—"

"She learned when she was sixteen. I'm not sure when she sought Warkworth out. Did Warkworth know you were her lover?"

"Good god, I hope not. Even more now I know he was her father and not her lover. Allegra said there was no reason for him to know, and she had a right to do as she wished."

"And when she married?"

"She told me she'd made the prudent choice." His frown deepened. "She looked—not unhappy, but resigned. That ended things between us. I went back to Brazil. When I saw her later in the Argentine, she said she'd been wrong to try domesticity, though she hadn't really had much choice at the time."

"Did she say anything else about her husband and children?"

"That she didn't want to discuss the past. It made sense to me at the time. Now that I have a family myself—I find it harder to comprehend."

So did Kitty, but this was not the moment she wanted to establish fellow feeling with Philip. "Why did Allegra want to see you now?"

Philip glanced away, grimaced, looked back at Kitty. "She had more questions about Ashford."

"Meaning Edward. My husband."

"Yes."

"Did she still think I killed him?"

"She didn't say, specifically. She wanted me to get her war office records of transfers to the Argentine at the time Ashford was there."

"Because she thought they contained information about who had killed Edward? Or what he'd been doing in the Argentine?"

"Both, perhaps. She didn't say. And I was too busy digesting her demand to think of asking."

"She demanded you get her the papers?"

"You could say so."

"Or she threatened you? Don't prevaricate, Philip. I liked

Alejandra, and I have sympathy for what we've learned about Allegra. But we also know she was prone to blackmail."

"She may have mentioned certain things she could share with Isabel."

"What did you say to her?"

"What could I say? Isabel knows a fraction of my past. I don't care to have her know the rest of it. She's understanding—but there's a limit to anyone's understanding. So I told Allegra I'd do my best to get her the information she wanted."

"Did you follow through on it?"

"I didn't have a chance."

"Did you intend to follow through on it?"

Philip's jaw tightened. He glanced out the window again. "It could be called treason, taking government records. Especially giving them to the mistress of a rebel leader from another country."

"Yes, I know. Allegra had made an impossible demand of you."

"She had. So I'd bought myself time, but I hadn't decided what I was going to do." Philip dragged his gaze back to Kitty's own, defiant yet resigned. "Which, of course, gives me an excellent motive to have murdered her."

"Rannoch." Lord Warkworth came forwards across his study with his hand extended. "It's good to see you. I've been following your career in Parliament with interest. Though I'm sorry we lost you from the diplomatic corps."

"You're kind, sir," Malcolm said. "I enjoyed working with you when our paths crossed." That was true, as far as it went. Though having just heard Mélanie and Kitty's account of their meeting with Ralph Allam, and Kitty's of her talk with Philip Ledgwood, his feelings were rather less cordial. Knowing Warkworth was Allegra Roth's father, the resemblance to the woman

Malcolm had seen dead on the floor of the Three Queens was plain in Warkworth's graying blond hair and fine-boned features.

"But you tired of a life abroad?" Warkworth asked, waving a hand towards the leather-covered chairs by the fire. His study was more elegant and less functional than Hubert's, with deep-cushioned leather chairs, gilded woodwork, and a handsome drinks trolley.

"To a degree. We wanted to put down roots as a family. But more and more I tired of arguing positions that weren't mine. And that were often diametrically opposed to what I believed."

"Ah." Warkworth poured two glasses of port and gave one to Malcolm. "You were always more of a firebrand than one would think in someone so controlled. But as I understand it, you're still putting your skills in intelligence to use."

"At times." Rather frequent times, as it happened. He should probably give up the pretense that he'd left the intelligence game. Malcolm accepted a glass of port and sat in one of the chairs. "It's an investigation that's brought me here."

Warkworth, still standing by the drinks trolley, raised his brows.

"Tell me what you know about Allegra Roth."

Warkworth spun away and clunked down the decanter. "Damnation. I should have known."

"Yes," Malcolm said. "You should have done. How much do you know?"

Warkworth's shoulders tightened beneath the impeccable blue superfine of his coat, but he didn't look over his shoulder at Malcolm. "She was killed. The night before last."

"So you still followed what happened to her."

"Of course. I'm not a monster."

"Had you seen her since she'd come back to Britain?"

Warkworth drew in and released his breath. "Once."

"When?"

"A week since. Perhaps a bit longer." Warkworth turned back to Malcolm and twitched his shirt cuffs straight.

"Why did she want to see you?"

"It had been years. She wanted to catch up. I wanted to see her. Is that so hard to believe?"

"No. But you didn't meet her until she was sixteen, from what we understand."

"Who told you?" Warkworth's voice was steady, but a bit rough.

"Your son."

Warkworth started, which was what Malcolm had intended. "Hartwick has no notion—"

"Not your heir. Ralph Allam. You know about him?"

"The thief from Seven Dials."

"Among other things. He said you'd never met."

"No." Warkworth picked up his glass and took a swallow. "I can't even be sure he's my son, though Allegra seemed to believe it was true. One can hardly keep track of all such accidents."

Malcolm clenched his fingers round his glass. It wouldn't help matters to toss the contents in Warkworth's face. "I wouldn't know. Being the product of such an accident myself."

Warkworth, who had the diplomat's gift of answering anything, seemed unsure what to say. Good.

"Raoul O'Roarke is my father. We neither of us make any secret about it. In fact, I quite prefer claiming him to my supposed father."

From Warkworth's expression, Malcolm might have emptied a chamber pot in the middle of the drawing room carpet. "That's hardly the same—"

"It's a parental relationship outside of marriage. Personally, I'd take being a parent seriously whether I was married or not. But not everyone views it that way."

Warkworth tossed down the contents of his glass and then refilled it. "You're young, Rannoch. And you've always been an idealist. But I think I need hardly tell you that there are different sorts of liaisons. Your—O'Roarke would surely agree when it comes to what he shared with your mother."

"You'd have to ask him, but I don't think he'd take a by-blow from a tumble in a tavern less seriously than he takes me. However, I take it your relationship with Allegra's mother meant more to you than a tumble?"

"That's hardly any concern of yours."

"It wouldn't be, if Allegra hadn't been murdered."

"Am I to understand you're working with Bow Street?"

"Would you prefer to talk to Bow Street?"

Warkworth took a more measured sip and seated himself across from Malcolm. "Allegra's mother meant a great deal to me."

"You hadn't seen Allegra when she was growing up?"

"That would hardly have been prudent. Her mother had begun a new life. Allegra's mother was dear to me. When she found herself with child, marriage seemed the best alternative."

"You were already married."

"Yes, and I couldn't—In any case, her marriage ended our relationship. She made it clear her husband would be Allegra's father. But she sent me news from time to time. When Allegra was sixteen, she sought me out. She'd worked out I might be her father."

"And you admitted you were."

"It might have been better for her if I hadn't done. But I couldn't bring myself to deny it. I said it was better for her to have the life she had. But I agreed to correspond with her. I sent her gifts from time to time. The sort of things I'd have given my own —my other—daughters. Then she wrote to tell me she'd run off to be an opera singer. I can't say I was pleased, though I was hardly surprised. Allegra hadn't been happy in her middle-class life, however Radical her mother and stepfather. She didn't write to me much for some months. But then she told me she'd broken with Tristram Gresham and was on her own in London. She was in need of help. And there was no reason not to help her, at that point."

"And you put her to work for you."

Warkworth hesitated. "Who told you that?"

"No one directly. I worked it out for myself. Philip Ledgwood was communicating between you and Allegra. He thought it was because she was your mistress. But obviously it wasn't."

"I still had my wife to consider. And my children."

"Your legitimate children."

"Quite. One wants to avoid public embarrassment. I couldn't formally acknowledge Allegra."

"Easier to have rumors that she was your mistress than your daughter. But it was more than that, wasn't it? The reason for the secrecy. You had Allegra spying for you."

"Spying? I'm not Carfax—Hubert Mallinson." Warkworth settled back in his chair and crossed his legs. "And in full disclosure, I did know Allegra was working for Hubert Mallinson by that time. She admitted it to me."

"Did you suggest she go to work for him?"

"Why on earth would I turn my daughter into a spy?"

"Because I suspect you wanted a source on what Hubert was doing. So you set Allegra up to be a double agent for you."

"A double agent?" Warkworth shook his head. "Rannoch, Hubert and I are on the same side."

"Since when have there only been two sides? And since when have people on the same side not spied on each other? I saw the tension between Hubert and Castlereagh. I reported to both men. At times, I think each would have been hard pressed to say who they thought was a greater threat, the other or Napoleon Bonaparte."

Warkworth grimaced. "I'm not Castlereagh."

"No. But you've been a force in diplomacy for years. You've been rumored as a possible foreign secretary. And you don't have the official intelligence channels that Castlereagh does." Malcolm was not feeling remotely sympathetic to Warkworth, but he eased one arm onto his chair arm and leaned forwards in a confiding posture. "Believe me, I can understand the impulse to want to know what Hubert was doing."

Warkworth took a drink of port. "Allegra was clever. She found a way to put that cleverness to use."

"Did you counsel her to marry Jeremy Roth?"

"She was in trouble. She had few options."

"You could have offered to protect her and the child."

"I wouldn't have let her starve. But a woman with an illegitimate child has many options in life closed off to her."

"Like Ralph Allam's mother."

"Who?"

"Your son."

"Oh. At that level of society, the issues are hardly the same. But in Allegra's case, marriage to Roth made sense. Just as marriage had made sense for her mother."

"Do you know who the father of her child was?"

"No." Warkworth looked into his glass. "I would hardly ask such a question of my daughter. And she didn't confide in me."

"Did you also counsel Allegra to leave that marriage and run off with Esquivel?"

Warkworth sighed and set his glass down on the small round table beside his chair. "Allegra would have been quite happy as a diplomatic or political hostess, I think. But she was withering in marriage to a man like Roth. She needed to get away. "

"Away from your grandchildren?"

Warkworth winced. "Roth is a good father. A better father than Allegra was a mother, I confess."

"You met Roth?"

"No. But Allegra confessed as much to me. She was remarkably clear-eyed about her deficiencies as a mother. I knew she'd be happier with Esquivel."

"And you wanted information on the Argentine."

Warkworth crossed his legs and reached for his glass. "Allegra came alive when she became an agent. You should appreciate that. From what I observed, the same was true of you."

"If you mean I stopped being numb to everything, you're right. But I wouldn't say I came alive. In fact, I moved so far away from myself I was almost lost completely."

Warkworth returned Malcolm's gaze, his own level as a dueling pistol. "That wasn't the case for Allegra."

"And as I said you wanted information on the Argentine."

"Carfax—Hubert—wanted information on the Argentine."

"And you wanted to know what Hubert was doing."

"It's an important region. It will be increasingly important in the future. So we both had reason to be interested. I'd met Esquivel. I thought Allegra would be happy with him. When I went to the Argentine myself, I saw that. "

"Does Hubert know you're Allegra's father?"

"No. Not unless Allegra told him. And I don't think she would. It shouldn't have mattered. Allegra was very professional about her work."

"What did she say when she came to see you last week?"

Warkworth turned his glass between his fingers. "She updated me on Esquivel's reasons for being in England. The shipping company he was attempting to start. She said she wished to remain quiet while she was in Britain. That it would only open old wounds for her to see Roth or her children."

"And yet in the end she attempted to see Roth."

"Yes. I don't know why." Warkworth's brows drew together. "One can make obvious assumptions from how the interview ended."

"The interview never occurred. Allegra was dead when Roth got there."

"So he says."

"You have reason to believe otherwise?"

"Only my natural assumptions from what I know of the situation. It wouldn't help anything for me to involve myself."

"You mean, risk your position."

"As Roth's friend, I would think you would appreciate my not attempting to exert undue influence. I certainly could speak with Sidmouth. I haven't."

It was a veiled threat. But at the same time, a good point about the power he could exert but had not attempted to use. "I assume you want to learn what happened to your daughter."

"Of course I do." Warkworth's fingers tightened on his glass. "I know your skills, Rannoch. Though you're a friend of Roth's, I trust you to investigate fairly. That's why I'm putting up with this."

"Did Allegra give you any reason to believe she was afraid of anyone on her last visit?"

"Afraid? Allegra was one of the least fearful people I've ever known." Pride tinged his voice.

"Even the bravest people can be wary of a threat. What did she say about Esquivel?"

"That she loved him. And it was harder than ever to lie to him."

Malcolm held his glass steady in his fingers. "Did you consider suggesting she stop spying on him?"

"Allegra wouldn't have wanted to. And I don't think she'd have been happy if she had done. She lived for the mission."

Malcolm forced himself to take a drink of port. It was a good vintage, but it cloyed on his tongue. "Did she have reason to think he was suspicious of her?"

"Not from what she told me." Warkworth's gaze hardened. "You think Esquivel killed her?"

"I think he has to be considered as a suspect. As, I admit, does Roth."

"She didn't indicate any worry that he was on to her. She did say he could be jealous, at times."

Malcolm swallowed the last of his port. "You'll contact me if you remember more?"

"Of course." Warkworth got to his feet as Malcolm did. "Rannoch," he said, as Malcolm moved to the door.

Malcolm turned back to face the older man.

"Allegra was my daughter," Warkworth said in a voice at once soft and hard. "Whatever I've done, don't think I ever forget that."

CHAPTER 42

*L*aura was by the library fire, having scones and tea with the children, when Valentin showed Judith in. Jessica jumped up and ran to hug her cousin. "Where's Serena?"

"She's with her grandparents." Judith bent to hug Jessica. "I just stopped in to see if Mélanie or Malcolm were at home."

"They're Investigating," Colin said.

"I'm not quite sure when they'll be back," Laura said, "but everyone turns up in Berkeley Square to compare notes fairly regularly." She'd recently returned from making inquiries round Mivart's. "Do you want to wait for them?"

"Yes. No. I shouldn't bother them, with everything going on. Everything you're dealing with."

"You're rather at the heart of what we're dealing with. The children were about to start a game of lottery tickets. I'm sure they'll let me sit this round out and have a cup of tea with you." Laura met Emily's gaze and then Colin's. They both understood. Quick nonverbal communication was a family talent.

Laura moved the tea tray to a table and chairs further down the room. They settled themselves on the tapestry chairs. Judith seemed at once relieved to talk and held in, as though afraid of what she might reveal. Laura had always liked Fanny's second daughter, but Judith was seemingly everything Laura had not been herself. Content with her life. Able to bend society to her will rather than rebelling against it. The sort who succeeded effortlessly at the game without even acknowledging a game was being played, and without hurting others in the process. Judith might have been insufferable were it not for her quick sense of humor and ready warmth.

Laura poured a cup of tea and gave it to Judith. "Has something else happened? You needn't talk to me if you'd prefer not to. We can always join the lottery tickets game."

"No. I'd quite like to talk to you. But it's nothing, really. That is, I don't think it impacts the investigation." Judith curled her hands round the cup. "But it impacts me. I sent to Richmond for Bobby's papers yesterday, because even before I knew Jeremy was spying on me, I knew Bobby had known Marco Esquivel. I've been going through them. Searching for what Jeremy might have discovered. I found some papers I need to show Malcolm or Mélanie. I'm not sure what to make of those. But I also found Bobby's letters from Marco Esquivel, and some drafts of letters Bobby was going to send to Mr. Esquivel. Bobby invested in Esquivel's shipping venture. We all already knew that from what Jeremy said. What I didn't realize was how deeply interested Bobby was in the idea. He wrote to Esquivel about traveling to the Argentine and overseeing the shipping company personally." Judith hunched her shoulders, pulling at the puffed sleeves of her gown, and took a drink of tea.

"He hadn't talked to you about that?" Laura said.

"No. He'd never breathed a word of any of it. He'd barely even mentioned Marco Esquivel. And there he was, planning a journey that would take months. He said—" Judith hesitated, took a drink of tea, seemed to force the words out. "That he needed to remember what it was to be alive."

"People can feel the need to find occupation. A focus for their life," Laura said. "It doesn't mean they're unhappy with their spouse and children. Look at my becoming a writer. Look at Mélanie's becoming a playwright."

"Yes, but neither of you sailed to another continent to do it. I don't think either of you would."

"No," Laura agreed. "But Raoul goes to Spain regularly. Not as far as the Argentine, but it does feel a world away. I miss him terribly. But I don't think it means he feels less for me."

Judith picked up a wedge of lemon and squeezed it into her tea. "Do you ever—"

"Worry he's restless?" Laura felt herself smile. "I worry he'd be miserable if he couldn't continue his work. If he couldn't be himself. If I had any doubts about marrying him, it was the fear that it would change him into someone he didn't want to be. But I didn't let that stop me. In fact, I sometimes think I was rather selfish."

"He loves you," Judith said. "It's quite obvious just looking at the two of you. Surely you don't doubt he loves you."

"No." Laura felt herself smile. "Not after I was past the anxieties of the first stages of being in love. I had some rather ridiculous imaginings at the start." Thinking he might have another mistress. Wondering how much he was over Mélanie.

"And you can't think he isn't happy with you."

Laura took a drink of tea. Perhaps it had stewed too long. It had a bitter bite. "No, but I wonder sometimes if I've turned him into someone he wouldn't have chosen to be." She didn't put that into words often. In fact, this might be the first time she ever had done.

"Well, he might not have chosen to be the person he is now if he hadn't fallen in love with you. That doesn't mean he regrets it."

"No." Laura splashed milk into her tea. "I don't think so."

"In fact, he's ridiculously lucky he found you."

Laura laughed, oddly reassured. "Love is important. But I don't think it means one person can find everything they want in another. I'm not even sure that's possible. Let alone advisable."

"But it doesn't mean one person should run halfway across the world from the other."

"A point." Laura stirred her tea, watching the color even out. "Have you thought—"

"That Bobby might have intended me to go to the Argentine with him? I did wonder, but it's quite clear he didn't. Mr. Esquivel says in one letter that it's a dangerous place for a young family. There's a draft of a reply from Bobby saying he understands that. That a break from family life might be just what he needs." Judith clunked her teacup down. Tea spattered into the saucer. "The truth is, I knew I was bored with married life. I didn't realize Bobby was as well. Or I suspected it, but I didn't want to admit it. And I don't know why, when I was perfectly able to admit I was bored myself, and I'm not even sure I loved him, it bothers me that he was bored and may not have loved me." She tugged a handkerchief from her sleeve and blotted the spilt tea. "But it does."

"No one ever claimed love was rational." Laura lifted the teapot to refill their cups.

"I'm not sure I ever loved Bobby."

"You thought you did." Laura filled the cups and set the teapot down. "There are different types of love, and infatuation is certainly one."

"I told myself the honeymoon couldn't last forever, that we were settling in to being married, to running a household, adjusting to having a baby. I even told myself it was good for a husband and wife to have some separate interests."

Laura took a sip of tea. Less bitter now. "I don't think you're wrong there."

"Yes, but I was thinking more of riding or fishing than a shipping company in the Argentine. Now I can't help but wonder—if he'd been happier at home, if he hadn't felt the need to go out so much, perhaps he wouldn't have been riding that day, perhaps he wouldn't have been riding so recklessly—"

"Judith, darling, no." Laura moved to the sofa beside Judith and put her arm round her. "We all make choices. Bobby was responsible for his own life and I'm sure he'd be the first to tell you so. It's so easy to feel guilt when we lose someone. I can't tell you the guilt I feel about my own first husband, with much more cause than you. If you let yourself dwell in that, it will corrode until there's nothing left of yourself."

Judith turned a tear-stained face to her, at once woman and little girl. "I was so busy being dissatisfied myself that I didn't pay nearly enough heed to Bobby."

Laura gave Judith her handkerchief. "Well, for that matter, Bobby could have paid more heed to you instead of thinking of running off to the Argentine."

Judith blotted her eyes. "I wish I could talk to him. I wouldn't want to leave my family, but I'd have quite liked to have an adventure. I don't think Bobby saw me any more clearly than I saw him." She reached for her tea and took another sip. "I knew I wasn't much of a success as a wife, but I didn't think I'd driven my husband away."

"Bobby was confronting parenthood and marriage, and perhaps wanted to escape into his youth. For all you know, he might have got on the boat for the Argentine and realized what a hash he was making of life and how much he'd miss you and Serena, and have got off at the first port to head home."

Judith took a drink of tea. "And the dreadful thing is, if he had done, I might not have been best pleased. I might have been enjoying my freedom."

"Well, then." Laura picked up her own cup. "You have your freedom. Mourn Bobby, but don't let the fact that tragedy brought about that freedom prevent you from enjoying it."

Judith picked up another lemon wedge. "That sounds callous."

"My darling. Life is full of challenges. No one who loved you would blame you for making the most of what you have, in the face of those challenges. I don't know what would have become of your marriage if Bobby had lived. But I'm quite sure he wouldn't want you to be unhappy."

"No." Judith smiled suddenly. "I can almost hear him telling me not to be a silly goose." She frowned into her tea. "I don't like to think about what might have happened if I'd got to know Jeremy properly while Bobby was still alive. Of course, Jeremy would never have approached me if he hadn't been bent on spying on me."

"Would you prefer that he hadn't?" Laura asked.

Judith's shoulders straightened. She frowned. "I'd prefer that he hadn't been spying on me."

"Well, yes, I can quite understand that. But if his not spying on you had meant you'd never have been more than polite acquaintances, would you have preferred that?"

Judith's delicate brows rose. "I should say I'd prefer not to have been lied to and used, shouldn't I? Not to have had a love affair that was based on a mirage. But I wouldn't give up those memories for anything." She squeezed the lemon into her tea. "What a contradictory person I am."

"Not at all. If I hadn't been arrested for the Duke of Trenchard's murder, I'm not sure Raoul and I would ever have broken through layers of reticence. I'll never say I was glad to have been in Newgate. And whatever I thought of Trenchard, I'm not happy he was murdered. But I can still be grateful for where that hideous mess got us."

"Raoul wasn't lying to you."

"Not then, at least. In fact, we were both able to be rather surprisingly honest with each other. But I was lying when I met him. I was lying to Malcolm and Mélanie when I met them." She hesitated a moment. But it wasn't really a secret anymore. And it might help Judith to hear it. "And spying on them."

"Because Emily was being used against you," Judith said. "No one's ever quite spelled it out for me, but that's what I've pieced together."

"You're clever." Laura cast a glance down the library. Emily had Clara on her lap. Sometimes, even now, her throat stopped at the sight of her elder daughter, how much she had missed, how amazing it was to have her back. "Yes. I'm not sure that excuses it. In the end, I found it intolerable."

"I think I could forgive Jeremy if he spied on me because the boys were being threatened."

"He was looking for information about the boys' mother."

Judith stared into her cup. "I have enough questions about Bobby; I should be able to understand his having questions about Allegra. But the thing is, he got close to me to learn things about her. It's not so much whether or not I can forgive that, as that he didn't really love me. That's incontrovertible."

"Is it? When Raoul and I first knew each other, I was spying on the Rannochs, and on him by extension, and he was trying to work out who I was, because he didn't trust me and he was concerned for Mélanie and Malcolm. But that didn't stop us from falling in love."

"Yes, but you—" Judith bit back the words, then seemed to force them out. "You really were in love."

"Are you sure Jeremy wasn't really in love with you? I'm not saying it excuses what he did. But it might be worth considering."

Judith turned her cup on its saucer. "He says he was. I think he may even believe he was. But I also think it's obvious he's still in love with Allegra. That's why he went to such lengths to learn about her."

"There could be all sort of reasons for that. Kitty has questions about Edward Ashford's death now, and she's determined to answer them. But she says she was never remotely in love with him, and I quite believe her."

"Jeremy was in love with Allegra. And I know Jeremy enough to know that sort of love doesn't stop."

Laura set down her teacup, careful not to jostle the tea. "People can love more than one person at once. And I don't mean infidelity. I mean echoes of an old love can still be there when one builds a new love. They may not ever fully go away. It doesn't make the new love any less real. I suspect you still have some feelings for Bobby."

"Well, yes—" Judith frowned. "I hadn't quite thought of it that way. Because what's between us is so much simpler on my side."

"I don't think love is ever simple."

"More straightforward then." Judith looked into her cup, then lifted her gaze to meet Laura's own. "I don't really feel I know either of them at this point, Bobby or Jeremy. But the devil of it is, I'm still in love with Jeremy. I can't deny it. If—"

She broke off as the door opened. Mélanie, Kitty, and Harry stepped into the room. The children fell on them with questions. And then, in the midst of the chaos of answers and scones and more tea, Malcolm returned as well. Laura saw Judith go over to her cousin, with determination but also hesitation, as though she was afraid of what she might be stepping into. "May I talk to you?"

Malcolm looked at his cousin. "Of course. Let's go into the study."

"Don't look at me like that, Malcolm. I'm not going to break." Judith pulled a chair up next to his desk when they were in the study. "Everyone's walking on eggshells round me, and it's silly. What's happened to me is actually rather commonplace. People fall in love under misapprehensions. In this family, I imagine people fall in love with people spying on them."

"I wouldn't say it's a common occurrence." Malcolm managed to keep his face straight.

"In any case, what's happened to me should hardly be a matter of concern right now. Laura talked to me, which helped quite bit.

But I don't need sympathy from you. Allegra Roth was murdered, she deserves justice. And Jeremy is in danger until the murder is solved. He also won't have any peace until it is. Whatever I think about Jeremy—which I'm still not sure—I want him to have as much peace about Allegra as he can. And I want him to be safe."

"So do I."

"I want you to focus on that. And I want to help, if I can." Judith sat back in her chair, hesitated. "There's not much I can do. So I went through Bobby's papers. I was looking to see if anything had got stuck in the lining, and then suddenly the whole bottom of the writing case sprang back. It had a secret compartment. And I found these."

She held out a stack of papers. In code. And again, it was a code Malcolm knew.

"Do you know what it means?" Judith asked.

"No." Malcolm controlled his voice. "But I need to talk to Hubert."

$\mathscr{M}$alcolm slammed the door of the sitting room at White's shut.

Hubert set down his paper with a sigh. "What are you doing here, Malcolm? I thought this was one place I could be free of you."

"Granville brought me in." Malcolm strode across the sitting room. "Can't you bloody get yourself some new codes?"

"The ones you wrote are excellent. And you'd just break the new ones."

"Did you have Bobby Derwent spying on Marco Esquivel?"

Hubert folded the newspaper. "Was he supposed to be off limits because he married into your family? Given our families, that would put quite a few agents off limits. And since when have any of us agreed to abide by rules like that? You've been quick to use my son, his lover, my eldest and youngest daughters, and certainly my nephew. And his wife."

"Don't you dare claim Julien and Kitty. They make their own rules." Malcolm dragged a chair closer to Hubert and dropped into it. "Bobby was a civilian."

"Bobby Derwent was a young man with a taste for adventure

who had been giving me useful information since he was at Cambridge."

A chill shot through Malcolm. As though a bucket of icy water had been dumped on him in a game at a country fair. "So when Bobby proposed to Judith—"

Hubert leaned back in his chair. "He was already working for me. He had friends at Cambridge whom I was interested in."

"As Oliver had at Oxford." Malcolm would never quite get past the way Hubert had used one of Malcolm's own best friends, who had later married one of Hubert's daughters, against Malcolm and his friends.

"In some ways. Your friends weren't the only case of discontent among undergraduates that I found it advisable to follow. Though you certainly stood out. But Bobby ran with a hotheaded set as well."

"We weren't—

"Hotheaded? No, coldly analytical may be more to the point. And much more dangerous. Tanner's less of a risk now that he's my son-in-law to all intents and purposes. The Cambridge group wasn't a risk on your level. But Bobby's information was still useful."

"So when he married Judith—"

Hubert picked up the cup of coffee on the table beside his chair. "Are you asking me if I orchestrated it? No. That would be a bit beyond me. Did I think it could be advantageous?" He took a drink of coffee. "Can you imagine I wouldn't?"

Scenes shot through Malcolm's memory. Judith and Bobby on the settee in the Berkeley Square library holding hands. Bobby playing billiards with Harry and Julien. Bobby and Judith playing with the children on the hearth rug while he and Mel and the others talked about their latest investigation. What had they said —to Bobby's face, or that he could have overheard without even trying very hard? "So he was spying on all of us at family parties?"

"Malcolm. *I've* been at a number of those family parties."

"And don't for a moment think I didn't wonder if you were spying on us."

"And the other way round." Hubert set down his coffee cup. "Marco Esquivel is a very dangerous man."

"Define dangerous."

"He could help set the Argentine on a course ruinous to British interests."

"What about Argentine interests?"

"Why on earth should I care about Argentine interests?"

"Why indeed?"

"I needed information on Esquivel. Bobby was perfectly positioned to provide it. So was Allegra Roth."

"And now they're both dead. As is Edward Ashford, whom you were spying on."

"I hope you aren't suggesting I had anything to do with that."

"I wouldn't put it past you." Malcolm regarded his former spymaster. "You didn't blink at the idea that Bobby might have been murdered."

"When an agent dies in an accident, one can't but wonder. But I had no reason at that point to think he had particular enemies. Even if Esquivel had learned the truth, Esquivel wasn't here."

"He could have sent someone. Hired someone here."

Hubert frowned for a moment. "Possibly. I didn't see Esquivel as a killer. At least, not then."

"Do you have reason to think he is now?"

"Only the fact that his mistress was murdered, and you've told me the spouses and lovers of a victim are always the first suspects. That puts him and Jeremy Roth at the center of things."

"In theory."

"Are you saying you don't suspect either of them?"

"I have to suspect both of them. I have a hard time seeing either as a killer. In Roth's case, I admit to bias—though I also have almost a decade of knowledge of him. In Esquivel's case, it's based on my impression from meeting him."

"And you agree with him politically."

"That's true. But it wouldn't bias me."

"Everyone has biases. We're more inclined to see those we agree with as sympathetic."

"It would be easier for Roth if Esquivel were clearly guilty." Malcolm hesitated a moment. "Raoul described Esquivel's face when he learned the woman he loved was spying on him. Raoul said if Esquivel already knew, it was masterful acting."

"Talking of biases." Hubert settled back in his chair, elbows behind him. "You have a lot of reasons to feel empathy for Esquivel."

Malcolm returned his former spymaster's gaze, willing every muscle in his body to stay steady. "I don't see how one could not feel empathy for him. But every case is different."

Hubert reached for his coffee again and took a thoughtful sip. "It's a remarkable thing," he said.

"What?"

"Forgiveness. I don't think Amelia will ever forgive me. I don't, objectively, think that she should. But you seem to have mastered it."

Wariness settled over Malcolm like the suit of armor at Dunmykel that had fascinated him as a child. But there were things he could say to Hubert now. And things it seemed wrong not to say. "I wouldn't say I've forgiven Mel. I understand her. I know who she is, better than I did before. And because of that, I can understand why she did what she did." It was by far the most revealing thing he had said to Hubert in years. Perhaps ever. Once the very thought of discussing Mélanie's past with Hubert would have had him break out in a cold sweat and contact Bertrand de Laclos to smuggle his family out of Britain. As he had in fact done. A lot had changed. Because Mel had a pardon. But also because his relationship to Hubert had changed.

"So you think she was right to do what she did?" Hubert sounded genuinely interested.

"Right's a funny word. She was doing her job. Rather better than I ever did mine. But then, that's why it's a good thing I'm not an agent anymore."

"You were the best agent I ever had. With the possible exceptions of Julien and Kitty."

"I'm relieved to hear you use the past tense."

"Slip of the tongue. You have a good sense of values, Malcolm. And I don't mean your nonsense about the rights of man."

When Malcolm was a boy visiting the Mallinsons on school holidays, he'd been amazed at a family far more coherent than his own. Later, as he got to know Hubert better, he saw the pressure Hubert put on his son. When he went to work for Hubert himself, he'd wondered if Hubert even knew the meaning of the word family. Now Hubert's gaze said he valued something he'd lost, something that Malcolm had mastered better than he had himself.

"Bobby," Malcolm said. "Who else was he spying on?"

"I wouldn't say spying. Bobby wasn't a trained agent. He was still giving me interesting information about Beardsley and Rowley. But mostly Esquivel."

"He and Beardsley, Rowley, and Esquivel were friends."

"You and Oliver were friends."

"Oliver was poor and ambitious. Bobby had a very comfortable fortune. And no ambitions I knew of."

"He was restless. Wanted something to do to give his life focus. I'd think you'd understand that."

"So he thought he was saving Britain?"

"Is it so impossible to imagine a young British man finding that a laudable objective?"

"That depends on the person. I don't think you ever saw it in such simple terms."

"I've never been one for causes. But some people find them meaningful. I'd think you, of all people, would understand that."

"I never saw working for you as a cause."

"No, you left me because you rediscovered the dangerous

cause that drove you as a young man. And I assume you're happier for it."

"Without question."

"Well, then. Is it so hard to imagine Bobby found a cause that was opposed to yours and your friends'?"

"He didn't seem like that type."

"What type?"

"Either the reckless do-or-die-for-my-country type or the Machiavellian schemer like you."

"Perhaps you misread him. Assumed certain things because Fanny's daughter fell in love with him and he married into your family."

"Perhaps."

Hubert set down his coffee cup. "I'm sorry for Judith."

It was not something Hubert would have said a few years ago. It might indicate his evolution when it came to personal relationships. It might also be fishing for information. Bow Street and the home office knew about Judith and Roth. So presumably Hubert did too.

"It's challenging," Malcolm said. "She's one of the few in the family who hasn't had to contend with espionage until now."

Hubert reached for his coffee again. "How did you tumble to it, in any case?" he asked in a voice of mild interest. "It seems on the edge of your investigation."

"Judith looked for letters between Esquivel and Bobby. I still know your codes."

"Ah." Hubert took a drink of coffee. His spectacle lenses had never looked more opaque. "And I suppose Judith was looking because of her concern for Roth. No sense pretending I don't know."

"When did you learn?"

"Only yesterday. Higgins has been enterprising in turning over aspects of Roth's life. I must say, I was surprised."

"So was I.

"I understand there's concern at the home office."

"Fanny always draws notice. And Judith is perhaps particularly notable among her children. Not a wise entanglement for Roth. But then, romantic entanglements seldom are wise."

Hubert took a drink of coffee. "For once we are quite in agreement."

~

"FIRST I LEARNED my husband wanted to run off and have adventures because he couldn't stand domesticity. At least not with me." Judith's gaze was wide and yet something about her eyes held a worldly wisdom that hadn't been there a day before. Mélanie had watched Judith grow from fifteen to two-and-twenty, but in some ways, it seemed she had aged more in the past day. "Now you're telling me he was a spy and I didn't know it?"

"Apparently Hubert Mallinson recruited him," Malcolm said. "To get information on Marco Esquivel."

Judith folded her hands in her lap. Her knuckles had gone white. "So Bobby wasn't just spying. He was spying on a friend."

"In the service of his country," Mélanie said. Which was what she'd been doing. In the service of her country and a cause she believed in. They were in the Berkeley Square library, she, Malcolm, Julien, Kitty, Laura, and Judith. Harry had gone to make more inquires of military contacts, and Raoul still wasn't back.

Judith snorted. "We all know what Hubert Mallinson is."

"We do, but Bobby may not have done necessarily," Malcolm said. "He might have believed he was helping Britain."

"I'd have thought that a week ago," Judith said. "Even a few days ago. But I'm no longer sure I knew Bobby at all." She loosed her hands, but only to grip her elbows, arms folded in front of her. "If he was working for Hubert Mallinson, do you think he married me to spy on all of you?"

Malcolm cast a quick glance at Mélanie. "Hubert says not."

"Malcolm, since when do you believe anything Hubert Mallinson says?" Judith asked.

"It seems highly unlikely."

"But you can't be sure."

Malcolm met his cousin's gaze. "At this point, we can't be sure of anything."

Judith shook her head. "I'd realized Bobby and I weren't as in love as we thought we were. But I thought he was a good person."

"Spies can be good people," Julien said from a corner of the settee. "Not claiming I am myself—just a general observation. I know quite a few spies who are good people."

"He was spying on his friend." Judith gave the last word a crescendo. "I'm all for understanding complex motives, but it's difficult to forgive that."

"Alejandra was spying on Esquivel too," Julien said. "Poor devil."

Judith looked among them. "Do you think—"

"There's no reason to think Bobby was murdered," Malcolm said. "But—"

"What?" Judith asked.

"We recently learned my first husband's death may not have been accidental," Kitty said. "Though it's difficult to put together a reason someone would have killed both of them and Allegra Roth."

"And attacked you."

"Assuming they're all connected," Malcolm said. "They might not be, and they might still all be murders or attempted murders."

Judith swung her gaze to him. The worldly wisdom in her eyes had been replaced by shock.

"I'm not saying it's likely," Malcolm said. "But it's a possibility we have to consider."

Judith drew back in her chair, still gripping her elbows. "Surely this at least proves Jeremy is innocent. He'd have had no reason to attack Kitty's husband. Or Bobby. Well, not then. You know what I mean."

"It's a new avenue to pursue," Mélanie said. "But it won't persuade Bow Street of anything. And we don't even have proof of most of this."

"Shouldn't we tell Mr. Esquivel about Bobby? He's already lost the woman he loves. I know it will be hard to hear, but surely he deserves to know. Unless"—Judith looked among them—"you think he turned on Bobby and Allegra Roth?"

"It's always been possible he killed Allegra Roth," Malcolm said. "Bobby's death was very different. And we don't even know it was murder. His horse would have had to be tampered with."

"But if Esquivel's the sort who gets angry at betrayal—they both betrayed him."

"So they did," Malcolm said.

Judith met her cousin's gaze, at once pleading for answers and afraid to face them.

"It's a possibility," Malcolm said. "But Harry and Cordy could tell you it's not nearly enough for a good thesis. Let alone anything close to proof."

Judith nodded. "So what now?"

"I think Mélanie and I established some trust with Mandy at the Three Queens." Kitty looked at Julien. "I know Mélanie has to go to the Tavistock, but if you come back with me, we may be able to learn more."

Julien nodded.

Mélanie reached down to pet Berowne and sent a mental apology to her characters for wishing rehearsal at the devil.

"I'll see if Palmerston can tell me anything about what Allegra Roth may have been looking for in the war office records she asked Ledgwood to steal," Malcolm said. "Hopefully we'll hear from Allie about the coded paper from the Agrippina bust soon."

"I'll stay here," Judith said. "At least I'll be close to information when we get it."

~

ALINE HESITATED JUST inside the library door. "I came to update Malcolm and Mélanie and the others on the paper I was decoding."

"Have you broken the code?" Judith asked her sister.

"Yes. It was complicated. Whoever created it had considerable skills—and was very determined to keep the message secret."

"You can't tell who?"

"No. Truth to tell, I can't tell what the message means. Hopefully they can." Aline moved to the settee, though she seemed unsure if she should properly settle in the room. It wasn't the first such uncomfortable moment Judith had had with her sister.

"I suppose you've heard about Jeremy and me," Judith said.

"A bit," Aline said. "Because Malcolm thought I needed to know, depending on what the paper had to do with."

"Because Bobby was about to run off to the Argentine."

"We don't know that."

"He put it in writing. At least that he was thinking about it."

"Which isn't the same as doing it."

"Tell me that if Geoff tries to run off. Which he wouldn't. Which is rather the point." Judith regarded her elder sister. "I used to feel sorry for you."

"I can understand that. I wasn't interested in any of the things that interested you."

"Not completely. We both like the theatre and music. But I thought it was sad that you didn't like to go out. In fact before my debut, I thought having a debut was entirely wasted on you."

"And there were many times I'd have much preferred to have you take my place. I'm sure I seemed sadly dull."

"No, but I kept thinking all the fun was wasted on you, and how sad it was you'd never get married. I mean, you kept *saying* you never would."

"So I did. I meant it."

"And then when you married Geoff—"

"You thought how sad it was I was marrying a fusty, middle-aged man."

"No! Well, not precisely. But I wasn't even sixteen. Even Malcolm seemed old. And you were still in Vienna when I first heard you were engaged. It was different when I saw you together. It was quite obvious what you felt for each other. Even to a self-involved teenager. I was glad you were happy. But I still rather marveled that you could be happy with a life so different from what I wanted myself. It was only later, after I'd been married for a time, that I started to envy you."

"Me?" Aline asked.

"Yes. Because you seemed to have it all worked out. You hadn't even been looking for a husband, you'd been avoiding it, and yet you managed to have a marriage that worked."

Aline's brows drew together (how often Judith had lamented that her sister wouldn't pluck her brows, though it now occurred to her that they were very pretty as they were, if a bit lopsided). "I don't think there's any such thing as having a marriage that works. I mean, it can work for a time. But I don't know that one can ever be sure it always will. Geoff had been a bachelor living on his own ever since university. I think he found it a bit disconcerting to live with someone else, at first. Fortunately, I like being on my own and wouldn't want someone fussing over me, so that works fairly well. But we've both had to make adjustments. It's worth it, though."

"That's the thing," Judith said. "I don't know that Bobby or I had to adjust nearly as much. We still had a large house and we could do much as we wanted. And even then, it didn't seem worth it." She stared at her hands. "I'm not even sure precisely *what* didn't seem worth it. It was simply that I would look at him across the breakfast table or in the drawing room after dinner—or sometimes across my pillow—and feel vaguely discontented. And there'd be these silences when neither of us seemed to have much to say. It sounds very foolish now. A lot of people muddle through on less."

"But one shouldn't have to," Aline said.

Judith's gaze shot to her sister's face.

"Not that marriage will ever be easy all the time," Aline said. "And not that there won't be difficult moments. But it shouldn't be something one simply endures day in, day out."

"I sometimes think it's that I was selfish and spoilt. Everyone always said I was."

"Not everyone. Just your elder sister and brother on occasion. You've always had a generous heart, Judith. And you deserve to be happy. Never think you don't."

Judith glanced away. "That's kind, Allie."

Aline tucked a strand of her ash-brown hair behind her ear. "I didn't say it to be kind. I said it because it's true."

CHAPTER 44

"Malcolm." Harry Palmerston, secretary-at-war, shifted a sheaf of papers off the chair beside his desk. "I thought you were buried in one of your investigations. Something lurid in Seven Dials."

"That's why I'm here, actually." Malcolm dropped into the chair. "What do you know about Edward Ashford?"

Palmerston added the papers to one of the numerous stacks on his desk. "Didn't know him well. Didn't think much of him. Especially not of the way he treated his wife."

"No." Malcolm settled back in his chair. Kitty had flirted with Palmerston when she first came to England, as part of her effort to get British support for the Liberal rebellion in Spain. At one point, Malcolm had suspected she meant to go further.

Palmerston gave a wry smile. "I'm very fond of Kitty, but it never went beyond that. Probably a good thing, considering the way she and Julien look at each other. I understand the pangs of jealousy too well to get in between a relationship like that." Palmerston's own relationship with his longtime mistress Emily Cowper was as tempestuous as it was enduring. From what Malcolm had seen, Palmerston's infidelities tended to be a reaction to Emily's. "Are Kitty and Julien mixed up in your case?" Palmerston asked.

"The murder victim had spent time in the Argentine, and Kitty and Julien knew her there. She also knew Edward Ashford. And now there are questions about Ashford's death."

Palmerston's brows drew together, but he didn't look as surprised as Malcolm would have expected.

"Had you heard anything?" Malcolm asked.

"Not about Ashford's death. But there was quite a bit of worry about Ashford at the time he died. Rumors about investments in a silver mine scheme. Whatever support we're getting to the Argentine rebels has to be strictly unofficial and isn't tracked by the war office. But more funds were being sent to Ashford than he should have needed for his vaguely defined mission. At first, I thought Carfax—Hubert Mallinson—was using Ashford to funnel funds to the rebels. But from some questions Carfax asked, I don't think he was."

"Nor do I," Malcolm said. "Hubert was investigating Ashford over the silver mine. And I don't think Ashford was involved in arming the rebels."

Palmerston nodded. "It seemed a bit blatant for even for Hubert Mallinson to funnel secret payments in defiance of an international treaty directly through the war office to an army officer. When I heard the rumors about the silver mine, I suspected someone was funneling funds for the mine scheme to Ashford that way. But I never thought he was in on it alone."

"Someone was putting government money into the mine?"

"Diverting government funds to front the money to get things started, so they could encourage other investors. And if I'm right, it was done with more than one mine."

"Do you know who might have been behind it?"

Palmerston shifted in his chair. "I never heard anything definite, but at a guess, Warkworth. He'd pulled strings to clear up more than one scandal for Ashford through the years."

Malcolm schooled his face not to betray shock. "I didn't realize they knew each other. But then, Ashford hardly confided in me. He didn't confide much in his own wife. Perhaps her least of all."

"Ashford had an uncle who was at school with Warkworth."

"Of course. It comes back to school ties so often."

"That's where we often make our closest friends. It's that way for me with my Harrow friends, and I suspect for you."

"In some cases." Malcolm leaned back against the hard slats of his chair. "Allegra Roth, the murder victim, was asking questions about war office records relating to Ashford. This could explain what she was looking for."

"You think she was on to Warkworth?"

"She was Warkworth's illegitimate daughter. And also spying for him."

Palmerston whistled, then got up and went to a shelf of ledgers. "A great many secrets can hide in military accounts. In any case, after Ashford died the whole silver mine scheme faded away. I think there were some quiet payments to people who had been affected. But I can't believe he was in on it alone."

"Your observations tend to be keen," Malcolm said. Palmerston was a bit of an outsider in the Tory establishment, but—despite or perhaps because of that—he picked up on things. "Did you ever hear a suggestion that Ashford's death wasn't natural?"

Palmerston pulled out a ledger, shook the dust off it, put it back. "Nothing more than a comment that it was timely."

"Fitzroy Somerset said you and he overheard Castlereagh and Wellington saying it would be wiser not to ask questions."

"I should have known Fitzroy would remember. Yes." Palmerston glanced at Malcolm over his shoulder. "It's suggestive."

"So it is."

Palmerston reached for another ledger. "Let's see if we can find what Allegra Roth was curious about."

～

385

"You're back." The fair-haired young woman with the green eyes stopped by the table at the Three Queens where Kitty was sitting. "Did you and your friend find Ralph?"

"We did." Kitty turned up the collar of her spencer. She had put the spencer and hat she'd worn on her first visit to the Three Queens back on over the bronze-green bombazine walking dress she'd put on to call on Philip Ledgwood. She could blend in, but she wasn't precisely the woman she'd been on her first visit. Which was the point. "He was surprisingly agreeable. And he seems to be fond of you."

The fair-haired woman humphed and folded her arms across her chest, but for a moment something sparked in her eyes.

"He said your name is Mandy."

"It is." Mandy's gaze took in the emerald satin appliqué on Kitty's bodice. "You didn't really want to see him about your friend's money, did you?"

"No. Not precisely."

"Your friend—whose name I'm guessing isn't really Molly—didn't come back with you?"

"Not this time." Kitty considered, then looked at Julien, who was at the bar procuring beer and listening for information. It was a risk, but the only way to do this was honestly. "My husband did."

Mandy spun round to look at Julien. Her gaze narrowed. "He looks familiar." She stared at Kitty. "You were here with him. That night. The night the lady was killed. I should have realized before, but I got a better look at him than you that night." Her shoulders went taut. "What were you doing in Seven Dials then? What are you doing here now?"

Nothing for it but to risk it. "Investigating."

Kitty was prepared for Mandy to bolt, but she held her ground. "You don't work for Bow Street?"

"No. We're friends of the murdered lady's husband."

Mandy dropped into a chair at the table. "That's why you wanted to talk to Ralph?"

"Yes. He knew her. He admitted it to us. He wasn't her lover—"

"Yes, I know. She was his sister."

That Ralph Allam had admitted that to Mandy said a lot about his feelings for her. Just as it had said a lot about Julien's feelings for Kitty when he'd admitted who he was years ago in Buenos Aires.

Kitty met Julien's gaze across the room. He'd been deliberately hanging back by the bar. Now he approached through the crowd with three pints of ale.

"My husband," Kitty said. "Julien Mallinson. I'm Kitty, by the way. This is Mandy, darling."

Julien inclined his head and gave Mandy a pint.

"For what it's worth," Kitty said, "Ralph was away on business for Allegra these past few days."

Mandy took a drink of ale. "Poison. He might have said. Men." She looked at Julien. "No offense."

"None taken."

"Your wife says you know Allegra's husband."

"We do. And we want to learn what happened to her."

Mandy dragged her pint closer. "No one wants to talk about her. She was close to Ralph and this is Ralph's place. Most people here are Ralph's friends."

"That's a lot of loyalty," Julien said.

Mandy shrugged and looked into her pint. "He may not be so bad as I made out to your wife and her friend earlier today. I was mad. I s'pose it's not his fault if he's got tired of me."

"I haven't met Mr. Allam, but if you'll permit me to say so, a man may have a number of reasons for giving a lady the idea that their relationship has no future. His own qualms. Even possibly concern for her."

Mandy snorted, but her gaze was thoughtful.

"I know you have no reason to believe me," Kitty said. "But Ralph talked to us about Allegra today."

Mandy took a drink of ale. "I do believe you, actually. For one thing, you knew she was his sister, and I don't know anyone but me who knew that."

"You were here that night," Julien said. "The night Allegra Roth was killed. I remember seeing you."

"I saw you then too. And your wife, though not as well. I didn't know Ralph's sister had been killed then." Mandy hunched her shoulders.

"Did you see Allegra come into the pub?" Kitty asked.

"Yes. That is, I thought it was her. She had the hood of her cloak shadowing her face. I'd only seen her once before. And I'd never talked to her. She never talked to anyone, just came in and went upstairs."

"Did you see anyone else go upstairs after she did?" Julien asked.

"Only that man. The one they now say is her husband. And then another man, a gentleman, and then the two of you. Later you all three came back downstairs. The other man's a friend of yours too, isn't he?"

"Yes," Kitty said.

"And then a fourth man came. That runner Higgins, we know now. He's been round here asking questions. Truth to tell, his questions made everyone even less inclined to talk."

"I'm not surprised," Julien said. "But you didn't see anyone else go upstairs after Allegra arrived and before her husband did?"

"Not up the main stairs." Mandy took another drink of ale, grip tight on the tankard. "But I went into the kitchen for a bit. There are back stairs that go down past the kitchen. People use them sometimes if they want to slip in and out unseen. Even at a place like the Three Queens there are people like that."

"There are people like that everywhere," Julien said. "What did you see?"

"Just a glimpse. A man in a greatcoat going up the stairs. Tall. He had a hat on. Couldn't make out more. Didn't think much of it.

Some men slip in to meet a lover in secret. Some to deal goods they don't want anyone to know about. But now—"

"Quite," Julien said.

"I was waiting for Ralph," Mandy said. "I wanted to tell him. Before I told Higgins. Who I didn't want to tell at all."

The door banged open. Ralph Allam strode into the taproom, cast a glance round, and went straight to their table. His gaze fastened on Mandy for a moment, then jerked to Kitty. "Somehow I'm not surprised to see you here."

"You shouldn't be," Kitty said. "This time I've brought my husband."

Allam inclined his head. Then his gaze shot to Mandy. "You all right?"

"I can take care of myself."

"Never said you couldn't." Ralph's gaze lingered on her face. "But you can't blame me for worrying."

"It's a worrying time," Julien said. "My wife could tell you I've been driving her mad with my concerns the past two days."

Mandy considered him, arms folded. "Your wife said earlier that she's not a romantic. Now I've met you, I think that was one more pretense."

"One can only hope so," Julien said.

CHAPTER 45

"*Y*ou *and Gideon make it look so easy,*" Letty Blanchard said, in just the tones Mélanie had imagined.

"*Marriage?*" Manon laughed. "*Don't forget we're both skilled at deception.*"

"*That sounds beastly.*"

"*I never said it wasn't worth it. The best things in life take work.*"

"Too trite?" Mélanie whispered to Simon.

"True, I'd say." Simon was watching the actors with his legs stretched out and arms folded.

Mélanie made a note on the script in front of her. Gaze on the page, she didn't see Tim until he was standing beside the table with the same caution that Valentin showed when interrupting her at home with the news of a caller. "A Miss Caldwell came to the stage door," he murmured, bending down. "She apologizes but hopes she can speak with you."

Mélanie exchanged a look with Simon. "This could be important." One thing to leave the case for rehearsal. Another to ignore the case when it followed her.

"I'll take notes for you," Simon promised. "Why don't you talk in the green room?"

The green room was empty, but the tea was still hot. Mélanie poured two cups, just as she would in Berkeley Square, though the cups were earthenware and the tea a rougher brew.

"I'm sorry to interrupt you again," Cressida Caldwell said, accepting a cup.

"In the circumstances, I'm grateful that you came." Mélanie settled beside Miss Caldwell on a shield-back chair that showed three chipped coats of paint from three different productions. "You remembered something else about your sister?"

"Yes. Not precisely." Miss Caldwell took a sip of tea. "Did you find Ralph Allam?"

"We did." Mélanie took a sip from her own cup. "You didn't mention that he was Allegra's brother."

Cressida Caldwell's gaze widened. "That's because I had no idea. So his father—"

"Was also Allegra's. According to him. Lord Warkworth."

Miss Caldwell's fingers tightened on her cup. "Good heavens."

"You know him?" It was not inconceivable that she did, and even that he had been one of Miss Caldwell's lovers.

"I've heard his name. Did Allam say they had met him?"

"He said Allegra had. And Lord Warkworth confirmed that to my husband. Apparently, Allegra found both Warkworth and Allam when she was sixteen. But Warkworth only acknowledged Allegra."

"Not surprising, perhaps. Though it hardly makes me think well of Warkworth." Miss Caldwell took a fortifying sip of tea. "I wasn't entirely forthcoming about what Allegra said when she came to see me recently." Miss Caldwell shifted on the frayed tapestry settee, sending a fringed cushion tumbling to the floor. An unusual show of discomfort. She had the elegant physical control of a dancer most of the time. Obviously cultivated, and yet she made it seem effortless. "Allegra wanted me to exert influence. On one of my lovers."

It was more of a surprise than perhaps it should have been.

Allegra Roth had obviously been involved in a number of schemes. "To do what?" Mélanie asked.

"She wanted to talk to him. Without Marco Esquivel's knowing."

Mélanie took a sip of tea. "Do you know why?"

"She wouldn't tell me. I couldn't but be suspicious. She said it would be easy enough for me to persuade a besotted man, and it was a small favor to do for a sister." Miss Caldwell set her teacup down. "That was Allegra all over, turning sweet when she wanted something. I said sisterly favors had never been part of our relationship from when we were five and six, and why on earth should I accommodate her? That was when Allegra's face turned hard. You know Rosina's aria from the barber opera? About how she's all sweetness and light until someone crosses her will and then she's a termagant? That's Allegra to the life. I could scarcely stop laughing the first time I heard that song. When Allegra was a girl, she'd have a tantrum, like Rosina does, if she was crossed. She was more controlled now. She simply straightened her back and said that if I wouldn't oblige her, she'd reveal certain information about Vincent's parentage." Miss Caldwell picked up the cushion that had tumbled to the floor and smoothed the fringe. "Morals mean nothing to me. It's no secret I was not married to Vincent's father. But I have my reasons for not wishing his parentage to be known."

"That's understandable," Mélanie said. And none of her business. Unless, of course, his parentage proved to impinge on the reasons Allegra Roth had been killed. But for now, it was more important to keep Cressida Caldwell's confidence and keep her talking. "What did you say to your stepsister's threat?"

Miss Caldwell jerked her hand back. Her nail caught on the fringe. "That she should know better than to think threats would work with me. When had they ever done so? I reminded her that I knew a number of secrets about her. "

"Do you know the father of her elder child?" Mélanie asked. "Jeremy has admitted it isn't he. Not biologically."

Miss Caldwell gave a smile that was sharp round the edges. "It must seem very odd, all the questionable parentages. Perhaps inevitable in a life such as we lead, but not what one would expect in Mayfair."

"On the contrary. Many ladies in Mayfair make it a point to father each of their children with a different gentleman. Though usually the eldest son is the husband's. Believe me, a number of my friends are in similar tangles." Such as Emily Cowper, who seemed quite comfortable with it, as did her husband. And Laura, Cordelia, and Kitty, for whom it was far more complicated. As it was for Mélanie herself.

"I don't think many of my lovers realize how freely their wives are behaving. Though some talk quite openly about it. Some with regret, some with what I might call easy affection. I rather admire those. Though it's not what I'd care for in a marriage. Assuming I ever married, which seems the height of absurdity. I have my suspicions about Allegra's firstborn's parentage. I can't be certain. When I threatened Allegra with that knowledge—which seemed only fair game—she said I could do what I would, she was determined and she would still counter with every bit of power at her disposal."

"Forgive me," Mélanie said. "But is the gentleman she wanted you to arrange a meeting with, the man with whom you'd let yourself fall in love?"

Miss Caldwell's brilliant green eyes widened. "How did you know?"

"I didn't, but it seemed a good theory. Because obviously, manipulating him bothered you on a very deep level."

Miss Caldwell glanced at the window. The cool light fell across her face, picking out fine lines in her skin and accentuating her delicate bone structure. "Is that so very much to ask? To keep one relationship—pure sounds absurd. But free of deceit and manipulation. I deserve that. He deserves that. Even if it's bound to end, we should be able to keep the memories. Someday the memories are all that I will have."

"Forgive me," Mélanie said again. "But if Allegra wanted to talk privately with your lover—who is he?"

Miss Caldwell met her gaze. "A courtesan's first lesson is to keep her affairs discreet. Except for the ones she finds it convenient to flaunt. But you were bound to ask. And I'm sure you could uncover the truth if you put your mind to it. He's William Beardsley."

Mélanie set down her teacup. "Did you know—"

"That William was at Cambridge with Marco Esquivel? Yes, but it had hardly seemed relevant to me before that day, as I didn't know about my sister and Marco Esquivel."

"Why do you think Allegra wanted to talk with him?"

"I don't know. I asked her why she couldn't go through Esquivel, and she said he tried to keep her away from his friends because they knew his wife. But she wouldn't tell me what she wanted with William. I was afraid she wanted to exert political influence. I can't guess at what, but I'm all the more convinced I was right not to agree." Miss Caldwell's gaze narrowed. "Your husband is a Radical MP. I've heard William speak of him with admiration. And of you."

"He's been to our house on occasion. And I've heard him speak. He has a powerful style. And keen insights, from what I've seen in his work drafting a bill."

"He said you help drafting language. That it was far better to meet at your home in Berkeley Square than at Brooks's, because you could be part of the discussion." Miss Caldwell stared down at the cushion, canvas painted to resemble damask. "That must be quite remarkable. To be so involved in something that could shape the world."

"My husband would say if we're lucky, we'll make the smallest difference round the edges. But it's one of the things that brought my husband and me closer together." Which was true. They might have begun with her spying on him. But working together, whether on investigations or speeches or articles, had given them a foundation to stay together.

Miss Caldwell picked at the fringe on the cushion. "William's read some of his speeches to me. I've even helped him a bit. It quite fascinates me, how he uses language to persuade people. Not entirely different from what a courtesan does."

"Or a playwright."

Miss Caldwell reached her tea. "I'm hardly a Radical. But I haven't entirely abandoned the principles I was raised on. In fact, I quite believe in them, in theory. I just have no desire to live in poverty until we get to a more just world. I may have sunk into cynicism in recent years, but there's something about William that shakes me out of it. He has a way of making me believe, at least when I'm with him." She took a drink of tea. "I believe enough to want him to have a career where he can do all he can to make the world a better place. So I know that eventually he'll have to marry and have a political hostess who can help him advance in his career. I'm sure you understand that."

Mélanie took a quick sip of tea. The familiar blend had an unexpectedly sharp bite. "I'm not as much of a political hostess as I once was. My husband says he's never going to be prime minister in any case, so it doesn't matter."

"But don't you want him to have every advantage possible? William talks of him as though he could change the world."

The tea roiled in her stomach. "Yes. While at the same time, I want things for myself. And for our children. It's a constant muddle balancing it all."

"But you manage?" Miss Caldwell's voice held genuine curiosity.

"Sometimes, for a few moments. Then one piece tends to go tumbling down and I have to scramble to catch it."

"You make it look easy."

Mélanie laughed. "That's acting. You should understand."

Miss Caldwell gave a smile of acknowledgement. "I do, at that. But I know what William needs for his life and his work. And it isn't me. I'll do my best to extricate us both without bitter feelings. It took a long time for me to indulge in a flirtation with a fairy tale. I'm quite sure I never will again. I believe in William. I'm not going to stand in his way. And I wasn't going to let Allegra do so either."

"So you refused her ultimatum."

"Categorically. Allegra lost her temper then, and we called each other all sorts of names, just like we did when we were girls. Finally, I rang for Simpkins and asked him to show her out."

"Did she leave?"

"Even Allegra isn't quite so bold as to risk refusing to leave. Or rather, she might have been when she was younger, but now she knows I'm fully capable of having Simpkins carry her bodily from the house." Miss Caldwell's brows drew together. "I rather regret we didn't have the chance to put that to the test."

"Did you hear from her again?"

"No. I lived on tenterhooks, wondering what she'd do to expose secrets about Vincent. Until I learned she'd been killed. Which was a new shock, but at least ended the blackmail threat." Miss Caldwell set down her teacup. "Which I suppose means I had as good a motive to have been behind her murder as anyone."

The door opened on Miss Caldwell's words. "Forgive me. But Simon said I would find you here."

Mélanie looked round to find herself staring at William Beardsley. Who had stopped short on the threshold. "Cressy."

"William." Miss Caldwell held her teacup steady as though by an act of will. "I had some things to say to Mrs. Rannoch about my stepsister."

"Your—"

"Allegra Roth."

His eyes widened. "I didn't—"

"No, of course you didn't know. I generally avoid talking about Allie when I don't have to. And I had no notion her lover was your friend Esquivel. But if you are here, you must have things to say to Mrs. Rannoch as well. I'll make myself scarce."

"No." Beardsley took a quick step forwards. "I have no secrets from you, Cressy."

"William, darling. Everyone has secrets."

"If Allegra Roth was your stepsister, all the more reason for you to stay." Beardsley turned to Mélanie. "I came here hoping to find you. I know the Tavistock—"

"From Leveller meetings."

"Yes." He pulled a chair close to the two of them and sat. "I wouldn't have thought it would have to do with Mrs. Roth's murder. But Marco told me Mrs. Roth had been asking questions about Edward Ashford's death. And that put me in mind of something."

"Something you'd heard about Captain Ashford?" Mélanie asked.

"Something Bobby Derwent said to me. About three years ago. We were riding in the park. He looked a bit abstracted. Unusual for Bobby. I asked if something was wrong. He said no. Not precisely. Then he asked if I knew Edward Ashford. I said I'd met him once—there was a bit of distance between our families, but one of my cousins was in the same regiment. And I thought I remembered Ashford had gone to the Argentine. Bobby said he had, and did I think Ashford was trustworthy. I said, not particularly, based on what I'd heard. I asked Bobby why it mattered. He said that Ashford was involved in something and it was hard to tell what to make of it."

"You don't sound surprised," Mélanie said. "You knew Bobby was gathering intelligence?"

"I—suspected. Truth to tell, it's one of the reasons I stopped seeing him as often. I was involved with the Levellers, and I suspected Bobby was giving information to someone in the government."

Beside Beardsley, Cressida Caldwell had gone still. "Edward Ashford? An army officer?"

"Yes," Beardsley said. "Do you know him?"

"No, but Allegra did."

"In the Argentine," Mélanie said. "We believe they were lovers."

"I'm not surprised. But Allegra knew Captain Ashford long before that. In London, over a decade ago. After she left Gresham and came back from Scotland, before she married Jeremy. I'm quite sure Ashford was the father of her eldest child."

KITTY STARED down at the papers on the library table. She and Julien had returned to Berkeley Square to find Malcolm studying the decoded paper from the Agrippina bust with Aline and Judith. But it was the coded original, which she had not seen before, that caught Kitty's attention.

"Do you understand?" Judith asked. "We don't know what to make of it."

"I haven't even read the decoded version," Kitty said. "It's the original. I know that handwriting. It's Edward's."

"Allegra got this from your husband?" Judith asked.

"It appears that way. I didn't know Edward was so good at codes." Kitty reached for Aline's decoded version.

Gretna Green. 10 March 1785. Records removed. Stayed at the White Hart. May be a journal. Ask Beardsley.

"It sounds like a wedding," Judith said. "Were Allegra's parents really married?"

"Not Allegra's," Malcolm said. "It's five years too early."

"So it is," Julien said. "But I think perhaps—" He broke off as

Valentin ushered a new arrival into the library. Mandy, Kitty realized with a start of surprise.

"I'm so sorry." Mandy hurried into the room, a faded green velvet bonnet slipping back on her shoulders. "I didn't know where else to go. It's Ralph."

"He's been attacked?" Julien moved to her side.

"No. But after you left the Three Queens, I told him about the man in the greatcoat I saw the night Allegra was killed. He got awfully quiet. Then he went to the backstairs where I'd seen the man."

"Did he find anything?" Julien asked. Kitty knew her husband had searched those stairs himself.

"No. Well, there are blood stains, but I think you knew that. Then he asked in the kitchen if anyone had seen anything. No one had seen the man I saw, but Betty admitted to finding a handkerchief on the stairs the day after the murder. She was keeping it, but she let Ralph see it. He got the oddest look on his face when she showed it to him. Like he was frozen."

"Did it have initials?" Kitty asked. "A crest?"

"It had a letter in the corner. I can read a bit, but it was too curly to make out—maybe a V or a W or even a U. But it was the smell that seemed to stop Ralph. Sort of woods and spices. Ralph held the handkerchief for a long time. Then he said he had to go." Mandy folded her arms across her chest. "He kissed me before he left. It felt like goodbye."

Julien was already moving to the door.

"Do you know where he went?" Mandy asked.

"I think so. Or at least who he's gone to find. And if I'm right, we can't delay."

CHAPTER 46

Of course. Mélanie stared at Cressida Caldwell. And yet, at the same time—good god.

"I take it that's significant," Miss Caldwell said. "Is Captain Ashford in England?"

"Captain Ashford died over two years ago," Mélanie said. "Allegra apparently had a theory that he was murdered. And his widow was attacked the same night she was killed."

"You know his widow?"

"She's Kitty Mallinson whom you met this afternoon."

"Good god. And despite having been attacked the night before last she went to Seven Dials with you today?"

"Kitty doesn't scare easily."

"I saw that. But I think I underestimated both of you. Allegra's murder is connected to Captain Ashford's murder?"

"It seems increasingly likely."

Miss Caldwell sat back on the settee. "I thought Allegra couldn't surprise me. But in the past half hour I've learned that she really did have a mysterious father, if what you say about Lord Warkworth is true—"

"Warkworth?" Beardsley's shoulders jerked taut. "He's connected to Miss Vargas? Mrs. Roth, that is?"

"He admits to being her father," Mélanie said. "You know him?"

Beardsley's fingers tightened on his gray pantaloons. "I've met him on a few unavoidable occasions. It's always awkward. Given that he killed my uncle."

Mélanie saw her own shock echoed on Miss Caldwell's face.

"It wasn't murder," Beardsley said. "Or perhaps it depends on one's definition. My uncle and Warkworth were friends at Eton and Cambridge. Did the Grand Tour together. Then they had a falling out before I was born. They fought a duel and Warkworth killed my uncle. Warkworth went abroad for a time, but the whole thing was hushed up. I heard rumors it was something about a girl and that Warkworth accused my uncle of deceiving him and serving him a despicable turn. My parents either didn't know more, or wouldn't tell me. Granted, my uncle was fool enough to engage in a duel, but it still doesn't endear Warkworth to me."

"Understandably." Miss Caldwell leaned over and touched his hand.

"From what my husband reported today, Warkworth sounds a thoroughly disagreeable man," Mélanie said. "Though apparently he was fond of Allegra." She looked at Beardsley. "You said one of your cousins was in the same regiment as Captain Ashford. Was he—"

"My uncle's son," Beardsley said. "He was a baby at the time of the duel."

"And apparently Edward Ashford's uncle was friends with Warkworth as well."

"Yes." Beardsley's mouth tightened. "John Ashford was Warkworth's second in the duel."

Miss Caldwell looked at her lover as though hesitating on a precipice. "Allegra wanted to talk to you. She wanted me to set it up."

"About the duel?"

"She wouldn't say what it was about. But the duel is a connection you have to Lord Warkworth, even if it's in the past. And to Edward Ashford, in a roundabout way, if his uncle was involved. Though I would think she'd want to talk to your cousin if she was curious about the duel. Perhaps she wanted you to introduce her to your cousin."

"My cousin was posted to India two years ago," Beardsley said. "He left his father's papers with me. But it's hard to see why Mrs. Roth would have been interested in such ancient history. And if Warkworth is her father, you'd think she'd have wanted to protect him."

"It's hard to fit the pieces together," Mélanie agreed. "Perhaps —" She broke off as the door opened again.

Manon paused on the threshold. "Sorry. I came up because I forgot my shawl." She picked a flowered pink silk shawl up from the sofa. "But I couldn't help hearing you mention Lord Warkworth?"

"Do you know him?" Mélanie asked. One never knew where one would find connections in an investigation. Manon was married to Crispin, Viscount Harleton, and they moved in Mayfair circles, though as an actress Manon wasn't invited some places.

Manon wrapped the shawl round her shoulders. "I've met him once or twice. Not with Crispin. He's seeing Eliza Bentley."

"I didn't realize," Mélanie said. Eliza, who had joined the Tavistock company recently, was playing Manon's maid in the new play.

"He doesn't come to rehearsals and he isn't in the green room often," Manon said. "But he'll come round to her dressing room at unexpected moments. The few times I've encountered him, he's looked at me as though I don't exist. I can't but think he'd treat me differently if he knew I was also Viscountess Harleton, but I'm not inclined to tell him. Without ever having spoken much with him, I can tell the type."

Cressida Caldwell met Manon's gaze. Whatever some might say, actresses were not courtesans. But the two women probably had a number of experiences in common. "I've never met Lord Warkworth," Cressida said. "But I know the type as well."

Beardsley's mouth tightened. "Men like Warkworth aren't worthy of the term gentleman. If I believed in the term at all."

Mélanie stared at a framed program for *School for Scandal* on the wall, picturing the scene in the alley outside the Tavistock after Kitty had been attacked. Simon asking questions of Tim. Manon holding Jessica, Colin clinging close to her. Brandon behind them, concerned. And next to him a slender girl with nut-brown hair. Eliza Bentley. Mélanie's memory focused in on her eyes. Wide with shock and fear. Which Mélanie had put down to the unexpected events of the night. But given what they knew now—

A crash sounded from downstairs in the theatre. Followed by a scream.

Mélanie raced downstairs in the direction of the scream, Cressida, Beardsley, and Manon following. More thuds sounded at the base of the stairs. From a dressing room off the passage at stage level. She jerked open the door to see Ralph Allam with his hands round the throat of a tall man with graying fair hair, while Eliza Bentley screamed on the sidelines. Footsteps thudded behind them. Julien, Kitty, and Malcolm burst into the room.

"Allam," Julien said.

Allam went still for a moment. As Julien once had when Kitty had stopped him from strangling Alistair Rannoch.

"You don't want to do this," Julien said in a voice taut as a garroting rope. "He deserves everything you can do to him and more. But you don't deserve what it will do to you."

Ralph Allam stared at Julien. Then he hurled the man, whom Mélanie now recognized as Lord Warkworth, across the room and took a step back.

Warkworth staggered backwards. He went still for a moment,

eyes blazing, face contorted with fury. Then he lunged at Allam. "You bastard!"

Allam went down under the force of Warkworth's assault. Warkworth's head struck the iron-bound corner of the dressing table as they fell.

For a moment both men lay still. Allam pushed himself away and reached for Warkworth's hand. It was limp in his grip. Allam pushed himself to his knees and looked at the bloody gash in the side of Warkworth's head. "What does this mean?"

"It means you're the Earl of Warkworth," Julien said.

llam stared at Julien. "What the hell—?"

But before Julien could respond, Simon appeared in the doorway. "What the devil—"

"I'm sorry." Mélanie looked up from checking Warkworth for a pulse. "There's been another death at your theatre. We're going to have to send for Bow Street again."

Julien put a hand on Allam's arm as Allam gave a jerk of alarm. "Warkworth attacked you. We all saw it."

Eliza Bentley, who had gone stone still, suddenly began to shake. "I didn't know," she said. "I swear I didn't."

"Of course not." Mélanie moved to Eliza's side and put an arm round her. "But you saw something the night Kitty was attacked. You were scared."

Eliza gripped her elbows, arms folded protectively over her pleated taffeta bodice. "He came into the White Rose during my dinner break. He'd meet me there sometimes. But he was odd that night. His gaze kept darting everywhere but at me. When I brushed against him there was something heavy in the pocket of his greatcoat. I think it may have been a pistol. We had a table by the fire, but he kept his greatcoat on. And then later when he moved his arm, I saw blood on his shirt cuff." Her gaze went to Kitty, who was standing by Julien. "But that was before Lady Carfax was attacked."

"It wasn't her blood," Allam said in a voice like a knife on granite. "It was Allegra's. What kind of monster kills his own child?"

"I can't answer that," Malcolm said. "But after we talk to Bow Street, we'll get you as many answers as we can."

~

WARKWORTH'S WORDS echoed in Malcolm's head. "*Allegra was my daughter. Whatever I've done, don't think I ever forget that.*"

They now held a chilling implication.

Hours after the Earl of Warkworth had fallen and struck his head and died, they knew more, though questions still lingered. Higgins had had little choice but to accept the explanation of Lord Warkworth's death given by multiple witnesses, including another earl and two MPs. He was less inclined to accept the theory that Warkworth had murdered Allegra Roth, though he had agreed to follow lines of inquiry they suggested.

Now they were all gathered in the Berkeley Square library. Malcolm, Mélanie, Julien, Kitty, Laura, Judith, Aline, Cressida Caldwell. Raoul was still out, but Harry and Cordy had arrived in response to a summons from Malcolm. As had Roth, who was sitting alone, removed from Judith. William Beardsley had gone home to look through his uncle's papers, and returned with more answers to the puzzle. Like Roth, he was sitting on a straight-backed chair. Cressida Caldwell had seated herself on the settee with Laura and Judith, a bit removed from him. Ralph Allam sat on the sofa beside Mandy, who was holding tightly to his hand. Questions clustered in his gaze.

"We're piecing it together," Julien said to Allam. "But it seems your father, Lord Warkworth, married your mother, Grace Allam, in Scotland in 1785."

Allam shook his head. "My mum only told me bits and pieces about my supposed father. One time she told me he was a gentleman, like I said. Another that she'd thought she was married when she went off with him. But she said it turned out to be sham. I more than half thought even the sham marriage was a story."

"I think Warkworth thought it was a sham," Malcolm said. "But his friend Beardsley—William Beardsley's uncle—got a real clergyman, not even a blacksmith, like so many Gretna Green marriages—and paperwork."

"That's clear from my uncle's journal," William said. "I'm sorry to say, none of us ever thought to look at it. Once I knew where to look, the entries were quite plain."

"And even without the clergyman, they were in Scotland, and Beardsley witnessed the vows, which is all it would take to make the marriage valid if Beardsley testified to it," Malcolm said.

"Why the devil would he do that?" Allam asked. "Make the marriage valid when his friend didn't want it? You lot stick together."

"I'd like to think it was because he had sympathy for your mother and was angry at Warkworth's trying to deceive her," Beardsley said. "His journal's more facts than feelings, but there are hints of that. Also, he and Warkworth seem to have been rivals for your mother. I did hear that Warkworth claimed my uncle had deceived him and, in Warkworth's words, served him a despicable turn. Warkworth and my uncle fought a duel not long after, and Warkworth killed my uncle. The start, it seems, of his ruthless attempt to cover up the past."

Allam sat back, the reality sinking into his eyes. "How did Allegra learn any of this?"

Kitty took a sip of whisky. "She had an affair with Edward Ashford. Who was my first husband. Edward was apparently working for Warkworth, so they may even have met through Warkworth. I didn't know it at the time, but Edward seems to have wanted to go to the Argentine to set up a silver mine scheme for Warkworth."

"Warkworth was funneling government money to Ashford to set up mines and attract investors," Malcolm said. "Palmerston and I found evidence in war office accounts that Allegra was trying to get access to. But two and a half years ago the scheme was falling apart. Warkworth was going to put the blame on Ashford. Ashford's uncle had been friends with Warkworth and Beardsley and was Warkworth's second in their duel. Ashford pieced together what happened. He probably tried to blackmail Warkworth when he realized Warkworth was going to make him take the blame for the silver mine scheme. A fatal mistake. Instead of giving in to the blackmail, Warkworth decided Ashford was a liability and had him killed. But before that, Ashford told Allegra what he'd learned and gave her a coded paper with notes about his discoveries. He knew or suspected Beardsley's uncle had left written evidence."

"Allegra knew how valuable and dangerous the coded paper was, so she hid it in a marble Marco Esquivel was bringing back to England with them," Mélanie said. "Then without her knowing, Esquivel sent the marble to his classics tutor at Cambridge. That's what Allegra wanted you to recover."

"What I tried to take from your house," Allam said, looking from Harry to Cordy. "Sorry about that."

"My compliments on your skills," Harry said. "If we only could have exchanged stories that night, I'd gladly have shared the contents of the paper with you."

"You're quick on your feet," Allam said. "Is the old gentleman I bumped into all right?"

"Only shaken. That was far more excitement than we usually see on Hill Street."

"You're damnably forgiving, Davenport." Allam turned to Roth. "Do you know why Allegra wanted to see you?"

"I know rather less than you," Roth said. "But based on what

I've heard tonight, I'm starting to think she may have wanted my help as an investigator."

"I suspect so." Malcolm picked up the decanter to refill the whisky glasses. "But Warkworth learned what she was on to, and followed her to the Three Queens. Far safer than confronting her at Mivart's. He either tried to talk her into letting it go and failed, or knew he couldn't even try. Allegra wouldn't abandon her brother."

"My"—Allam's breath caught—"the man who fathered me was so determined not to claim me, he was willing to kill his own daughter."

"Our fathers don't define us," Julien said. "Mine was ready to see me hanged. Admittedly for a crime I had actually committed."

Allam tossed down a drink of whisky and then looked at Kitty. "You were attacked the night Allegra was killed."

Kitty nodded. "Warkworth must have either lingered near the Three Queens or paid someone to watch and report to him. In any case, he must have stayed nearby in Seven Dials. I'm guessing that when he realized I'd gone into the Three Queens, he panicked at what I might be able to piece together from what I knew from Edward. Allegra had learned the whole truth from Edward. Of course, Edward was rather closer to Allegra than to me, but Warkworth might not have known."

"He was right, in a way," Cordy said. "Once you learned Edward might have been murdered, you wouldn't let go of it."

"So Lord Warkworth tried to kill Lady Carfax too?" Mandy asked.

"In the circumstances, I think you should go on calling me Kitty," Kitty said with a quick smile. "I'm still not sure if he meant me to be killed or just scared off. Either way, he didn't attack me himself. He hired someone in Seven Dials, who must have followed us."

"Or Warkworth guessed we'd end up at the Tavistock," Julien said. "Call me arrogant, but I think we'd have realized if Purvis had followed us all the way to Mivart's, and back to Covent Garden, and then to the Tavistock. Warkworth knew Miss Bentley had a rehearsal. Even without knowing us well, it wouldn't be hard for him to guess the two of us and Malcolm would end up at the Tavistock to talk to Mélanie."

"So he met Miss Bentley at the White Rose in order to keep an eye on the Tavistock?" Mélanie said. She was sharing one of the Queen Anne chairs with Malcolm.

"I think so," Julien said. "And then shot Purvis when I was about to catch him."

"Do you think he'd planned to use the pistol on Allegra?" Allam asked in a tight voice.

"I doubt it," Malcolm said. "He probably brought it for general protection in Seven Dials."

"What about Bobby?" Judith asked. "Was Warkworth behind his death too?"

Malcolm met his cousin's gaze, wishing he could offer comfort as easily as he could to Colin or Jessica. "I'm not sure. Bobby seems to have been suspicious of Edward Ashford. He told Beardsley as much. So it's possible. But we have no proof."

Judith nodded. Roth tensed as though he wanted to move across the room to her, but he held himself in check. Aline gripped her sister's hand.

Mélanie looked from Malcolm to Julien and Kitty. "What I don't understand is how all of you got to the Tavistock. Though I'm very grateful you did."

"From what Mandy told us I guessed Allam had gone after Warkworth," Julien said. "We went to Warkworth's house first, and Kitty got one of the footmen to admit Warkworth was often to be found visiting his mistress at the Tavistock."

"I learned the same from one of the kitchen maids," Allam said. "That's how I got to the Tavistock. All these years of not wanting to meet him as my father, but when I knew he was my sister's killer I had to confront him."

"Because of the handkerchief?" Mandy asked.

Allam nodded. "It had a W in the corner, but it was the smell that convinced me. Allegra had described it very clearly when she first met him. She said she'd now always know when our father walked into a room." He stared at his hands." The bastard. I can't—"

"My grandmother was a slave," Julien said. "My mother was never properly accepted. But I'm Earl Carfax."

"You were raised for it."

"All the more reason for a man like you to claim his heritage. It's a bloody ridiculous system that should be dismantled, but for the time being, it needs shaking every way it can get."

The door opened as if to punctuate his words, and Raoul came into the library. He paused by the library table, taking in the company.

"You look as though you have news," Malcolm said.

"I thought so. But looking at all of you, I suspect you have more significant news." Raoul moved to the settee and sat on the arm beside Laura . "I found a doorman at Drury Lane who was in a pub on the edge of Seven Dials the night of the murder. He saw Eddy Purvis talking to a man he swears he recognizes as a regular in a box at the Drury Lane. He claims it's Lord Warkworth."

"That's not surprising," Mélanie said, "Because Warkworth murdered Allegra Roth. Have some whisky and we'll tell you. And introduce you to Allegra's brother."

CHAPTER 48

Hubert looked from Malcolm to Julien. "Your team worked as quickly as I'd have expected. Though I wasn't anticipating another noble family's succession being disrupted. I understand the new claimant to the Warkworth title is staying at Carfax House along with his mistress."

"Fiancée," Julien said. They were walking along the Serpentine in Hyde Park. Outdoor meetings could be convenient for agents, though Hubert was usually given to facing agents across his study. The air had a crisp bite, but patches of blue showed through the clouds and the snow had melted. "Allam proposed to Mandy the night Warkworth died. He said he'd been planning to for a long time, he'd just been scared."

"Not the most sensible choice," Hubert said. "A prudent marriage might have helped him gain entrée."

"I don't think Allam sees marriage as a transaction."

"He's going to need all the help he can get."

"I don't think you saw marriage as a transaction once either."

Hubert grunted. "You've taken on a complicated battle."

"I thought supporting our peers was very much what was

expected of our class," Julien said. "Hard to find someone who's more my peer than Allam, given our stories. Besides, I like him."

"Do you really think you can prove his title?"

Malcolm ducked beneath an overhanging branch. "Warkworth got rid of whatever marriage lines there were. We're seeing if we can trace the clergyman. But even without that, the entries in the Beardsley journal are very plain."

"Warkworth's son—his supposed heir—is being quite reasonable," Julien said. "He was well aware of his father's activities and had little respect for him. One sympathizes."

Malcolm studied Hubert in the slanting sunlight. The cool clarity of winter with a hint of spring. "You had to have suspected Warkworth was behind the silver mine scheme."

Hubert's gaze fixed on the winding water of the Serpentine. "Possibly."

"Bobby suspected Ashford was involved in something. He must have told you."

"Oh yes."

"Did Warkworth have him killed?" Malcolm asked.

Hubert put up a hand to adjust his spectacles. "I couldn't find evidence that the saddle had been tampered with. But it was damaged when Bobby fell so we might not be able to tell." He met Malcolm's gaze, his own remarkably open. "I'm sorry not to have more answers for Judith."

Malcolm nodded.

Hubert pushed his spectacles up again, though they didn't seem to have slipped. "Warkworth's estate was encumbered. His wife's—his supposed wife's—marriage portion was tied up for their children."

"He wasn't the first Englishman to see the promise of fortune in South America," Julien said. "Only his way of extracting it didn't involve plundering resources or selling goods or exploiting those born to the land but capitalizing on others' dreams of gilded glory. Or I suppose silvery glory to be accurate."

"And since we couldn't prove anything, and couldn't risk economic chaos or disrupting our alliances in South America, we had to cover up his crimes," Hubert said.

Malcolm regarded his former spymaster. "You wanted us to uncover evidence pointing to Warkworth and bring him down, but to keep your own hands clean in case it didn't work."

"Glad to see time in Parliament hasn't blunted your instincts, Malcolm."

Malcolm jammed his hands in his greatcoat pockets. "We might have had an easier time of it if you'd given us some clues."

"Warkworth had a lot of connections and influence. If I'd tried to take him down, I'd have made a lot of enemies, even if I'd succeeded. The two of you don't care about your influence. Besides, it took you less than forty-eight hours as it was. And not even an arrest to deal with."

"That was an accident," Julien said. "Though I can't say any of those of us who saw it is mourning Warkworth. And while he may have friends who miss him, his family aren't mourning him much, from what I've learned from his son."

"With my luck you'll get Allam into the Lords, where he'll cause more problems for me."

Julien grinned. "One can only hope, Uncle."

WILLIAM CAME into Cressida's sitting room quickly, with that impetuosity that always characterized him, whether speaking on the floor of the House of Commons or making love in her bed. Or other places. He came across the room, close enough that she could see the shaving cuts on his neck and smell the scent of his bay shaving soap, but not quite close enough to touch her. "I got your note. Did you really think it would work?"

"Of course." She gave her most dazzling smile. One could only hope it was enough to disguise the fact that she had felt as though she was writing that letter in her own blood. "My dear William. I have few rules, but one is that when I say a liaison is over, it is. I let ours go on far too long."

"Are you saying you were bored?"

"My sweet." She fell back on practiced language. "No. But I wanted to end it before either of us could become bored."

"I can't imagine ever becoming bored with you."

"Believe me, my dear, I've enjoyed it, but we've let ourselves linger, and now we've ended up in a sad tangle. I'm sorry for my sister's death, and angry at her at the same time, but perhaps she did us one favor. She showed us when it was time for the curtain to come down."

"Sometimes when the curtain comes down, there's a sequel. Mélanie Rannoch's latest play shows that."

"A sequel in which you marry and continue with your career."

"Precisely. I wouldn't say I need a wife, but I've come to realize I would quite like to be married."

It wasn't what she'd expected. It should be a relief. She would have to make herself act as though it was. "Well, then. We're in agreement."

"I hope so." Still not touching her, he dropped down on one knee. "Marry me, Cressy."

Shock held her motionless. Somehow, she had stumbled into a play. The sort of improbable play that a dramatist like Mélanie Rannoch could make convincing. Where couples put aside the obvious issues that would cloud their attempt at happiness and defied society and their families and the weight of the world to be together. She had felt the power of those moments, sitting in her box at the theatre, eyes unexpectedly wet, fingers tight on her opera glasses. And then later, over champagne at the Piazza, she'd shaken her head and told her friends—and her latest lover—how foolish it was, and that they'd not only not be able to defy the world, they'd be tired of each other within a month.

"William. My dear." She bent forwards, but didn't let herself touch him. "You can't know what this means to me. And you must believe I will always treasure what we had. Including the memory of this. But when you let yourself think clearly, you'll realize it would never work. And you'll be grateful to me for letting you go."

"You don't love me?" he said. A clear declarative question, not a plaintive request.

"My darling. Far too well to marry you."

"Don't talk rubbish, Cressy." He pushed himself to his feet. "That's the sort of thing rakes say to innocent young girls in plays not nearly as sophisticated as Mélanie Rannoch's. Your whole life has been about defying the world. Why hesitate to defy it with me?"

"Because while one may defy the world, one still has to live in it. And I don't like what it would do to you."

"That's my affair."

"And mine. I want you to succeed."

"Let me worry about that." He regarded her for a moment, his gaze tender and yet at the same time piercing, in that way it could be. "I wouldn't ask you to be anything you aren't. I don't need you to change into some sort of Mayfair hostess."

"I'll never be a Mayfair hostess. Except of the sort of parties I give here."

He frowned for a moment. "If you want to go on—"

That would be an easy out. To say she couldn't imagine fidelity. Because whatever he might claim, she didn't think—she was certain—he wouldn't be happy with a life that didn't include it. That would let both of them out, perhaps with a lingering aftertaste of bitterness, but with a clear line drawn. If she were sensible, she'd seize on one of the score of flowery letters she had from the viscount who had been her last protector, and tell William she was returning to him. She'd actually follow through and go out publicly with Lord Rothersmere and let him ogle her and slip his hand down her bodice in their box and spend the night in his bed, and that would be that. But somehow she couldn't bring herself to do it. It might be a clear break, but it would taint everything that had gone before. And just now she couldn't bear the thought of Rothersmere's hands on her.

"We've been happy," she said. "I haven't wanted anyone but you. It quite drove me to distraction. Let's leave it at that, before life intrudes."

"That's what you aren't explaining, Cressy. Why on earth we should leave it at that. I don't give a damn about society, or where we're invited, or who hosts parties in my home and who will attend them."

"I know. That's why you need a wife who does."

"A wife like that would bore me to tears."

And perhaps he'd the find the need to seek solace elsewhere. But not with her. Because flexible as her morals were, she realized she couldn't abide the thought of sharing William. "I imagine you'll be less bored than you think. You might find a wife like Mélanie Rannoch, who would help with your speeches."

"Mélanie Rannoch is brilliant. But she's stopped playing the hostess game as much. Rannoch says he doesn't want her to. Anyway, you can help with my speeches. You have."

Sitting up in bed, a candle beside them, the paper on a book on their knees, passing the pen back and forth. Some of her fondest memories. "You're an idealist, William. You believe in a better world. And I think you can go a long way towards creating it. But meanwhile, we have to live in the world we have."

"Don't I know it. And I want to live in it with you. It's not as though we'd be living in poverty either. You could bring a lot more to the marriage than I could, but I'm not exactly a pauper."

She laughed despite herself.

He grinned, and for a moment their gazes caught, and the shared laughter rippled between them. "I'm not such an idiot I'd insist on your abandoning everything and living off me," he said. "I'm glad you can still have the lifestyle you're accustomed to. By all means, leave everything in trust for Vincent, but there's no reason you shouldn't enjoy it." He frowned. "Is it Vincent? You don't trust me with Vincent?"

"No," she said without thinking. She tried to keep Vincent away from her lovers, but William was in the house enough it was impossible. She'd come back from a drive once to find William and Vincent building a fort in the parlor, and from then on they'd been fast friends. "You're a wonderful friend to Vincent. I'm grateful for it."

"Please don't talk rubbish about gratitude." He stepped back, arms folded across his chest. "If you don't want me. If this is a pleasant interlude and you're growing bored. If you can't imagine not sharing your bed with a multitude. I can understand your wanting that, but that's not the life I'd want with you. If any of those are true, I'd agree we were better off parting."

"Let's just say we're better off parting, and leave it at that." She gave way to impulse and touched his face.

That was a mistake. He caught her hand and pressed it to his lips. Warmth spread through her and curled round her heart. Round her heart? God, when had she started thinking like this?

"I'm all for choice," he said, fingers laced though her own. "Everyone should choose whom they take to bed, with or without vows being involved. Marriage makes the choice a bit harder to get out of. Women often get particularly little power in these choices. I'm trying to make this a reasoned choice. But at a certain point, it comes down to this." He tightened his grip on her hand and pulled her into his arms. "I love you, Cressy. I want to spend the rest of my life with you. With or without marriage, but I'm conventional enough I'd prefer marriage. I'm not going to love again. Not like this. I don't want to. And in the end, it should come down to whom we want to be with. So tell me. Do you love me?"

"I can't possibly marry you, William. I'm not the sort of woman who gets married."

"Since when have you let ideas about what kind of person is

supposed to do what stand in your way? For shame, Cressy. You're braver than that."

There was a light in his eyes. She'd seen it when he worked on a speech and honed in on his final argument. William was a master of rhetoric.

His arms tightened round her. "Do you love me? And don't give me any of that trite nonsense about 'too well to marry me.'"

She choked. "I love you, William. But I'm not mad."

"That's a pity. All the most interesting people are a bit mad. It's part of what made me fall in love with you."

His face was inches from her own. But those inches, so lightly covered, over a glass of champagne, in a box at the opera, across a pillow, were suddenly an insuperable barrier. "You'll regret it. Maybe not tonight. Maybe not tomorrow. But before long. And for the rest of your life."

"Says the woman who always told me she sought to live in the moment."

"Says the man who wants to change the world. You need to believe in the future to do that. You made me believe."

"My love." His eyes lit. "That's one of the most remarkable things you've said to me. Think of what we can do together."

"You don't need me."

"I need you with every fibre of my being, every moment of my life."

"This isn't a play. I'm not going to turn into a virtuous woman who repents of my past through the love of a good man."

"Of course not. And that would be a singularly trite play. Mélanie Rannoch would never write it."

She put her hands on his chest. "This is our life, William."

"Precisely. *Ours.*"

Their gazes caught and held. In the depths of his eyes, she caught a flash of a future she had never dreamt possible.

"Can you look at me and say you can imagine yourself in ten years without me?" he said.

She closed her eyes. "I can scarcely imagine ten minutes without you, you provoking man. For one thing, you never stop talking long enough for me to think."

His face relaxed into a smile. "Oh well. That's a calculated politician's technique. I learnt it from Rannoch. But if it comes halfway near working with you—"

"Oh, do shut up, William. And kiss me." She closed the impossible distance between them and put her mouth to his.

He went still for a moment. Then his arms closed round her as she molded herself to him. One hand slid up her back to tangle in her hair. A long while later, he lifted his head. "Yes?"

The light of the candles flashed in his eyes. She was probably mad. But then, as he'd said, she always had been. "Yes."

CHAPTER 49

"Lady Car—Kitty." Roth hesitated just inside the Berkeley Square hall.

"Do come in." Kitty held out a hand to take his hat. "Raoul and Laura asked me to come out and greet you. They're in the midst of a very elaborate puppet show. It's Valentin's afternoon off. Mélanie's at the theatre and Malcolm and Julien went to talk to Hubert. Oh, and Judith will be down shortly. Serena's just waking up from a nap."

"Thank you." Roth hesitated a moment longer, then shrugged out of his greatcoat. "She said—"

"Yes, I know. She very much wants to talk to you." They went into the library and paused to admire the puppet show Raoul and Laura were staging with the children. "In truth," Kitty said, as she and Roth settled themselves by the fire where they had spoken once before, "I was hoping for a moment to talk to you. There's so much we haven't had a chance to talk about."

"There's been a lot to attend to," Roth said. "And I've been back at work."

Warkworth hadn't been publicly named Allegra Roth's killer to spare his family (not to mention the scandal in the government and diplomatic community, Kitty suspected), but Roth had been formally cleared of suspicion. He had been in Berkeley Square briefly a couple of times since the end of the case, but Kitty had not had a chance to talk to him about one of the major revelations.

She glanced at the puppet show. Genny was on her stomach, working a lever in the puppet theatre. Leo was adjusting a piece of scenery, while Timothy tried to get a crown to stay on one of the puppets. "I must say one thing I didn't anticipate was that we would learn Samuel is my children's half-brother, " she said. Technically he was only Timothy's half-brother, but there was no sense in going into that. "This settles one thing. You'll never be able to be free of us."

Roth gave an unexpected laugh. "You're amazing, Kitty. I can imagine few who would laugh at the circumstances."

"How can I do anything else? It shouldn't be so surprising. I knew about Edward's affairs. We knew Edward knew Allegra in the Argentine. It's a bit of a surprise that they knew each other in Britain before. But it's hardly the greatest surprise I've had. I knew Edward had been back to London on a visit then. We weren't long married, but I don't think Allegra was his first affair since our marriage." She watched Roth for a moment. "Biology is perhaps the last thing that makes a parent. But I confess I rather like that Samuel is my children's sibling. Even if they never know."

"He'll need to know," Roth said. "One day."

"It won't make a difference," Kitty said. "Children have a way of knowing who their real parents are." She looked round as the door opened. "Oh, here's Judith. I'll leave you to talk."

JUDITH SMILED at Kitty and set Serena down to run and join the other children. Jeremy got to his feet. "Thank you for agreeing to see me. I realize I have no right to be here."

422

Judith moved to one of the chairs by the fire. "Berkeley Square isn't a colony breaking away from its colonizer."

"You know what I mean." Jeremy returned to the settee, a little stiffly. "There's no reason to think you'd receive me. By rights, you shouldn't."

"What was between us was never so formal. And I hope I'll always have time for a friend."

"Is that what we are? Friends?"

"I'm not sure what we are." Judith clasped her hands, holding herself in check. If she let go, she was quite sure she'd do something embarrassing. Like fling herself into his arms.

"To say I'm sorry seems entirely inadequate. But I'm sorrier than I can say that I pulled you into this."

"I'm not," Judith said. "If it weren't for Allegra and Esquivel and Bobby, you'd never have crossed the room to talk to me. And for all the tangle that caused, I'm inestimably glad you did. Because even when it hurt the most, I somehow knew someday I'd be grateful for the memories."

"I'm relieved to hear that. It's far more than I deserve."

"Do you want something?" She gestured towards the decanters.

"I don't want to—"

"Please. If we're going to talk more, I need something." She went to the decanters and poured two glasses of Malcolm and Mélanie's excellent sherry. "I'm not the woman I was that day you came over to talk to me." She put one of the glasses in his hand. "For that, I owe you my thanks."

"A bitter lesson."

"No. Or not entirely. For you it may have been the side effect of a mission. For me it was more."

"You can't think—can you really still think that's all it was to me?"

"I'm not sure." She took a sip of sherry, deeper than she intended. "Sometimes I think there was more. That I couldn't have been so deceived. Others, I think I was too in love to see anything clearly. I saw what I wanted because I wanted it so much." She watched him for a moment in the soft glow of the firelight. Light could hide as much as it revealed. "Is that how it was for you with Allegra?"

"I don't think I was ever properly in love with Allegra. I was fond of her. I desired her. I cared for her. But it wasn't ever—I don't think I understood what love could be until us."

"That sounds very gallant."

"I've never been gallant in my life."

She took a sip of sherry. "You're back at work."

"Yes. A bit awkward, but I've always been something of an outsider at Bow Street. All in all, most of my colleagues are treating me very decently."

"How are the boys?"

"They're—as well as possible, I suppose. Though I'm honestly not sure what possible means."

"I miss them. Even though you never really wanted me round them much."

"Don't talk rubbish, Judith."

"It's true. You almost never talk about them, and once we were together you were careful not to bring them round me much."

"I could hardly have brought them on an assignation."

"But when we were in Berkeley Square and they'd come running over to me like they used to, you seemed to want to hurry them away. Don't deny it."

Jeremy hesitated. "I suppose I was afraid of giving something away in front of them. I'm not always the best at containing my feelings. And they've been through a lot. They're fond of you. Very fond. I didn't want them to get even fonder and lose someone else."

"Because you assumed we were going to end. And then I wouldn't want to see you again? I suppose that makes sense, given that our affair was a mission. Missions come to an end. At least that seems to be the case from what my spy relatives tell me."

"Our affair was a lot of things, Judith. But it wasn't a mission."

"All right." Judith scanned his face. She didn't know whether it was his insistence or her own wishful thinking, or just possibly the first glimmerings of understanding, but she was willing to entertain the possibility that that was true. "If that's the case, then what? You were convinced what was between us had to end?"

He looked into her eyes. His own were dark and steady. Opaque and yet somehow she had the sense they could be smashed with a word. "Where else was it going to go?"

"It was quite delightful. And it wouldn't be the only permanent relationship we know of that began with a spy mission. Laura told me some quite illuminating things about her and Raoul. And while I've never quite been able to work out all the particulars, I'm fairly certain Mélanie and Malcolm began as a mission. I remember when Malcolm first brought her to England. You could feel what was between them. It was almost palpable in the air. But it was as if they were holding it in check. In any case, if spy missions didn't stand in their way—"

"Judith, I was in no position—"

"You were married. But that didn't stop Raoul and Laura. I mean, I think they're very happy they're married, but I'm quite sure they'd have stayed together regardless. Did you really think Fanny Dacre-Hammond's daughter would have objected to living in sin?"

"You can't seriously think I'd have asked you—"

"You were willing to bed me in secret but not to let the world know?"

"Isn't that the way love affairs are carried out in the beau monde? It doesn't matter whom one sleeps with as long as one doesn't flaunt it publicly?"

"Well, not precisely. It's all right for the public to know—like they do about Emily Cowper and Palmerston, like they did about Mama and goodness knows who—so long as one doesn't make a public display of it like Caro Lamb. But that assumes we care about the beau monde, which I know you don't. I suppose now that you're free you're going to refuse to marry me as well."

Jeremy's glass tilted in his fingers. "Who said anything about marriage?"

"You certainly didn't. I suppose I shouldn't be surprised you don't want to compromise your principles."

"Compromise my *what?*"

"Jeremy, you can't deny you despise the world I come from."

"I never said—"

"No, you have better manners than that. But you can't deny you have complete contempt for the beau monde."

"I wouldn't say that."

"But you'd think it?"

"I'll admit I was quick to judgment in the beginning."

"It took you forever to even be comfortable coming to Berkeley Square as a guest."

"Because it's not my world."

"And you think we're shallow and selfish and out of touch with ordinary people. You aren't far wrong, if you think of the beau monde in a lump. But I think you've learned some of us are different."

"Of course I have. I'll admit to prejudices. And I'll always feel a bit awkward. But the Rannochs and their friends are now some of my best friends."

"So I think you could learn to live in that world, against your principles. Look at Raoul. He's a revolutionary—"

"Who was born to aristocrats. It's different."

"Since when have you cared what anyone thinks of you? You're gloriously free of worrying about such things. So it shouldn't bother you if anyone thinks you've married me for my money. I wouldn't force you to be part of this world. But I do insist we use my fortune. It would be very foolish not to. And you're far too pragmatic for that. I'm sure there's a great deal I don't understand about poverty, and a great deal I can learn to do, but I don't think our and our children's living in poverty will help anything."

Jeremy shook his head. His mouth curved with a tenderness that brought a lump to her throat. "My darling. I don't doubt that you could do anything you put your mind to. And I know your family's capacity for breaking rules. But some lines can't be crossed."

"Jeremy." Judith stared at him. "Are you, of all people, going to say you're bound by class lines?"

"No. But I can imagine how you will likely feel in a few months or a few years—"

"My family won't cast us off. And you already like them. I think."

"Of course I do."

"Well, then."

"Judith. I'm not going to pull you into something you'll regret."

Judith moved to the settee and put her hands on his chest. Not long ago she had thought she'd never touch him again. But now it felt natural. "Don't you think I should be able to say what I might regret? And you aren't pulling me into anything. I'm attempting to drag you by your fingernails."

"My darling, in a few years—"

"I hope to goodness we'll be happily married and beyond this." Judith put her mouth to his. "Stop being an idiot, Jeremy. And marry me."

CHAPTER 50

"*D*o you think it will get easier?*" Manon asked.

"*I'm not sure,*" Brandon said. "*But I don't think it will ever be dull.*" He held out his hands and Manon stepped into his arms.

Watching from the table to the side, for the first time Mélanie felt the last scene was working. She lifted her teacup in a silent toast and caught a stir of movement in the wings. Jessica darted out of the shadows and ran to her, followed by Malcolm.

"Mummy!" Jessica threw her arms round Mélanie. "Daddy said I could come if I was quiet."

Mélanie hugged her daughter and smiled at Malcolm. "How long have you been here?"

"For the last scene. It's good."

"That's the first time I've felt that scene landed right." Mélanie pulled Jessica onto her lap. "Did you and Julien talk to Hubert?" she asked, as Jessica picked up her pencil and began drawing on a blank sheet of paper.

"Yes. As usual, he didn't admit much. Then we looked in at Brooks's. Beardsley found us there. He and Cressida Caldwell are betrothed."

"I'm so glad she was sensible about it. I thought he'd be sensible after seeing them together."

"Yes, so did I. He said it was quite a challenge to persuade her. Then I went back to Berkeley Square. I found Roth there."

"Judith said they'd arranged to talk. How did it go?"

Jessica, who had seemed totally absorbed in drawing, set down the pencil. "They're getting married."

This time Mélanie started. She put her arms round Jessica so her daughter wouldn't slip off her lap. "I hoped—but I didn't think anything would happen so quickly."

"Nor did I," Malcolm said. "Nor did Roth, apparently. He was still looking rather thunderstruck when Jessica and I left. I gather Judith had as hard a time persuading him as Beardsley did Miss Caldwell. She was always determined."

"Judith says I can be a bridesmaid." Jessica was drawing again. "But it won't be for a while. He has to talk to Samuel and Dorian." She looked across the room where the company were gathered round the refreshment table. "May I talk to Roxane and Clarisse? And get some biscuits?"

"Bring some back for us."

Jessica grinned and ran over to Manon's daughters. Malcolm smiled as he watched her. "Another case concluded."

"I missed too much of it."

"If you hadn't been at the theatre, we wouldn't have learned about Warkworth and Eliza Bentley." He looked down at Jessica's drawing. "She's drawing a stage."

"She's writing a play in pictures. I've promised to put them all together for her."

"Like her mother." Malcolm tugged the picture into the light of the lamp on the table to study it better. "She couldn't wait to come when I said I was going to the Tavistock. She's at home here. Like you."

Mélanie reached for her tea and forced down a sip. "It has to bother you sometimes, Malcolm."

"What?"

No way to say it but bluntly. "That we don't share everything we used to."

He hitched himself up on the edge of the table. "Are there moments I miss you? Of course. Are there moments I'm a selfish idiot and wish you were always there when I looked round? Guilty. Am I immeasurably proud of you?" He touched her hand. "I can't say how much."

Mélanie smiled up at him and felt a prickle behind her eyes. "How do you always know just what to say, darling? Perhaps I should have turned to you for my last scene."

"Hardly. But you might ask me for help, if you ever need it. I'm not a playwright. But I did grow up on plays. And we've always done quite well collaborating. There's no reason that should mean just your helping me."

She squeezed his hand. "You're amazing, Malcolm."

He turned his hand to twine his fingers round hers. "I'm married to an amazing playwright."

"I FEEL FOR THEM," Julien said, looking across the Berkeley Square library at Jeremy and Judith, who were talking to Sandy and Bet and Justine and Gerry. "I keenly remember the horror of everyone offering congratulations and looking smugly satisfied that we'd discovered connubial bliss."

Kitty tucked her hand through his arm. "Poor darling."

"You were more horrified than I was. I was too busy worrying you'd back out of it."

Mélanie undid the wire cap on a bottle of champagne. "It feels rather like being on stage without a role to hide behind."

Julien's gaze took in Mélanie, Malcolm, Laura, Raoul, Harry, and Cordy, who were gathered round the drinks table. "Of course, as Roth and Judith will discover, the really annoying thing about the smug satisfaction you all showed is that you were right."

"I categorically deny ever looking smug." Malcolm handed Mélanie a towel as she wrestled with the champagne cork.

"It seems an oddly appropriate conclusion to the case." Cordelia slid her arm round Harry. "This case was about marriage."

"Was it?" Harry said. "I thought it was about revolutions and colonization."

"There could be said to be parallels between the two," Raoul said. "I once heard Fanny say exclusive rights were the province of colonial powers, not consenting adults. Though that was before Archie."

"Are you comparing marriage to being colonized?" Laura asked.

"Not with the right person." Raoul kissed her hand.

Mélanie popped open the champagne and refilled glasses.

"It's funny," Cordelia said. "It seems quite clear now that Jeremy's and Allegra's marrying wasn't a good idea. And it seems equally clear to all of us that this is different."

"The cast of characters does make a difference," Mélanie said.

"And the timing," Kitty added.

A shout of laughter came from the children, who were organizing another puppet show. Manon and her husband Crispin, Blanca and Addison, and Harriet Roth were with them, along with and Cressida Caldwell and William Beardsley. Cressida's son Vincent looked perfectly at home with the other children. Laura smiled at them, then glanced towards the fireplace. "Ralph and Mandy look happy. And a bit less overwhelmed."

Mélanie set down the champagne bottle followed the direction of Laura's gaze. Allam and Mandy were talking to Frances and Archie and David and Simon. "Fanny's good at putting people at ease. Well, they all are, really."

Julien took a drink of champagne. "It occurs to me that it may actually be good preparation for surviving the House of Lords."

"What?" Mélanie asked.

Julien lifted his champagne glass towards Allam and Mandy in a silent toast. "Growing up in Seven Dials."

HISTORICAL NOTES

Marco Esquivel is fictional, but Carlos María de Alvear and José de San Martín were very real and both involved in the Sociedad de los Caballeros Racionales/The Lodge of the Rational Knights. They were both in London in 1811 and attended lodge meetings at the home of Venezuelan revolutionary leader Francisco de Miranda, who was then in London as well. Shortly after, Alvear, San Martín, and others sailed to Buenos Aires on the British ship *George Canning*. Some historians have theorized that San Martín may have been a British agent, though others disagree. The Argentine revolutionary government received a loan from British merchants in 1821.

The term La Argentina was used for what is now Argentina going back to the seventeenth century, though officially the Spanish called it the Viceroyalty of the Río de la Plata and then it was called the United Provinces of the Río de la Plata by the revolutionary government. The term Argentine Republic was first used in the 1826 constitution. The term the Argentine was commonly used by the British.

The Portuguese royal family and court did escape to Brazil in 1807, just ahead of the French. Lord Strangford was involved in their flight, though Henry Brougham (who appears elsewhere in the Rannoch Fraser Mysteries) did indeed claim Strangford had exaggerated his role.

George Thomas Love's *A Five Year Residence in Buenos Ayres, During the Years 1820 – 1825* (London: G. Herbert, 1825), provides a fascinating glimpse in Buenos Aires at the time through the eyes of a British expat. Patrick Wilcken's *Empire Adrift: The Portuguese Court in Rio de Janeiro 1808-1821* (London: Bloomsbury, 2004) is not only a wonderful account of the Portuguese court's time in Brazil but of many of the issues and conflicts in that part of South America at the time.

The Seven Dials Affair
About This Guide
The suggested questions are included
to enhance your group's reading of
Tracy Grant's *The Seven Dials Affair*

.

1. Allegra Roth and Marco Esquivel both left their
   children to pursue their work in the Argentine. How do
   you feel about their actions? Are you more sympathetic
   to one of them than the other? How do their actions
   compare to Raoul's being away from Malcolm and now
   at times Emily and Clara?
2. What do you think drove Allegra/Alejandra? Do you
   think she loved Esquivel?
3. Roth confronts his past in the book, but Kitty, Malcolm,
   and Raoul also confront issues from their pasts. Do you
   think each of them is more or less at peace with the past
   by the end of the investigation?

4. Mélanie continues to juggle being a playwright, an investigator, a mother, and a wife. How does her juggling compare with that of modern parents? Why do you think she was reluctant to let Malcolm see the play?

5. What do you think lies ahead for Judith and Roth?

6. Allegra struggled with the options available for a woman in her era. How do her struggles and choices compare with Mélanie's, Kitty's, Cordelia's, Laura's, Cressida Caldwell's?

7. What do you think lies ahead for Cressida Caldwell and William Beardsley?

8. Allegra's spying on Esquivel is a parallel to Mélanie's spying on Malcolm and also to Roth's spying on Judith. What are the similarities and differences among the three?

9. How do you think Kitty and Raoul help each other in their scene?

10. Do you think Ralph Allam will become Earl of Warkworth with Mandy his countess? What sort of life will they have? Was Julien right that growing up in Seven Dials will be good preparation for the House of Lords?

Traditional Regencies

WIDOW'S GAMBIT

FRIVOLOUS PRETENCE

THE COURTING OF PHILIPPA

Lescaut Quartet

DARK ANGEL

SHORES OF DESIRE

SHADOWS OF THE HEART

RIGHTFULLY HIS

The Rannoch Fraser Mysteries

HIS SPANISH BRIDE

LONDON INTERLUDE

VIENNA WALTZ

IMPERIAL SCANDAL

THE PARIS AFFAIR

THE PARIS PLOT

BENEATH A SILENT MOON

THE BERKELEY SQUARE AFFAIR

THE MAYFAIR AFFAIR

INCIDENT IN BERKELEY SQUARE

LONDON GAMBIT

MISSION FOR A QUEEN

GILDED DECEIT

MIDWINTER INTRIGUE

THE DUKE'S GAMBIT

SECRETS OF A LADY

THE MASK OF NIGHT

THE DARLINGTON LETTERS

THE GLENISTER PAPERS

A MIDWINTER'S MASQUERADE

THE TAVISTOCK PLOT

THE CARFAX INTRIGUE

THE WESTMINSTER INTRIGUE

THE APSLEY HOUSE INCIDENT

THE WHITEHALL CONSPIRACY

THE SEVEN DIALS AFFAIR

ABOUT THE AUTHOR

Photo by Kristen Loken, https:// kristenloken.com

Tracy Grant studied British history at Stanford University and received the Firestone Award for Excellence in Research for her honors thesis on shifting conceptions of honor in late-fifteenth-century England. She lives in the San Francisco Bay Area with her young daughter and four cats. In addition to writing, Tracy works for the Merola Opera Program, a professional training program for opera singers, pianists, and stage directors. Her real-life heroine is her daughter Mélanie, who is very cooperative about Mummy's writing time and is starting to write herself. She is currently at work on her next book chronicling the adventures of Malcolm and Mélanie Suzanne Rannoch. Visit her on the web at www.tracygrant.org.

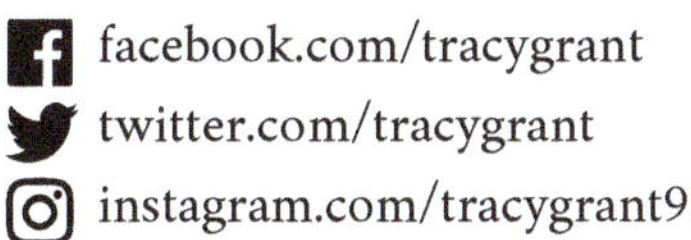

facebook.com/tracygrant

twitter.com/tracygrant

instagram.com/tracygrant93